RENEGADES OF SKAYTHE

Volume II

by Deby Fredericks

A character index can be found in the back of the book.

Indicia

Minstrels of Skaythe

Where dark sorcery rules, they seek to restore a
forbidden power — hope!

Book I — The Tower in the Mist
Book II — Dancer in the Grove of Ghosts
Book III — The Ice Witch of Fang Marsh
Book IV — The Renegade of Opshar
Book V — Prisoners of the Wailing Tower
Book VI — The Tale of the Drakanox (forthcoming)

More by Deby Fredericks

E-books
The Weight of Their Souls
The Gellboar
*Wyrmflight, a Hoard of Dragon Lore**

Wolfsinger Publishing
*The Seven Exalted Orders**
*Trials of the Eighth Order (forthcoming)**

Dragon Moon Press
The Magister's Mask
The Necromancer's Bones
Too Many Princes

More by Lucy D. Ford

E-books
*Aunt Ursula's Atlas**
*Masters of Air & Fire**

*Also available in paperback

The Shining Ones

as told by Keilos

This is a story that is dangerous to know. It comes from so long ago that it was all but forgotten. I heard it from a very old woman who was assassinated not long after. And I have never told it to anyone, because of the risk.

In ancient times, it is said, all people were magical. There was no division of mages and commoners, of rich and poor, or even of men and women. We call those people the Shining Ones. Knowing that all were equally blessed, they shared a mutual purpose to bring happiness and welfare to every person.

The Shining Ones raised up a great civilization. It boasted every marvel that magic could provide. No one wanted for food or companionship, for all things were held in common. Nor were the people judged for any failings. Weakness was met with compassion rather than anger. Error aroused not disgust but forgiveness.

The cities of the Shining Ones prospered and grew to cover all of Skaythe. Even now, some of their works endure. Their ancient roads stitch our world together long after their time.

But we know that for every light there is a shadow. After the summer, winter must come. The Shining Ones, too, had their opposite. These were the vicious Devourers.

The Devourers came from everywhere, and from nowhere. They fed upon magic, and all the things of magic. The Shining Ones could not fight them, for their spells were consumed. They could not hide, for their very essence was magical and the Devourers were drawn to slaughter them.

Soon the Shining Ones were gone forever. Their

great cities crumbled, and everything they had made was swept away.

There had been those few who were born without magic, or whose power was malformed in some way. These defectives were regarded with pity and maintained with all kindness. After the Devourers, they were all that was left.

Alas, these were no Shining Ones. Some did not wish to share in common. They seized what they wanted to keep it for themselves. So were the rich divided from the poor. Some desired to hold and control the ones they loved. So were the men divided from the women. And some, who yet held a feeble ember of magic, set themselves up as rulers over those who had none. So were the mages divided from the commons.

This is the end of the story. For the Shining Ones are lost, and now we must struggle in the dregs of our world that the Devourers left behind.

Why was this story lost? Why is it dangerous to know it now?

For every light there is a shadow, and that shadow is within all people. Who would take on the pain of knowing how much has been lost? And who would dare to imagine, in this world of suffering and cruelty, that there is another way?

Once you hear this story, it grows within your heart. It drives you to defy common sense. We minstrels were cursed when we heard it. Now we wander the roads of Skaythe and try, in small ways, to defy the darkness that covers our land.

One day it will be our undoing. Or, it may be the salvation of all Skaythe.

THE RENEGADE
OF OPSHAR

by Deby Fredericks

Dedication

For Daron, who else?

The Renegade of Opshar

I

An Insignificant Village

For as long as he could remember, Berisan had lived by one rule: Don't Get Caught.

And so he found himself in a far corner of Skaythe, playing a two-reed pipe in the futile hope of attracting a coin or two. The oval market plaza had been packed hard by generations of farmers' boots. Berisan crouched there, in the burning sun. He had folded his leather cloak to make a sort of pad, but it wasn't much help. He had to shift, easing the tingle of lost circulation in his folded legs. Even with the cover of a reed hat, he couldn't stop sweating.

Early in the day, he'd managed to catch a couple of coins, but now the noonday heat withered everything. His mouth was too dry to produce more than a few tired notes. Villagers scurried past, intent on their own affairs. No one spared a glance for the beggar in his ragged clothes.

Opshar was an insignificant village, barely visible in the grassy expanse of Pulgoll. That was not all bad. For a renegade mage, always on the run, an insignificant place was what he needed. There was less chance the hunter-guards would sniff him out here. Even if the villagers mostly ignored him, Berisan hoped to scratch up enough coin to pay for a bed in the tavern that dominated the far edge of the plaza. Maybe he could even get a bath that wasn't drenched in the river's chill.

If that failed, Pulgoll still held possibilities. Shark-tooth mountains jutted on both sides of the valley, but the land between was soft and green. Though the farmers guarded their fields against what they assumed was a thieving beggar, the river offered wild grain, crayfish, turtle eggs, and more.

Berisan just hoped he had run far enough to find a measure of safety. He was tired of the endless road. He longed to hide himself, the way silt-fish did when they burrowed into the mud.

True, there had been signs of bandit activity along the way. A cart at the roadside, broken and burned. Logs stacked on a hill where few other trees grew. What purpose could there be but to block the road for an ambush? Still, none of that was recent. If it had been, Berisan would have wandered elsewhere.

"Apricots, Cherries, fresh picked," chanted the young woman in the next space over. She had a blanket spread out, held down by baskets of the self-same fruit. The hot sun was beginning to shrivel them. Occasionally she swept a whisk over the bowls to discourage flies.

Berisan had been trying not to stare. The woman was lovely, with a wide brown face and piercing black eyes. Two glossy braids coiled together on top of her head. Also, he couldn't help noticing how well her breasts filled the tight bodice of her peasant dress. After a while, when she stood to pass over the sold apricots, he had noticed that she was many months pregnant.

You would expect such a beauty to have a man nearby, a husband or lover taking good care of her. Yet she had been alone all morning. Her expression, when no customers were at hand, showed no hope of anyone joining her. Berisan knew better than to get involved with a stranger's business, but he couldn't help feeling a bit of concern for her.

Perhaps because he was a fugitive himself, he began to notice how the woman's almond eyes darted toward any movement. Those quick, wary glances said she was watching for trouble. What was she afraid of?

Yamaya never knew what to expect when she came into Opshar. Her name and face might be known, but she wasn't trusted. It had only been three months since she and Gabrith escaped the mountains in search of a better life for their coming child. They had been lucky to find a farm down the valley, near the Weeping Falls. Though long abandoned, it had a handful of fruit trees still alive. Aulgrip, the village headman, had been glad enough to let them dig the fields there.

Still, three months wasn't nearly enough time to knit themselves into an isolated community. Especially one so at odds with their former ways. Gabrith had made repairs to the old farmer's shack as best he could, but now he was gone. Yamaya was left to tend the sparse fields and make the place fit to raise a baby.

Most days, she didn't mind being alone. People would ask questions, and there were things she didn't want anyone to know. Besides which, the fruit trees wouldn't question her life choices. Still, she needed some things to get by until the sweet potatoes came in. River grain and smoked fish would add to the scanty vegetable harvest. With thread and a bit of cloth, she could sew diapers and patch her peasant dress.

Without Gabrith, there was no one else to do the bartering. So at first light Yamaya had packed her baskets with the last of the apricots and the first of the cherries. It was a long walk up the valley, but the day's trading had been decent. Everyone liked cherries, and they wouldn't grow in the soggy ground by the river. The girl in the fishermen's stall shared a bit of gossip — a first.

Even Aulgrip had asked a few questions about her plans, now that Gabrith was dead. Yamaya meant to stay on. She had nowhere else to go. It was hard for her to tell if Aulgrip liked that answer. His reaction had left Yamaya unsettled. She would be glad enough to pack up her leftover fruit and take it back, to dry for her own use. The only task left for her was to have a word with Gordemir, the carpenter, about getting a cradle made.

In her previous life, Yamaya had developed an instinct for when trouble was near. It pricked at her now. Dark eyes flicked around the square, seeking where it might come from. The townsfolk moved about their business. No one seemed to care about her.

There was that man, next over. An outsider, like her. Yamaya had seen him ogling her, though never for long enough that she could object. He seemed to be nothing but a beggar. Hunched over beneath his woven hat, playing a wandering tune on a two-reed pipe. Untrimmed hair and scruff of beard. Dusty shirt with torn sleeves. Trousers worn down at the cuffs.

Yet he didn't cringe. Beggars always braced for the blows that were sure to come. According to Lillia, the fisherman's daughter, the fellow had been hanging around Opshar for a few days now. Despite the condition of his clothes, he appeared quite fit. Hardly a starved and helpless beggar, to Yamaya's eye.

More, his music was actually melodic. No shrill squeaking from those pipes. Opshar had no good musicians, at least that Yamaya had seen. Their time was better spent fishing or hoeing or weaving or smithing. Early on, the tunes had drawn a few of the townsfolk closer. If they spent a little longer at Yamaya's fruit baskets, she could hardly complain.

All the same, something wasn't quite right. The man could be a spy, sent by the Count of Deeve, over the mountains. Or maybe he worked for the hunter-guards, seeking rumors of rogue mages. Whichever, Yamaya didn't like it. So when his eyes strayed over to her blanket again, she scowled.

"What do you want?"

Yamaya had spent years perfecting that tone of voice. Most people backed off when she used it. The beggar ducked his head a little, more a nod of respect than a fearful flinch.

"I was wondering if you need any help." The words were smooth and neutral. A trained voice.

"No thanks."

Now she knew this was no beggar. Beggars whined and pleaded for charity. Victims of banditry groveled and offered to pay for their lives. His being here was definitely a plot of some kind.

After a moment, he pointed out, "You are alone."

That was so obvious, Yamaya almost didn't bother replying. Finally she spat, "That doesn't mean I need help."

Quickly, she covered her fruit baskets and began to tie the lids down. This had to be a hunter-guard, sniffing after Gabrith — and good luck with that — but she wouldn't sit here while he pried for information.

The beggar's hat shifted as he turned his head to search the square with his eyes. "No man is with you. Did he abandon you?"

He almost sounded kindly. Yamaya didn't trust it. "Mind your own business." She lifted her drab green skirt a little, showing the sheathed knife on her outside thigh.

The beggar shrugged a little as she flicked the cloth back down. Crouching, she leaned over her bulging stomach to pack her things away. Yamaya had decided that this would be a good time to go see Gordemir. The tail end of business wasn't worth risking whatever this false beggar had in mind.

"I'm only looking for work." He spoke slowly, offering a word at a time to see if she stabbed it. "A dry place to sleep. If you need a pair of hands..."

"Let it go, hunter-guard," she warned.

She glimpsed a startled expression. Then dark eyes crinkled as he laughed. "That, I am not."

The reaction didn't feel fake, but Yamaya didn't care. She snatched up her blanket and shook a cloud of dust over this annoying, perilous beggar. He coughed obligingly.

Before she could get the blanket folded, a new voice

trumpeted. "Yamaya! Is everything all right?"

Berisan had been considering moving on from the square. No one was tossing any coin his way, and he had his own problems to worry about. Yet he couldn't make himself do it. The people of Skaythe might be notoriously callous, but this was a pregnant woman. A fierce one, evidently, but still.

Berisan was a minstrel, sworn to follow the code of his old teacher, Ar-Thea. Dar-Gothull's regime ruled over Skaythe with iron cruelty, tainting everything with his malice. It was the minstrels' calling to work against the regime by showing generosity instead of selfishness, compassion instead of suspicion. That was what made him a renegade.

Thus, Berisan couldn't turn his back, even though he risked everything if he was caught. He spoke slowly, hoping to smooth the jagged edges of suspicion that lurked in her thoughts. If he gave her time to think, she might accept his help. For this young woman, Yamaya, clearly needed it.

Now, here came someone to help her. This was Berisan's opportunity to back away. Yet instead of relief, surprise flitted across her face.

Berisan had already noticed the young man who strutted up to them. You could hardly avoid noticing, since he stuck out among the plainly dressed farmers and workmen of Opshar. Everything he wore was new and finely made. Trousers stitched with a running pattern, shirt so white that he couldn't ever have done a hard day's work in it. A whiff of sweet oil hinted at how he smoothed his black hair into a topknot like that worn in county capitals. There was even a small nose ring, silver gleaming against his smooth brown skin. So too, his loud voice was meant to be heard by everyone around him.

"Is he bothering you?" The fellow peered down at Berisan, folding his arms with what he must have imagined to be an intimidating air.

"It's nothing, Kinson." Yamaya continued stuffing fruit baskets into her waypack. Kinson made no move to assist her. He quickly seemed to forget Berisan was there, either.

"Surely you don't have to leave so soon," he coaxed. "I was hoping you could go for a walk with me. Father gave me some time off from the shop."

"I will be walking," Yamaya retorted. "It's a long way back to Weeping Falls." She struggled a little to get her waypack on.

Berisan resumed playing his double pipe and tried not to listen to their conversation. The dynamic between these two was strange, and it was hard to ignore when it went on five feet away from him.

"Don't you see, you don't have to go there alone. I'll help you." Kinson tried to flirt, yet still didn't offer to take the heavy pack.

"You?" Yamaya smiled with a sly edge. "You'd get your clothes dirty."

Kinson chuckled, but with a trace of indignation. "You know my father's the tailor. If I don't look good, his business will suffer."

Berisan kept his head down. He couldn't help wondering what customers a fine tailor had in this insignificant town. Most of the villagers were dressed more practically, in sturdy dresses or trousers.

"There's no tailor shop on my farm," Yamaya teased. To Berisan's ear, the flirtation rang hollow.

"I know that," Kinson said, earnestly exasperated. "But it isn't right that you have to do it all alone. Gabrith died too soon."

"Yes. He did," Yamaya answered quietly. She shrugged, an uneasy movement. "What's my alternative? I can't move the farm to town."

Yamaya was widowed? That explained some things, especially why she seemed so uncomfortable. Her husband must not be long dead, and this man was all dressed up to court her.

"Then let me help you," Kinson said. "And my brothers. Father won't mind. It'll be a good chance to watch over the countryside outside of Opshar."

"That's nice of you. I'll keep it in mind for the future." Yet something changed in Yamaya's posture. A subtle shift in balance that added space between them. Kinson didn't seem to notice.

"You really should." He smiled, with every expectation of victory.

Yamaya kept a coy face on — that was every woman's best defense, to let men think you liked them — but her mind was racing. Kinson had never shown a bit of interest in her before. Only now, when she was ugly and bloated with another man's child, he wanted to walk her around town.

Yet, hadn't she just been feeling like an outsider? Bemoaning that she had a farm to run all on her own? Here was an offer of help. One with advantages, at that. Kinson's uncle, Aulgrip, was the village headman. He ran the tavern and knew everyone's business. Kinson's father, the tailor, was Aulgrip's brother. Another uncle ran the smithy. They were all key figures in Opshar.

The memory of Yamaya's second-mother whispered in her ear, "Always make connections when you can."

It was the basic expectation of every woman in Skaythe. Be sweet to the men, no matter what they did. Take them to your bed. Bind them to your family with children. It was exactly how she got tangled up with Gabrith, back when they both were under her second-father's thumb.

Just the same, Kinson's connection dangled. Could

she afford to let it go by? It wasn't as if she knew him well enough to like or dislike him.

So she said, "There is one thing, if you don't mind. I need to talk to Gordemir about a cradle. Will you walk me that far?"

"Gladly!" He offered his arm. Yamaya pretended to be pleased, and held on. At least it helped balance her heavy pack.

As soon as they reached the carpenter's shop, Yamaya saw her strategy pay off. Gordemir hurried up to the counter, brushing off sawdust, when he saw who was there. When Kinson informed Gordemir what Yamaya needed, his black eyes flicked between them like a bee seeking nectar in a flower patch. He went easy on the bargaining, no doubt expecting that Headman Aulgrip would hear about his generosity. Gordemir even accepted the rest of Yamaya's cherries as a first payment.

As for Kinson, Yamaya thought he enjoyed pulling strings. He shook Gordemir's hand vigorously, and smirked as he held the door for Yamaya. "I'll see you again soon?" Then he hurried back to the tailor's shop without waiting for her agreement.

Yamaya crossed the market plaza. For all that she'd traded the cherries away, her waypack dragged on her back. Gordemir obviously thought she and Kinson were a couple. Soon everyone in Opshar was going to "know" that. It was intensely irritating. Yamaya just wasn't sure why.

Ahead of her, the beggar kept playing his two-reed pipe. Eyeing him, she recalled how he and Kinson both offered to help with her farm. Almost exactly the same words, yet they sounded very different to her ears.

Well, as long as she was making connections, what if she considered the beggar? He had already told her what he wanted: "a dry place to sleep." On the surface, he didn't have much to offer. Yamaya knew he was hiding something, too. She would be gambling that his secrets didn't bite her in the ass one day.

There was also a risk of offending Kinson. And through him, the village. Long-term, that mattered more than her niggling worries.

The problem was, Yamaya didn't understand what Kinson wanted. He was reaching down to her, just as she would be to that beggar. Thinking back, she had never had the sense that Kinson was attracted to her. Of course, he wouldn't have approached her when she was with Gabrith. At least he had that much sense.

Why was he in a hurry now? Parading her before the town. Staking a claim. Old irritations pricked at Yamaya's mind. She wasn't some prize to be argued over!

What Yamaya wanted — what she needed — was to get away from the mountains. She'd eloped with Gabrith on his promise that they both would give up that life. The lowlands had been a big change. Living in a drafty old cottage. Digging, planting, pruning. Sitting under the apricot tree with her sewing. Fingers cramped, back aching, but soothed by the knowledge that they wouldn't have to fight for their lives that day. Those few weeks had passed too quickly.

If Yamaya wanted to have any freedom, the beggar might be a better choice. She had already made it clear she was able to defend herself. She could use him, and he wouldn't dare speak up. Later, if things worked out as Kinson seemed to wish, they could send him on his way.

"*Do both,*" Bekkera's voice murmured from memory. "*Let Kinson know his fancy clothes and string-pulling aren't enough. If he wants you, make him work for it.*"

Yamaya had had many disagreements with her second-mother, but it was hard to fault the reasoning. She had options, even if Kinson didn't see them.

When she reached the beggar, she paused. "What's your name?"

His reed hat tilted up, but he didn't quite look at her. "Sand."

"Sand." That wasn't a real name. Maybe she shouldn't have been surprised. "Have you done any farming?"

"I've gardened. A lot," he added with shades of some private joke.

"Well, that's something." Yamaya noticed that he didn't beg for the work, or brag to make himself look better. He sat relaxed, pipes across his lap, and waited for her decision. It was odd. Not necessarily bad, but odd.

"Shall I come with you, then?" At last he met her gaze. He had a broad, square face, neither handsome nor plain. The dark eyes were alert, but calm.

"You're hired. For now."

At her words, Sand rolled to his feet. Yamaya noted his uncommon grace. She couldn't have done better herself, at least before she got pregnant. If she needed a reminder to be careful about this man, there it was. Still, she only needed him long enough to figure out what Kinson wanted. If she was lucky, she would never discover the truth of this beggar.

As he shook out his leather cloak, Yamaya let her gaze wander about the square. Nobody appeared to be watching, but she knew how false that impression could be. Besides, on a battlefield, the feint was often more important than the strike.

"*Let's see your next move, Kinson,*" she thought.

II

Weeping Falls

Berisan stowed his pipes, pleased at this turn of events. Tonight he would sleep under a roof, something you didn't fully appreciate until you'd spent a few nights outdoors. More, he would be in a position to help someone who really needed it. That was a goal truly worthy of his heritage.

Noting how Yamaya shifted her back under the weight of her waypack, he extended a questioning hand.

"Shall I carry that for you..." He hesitated, not sure what to call her. Not lady or mistress, since she was not of noble birth. He filled in with "...Boss?"

Yamaya answered with a curt laugh. "Not boss. Farmer."

She shrugged her pack off and shoved it at him. A glimpse of her murky thoughts suggested she was as unused to receiving even so simple a kindness. Berisan put both straps of his waypack over one shoulder, and both of hers over the other. It took a bit of shifting to balance the two. Before the minstrel troupe had had to split up, they used to pack their things on Tisha's gray donkey, Riprap. Now that he carried so much, Berisan recalled the beast of burden with greater sympathy and respect.

In silence, he followed his new employer through the village, heading generally westward. Booted feet shuffled over streets of packed earth. Each house stood shoulder to shoulder with the others. Behind them, Berisan glimpsed large vegetable gardens or pigs in sturdy pens. The spice of dust and animal droppings reminded him of his childhood home in Kamuril. In those days, a walled garden had been his whole world. The skills he had learned, however reluctantly, would serve him again.

Like most of the small villages across Skaythe, Opshar did not have a wall to protect it. Such defenses were reserved for the counts' capitals, where there were resources to maintain them. Peasant folk had to cope by building close beside each other, forming an irregular barrier.

The village street dwindled to a narrow lane, barely wide enough for a farm wagon to pass. Beyond the cluster of houses, farm fields and pastures spread out like a quilt embroidered in every possible shade of green. The river looped across and around them, like the badly mended tear in Berisan's cloak.

Not knowing their exact destination, he could expect that his newly hired employer knew the way. He used the time to study her. He couldn't see Yamaya's face, but there were a few hints from behind. Even with the weight of her belly, she stalked with an athletic, controlled stride. Head up, coiled black braids gleaming as she turned her head, ever watchful. Of course, Skaythe could be dangerous for anyone traveling alone. Still, the extent of her caution seemed out of place in the peaceful countryside.

Berisan's curiosity swelled. Who was this widowed farm wife, truly? What had happened to her husband? It would be stupid not to ask any questions about what came next.

"Farmer?"

"What." Yamaya darted a sharp glance over her shoulder.

"What kind of farm is it? And what duties will I have?"

"We have the fruit trees, a few sweet potatoes, some vegetables. Enough to eat, but not much more." She seemed to relax a little, speaking of this.

"I saw you can trade the fruit," Berisan said.

Yamaya nodded. "I've gathered a few herbs, for medicines. Haven't been able to root them yet."

"Do you have any animals?" Most farms at least had chickens, or a pig.

"That's what I need you for, " she tossed over her shoulder. "A handyman, to finish some of Gabrith's projects. He was working on a chicken run."

Her voice trailed off, bleak. Berisan's heart went out to her. "What happened? If I may ask."

"A fever." Yamaya's back was rigid. Almost to herself, she muttered, "After everything we went through, a stupid fever took him."

"That's rough," Berisan sympathized. It was common enough for diseases to sweep through local areas.

"Save your pity." She walked faster, leaving him a little behind.

Yamaya's words were vague, but she couldn't hide the flashes of memory. Lurking among foliage, two bone hafts slightly sticky in her sweaty fists. Shrieking as they sprang the ambush. But also, a figure at her side. Short robes to the knee, a leather jerkin beneath. Fire flared from his hands. Gabrith.

Now that was something. It seemed her husband had been a mage, like Berisan. And Yamaya had been some kind of fighter. It explained her walk, and those knives. The handle he had glimpsed was deer horn, too. It was unusual for women to fight, but not extremely rare. Especially in areas where there weren't many young men. What surprised him more was that Yamaya's late husband had apparently been a rogue mage.

As a renegade himself, Berisan understood all too well the deadly crossroads an untutored mage stood at. The power of life or death in your hands. Wealth and prestige, if you were ruthless enough to claim them. Yet, if you lacked the connections to be sanctioned by the regime, it was a precarious gift. The common people suffered so much at the hands of Dar-Gothull's followers. They hated all mages on principle. Even a small bounty meant swift betrayal to the hunter-guards.

Berisan and his brother Alemin had faced this exact challenge, growing up. Their family had hidden them out of love, and lived every day with the fear of being exposed as traitors. Despite being older, Alemin never seemed to fully realize the danger. It was always Berisan who looked out for the two of them. They had been very lucky that the roving mage, Ar-Thea, offered them a place among her household.

Without the training of that gentle mage, Berisan could have ended up just like Gabrith. A rogue mage, living in fear. Eager to throw in with whatever group was ambitious enough to want his power, and strong enough to protect him. Thinking back to the signs of banditry he had seen on the way to Opshar, Berisan was fairly certain that Yamaya and Gabrith hadn't been part of any regular military.

That wasn't good news, yet there was the babe she carried. The offspring of a mage would be born into the same darkness his father had known. Perhaps, if Berisan was able, he could teach that child a better way.

"We'll rest here." Yamaya's curt voice cut into his thoughts.

Their trail had turned from the river into an area of rolling land somewhere between low hills and large hummocks. A chattering stream ran down toward the river, crossed by a bridge made of driftwood lashed together. On the far side, a bigger log had been carved open to make a rough bench. Berisan was glad enough to stop. His head and both feet throbbed. He let his burdens roll onto it, and straightened to stretch his back.

He thought that Yamaya would sit, but she started to shuffle down toward the water. Instinctive fear pierced him, that she would lose her balance on the muddy bank.

"Are you getting water?" He jumped up again. "I'll bring it. Go ahead, sit. "

"What are you doing?" Obsidian eyes stabbed him with a combination of irritation and embarrassment.

"Just being a good worker," he answered cheerfully.

"I didn't hire you for a nursemaid!"

"If something happens to you, I won't have much of a job, will I?" Berisan grabbed the water skin that dangled from his pack and slid down the bank to fill it. You now could add puzzled gratitude to the list of Yamaya's emotions.

Yamaya watched in confusion as this uppity beggar fetched her water. Just as with Kinson's sudden interest, she wasn't sure what she was seeing. When she picked a beggar for her farm hand, she expected him to do the least work he could get away with, while eating into her food stores. Nobody was this helpful. Not without a reason.

But of course, she did know what she was seeing.

You could always tell a mage. Her second-father, Huld, had taught her, starting when she was about nine, how to pick out the fighters from the rabble. It was the way they stood. Not with blustering bravado or jittering with nerves. A dangerous fighter was relaxed, ready to move or strike.

Mages were like that. They had power to strike over any distance, and no one could stop them. What did they have to fear? Nothing, except for another mage.

Yamaya ought to know, after living with one for two years. Gabrith even spoke of her as his wife, not as a temporary playmate, like most of Huld's men. They hadn't been married at the temple in Pulgoll, but Huld had been glad enough to accept his claim, along with Gabrith's loyalty.

Now Gabrith was dead, and here came this stranger who was and was not like him. Not as forceful, to be sure. Gabrith had been fierce and direct. One was never in doubt about his intentions. Sand passed over the waterskin with his face a little turned away, deflecting her gaze. He was a calm man, confident without arrogance. One who understood fear but was not governed by it.

Still, Yamaya knew. And she wondered, what curse was it that attracted all these mages to her side?

"Let's go before we stiffen up," Yamaya declared.

"All right." Berisan's back complained as he straightened with the two waypacks over his shoulders, but that just showed she was right. Besides, he was curious to see this farm of hers. The place where he planned to burrow in and elude the ever-watchful hunter-guards.

Beyond that small stream, their trail angled up a shallow ridge above the Pulgoll Valley. The shape reminded him of a horse's neck, slightly arched, with short grass on the sides and a fringe of trees along the top, like a mane. Below them, on the right, the river had straightened out to flow directly across marshy ground where reeds grew thickly. The main watercourse was exceptionally clear. Even downstream of the village, there wasn't a bit of mud to sully the current. The bottom was smooth and sandy, without so much as a submerged rock breaking the mirrored brightness.

He labored upward, breathing steadily. As they climbed, Berisan recognized something unnatural about the riverbed. One of the Shining Ones' highways ran beneath it. Or rather, the water had found the easier course and flowed over the top of the roadway. Ahead of them, it ended in a perfectly round pond, right where the land came to a sort of edge. Sunlight glittered over its face. Rising mist hinted at waterfalls where the water tipped over the far side of the ancient paving.

Distracted by this enchanting vista, Berisan didn't see the farm at first. The trail steepened and turned, forcing him to watch his footing. Now he saw that the row of trees on the crest of the ridge were fruit trees. Old ones, badly in need of pruning. A small cottage nestled among them, nearly hidden by the tangled branches.

He found enough breath to ask, "Is that it?"

"That's it. Weeping Falls."

Berisan couldn't quite place her tone. Was it pride, or sarcasm? As they drew closer, the overall impression was of long neglect. The ill-tended trees, he had already noted, but there were also bloodthorn thickets around the foundation, and rascalweed stalks stood tall along the hillside.

When they reached the place, he saw the cottage's foundation and lower half were made with rounded chunks of stone. The curved edge of a cistern swelled out from the back of it. Rough old boards formed the upper half of it. Some of these were missing, with oddly shaped sections of driftwood wedged into the gaps. The overhanging roof was of thatch, shaped with an inward tilt to funnel rain water into the cistern.

Farther under the trees, he saw a lean-to inside a partial fence. That must be the chicken run Yamaya had mentioned Gabrith working on.

The farmer herself marched up a trio of stone steps into the shadows of the cottage. Not knowing where she wanted her waypack, Berisan followed her inside. The floor was a flattened oval of river stones, but covered with thick mats. He faintly scented the sweetness of the reeds they were woven from. Near the center, a square hearth was sunken in the floor. There was a low work table beside it. On the right side, wooden shelves held clay pots and reed baskets that likely contained foodstuffs.

"Set mine there." Yamaya gestured to the left half of the oval, where bedding had been rolled up to clear the floor for the day's work. "You can use the lean-to. We were going to get some chickens, but it isn't ready yet."

"Thank you." Berisan set her waypack down and took his own toward the rough shelter.

Like the cottage, the lean-to had a stone foundation and overhanging roof. Though dusty, the structure appeared sturdy enough to keep off all but the worst weather. Yamaya said chickens, but it might even have been large enough to house a cow or goat. A pile of dried, cut weeds had been tossed into the back angle. Nesting material for the chickens, no doubt. Still, it would make a better bed than the damp ground Berisan was used to sleeping on.

The incomplete fence was of woven branches, some of them apparently hacked off the nearest tree. From the downed fruit littering the ground, it was an apricot tree. Berisan marked it as his first task to rake that up. He didn't want to deal with flies and other vermin coming to feast on rotten fruit.

He set his waypack down near the back of the lean-to and focused for a moment. Golden energies swirled and settled around it. No one but another mage could see them, but anyone who approached the pack would feel a sense of deep unease. That they were being stared at by someone they couldn't see. If they didn't leave the pack alone, the dread would continue to intensify. Berisan's old teacher, Ar-Thea, might not have approved. She taught that it was evil to disturb the thoughts of others. But he was alone now, without his fellow minstrels for safety. It was better not to take chances.

With that handled, Berisan walked about to get a feel for the place.

A gradual slope fell away below the ridge top. Several terraced fields were edged by more river stones. He could see that the land had been shaped, gently, to direct the frequent rains into the fields. There were low mounds of foliage in neat rows — sweet potatoes — and a few other vegetables. They looked healthy enough, but too many stalks of rascalweed jutted up. That would be his second task.

Gazing past the cottage, he saw the other side of that perfectly round lake. At some point in the past, the land had slumped away beneath the ancient paving, so that sheets of water flowed unevenly over the lip. This must be Weeping Falls. Misty patches of rainbow hovered where the water cascaded down dozens of rocky layers toward a marshy area far below. Even from this distance, Berisan could see many exposed river stones. That explained where the original builders of this farm had acquired their construction materials.

When he came back to the cottage, Yamaya was on the porch. She spoke with a waspish snap. "Does everything meet your standards?"

"Just seeing what might need to be done." Berisan spoke soothingly. From the way she rubbed her lower back, the weight of the babe troubled her. "Were you here long, before..."

"Three months ago, we came down from the mountains." Yamaya's dark eyes moved past Berisan, taking in the fruit trees and terraced fields. "That was no fit life."

No fit life for their unborn child. Yamaya didn't say the words, but Berisan heard them all the same.

"He wanted this," she said, thinking of Gabrith now. "We both did, but he wanted it more." Though her expression was stony, Yamaya spoke with the softness of regret. "The time was too short."

Berisan nodded. "It always is."

His friends, Ar-Thea's other apprentices, were far from him now. By what Yamaya said, they had been forced to part ways at nearly the same time she and Gabrith had left those mountains she was being so careful not to name.

Anything could have happened in the months since the minstrels parted. Hunter-guards. A rival mage. Even a random fever. There was nothing Berisan could do about it, but still he wondered. Would he ever see them again?

The afternoon was all but gone, fiery rays of sunset beginning to smolder all over the hillside. Yamaya knelt at the back of the cottage. Brooding, she peeled back the mat and lifted the lid. A clay pot brought up water for cooking the river grain. She replaced the lid and mat, and brought the water to the fire.

Sand had found Gabrith's hatchet. She heard him outside, cutting wood into proper sized pieces for the fire. The sound of it both alerted and reassured her. Yamaya hadn't worried about being alone since she was a little girl. She was too much a fighter. Or maybe, she hadn't thought about it, until she was no longer alone.

Yamaya readily admitted that she was glad to let someone else handle such a splintery chore. It meant she only had to awaken a small blaze from the morning's embers. While she waited for the fire to be ready, she measured river grain into the cooking pot and chopped a few vegetables and a bit of smoked fish to mix with it.

It had been a while since she fed more than herself. Yamaya hesitated over the quantity, and added another handful of grain. Men would forgive a lot of things if you fed them well. Smoke wafted into her eyes and made her blink.

Why was she worried about what Sand thought, anyway? He was just a hired hand, and she was supposed to be free of the need to please the men around her. It was the only good thing about losing Gabrith.

Anyway, it would be strange enough to have company with her food, after weeks alone. Maybe Yamaya had made a mistake with this man, Sand. He asked so many questions.

All right, it was reasonable to ask. Irritably, she allowed that. The weird thing was that he actually seemed interested in her answers. In Yamaya's experience, men only wanted to tell you what to do. They never cared what the woman thought about it.

Now, with Gabrith gone, this farm was hers alone. Yamaya was the one who should be in control. She stirred the cooking pot, determined that she would be the one asking questions from now on. Let him struggle to come up with the answers.

So when she called him for the meal, she passed a question along with his bowl of food.

"Well, Sand. What about you? I know you aren't from Pulgoll. How did you get here?"

It was gratifying, in a petty way, to see his friendly face close in a little. Yamaya chewed her river grain, and waited.

"Originally? Kamuril," he answered.

"Never heard of it," Yamaya was forced to admit.

"It's west of here," he provided after a moment's hesitation.

"Must be a long way."

He shrugged. "It's on the other side of Skaythe."

A greater distance than Yamaya could imagine, but it didn't explain how he got to Pulgoll. "And? How did you get here?"

He smiled faintly. "I walked."

"Oh? I was sure that you flew," Yamaya retorted. Some mages could do that, at least according to the tales.

"If only. My feet wouldn't be so sore." Sand's eyes crinkled with laughter, but he admitted nothing. He gazed toward the far western horizon, where the sea seethed with sunset's blaze. "I didn't realize we're so close to the ocean. I guess there isn't much farther I could go."

It was a nice try at changing the subject, but Yamaya wasn't having it. "Getting away from something?"

He gave that little shrug again. "Aren't we all?"

Yamaya felt the barb of his subtle accusation. "Someone's after you."

She spoke out of spite, and thought he would get angry. Maybe she wanted him to. She knew how to respond to that. Sand just ducked his head over his bowl of food.

"It's better for you not to know." As in the market square, he seemed to choose his words. "Except that I am not a hunter-guard. I wasn't after your husband."

Yamaya bristled. How would he know that? "Then you're a spy," she accused.

"No. I'm just trying to stay alive." Sand set the empty dish down on the table. "Thank you for a roof over my head, and the food. It was delicious."

Yamaya glared at his back as he started down the steps. Sand needed to be reminded who was in charge here. "Just a minute."

He turned, wary. She jabbed a finger at her pantry shelf. "See that bottle? Never touch it."

You could hardly miss the bottle. It was the only glass object she had. Thick and crude it might be, but glass was expensive. It stood tall and shining among the reed baskets and clay jars around it. Dark amber liquid glinted inside. It looked like nothing more than some fermented apricot juice.

Sand's mouth opened, his expression faintly indignant. Yamaya could practically hear his protest that he would never get into her stores. Then he paused, and asked, "What is it?"

"Sleeping syrup. I had to gather the barbtails myself, and there aren't many around here."

He eyed her for a moment, then slowly asked, "Barbtail?"

"I'm making it for pain, when the baby comes." Barbtail had other uses, too. The herb was something of a secret weapon among the women of the mountains. Bekkera had taught Yamaya the recipe when she came of age. "That's why I'm saving it up. This is my first baby. I don't know how much I'll need."

Sand's face was a careful blank. "Will it be long, then?"

"Two months. Three at most." Yamaya had no reason to lie about that.

He nodded. "I'll keep my eyes open for barbtails when I go about to look for more wood. Will you need anything else tonight?"

"I don't think so." His quiet embarrassment was satisfaction enough, for now.

Berisan's belly was thick with the first hot meal he'd had in forever. His legs were tight after long walking. Especially, his head was foggy and ready for sleep.

The heaps of dried vegetation under the lean-to needed a bit of work to make them comfortable. Boards creaked and weeds crackled as Berisan trod the pile down. He laid his sleeping mat over the top and lowered himself onto the scant cushion. With his leather cloak wrapped around him, he linked hands behind his head and gazed upward to watch the daylight fade.

Being under a lean-to was better than sleeping under the sky, but he could still hear the wind slithering through the apricot leaves. There was an occasional moist thud as over-ripe fruit fell to the ground. Maybe that was what made him so restless.

More likely it was the barbtail syrup. Ar-Thea had been an herbalist, and not just as her excuse for a wandering lifestyle. It had been her true profession. Berisan had already been good with plants, since he and Alemin had grown up hiding behind the walls of their family's big garden. His time with Ar-Thea had only sharpened his interest.

Because of his training, Berisan knew very well that barbtail was no mere sleeping syrup. It was a poison. Ar-Thea would never have kept something like that in her kitchen. It should have been locked away, and he was anxious just knowing that Yamaya was so careless.

Ar-Thea would also have told him not to pass judgment. There weren't many ways to relieve severe pain. Yamaya was only taking care of herself. At least she had warned him about the barbtail syrup.

Remembering Ar-Thea's kindly ways was a comfort, but was also a mournful reminder of what Berisan had lost. For much of his life, he and Alemin had been horrific oddities. They had been born magelings in a family with no other mages. By Dar-Gothull's cruel laws, all young mages had to be trained in a temple school. There, they were goaded into ruthless competition that supposedly forced them to master their power. Yet there were dreadful rumors about what happened to magelings who weren't strong enough to learn.

Rather than lose both his sons, their father had kept them hidden away behind the walls of the family's garden. If anyone ever visited the house, they had to wait in the root cellar. That was where Berisan had learned the over-riding commandment: *don't get caught*. No one must ever know of their power.

The brothers grew up safe, but trapped. As they got older, the house and garden had become more and more a stifling prison. Ar-Thea's arrival had changed all that. She had taught them to accept themselves as the first step toward control. While part of her roaming band — the six apprentices she called her family — the brothers had experienced a wider world. Ar-Thea had shown them that violence was not the only way. Her potions and remedies brought rewards far beyond the scant coin she earned. Certainly beyond the soul-destroying corrosion that lay beneath most mages' power.

In the end, Ar-Thea had been branded as a renegade — one who rejected and subverted Dar-Gothull's tyrannical rule. She, who had only done kindness, had been accused and condemned in secret. Her crime? To seek out six magelings and divert them from the horror of the temple schools.

Their mentor must have sensed her fate. A few days before the count and all the hunter-guards descended, she had sent them all away. In farewell, she had given them one last gift. A story. One that was impossible, and inspiring, dangerous to know.

In their grief, the six apprentices had chosen to take up her work. They became minstrels, a traveling circus that moved through the lowest and most desperate places, bringing hope where they could. In that small way, they fought back against the endless wrongs of Dar-Gothull's cruel reign.

Berisan threw his cloak off and called forth a witchlight. Beneath its soft glow, he dug into his waypack. Down at the bottom, he had a set of eight juggling knives. They looked like steel, with gaudy gems in a golden hilt, but that was merely stagecraft. Paint and carving to enchant an audience. Berisan turned them slowly, remembering the excitement of the cheering crowd. He flipped one and felt it slap into his palm.

Alemin had been obsessed with the juggling. At any idle moment, he would be practicing. In addition to the brothers' act, there was Tisha, the dancer, and Meven, the puppeteer. Keilos on his lute and Lorrah on her violin made music to bring it all to life.

It had been a risk, their traveling minstrel show. Even with their mentor's fate in mind, it had seemed worth taking. For two years, they roamed Skaythe and did what they could to comfort the masses crushed by Dar-Gothull's reign. Until Keilos received his prophecy of disaster, and they scattered to hide themselves.

Berisan tossed the knives a few more times, while loneliness gnawed at his heart. Then slowly he put them away. Juggling wasn't the same without his brother. Being separated hurt, especially when he stopped to think about it.

These days, Berisan wandered alone. Without his friends, the old fear crushed him with its desperate imperative: *don't get caught.* Most days, he trudged with helpless futility. A lone beggar couldn't do much good for the people. Ar-Thea's dream of a better future for Skaythe had faded to a dying ember.

Since his chance meeting with Yamaya, that ember flickered to life. Berisan had been so afraid that he risked forgetting his purpose. No longer.

A woman alone, widowed and pregnant. This farm was all she had, but trying to keep it would take more than she had could give. Fierce as she was — unwelcoming, even — he couldn't call himself a minstrel if he ignored her plight.

The separation from his friends wasn't supposed to be permanent. They planned to gather again in six months — four months, now — and renew their efforts at change. Assuming no hunter-guards or other disasters forced him to flee, Berisan could stay that long.

Yamaya might not know it, but she didn't need her poison. She had Berisan on her side.

III

Enemies, Old and New

A farmer's days were always long. Yamaya had come to know that well. Ever since she and Gabrith moved into the abandoned cottage, something they tried to repair would always be falling over, or something else would be sprouting in the wrong place and need to be dug out. That didn't exactly change with a hired hand. Yamaya still sweated and toiled, and fell onto her mat at night in exhausted slumber.

But there was no mistaking the difference it made when someone worked along with her.

For all she suspected Sand was a mage, he was also a natural farm worker. He dug the weeds without being reminded, then chopped them small before packing them around the melons and sweet potatoes to preserve the moisture in the soil. That was something Yamaya would never have thought of. After several days without rain, he joined her in trudging back and forth to the waterfall, carrying buckets and jugs to refill the cistern.

Sand thinned the crowded branches on the apricot trees and wove them together to extend Gabrith's fence around the future chicken run. When flies swarmed around the apricots Yamaya was drying in the sun, he rigged up a simple tent to shield them. Soon the farm started to look like someone actually lived there.

Yamaya had a hard time believing in her good fortune. She cultivated the vegetables in the mornings, and when the afternoons grew too hot, she worked on her sewing in the shade of the cherry trees. All the time, she watched Sand carefully, expecting some sign of theft or treachery. It was inevitable, after all. Nobody in Skaythe cared about other people.

Except for Sand, it seemed. When she was thirsty from working in the hot sun, he turned up with a pot of water. He juggled stones to make her smile. In the evenings, when the baby kicked the most, he played a gentle tune on his pipes that always seemed to calm the brat down. Only Gabrith had ever been so attentive. It reminded her of how much she had lost when he died.

Sand even brought her a small basket of moss, collected from near the waterfalls. "If one of us gets hurt," he explained, "we can pack the wound with it."

Yamaya already knew that. Perversely, she felt compelled to compete with his knowledge. "I can stuff diapers with it," she retorted, "or use it to line the cradle."

It had to be the magic. He was spying on her somehow. There were other signs, as well. Sometimes, in the night, she glimpsed light beneath the lean-to, a golden glow without any particular source. Disturbing as that was, Yamaya found herself getting used to it. She continually warned herself not to get complacent. That caution didn't keep her from becoming accustomed to company with the evening meal. They talked of superficial things, matters of running the farm.

She could almost forget this wasn't Gabrith. Then she felt guilt bite deep, as if she had turned away from his memory too soon. Ruthlessly, Yamaya reminded herself that it was Gabrith who had died. Willing or not, he had left her alone with a farm to run. It was no betrayal for her to keep building the legacy he wanted for their kid.

Despite her outward beauty, Yamaya was not an easy person to get close to. Berisan quickly realized that she wasn't open to a new friendship, let alone more than friendship. Even when she was alone, the woman never seemed to relax. Her brow was always tight, with a watchful darting glance. That didn't keep him from doing what he could to restore the neglected farm. Berisan knew he was making a difference, even if Yamaya found it difficult to admit. That held its own satisfaction.

One evening, as Yamaya prepared supper, she snapped at Berisan, "You eat too much. We'll have to go into town and trade for more river grain."

That wasn't fair, but there was no sense arguing. After nine days, he was becoming accustomed to the quickness of her anger. Of course, that hardly set her apart from the rest of Skaythe, who lived in constant fear of being attacked by mages, or bandits, or their count's guards.

Berisan thought for a moment, then said, "Now I'm hungry."

Yamaya's eyes were one of her best features, gleaming black but sharp as broken obsidian. At the moment, she was studying Berisan in a way that made him think she was considering the best method to kill him.

"You know best," he immediately amended. "What should we take with us for trade?"

"Cherries, of course."

As Berisan had hoped, the question diverted her to thoughts toward the helpful task of picking the most fruit and away from potential murder.

The following day saw him scampering up and down the three cherry trees, filling small baskets with fruit and passing them down to Yamaya. Once all her bushel baskets were filled to overflowing, she let him come to earth. They spent the hottest part of the afternoon in the shade, sorting cherries. The plumpest crimson fruit were packed for the market, while the rest were put aside to be dried, or boiled for juice.

The next morning's dawn was just breaking when

Yamaya packed a day's food for them. Their two waypacks were heavy with fresh fruit. Berisan would have carried them both, but Yamaya insisted she wasn't such a weakling. In silence, they trudged down the hillside trail, lured on by distant flickering lights in Opshar.

The sun was well up by the time they arrived there. Market stalls were set up all around the plaza, just as Berisan remembered. Some of the dealers had sturdy wooden stalls with colorful flags. Others, like Yamaya, simply spread their wares on blankets. The noise of calling out wares, echoed into cheerful cacophony on a pleasantly cool morning.

"Keep close," Yamaya ordered. "I'll get us a spot."

She strode ahead to the porch of the tavern. The headman sat at a table, organizing the affair. After passing over a coin Berisan hadn't known she had, Yamaya was granted a surprisingly good space, just a bit down and across from the inn. A shoemaker was on one side of them, and a group of fishermen were selling on the other. Their humble blanket appeared a bit out of place, at least to Berisan. Still, who was he to say? As a mere beggar, he had only been tolerated when he crept in on the far end.

So had Yamaya been, but today felt different. Perhaps it was the lively music of Berisan's pipes, once he had folded his leather cloak for a pad to sit on. Perhaps it was simply that the morning was still cool. People came eagerly to trade for Yamaya's cherries. The girl helping out in the fish stall leaned over to gossip, whenever she had a moment.

It looked to be a good day.

To Yamaya's ear, the increased friendliness was new. That made it somewhat suspicious. People came to her display, but there was still that sidelong moment, a decision being made. They liked cherries, true, but did they want to do business with an outsider? Today, for some reason, there was an added strain of interest mixed in.

Belatedly, she remembered that Kinson had shown an interest in her. It seemed that made her a curiosity. Even the fisher's girl seemed intent on talking to Yamaya. Yes, Lilia had been friendly before. She always wanted to hear about the world outside their small village.

Confirming Yamaya's suspicion, the younger girl leaned in to say, "Kinson has been asking about you."

"Oh?" Yamaya arched a brow, inviting further information.

"Who your family is, what anyone knows about you," Lilia went on.

Yamaya's family was something best not spoken of. Then the girl's bright eyes flicked past her. She stepped back, raising a hand to cover her giggles.

Yamaya wasn't surprised to spot that very man strolling down the steps from the tavern. Kinson wore an even finer tunic than the last time she'd seen him, and his boots shone dark with polish. He moved through the mingling villagers in the marketplace with swaggering purpose. Just slowly enough for everyone to see, Yamaya thought wryly.

One of the village women cut in front of him, blissfully unaware of his approach. Yamaya hid a smile when she saw the flash of annoyance across Kinson's brow. Let him stew for a moment. She had no intention of being at any man's beck and call.

"You're in the right place," she happily greeted the woman, whose name she thought might be Theda. "My cherries are the best in Pulgoll. How many can I get you?" Then, as if it was an afterthought, she tossed off to Kinson, "I'll be right with you."

Most people in the small villages didn't deal in coin, but in equal trades. If this was Theda, as Yamaya thought, then they had passed her husband's melon field on their way in to Opshar. The fruit was looking good. At first the woman deferred, but Yamaya then asked for things she knew Theda didn't have, like river grain.

"Unless you have a young hen to spare?" she added.

Theda shook her head, but eventually they reached a reasonable trade, a basket of Yamaya's cherries in exchange for equal weight of melons. It might be only one or two, but that was enough for a treat — and to save seeds for a crop of her own. Kinson loitered through all her bartering. Yamaya noted how he looked over her wares with an acquisitive air. Nor did she miss how he frowned at the sight of Sand, playing his double pipe softly on the other side of the blanket.

As soon as Theda stepped away, Kinson turned on a smile, though. "I've been looking for you." Was that meant to be flirtatious? There was a hint of childish sullenness in his tone. Yet again, Yamaya wondered what she was getting into. Then, just as quickly, she remembered her purpose. If she was going to live in Opshar, she had to make connections.

"I had to wait for more cherries to ripen," she breezily explained, and swept out a hand to indicate her trees' bounty. "Look at them now, though."

"Beautiful," Kinson flirted, and he bent to take one without offering payment. Sand looked up, or at least the brim of his hat rose a little. Kinson immediately frowned, popping the cherry into his mouth.

"Who is this man, Yamaya?"

"He's just a hired hand," Yamaya replied with her own tartness. What business was it of his? "And most of my customers offer something in trade."

"A hired hand?" Kinson ignored her warning. He looked at her with sad, disappointed eyes. "After I said my brothers will help you."

"You're all so busy in your shop," she parried. Compared to Gabrith, Kinson was vain and immature. Even Sand was more responsible. Lilia, in the booth behind him, hid her face to suppress giggles.

"That reminds me." Kinson brightened. "I wanted to bring you to my father's shop. You deserve a better dress." He gestured dismissively at her patched but sturdy dress.

"This one won't be spoiled when I work in the fields. It's already been torn and mended." Several times, in fact.

Even as she said so, Yamaya's mind darted. Kinson wanted her to meet his father already? That was making this more than mere flirtation. Why was he in such a hurry?

"That's why you need a new one. You should wear clothes that will make you look as pretty as you are," he cozened. Maybe he just wanted to get his hands on her.

Yamaya glanced away, pretending to blush. "How long will it fit me?" She gestured to take in her pregnant condition.

He shrugged a little "Oh, Father knows how to account for that." As with the issue of Sand's employment, he quickly moved past it. Did he accept her wishes, or hope to pretend that her wishes didn't exist?

"Won't you come?" Kinson cajoled. "It will be fun. Surely your hired hand can handle the trading for a little while."

Yamaya hesitated. She shifted a little, feeling the tightness of the leather straps concealing the sheathed knives beneath her skirt. She didn't trust Kinson's intentions, but if she wanted to know what he was up to, she might have to play along. For now.

Berisan played his double pipe, trying to focus on other customers who might be interested in trading for cherries, instead of the talk between Yamaya and her hoped-for beau. It wasn't easy. This man, Kinson, wasn't worth a moment of her time. He took her things without asking, right in front of the market. What else would he do when no one was around? Berisan couldn't understand why Yamaya put up with it. As he recalled, she had been quick enough to warn him away with steel after just a few words.

He ducked his chin a little, allowing the brim of his reed hat to block the sight of them. Berisan reminded himself that Yamaya was a few years younger, but she was his employer, not a child who needed to be watched over.

"Would you? Watch the stand for a while." Yamaya glanced down at him, calculation in her eyes. The surface of her thoughts did not glitter with infatuation. Instead, Berisan sensed a keen purpose. It seemed she had a plan.

So he said, in a neutral tone, "If you want, Farmer."

She nodded briskly, and turned to Kinson. Whatever she meant to say was lost in a sudden commotion. A woman's startled shriek pierced the marketplace babble. Then other scattered cries of protest were followed by the muted thunder of horse's hooves growing rapidly louder.

Yamaya reacted instantly, dropping to a crouch. One hand was deep in her pocket, while the other pressed to the blanket and helped her balance. Steely eyes raked the area, not with fear, but with expert skill at picking out hazards. Berisan had only a moment to take that in before the source of the disturbance became obvious.

Three horsemen trotted between the market stalls. Their clothing and tack were rough leathers and canvas, dull colors of earth and forest. Only, one of them waved a colorful scarf overhead as if it was some kind of trophy.

Kinson stepped back, cursing between his teeth. He almost planted a polished boot into one of Yamaya's cherry baskets.

"Careful." Berisan snatched it out of the way.

"You shut up." Kinson shoved Berisan's arm and caused several of the fruit to spill.

"Thief! Give it back!" A woman ran into the square after the riders. Jet black hair swirled over her shoulders, half fallen out of its braids. The bullying rider must have snatched the scarf off her head.

"Thief? I'm no thief. This rag got caught on my stirrup!" The fellow called out with joking indignation. The others guffawed along with him. The marketplace had gone deathly silent, allowing their voices to be heard easily.

"She shouldn't make such accusations," another complained.

Berisan held still, though his heart thudded in his chest. Those men were armed with swords, and beneath their loose outer shirts he glimpsed the rigid lines of leather jerkins.

He whispered to Yamaya, "Who are they?"

Intent on the unfolding scene, she made no reply. Berisan could only think that they were bandits.

"Here, have it back then." The one with the scarf dropped it in the dust, but as the woman ran to claim it he spurred his horse and made as if to trample her. A gasp went through the onlookers.

Berisan found himself on his feet. He lost track of what he meant to do when Yamaya rose and slipped behind him. Though startled, he immediately moved to shield her from view. Others around them were taking shelter, too. The shoemaker clawed sample boots off his counter, while others threw blankets over their products. The fisherman hastily shoved his daughter behind the barrels of fish.

"Stay out of sight," he hissed urgently.

"Yes, Papa." Berisan caught a flash of Lilia's face as she tucked her knees up to her chin. Just a while ago, those bright eyes had gleamed with humor. Now they were dark pools of fear.

Yamaya's fingers dug into Berisan's arm. "Your hat," she said in a barely audible growl. "I need it."

"*Don't let them find me,*" roiled in her thoughts. Berisan jerked on the cord beneath his chin and passed it over his shoulder without a word. Yamaya jammed it on over her coiled braids and crouched again to start snatching her cherries out of harm's way.

All around them, the villagers stared at those riders with hopeless fear and fury. The three thugs taunted the woman whose scarf they now tore beneath their horse's hooves.

"I thought you said it was yours," the third one sneered. "Don't you want it?"

Softly, Berisan asked Kinson, "Does this happen often?"

The man jerked away, shoulders slightly hunched. Though he refused to answer, his angry expression was its own reply. Kinson swallowed, and his dark eyes darted, looking for a way out.

Somehow one of the bandits had got hold of the woman's wrist. He dragged her effortlessly as his horse trotted into the plaza. The victim barely kept her feet. She still struggled, wailing a wordless keen of terror.

"Oh shut up!" The man kicked at her.

They stopped in front of the tavern steps. Their leader dismounted, bellowing toward the building. "Headman! Where are you?"

That was a very good question. Where was the headman? Berisan remembered him being quick enough to take Yamaya's coin. Now the tavern door was shut, and the only people left on the porch were cowering behind the rails.

Actually, that made perfect sense. A small village like this had no true soldiers to defend them against thugs like these. They were completely on their own.

The second attacker joined in. "She insulted us. We want justice!"

"Get out here, Aulgrip!" taunted the third.

Behind Berisan, Yamaya's voice was low and hard. "Do something."

Who did she mean? Berisan spared a glance to Kinson. It was clear from the tailor's fixed snarl while edging away that it wouldn't be him. That left it to Berisan.

Don't get caught. The old rule wrapped around his chest like iron chains. It squeezed the breath from his lungs.

Stay out of people's business. That was how you survived in Skaythe. If someone was hurting, or in danger, that didn't matter as long as it wasn't you. Yet, it was exactly the way of life Ar-Thea had rejected. Everything he and the other minstrels did was to prove that philosophy wrong. Unfortunately, his friends weren't here. Berisan would stand alone, and it was terrifying.

"Stop," the victim shrieked. "Let me go!"

Could he do something about this poor woman being dragged around? Oh, yes. But it would cost him. His secrecy, and the safety it brought him. Berisan's head felt tight and his legs were so tense that he felt a cramp coming on.

Wasn't this the core of Ar-Thea's teaching? Not just to talk about creating a better world, but to show people how it could be real. His own thoughts rebounded on him: these people had no one else to help them.

What was his safety worth, if it meant watching someone else suffer? More — Berisan had set himself to protect Yamaya in her vulnerable situation. Right now, it didn't seem like that protection was worth very much.

He glanced down, and was not surprised to meet a deadly frown. In Yamaya's mind, she snarled, "*Are you a mage or not?*"

He couldn't meet her gaze. For another agonizing moment, he watched as the three thugs taunted the headman while they terrorized his village. In his mind, Ar-Thea's gentle voice cautioned, "*You must never lash out in anger. Find a better way.*"

Berisan drew a deep breath, and stepped past Yamaya's blanket. Yes, he was angry at what the bandits were doing. He feared what it meant to give up the protection of his secrecy. But he couldn't lash out in fury. Yamaya and everyone else in Opshar deserved his help, no matter how insignificant their village might be. He had to show them that there was a better way.

The walk felt very long. Berisan was terribly exposed, bare-headed and squinting a little without his hat. He used the time to breathe slowly, gathering the power of *vitalis* so plentiful in the blazing sunlight. By the time he got around to the steps, the thugs were unleashing a chorus of taunts at the shuttered tavern.

"Hey, old man!" As his victim fought and cried, the leader raised his fist. "Get your ass out here! I'm gonna keep beating this bitch until you do!"

Quietly, slowly, Berisan said, "Please don't do that."

Why was Sand just standing there, Yamaya fumed. She knew he was a mage. With his power, he should be able to handle these three. Even Yamaya could have taken them on, if she hadn't been so great with child. Three-to-one wouldn't be the worst odds she had ever faced. Her hands slipped through the slits hidden in the folds of her peasant dress. The knobbled surface of her deer-horn dagger handle was ready beneath her fingers.

It should be so much easier for a mage. Gabrith would have blasted them with a flick of his hand. Despite that he knew them. Or maybe because of it.

Yet Sand stood there with hands at his side, flexing the fingers casually. Kinson was trying to sidle away. Both of them useless. What did they think was going to happen? Men like Mogrok and Tyar never learned until you hurt them.

Mogrok was braying something about making the headman come out when Sand finally moved. Yamaya's heart leaped. At last! She couldn't wait to see him rush in, blasting flames to make the horses run. Show those fools not to bother this village again! Then Yamaya would be safe, too. Sand just trudged across the plaza, a humble and unimposing figure. There wasn't so much as a spark of punishing flame.

She barely even heard Sand's voice when he said, "Please don't do that."

"What was that?" Mogrok turned with mocking slowness. Fist still raised, he let his gaze slide over Sand, and then past him, to Tyar. "Did you hear a whining noise? I thought it was a little cricket or something."

Tyar and Sabbin snickered. Then Sabbin started collecting the horse's reins, while Tyar advanced toward Sand. "What are you going to do, little cricket?"

"I was hoping we could talk about this," Sand said, slow and mild. "Please."

"Please," Sabbin snickered. "He said *please*."

"I'm new here," Sand told them. "Can you tell me what's going on?"

Yamaya's eyes narrowed as she assessed their reactions. Any of the men were bulkier than Sand. They were armed, and he bare-handed.

Yet his stance didn't look intimidated. He was relaxed, just like Huld used to tell her. Sand had to be doing something. Yamaya just couldn't figure out what it was.

The market crowd watched, breathless. Even Mogrok's victim was quieter as the imminent threat of a beating faded. Berisan could feel the communal dread of what these brutes would do to such a ragged beggar, because it was the same thing the bandits might do to them. At the same time, he sensed them daring to hope — but what they wished for was violence. They wanted him to make these thugs bleed. It was not a wish Berisan could fulfill.

"What's going on?" Mogrok's fierce laughter punctured the bubble of silence around the plaza. "What's going on is that the headman owes us tribute. He hasn't paid for a couple of months, so we're here to collect."

The merest rustle passed among the watchers. "*Is this true?*" Some were surprised by the accusation. Not all of them were, though. At Mogrok's gesture, one of the others grabbed the hostage. Mogrok swaggered forward.

Berisan kept a quiet face, but his eyes flicked, assessing where the men were and what cover might be nearby. It wasn't something he enjoyed, but these were skills he'd had to learn in his time on the road with the minstrels. The men were too close together, and too far from Berisan. He needed a little more time.

He asked, "How much do they owe you?"

Mogrok's black eyes glittered, greedy for even more coin. "It was three hundred, but like I said, they're behind on what they owe. So now it's five hundred."

Around the square, people blanched at the impossible sum. All of them together couldn't raise half of what Mogrok wanted. On the other hand, the thugs were almost close enough. Berisan inhaled, gathering his power. When he exhaled, *vitalis* flowed in ripples over the packed ground. Its sheer golden radiance was all but invisible in the brilliant sunlight.

Mogrok scowled as he drew near. Just for a second, he hesitated. Berisan wasn't cowering the way he expected. It set him on edge. Then the bandit stepped closer and leaned in, trying to dominate his pitiful opponent.

"You got that much on you, beggar?"

Berisan held his place. "I have fifteen." It was all he had gathered when he planned to rent a room above the tavern. "Let her go, and you'll at least have that much."

"Why, is she your girlfriend?" The fellow holding the hostage burst into crude laughter as he made kissing noises in the woman's ear. She wailed and started struggling again. Berisan glimpsed the rage in Mogrok's mind an instant before it erupted.

"Don't waste my time!" he bellowed, fist already hammering toward Berisan's face.

Berisan sidestepped with an acrobat's grace. The brute whirled to follow, teeth bared in a set smile. Murder was in his mind, but already *vitalis* wrapped around his sword hilt. Berisan made a beckoning and the blade flashed as it cleared the sheath. Mogrok staggered to a halt as it hung in the air.

"Hey!" Tyar shoved his hostage aside as he started toward them. Berisan swept a hand out. Coils of *vitalis* tangled the fellow's feet and he fell on his face with an angry yell.

"What the hells!" Mogrok cursed as the sword hovered above Berisan's shoulder. His face showed confusion, but then the instinctive fear of offending a mage.

"None of that, thanks," Berisan answered calmly. A wave of his hand sent the sword skittered over the dry ground in Yamaya's direction. He was certain she would know what to do with it.

Tyar stumbled to his feet. Berisan hooked his ankles and sent him sprawling again. When he turned back, Mogrok was almost on him, rushing with a wordless howl. Again Berisan sidestepped. His opponent was faster to pick it up this time, and turned with him.

"Stay out of my business," he roared as he lunged.

Berisan met him with a shove, palm-out, that projected a wedge of force a foot ahead of him. Mogrok effectively punched himself in the gut as he crashed into it. He staggered, groaning and coughing.

Before he could recover, Berisan summoned another wave of *vitalis*. He wrapped it around the man, huffed out a breath, and lifted him into the air. It wasn't easy; Mogrok was heavy, and he struggled to break free. Just for good measure, Berisan turned and caught Tyar, who was in the act of charging toward him.

Now he held two of the attackers up three or four feet above the ground. Unable to touch the packed earth, they couldn't attack him. They could only shout curses and struggle against the grip of something they couldn't see.

Berisan straightened, feeling a flush of victory. He'd found a way to stop them without hurting them. He allowed himself a brief grin, though he breathed heavily with effort. Several months ago, he and Keilos had had a long argument about whether this move was really possible. Someday, he wanted to tell his friend of this success.

IV

A Balancing Act

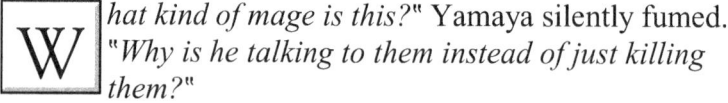

W|hat kind of mage is this?" Yamaya silently fumed. "Why is he talking to them instead of just killing them?"

Mogrok's sword flashed as it turned in the air. People standing nearby jumped back as it landed a few feet away from Yamaya's blanket. Cautiously, she glided forward. The blade was heavy and badly balanced, because Mogrok relied on brute force rather than skill. For all that, the edge was keen. She wrapped a spare scarf around it so that no one would get cut.

Another gasp went through the onlookers, and Yamaya's eyes jerked back to the fight. Somehow, Sand had both Mogrok and Tyar hanging up in the air. There was a kind of light around him, hard to see in the bright sunshine. The bandits fought and yelled, unable to free themselves from the unseen grip of a mage's power.

Yamaya didn't understand what was happening. Sure, Sand was deft in evading Mogrok's grapple, but why would he bother? Now he held them both up. He wasn't hurting them, and that mattered. Eventually he'd have to let them down, and the fight would begin again.

"What are you doing?" she wanted to yell. Gabrith would have roasted them both by now.

Battles were not for joking around. They had winners and losers. Yamaya knew men like these well. Such brutes never respected you until you made them bleed. If you held back, you'd find their hands all over you, whether you wanted them or not. And she knew these specific men even better. They were her second-father's fighting dogs, just as she used to be. Sand might think he was clever, but embarrassing them would only make them madder when they got their feet back under them.

Sand held the two bandits helpless in the air. The longer he held them, the more ridiculous they looked. Already, scattered titters spread through the crowd. This had better not be all he meant to do.

Sporadic laughter grew to a current that swept around the market. People who had been so afraid now felt powerful. The swift current turned to a dangerous tide. Villagers started to yell insults, and then throw things. Just a few at first, rocks and fruit and a small clay pot.

"Get back," yelled the third thug, he who held the horses' reins. "I'm warning you."

"You get back," a villager cried.

Someone else bellowed, "Get out of here!"

Larger objects began to fly. A green-gold melon, a metal jug. Valuable wares smashed on the ground, but those who owned them thought the loss was worth it. Mocking laughter swiftly built to a roar of the pent-up humiliation and revenge.

Berisan shouldn't have been surprised. It was only natural that people who had been frightened would want to retaliate. Maybe, the two bandits even deserved it. Despite what they'd done, his instinct was to block the assault, but he was already feeling the strain of holding them both. It wasn't possible to screen the missiles.

"Don't do that." Berisan focused his will and swept the plaza with his gaze. "I want to talk to them."

Just for a moment, the throng faltered. They wouldn't hesitate for long. He pleasantly turned to Mogrok, the red-faced and panting leader.

"Tell me again, what's the amount Aulgrip owes you?"

"Two hundred," he blurted, still struggling. "Two hundred! Put me down."

"All right, two hundred," Berisan repeated. That was quite a reduction from the five hundred, and a sign of Mogrok's opportunistic greed. "Does he owe it to you, or do you work for someone?" There was no sense trying to negotiate, if his boss was shortchanged and still came after the villagers.

"Quit asking me these questions," Mogrok demanded. "Just let us down."

"We'll stop fighting," Tyar vowed. Berisan tilted his head a little.

"Put you down?" He looked toward the river, debating whether he had enough strength carry them both over and drop them in the water. His head was starting to ache from holding this focus.

The avidly watching villagers correctly interpreted his thoughts and began to cat-call, "Toss them! Dump them in!"

"Shut up, you worthless gnats," Mogrok roared, but Berisan shifted his stance and began to stroll toward the river. The two men drifted helplessly after him.

Tyar cried out, "Huld! It's Huld from Cutrock Canyon."

The onlookers jumped back as Berisan approached them. He caught the eye of a man who was calling, "Give them a bath!"

"Is that a real person?" Berisan asked.

"Huld? Yeah, he's real," the fellow watched avidly. "Are you gonna do it?"

People yelled and cheered, urging Berisan to throw the two thugs into the clear, cold water.

Mogrok bellowed, "Don't you dare!"

That alone made Berisan want to douse him, but he really couldn't keep this up much longer. He would lose his grip, and they'd both be on top of him. So he turned back to his captives.

"Here's what I think. You're going to get on your horses and ride out of here," Berisan informed them. "I'll talk to Aulgrip about the two hundred. He'll get it to you however he usually does." He spread his hands a little. "Everyone gets something they want. All right?"

Mogrok's scowl was murderous, but Tyar exclaimed loudly, "Yes, yes! We'll tell Huld."

"That's all I ask."

Sand made a theatrical downward gesture and the two men settled out of the air. When their thrashing boots were a few inches above the ground, they dropped. Tyar stumbled a little, then darted back to Sabbin and the horses. Mogrok straightened and glowered at Sand, trying to reclaim some dignity.

"I want my sword back."

At those words, Yamaya sucked in a breath. She shouldn't have picked up the sword when Sand tossed it to her. That had been a mistake. If she didn't want them to get a good look at her, she should have left it on the ground. Stupid thing — but she had assumed Sand would kill them.

"As long as you don't use it here and now," Sand replied. What an idiot he was!

Yamaya felt a moment of panic as Mogrok stalked toward her, face dark with anger. Sand ambled after, maybe trying to keep in position to watch all three of them. Yamaya acted before Mogrok reached her, whipping the scarf off the blade and throwing it back in his direction. She made a show of handling it clumsily, as if she was a peasant woman and not an expert warrior in her own right.

"Careful with that, bitch!" Mogrok growled as the blade clanked against a stone. Yamaya jumped away as if he had scared her.

He half turned away, then paused in the act of sheathing his weapon. Black eyes pricked at her, trying to see her face. No, he was staring at the scarf she had used to cover the blade.

"Where'd you get that?"

"None of your business," Yamaya rasped, trying to disguise her voice. She tucked her chin, keeping the brim of the hat low, and stuffed the scarf into the crook of her arm.

"Let her alone," Sand said in his soft, slow way.

With a last suspicious glare, Mogrok stalked back toward the horses. Sabbin and Tyar watched, perhaps waiting for a cue to attack, but Sand again strolled after them. The thugs left the square at a sullen trot. Sand watched them leave for several long seconds. Then he headed into the crowd. People pulled away before him, so Yamaya could see him approach Farri, the newly freed hostage, who was trying to put her tangled hair back in order.

Meanwhile, the crowd seemed freed from the paralysis of their fear. People moved around, checking on each other's safety as they picked up things they had thrown. Yamaya absently returned a wooden tray to the potter's assistant. There was a lot of excited chatter, everyone still upset by what had happened. Puzzled, too. A lot of them had really wanted to see those bandits be tossed in the river. Mostly, they couldn't believe no one had been seriously hurt.

"Fool," Yamaya hissed under her breath. "You have no idea what you've done."

Fortunately, nothing of hers had been damaged. Yamaya surveyed the square and tried to decide if it was worth staying the rest of the day. She hadn't gotten the river grain she needed, and she hadn't seen whether Gordemir had made any progress on a cradle, but after a morning like this, would anyone be in a mood for trade?

"Yamaya," came a breathless whisper. Lilia was climbing out from behind the fish barrels now that the danger was past. "*That's* your hired hand?"

Sand was moving back toward them. Yamaya squinted, searching for any of the glow she thought she had seen. Though now he seemed no more than a common beggar, people veered aside to let him through. Mages were always to be feared, no matter what seeming kindness they did.

The girl gazed at Sand's ragged figure with awed fascination. Yamaya felt a moment's sadness. Even at the height of their passion, she had never looked at Gabrith that way. It almost seemed that she might have missed something.

She shook that feeling off and snapped, "Don't blame me for this."

Lilia just tossed her head, hands on hips. "You? I blame those bandits." Then she added, "Besides, you already have Kinson. Give the rest of us a chance."

"I do not," Yamaya huffed. "He just thinks —"

Sand was back. Yamaya noted a sheen of sweat on his brow, more than the day's heat would explain. He breathed slowly but deeply, as someone who didn't want to show how winded he really was. That was smart, to avoid revealing any weakness. Not that it did much good.

She crossed her arms. "Having fun, were you?"

That wiped the little smirk off his face, and he gave that half-shrug of his. "Maybe a little." Glancing around, he murmured, "Where's your friend?"

It took a moment for Yamaya to realize he meant Kinson. Indeed, there was no sign of her would-be suitor. She had been too intent on Mogrok and the others to even notice him leaving.

"If he wasn't going to fight, it's just as well that he got out of the way," she retorted. Not that a retreat was really a mark in Kinson's favor. And what was that edge in Sand's tone? Surely he wasn't jealous.

"You were so brave," Lilia interrupted. Her big, dark eyes were fixed adoringly on Sand. "Are you thirsty? We have water."

Sand hesitated for a startled moment. "Thanks, that's kind of you."

Lilia flushed happily and started digging into the back of her booth, no doubt hunting for a waterskin. Yamaya puffed out a breath. If this was any other man, she would have admired the girl's boldness, but it was just stupid to flirt with a mage.

Lilia's father seemed to feel the same way. "Hey!" He grabbed her arm. "Girl, what are you doing?"

Lilia yelped, but insisted, "He saved everyone."

The fisherman darted a glance at Sand. His chin jerked as he nodded, but he pressed his pouting daughter back. "Then let the man rest."

In a neutral tone, Sand answered, "Thank you, Lilia, but we have our own supplies." Then he side-eyed Yamaya. "Can I have my hat back yet?"

She passed it over, and ran a quick hand over her head to make sure the inky braids were still in place. All the while, complications raced each other to the forefront of her mind. She couldn't believe Huld's dogs had shown up, on just this day, to demand their protection money. Gabrith had taken her away from there, and they hadn't left on good terms. Yamaya didn't think Mogrok had recognized her, but he was definitely suspicious.

That wasn't the worst of it, though. Now, in an emergency, the villagers were happy about Sand's intervention, but harboring a rogue mage was bound to bring trouble. Not all of them were going to want him in their midst for very long.

Yamaya had her secrets. Sand had his. She had

known all along that secrets were going to bite them in the ass. She just didn't know how hard. Not yet.

Berisan thought he'd done well, turning those bandits away without hurting them. Ar-Thea would have been proud. Not so with Yamaya.

"Quit smirking," she growled. "Do you think this is over?"

Of course it wasn't. Only Berisan's practice as a showman allowed him to maintain this pretense of calm. After weeks of being so careful, he had revealed himself in front of the village. There were bound to be consequences. One of which was the heavy fatigue that always followed a strenuous casting. The slight vertigo dragged on him, demanding that he sit, while the habitual worry about discovery spurred him to stay on his feet. These peasant folk had been quick enough to vent their fury on the bandits, once they were helpless. They could turn on him just as well.

So Berisan breathed slowly, drawing in *vitalis* from the sun's powerful rays to replenish his strength. All the time, the eyes of watching villagers pierced him like needles. He didn't know if he was safe.

Still, that didn't seem to be exactly the problem Yamaya thought he had caused. When he felt a little stronger, he asked, "What do you mean?"

"Those men will be back. What then?" Behind her, the fisherman nodded dourly. She leaned in to whisper urgently, "Do you even know how many men Huld has in his camp?"

That was an odd thing to ask, and it raised even more questions in Berisan's mind. He especially wondered if Cutrock Canyon was somewhere in the mountains where she and Gabrith had come from.

Even more quietly, he asked, "Do you?"

It seemed he had touched a nerve. Yamaya went still,

then occupied herself with her colorful scarf. She held it up in the light, frowning slightly. The fabric was dyed with intricate swirls of brown, gold and green. Perfect for someone who needed to hide among trees and brush, he couldn't help thinking. She shook out the wrinkles from stuffing it behind her back, and started folding it into smaller and smaller rectangles.

The moment's silence allowed old instincts to creep up on him. Berisan found himself studying the area, seeking the fastest escape if need be. Then Yamaya's dark eyes fixed on a point across the square.

"Here comes your first problem," she muttered.

Berisan followed her gaze. Kinson was coming down the step from the tavern. Somehow he managed to strut along, even while he also groveled before the older gentleman who was with him. Their family resemblance was plain in the proud angle of their black eyes. Like Kinson, the elder was finely dressed in breeches and an embroidered vest. Gray streaked his topknot and the narrow trickle of beard from his squared-off chin.

"The headman," Berisan murmured. Worry knotted in his stomach, but he warded it off with a moment of sarcasm. "What could he possibly want to talk about?"

Yamaya snorted with sour humor.

Someone ran up to Aulgrip, forcing him to pause. Berisan wondered if he should seize the moment to escape. Then Kinson interrupted, pointing toward Yamaya's space with an agitated jerk. It was too late for sneaking off. Besides, he was here to show these people a better way. That conflict could be resolved without violence. It would undercut that lesson if he scampered away.

Narrowed eyes swept Berisan up and down as Aulgrip approached. It took no magecraft to sense his affronted dignity, or the indignation of the nephew who hovered behind his shoulder. Jealousy beat in Kinson's mind. *"Get rid of him. Then I'll have Yamaya to myself."*

His gall scraped at Berisan's nerves, but the headman was the one who mattered. Berisan thought he understood what Aulgrip needed to hear — that he wasn't there to take over, as mages did so often.

"Headman." Berisan relaxed and smiled, the way he did on the minstrels' stage.

"Mage." Aulgrip spat the accusation without a moment's hesitation. He must have decided on this tactic before he left the safety of his tavern. "Come. I will speak with you in private."

Berisan's stomach tightened further. If possible, he wanted to make this about something other than himself.

"Regrettably, no." He spread his hands to encompass everyone nearby. "This situation involves the whole village. Everyone deserves to know why those men were here."

Aulgrip's mouth tightened. He definitely didn't like being told no, but Berisan was right in thinking that the people were paying attention. The neighboring booths and displays were full of watchful eyes and ears. Kinson scowled, but Aulgrip was quick to seize what he must think was an opportunity.

"Then why don't you explain to the village what you were doing in our square, just now," he spoke loudly, in anticipation of triumph. Almost exactly like Mogrok had been doing.

"Your friend and neighbor Farri was attacked. I thought someone ought to help her."

"So you took matters into your own hands?" Aulgrip accused.

Berisan deflected the blame back at him. "I assume you know who they are, and what they wanted."

"How would I know what some ruffians are after?" The headman puffed his chest, outraged.

"They were yelling your name," Berisan answered gently. A swirl of agreement went through the onlookers.

Nobody could have missed hearing Mogrok's threats. "They said you owe them money."

"Everyone knows who the headman is," Kinson burst out. "Whatever they said, it was a lie."

An odd phrase, since Kinson had been right there listening to Mogrok's demands. Berisan focused on Aulgrip, keeping a reasonable expression. The headman's face darkened, and he hastily said, "The tavern covers it."

"I'm not judging that." Protection schemes were common across Skaythe. If it wasn't bandits making demands, it would be the Count's own men. Berisan offered Aulgrip a salve for his pride, if he wanted it. "You do what you have to do, to protect your people. Then they said you stopped paying. Was there a reason for that?"

"Who are you to ask all these questions?" Aulgrip demanded. His eyes were sharp as needles.

"It's your people who deserve answers, not me."

The crowd was focused on Aulgrip. Though Berisan heard a few mutters shared among them, no one spoke up. The headman's black gaze went past Berisan, to where Yamaya stood on the blanket. A few fruits were scattered outside the baskets. Her hands were in her skirt pockets — or, he suspected, on the hilts of her knives. She tilted her head a little.

"Was it because of Gabrith?" Her voice held a cold edge. "You thought Gabrith would protect you from them. So you stopped paying."

The headman glared in silent frustration as the muttering grew a little louder. It seemed most of the villagers hadn't known Gabrith was a mage, but Aulgrip obviously had known. Berisan could guess the rest. Just like Yamaya said, Aulgrip thought he could use the rogue mage as a replacement form of protection.

"I don't recall us discussing that, when we talked about moving into Weeping Falls," Yamaya went on.

A faint sneer passed over Aulgrip's face. "You weren't there." Why would they discuss it with a woman? It was something to be decided between the men.

Yamaya's eyes narrowed in a way that told Berisan some part of Aulgrip's statement wasn't true. He wondered what it was, but didn't want to get stuck on the details.

Soothingly, he put in, "I told those men I would ask you to pay what you owe. I really suggest that you do that."

"Why would I?" Aulgrip's manner suddenly turned spitefully smooth. "There's another mage here now, who can provide the same valuable service."

"No, Headman." The reversal left Berisan cold, his heart pounding. "You don't want that."

"Don't tell me that I want!" Aulgrip burst out. "This is partly your fault, after all. You interfered. Now you get to clean up the mess you made."

"I didn't make this mess," Berisan reasoned. Yamaya sniffed, as if that was the most stupid thing he'd said yet. He tried again. "I bought you time. You should use it to pay your debt."

"That's enough out of you!" Aulgrip shouted. "Do what you're told, or you'll find out how fast the hunter-guards come when they hear there's a dangerous mage around here."

He folded his arms with smug satisfaction, then strutted away with Kinson sulking at his heels. The villagers watched, some focused on Aulgrip and some on Berisan. They were like a pack of beaten hounds, he thought. They wanted to bite someone, but they hadn't decided who to bite yet.

Yamaya's question a short time again had been all too accurate. *"Do you think this is over?"*

Yet, incredibly, some of the people stared at him not with accusation, but with hope. They had just witnessed his power. At least a few actually believed he could keep them safe. Maybe, just maybe, he could still plant the seeds of Ar-Thea's dream.

Yamaya had been afraid the morning's events would sour everyone's appetite for trade. Instead, the afternoon brought more business than she could have asked for. Once the marketplace settled down, a steady flow of villagers came to her space. No doubt most of them were far more interested in getting a better look at Sand than they were in her fruit. Her so-called farm hand kept his hat down and played his pipes from time to time. Now that he'd wrecked everything, he thought to do that.

Between customers, they sniped at each other.

"I can't safeguard this village," Sand muttered. "We don't even live here. Weeping Falls is an hour's walk."

"Maybe you should have thought of that," she retorted.

"You wanted me to do something." For once, she could hear his irritation. That was almost better than his eerie calm.

The next customer was there, leaving Yamaya no choice but to smile and talk about cherries. Then there were others. Once they were gone, with a promise of soft fabric to trade, she had her say.

"Why did you let them leave?"

"Their friends would come looking for them," came the mumble from under his hat. "A couple of bodies would be harder to explain than a couple of embarrassed guys."

"A couple of bodies would be very easy to understand." Yamaya hadn't forgotten the way Mogrok squinted, trying to figure out if he knew her. "Embarrassing them will make them twice your enemy."

Sand's shoulders hunched a little. She scowled at the ridges of his reed hat. "You should have just killed them."

"I can't do that." His voice sounded strange.

"Gabrith would have."

"Not every mage has exactly the same craft."

Their conversation ended when Shalleya, the blacksmith's wife, came by to suggest they trade for a honing stone to sharpen their tools. That was another of Kinson's family, an aunt. Though she cheerfully accepted Shalleya's deal, Yamaya couldn't help recalling how Kinson had been absent since he trailed after Aulgrip.

"He must have changed his mind about the dress," she thought sarcastically.

She had said herself that Kinson was smart to make himself scarce if he didn't plan to fight. You could also call him a coward. It was even possible that he thought she and Sand were romantically involved. She muffled a snort at the very idea. If that was what they thought, Shalleya's offer could be a ploy to lure Yamaya away from Sand.

Ironically, Sand seemed to have cemented a relationship with the village far more effectively than Yamaya had by tolerating Kinson's flirtation. She would have admired his strategy, if she thought it had been one.

Then she recognized the song Sand was playing on his pipes. It was about a gang of bandits being hunted down one by one, and marched to the gallows. Despite herself, Yamaya swallowed a burst of fear. She wasn't a bandit! Not any more, and never again.

The longer the day went on, the more Berisan's anxiety grew. His gut churned, thinking of everything that could go wrong. It wasn't that he took Aulgrip's ultimatum seriously. Berisan hadn't agreed to fight his battles for him, and there wasn't much the man could do if he simply refused to come down from Weeping Falls Farm.

This village wasn't his responsibility. Except, as Yamaya so quickly pointed out, that he had gotten involved with their business. Some part of the mess was his to own. Whatever he hoped to achieve here, it all hinged on Ar-Thea's philosophy of shunning violence. What was he supposed to do if a whole troop of bandits showed up?

Or the hunter-guards. Count Ar-Kundrel would have a garrison at his main city of Pulgoll, and he wouldn't take kindly to rumors of a renegade mage in his territory. Berisan could probably slip away from them, if he had a head start.

This would be the time to do it. Tonight. He could grab his waypack and set off north, toward Dunsaph. Yamaya couldn't stop him any more than Aulgrip could. In fact, she would probably kick him down the waterfall steps to speed him on his way.

Even as he thought so, Berisan knew he couldn't do that. Not because of Aulgrip, or Ar-Kundrel. Because it meant abandoning Yamaya, still widowed and pregnant, still desperately in need of help, whether she was willing to admit it or not.

These fears circled around him like so many flies drawn to a pile of pitted apricots. All the while, Berisan was forced to sit still, playing his double pipe for customers who stared at him like an oddity. Thinking it would reassure them, he played a long ballad about bandits facing justice. Yamaya didn't seem to appreciate that. After a while, Berisan switched to a working song, something the fishermen might sing while casting their nets over the river.

As the day grew really hot, business slowed down enough that Yamaya was willing to pack up for the day. She informed Berisan that she had a list of houses where they could stop on the way back to Weeping Falls. The weight of cherries in their packs would be replaced with fabric and melons and river grain. She'd even bartered for a honing stone from the blacksmith. The tool would be useful, but Berisan didn't like the cozening way Shalleya had talked to Yamaya, as if she was a lost child in need of parents.

After making several stops and visiting with various villagers, Berisan's pack grew heavier and heavier. It was a relief that Yamaya felt happy about what she had traded for, but even more of a relief to get out of Opshar. This unimportant village had suddenly become a little too important.

Yamaya walked in front, moving faster at first that Berisan, who toiled with a heavy load. Eventually she slowed enough for him to voice some of the questions that could no longer be avoided.

"What do you think?" He left it open-ended, to see what she would say.

Yamaya's back stiffened. "About what?"

"Those men. How soon will they be back?"

"How should I know?" she evaded.

"You talked like you know a lot about them."

Yamaya didn't answer that, but stomped along the earthen trail with angry strides. Whatever she knew, he needed to know it, too. After a few minutes of swishing between the tall grass and reeds along the trail, he tried again.

"The bandits said this Huld sent them. Do you think that's true?"

Still the silence. Just when he thought she would remain mute, she grudgingly replied, "I don't know." Yamaya sounded as if she was thinking about it, not just trying to brush his words aside. "It wouldn't be his usual method. Huld mostly waylays caravans. Demanding tribute from villages, taking hostages — those things draw too much attention." Then she snorted scornfully. "The count thinks he's the only one who should be draining the life out of villages."

They had reached the small downhill stream. Berisan considered her words as their boots thunked on the boards. Yamaya settled on the rough hewn bench. Berisan would have liked to sit down, too, but he didn't want to be within stabbing range. He went down the bank to scoop some of the cool water. When he returned, wiping his chin, Yamaya handed him the food she had prepared that morning, a baked roll stuffed with chopped vegetables and fish.

"Thanks." Gratefully, Berisan bit into the cold bread. After inhaling a couple of bites, he asked, "So Mogrok was lying? Taking a bit extra for himself?"

"Maybe he would." Yamaya didn't admit that she knew the three bandits, even though it was obvious she did.

"Then, would Huld like having his name brought into this? Maybe we could get word to him..." Berisan suggested.

Yamaya shook her head. "No."

"If it kept the bandits from coming back," he argued. That would solve Berisan's problem of the village thinking he was obligated to them. He would have more time to focus on what he really hoped to achieve.

"I said no!"

He watched her, exasperated. It wasn't fair that she tried to hide things, while everything about him was blown wide open. Yamaya chewed furiously, and said nothing.

"Do you really think I can't guess?" Berisan asked quietly. "You know things about them. You didn't want them to see you."

Yamaya answered with a kind of grunt. Her defensive frown gave way to something more like pain as she rubbed a spot under her ribs. "Quit kicking me, brat," she grumbled.

Berisan winced and glanced away. Pregnant women's symptoms were outside his experience. If only Tisha were here. She was a born healer, much more the person Yamaya would need when her baby came. Unfortunately, Tisha wasn't here, and neither, apparently, was the information he needed. If those bandits came back, the knowledge might spare him, and maybe everyone in Opshar, a lot of trouble.

He could plunder Yamaya's thoughts, or just threaten to, but it would end any possibility of her really trusting him.

He'd given up enough chances like that today.

Anyway, that was out of bounds. Ar-Thea would never have approved of such a violation. Frustrating as it was, Berisan had to wait. Yamaya would tell him, or not tell him, when she was ready.

Uncomfortable, Sand began to study the grassy slope around them. Yamaya allowed herself a moment's satisfaction. She hadn't believed the kicking-baby ploy would work. Too many questions, this mage. Too quiet, too polite. His patience as he chewed his bread roll was almost too much. It unnerved her more than even his direct questioning did.

Gabrith would never her been so quiet and polite. That was just the problem, wasn't it? Gabrith was dead. Yamaya was left with Sand, who wanted to know all about her past life. She didn't owe him that. Those were things she had left behind, or lost. Yamaya had to put them out of her mind. She wasn't that person any more.

When the last crumb had disappeared and the waterskins had been refilled, she groaned and pushed on her knees to lift herself from the bench. Behind her, as they took up the trail again, Sand softly said, "It's better if you just tell me."

Yamaya walked away from that. It was all she could do.

V

Battles, Old and New

When they got back to the cottage on the ridge, Sand set the waypack down, gently and carefully, and left without another word. Yamaya busied herself with putting their provisions away. It hadn't been completely a lie that the baby was moving inside her. It just didn't hurt as much as she claimed. Unfortunately, the brat seemed to take her words as an invitation. All through the afternoon, it kept up the kicking, as if it knew she was upset and had decided to make things worse.

Since she had enough cloth now, Yamaya tried to settle herself by sewing the diapers. This had been one of the basic tasks at Cutrock Canyon. Someone always had a baby or toddler running around. If not her second-sisters, then one of the other women. When the rooms were clean and you had nothing else to do, you sewed more diapers.

First she smoothed the loose-woven fabric across the mats on the stone floor. She cut it into large squares and folded them, over and over, until they formed many-layered pads with a pocket in the middle. Yamaya stuffed the pockets with the moss Sand had brought from the waterfall, and made one more fold to keep the stuffing in.

From time to time she glimpsed Sand moving through the orchard or weeding out stubborn rascalweed stalks from the sweet potatoes. Sometimes he stood and gazed out over the fields without moving. She could guess what he was thinking about.

It seemed like Sand was taking Aulgrip's outrageous

demand seriously. She couldn't understand why — either the demand itself, or that Sand would ever agree to it. Yamaya knew what she had to hide from, but a mage had power. He should never have to hide. Besides, Aulgrip was the headman, with money and all his relatives to support him. Especially Doloram, the smith. Farm tools could do the job of weapons, if pressed. If the bunch of them were willing to stand together, Mogrok wouldn't have had a chance.

Yet Aulgrip demanded protection from Sand. He claimed that the tavern was profitable enough to pay the bribes, so why do that? Maybe he thought Sand had shamed him by protecting the villagers as he could not. Maybe he wanted revenge.

The baby started kicking again. Yamaya groaned and reached for a jar of salve. The skin of her belly felt tight enough without so much pressure. She checked to make sure Sand was out of view before she pulled up her skirt and rubbed the salve over her bulging belly.

"Gabrith would never have allowed such a coward to make him into a lackey," she complained to the infant moving within her.

As she got back to work, Yamaya considered that Sand wasn't the only one at risk from Aulgrip's scheming. It was one thing for her to have a farm worker who was secretly a mage, if she didn't know about it. But she did know, and she hadn't accused him in the marketplace or put him out of her service. That meant she herself could be accused of sheltering a rogue mage. If the count ever found out, he would burn her farm to ash.

It wouldn't surprise her at all if Aulgrip brought that up at some point.

If Yamaya was lucky, maybe Sand was planning to run off before Aulgrip had time to send to the count. He was only here for a dry place to sleep, or so he said. She didn't believe it though. His concern clearly went beyond self-interest.

Yamaya frowned as she jabbed the needle back and forth through the layers of moss and folded cloth, setting lines of stitching so the diapers would hold their shape on the baby's bottom. She still didn't understand why Sand took an interest in someone like her. Or why he had stepped in to help Farri when Mogrok threatened to beat her.

It was baffling. Yamaya didn't like that.

She should order him to leave. It was her farm, after all. Yet, even a brief glance at the plentiful wood pile and the weed-free fields reminded her why she wouldn't do that. One person alone couldn't run a farm. Uncomfortable as it might be, Yamaya needed him.

The other problem with Sand was that he asked good questions. Yamaya didn't think Mogrok had recognized her, not with the hat, but he sure had taken a double look at her scarf. That sturdy weaving of Norith's, and Jura's clever dyeing. You wouldn't find it anywhere but Cutrock Canyon. It was one of the few things Yamaya had kept from there. Such a small detail to betray her.

More questions unfolded, like the leaves of a fan palm. Did Mogrok care enough to figure out who she was? If she knew his character, he would be more focused on how Sand had shamed him. Yes, he would want revenge for that. Mogrok might not realize that Yamaya and Sand were in Opshar together. That wouldn't matter if he came after Sand and stumbled over Yamaya, too.

Grimly, she glanced over her shoulder. On the shelf, the bottle of barbtail syrup gleamed with silent menace. That was her reserve weapon. It would be great if she never needed it beyond the time of her birthing. Unfortunately, life had taught her not to hope for easy solutions.

After Berisan ran out of weeds to massacre, he still had energy to cast off. Frustration simmered within him, at the unfairness of this woman. He wanted to help Yamaya, but she wouldn't tell him what he needed to know in order to do that. Casting about for something else to do, he recalled that she needed more moss. He hadn't harvested near the waterfalls in a dozen days. That should be enough time for it to re-grow.

So he grabbed a basket and angled down the hillside below the cottage. Weeping Falls cast sheets of hissing spray to eddy around him with the shifting wind. On every side, rivulets went chattering down the slope. Loose stones shifted under his feet, so that he stumbled his way across the steep slide area. Berisan sensed little sparks flitting among the rocks — mice, lizards, insects, frightened by his unexpected passage. It was comforting to not feel so alone.

The rim of the circle pond had a slight overhang, and the moss grew thick beneath it. Streams of falling water battered Berisan's reed hat as he ducked through them. Damp mist seeped through his shirt as he worked his knife under plates of moss and slid them carefully into his basket. The steady work gave him a chance to order his thoughts, while the waterfall's spattering cut him off from the rest of the world.

When his basket was heavy with wet moss, Berisan returned through the curtain of spray. Moments later, a stone tumbled down past him, raising a skiff of dust. Berisan straightened, suddenly aware of his exposed position on the rubble slope. He barely glimpsed a pair of men crouched at the top of it. The waterfall's steady rush had blocked all sound of their approach. One of them held some kind of stick, or — no!

He saw only a flicker of movement before the arrow struck him.

As the afternoon light grew long, Yamaya packed the finished diapers away and set to work boiling river grain for supper. She was just starting to chop the vegetables that would go with it when she heard a faint shuffle of movement outside the cottage. Sand, coming back at last.

She called out to him, "Did you get any more cherries down?"

An all too familiar voice answered. "Nope."

Cursing herself, Yamaya went still. She should have recognized that the step was different. Or that Sand would have been cutting wood, not slinking around behind the house. Her thoughts darted, while her fighter's eye assessed the area, what obstacles there were and how she could use them. The kitchen knife had a broad blade and short handle. As a weapon, it was pitiful. Good thing it wasn't her only one.

"You'd better not be here for trouble," she stated coldly, "because I'll give it to you."

Steps approached, unhurried, until a bulky figure rounded the side of the cottage. A nasty smirk twisted Mogrok's lips.

"You always were the friendly one, Yamaya."

Berisan grunted, staggered by the impact. Somehow he kept his footing. Acting on instinct, he dropped into a crouch and tightened his fists, raising a protective barrier. His hat fell behind him, and the basket bounced down the slope, scattering the carefully collected moss.

A long wooden shaft stood out from his chest, between the collar bones and armpit. It was an obscenity, incomprehensible. His dazed mind sensed pressure more than pain — so far — but crimson stained his tunic in a spreading blot. The feathers of the fletching trembled as he caught several fast, shallow breaths.

Berisan tore his gaze from that as more stones galloped past. A few glanced off his barrier. The two men rushed down at him. The bandits from the village. Of course they were here.

He moaned, fighting to control his stomach and keep the barrier up at the same time. Every instinct was to yank at the arrow, that violation of his person, but he couldn't afford to faint with these two bandits coming at him.

With gritted teeth, Berisan wobbled upright. "*Hold the barrier,*" he focused in his mind. Their faces came closer, brown blobs distorted by grins of fierce glee.

He didn't want to hurt them. These men meant nothing, and Berisan had promised Ar-Thea that he wouldn't use his power in spite. Yet, there had been three bandits in Opshar. If these two were here, attacking him, it was obvious where the third one must be. Berisan had also promised himself to keep Yamaya safe.

"Are you sure," he grated out, "that you want to do this?"

Tyar did hesitate, after having been hoisted into the air once before. His partner snarled, "Don't let him talk! He'll just confuse you."

The archer stopped several paces up the slope, drawing another arrow and aiming it squarely at Berisan.

"You won't make fools of us again," Tyar yelled, and lunged at the gleaming barrier.

Reflex took over. Berisan shoved, pushing Tyar away, and then yanked at the stones where Sabbin stood, feet braced on the treacherous slope. The arrow flew wildly as he tottered and waved his arms.

"Look out, you idiot!" Tyar yelled, just before Sabbin lost his balance and crashed into him.

Desperately Berisan clawed at the loose rocks. He had to start as many of them rolling as he could. With a rumble, that part of the slope began to shift. Sword and arrows clattered on the stones. Sabbin grabbed at them, trying to keep his place, but the rocky wave crashed over him.

Berisan stumbled back, gasping at the pain that now exploded around the arrow in his flesh. Yelling and flailing, the two men rolled past him, toward the bottom of the long slope.

Yamaya fixed Mogrok with a grim eye. All the while, her mind was racing. The bandits had followed her here? But it only made sense. Cutrock Canyon was days away from Opshar. Then they'd have to crawl up to Huld and beg for help, and if he agreed, travel all the way back. That was too long to wait for revenge.

Mogrok and his cronies must have some watch post where they could look down on Opshar. All they had to do was wait until Sand left, and see where he went. Then watch a little longer until the two of them split up to do their chores.

That was so easy, she should have thought of it herself. She and Gabrith should have been roaming the hilltops near their farm, finding the spyholes and blocking them off. Yamaya would have to do that. Later.

If there was a later.

Mogrok kept up his unpleasant grin. "Aren't you at least going to say hello?"

"No."

It didn't matter if she clipped the word. Mogrok's leering eyes had fastened on her pregnant belly, and his grin widened into something even uglier.

"Oh, I see now," he crowed. "That's why you both left and didn't say goodbye."

Yamaya didn't bother answering. While Mogrok guffawed at her condition, she scraped the rest of the vegetables into the simmering pot with the chopping knife. There was supposed to be enough for her and Sand. And where was Sand? Yamaya tried to put that question out of her mind. He wasn't good for much in Opshar. She didn't know if she wanted him to come back. It might be better if she handled Mogrok herself.

When the brute stopped for a breath, she cut in, "We

did say goodbye."

Mogrok shook his head and with insincere complaint. "That's ballsy, to steal a man's daughter from his hearth."

"Huld gave me to Gabrith, remember?" Yamaya answered acidly. "His reward for a fight well fought. So when Gabrith was ready to move on, he decided to keep me. Huld wasn't happy, but —" She shrugged. "Best not to fight with the mage."

Mogrok made a little hiss between his teeth. He'd tried to get his hands on Yamaya more times than she wanted, and only stopped trying because Gabrith took her for himself.

"Where is he, anyway?" Mogrok made a show of looking around. "Get tired of your spiteful ways?"

"Died." Yamaya pointed toward the cherry grove. "I buried him over there. Go take a look."

Maybe Mogrok would get out of the doorway. Yamaya would have a better chance in an open yard than in the confined space of the cottage.

"You kill him?" Mogrok asked suspiciously.

"No." As if he cared, either.

Mogrok answered that with a curt laugh. "I guess you replaced him fast enough." Rather than stepping away, as she had hoped, the unwelcome visitor came up the steps to lean casually on the door frame. "Does that guy know it isn't his brat?"

Yamaya's temper rose at his sly accusation. "He's just a hired hand, and it's none of your business."

"You mean he was," Mogrok corrected with evil relish. "Sabbin and Tyar are down there having a word with him."

Mogrok's strategy made sense. Everyone at Cutrock Canyon knew Yamaya could fight, and they knew Sand could — do whatever he did. Better to take them on separately. Yet her whole body went rigid. If they put Sand out of action, she'd be in a world of trouble.

Regardless, Yamaya couldn't let herself be distracted. "Then I'll hire someone else." Kinson, if he still took an interest. "You can be on your way."

She made it an order, but Mogrok guffawed again.

"Oh, we'll see, we'll see. Since you're all alone now, I might have to help you get back home. Or maybe we'll just stick around."

He glanced around the farm and cottage in a proprietary way that made Yamaya seethe like the river grain in boiling water.

"It's not a bad little place you have here. Cutrock's getting a little crowded these days. Might be time for us to set up on our own." He met her glare with leering amusement. "What you got cooking there?"

"It isn't for you," she said. Yet something in those words triggered a memory.

"Don't be so sure. My boys will be up here as soon as they put a few arrows in your 'hired hand.'"

"*If* Sabbin and Tyar come back from that, you'll all be going. In fact, maybe you'd better go make sure they're okay." She didn't bother to hide the chopping knife in her hand.

"Don't even try it," he leaned forward menacingly. "Huld let you run wild for too long. It's time that you served me, like a woman should. Me and the boys. No more of your playing with knives."

Yamaya hardly even heard the threat. A harsh voice rasped in her memory. "*The first thing every brute will say is, 'Bring me food, woman. The next will be, bring me drink.'*" Bekkera had been exactly right, all those years ago.

"You'll serve me, Yamaya. If you don't want this place to burn, or something awful to happen to that mage's brat." His finger jabbed at her belly, and Yamaya's blood went cold at the threat. Certain of his victory, Mogrok gloated, "Now show me what's in that pot."

Before she was so heavy with child, Yamaya wouldn't have hesitated to take him on. Now she paused, assessing his words. The thatched roof was dry enough to burn, for certain. What she didn't know was if Mogrok meant the threat to destroy her home, or hurt her unborn child.

Talk, sure. Mogrok was good at that. Yamaya preferred action to words.

A steady breath came and went. Then she looked down, allowing him to think she was cowed.

"All right." She forced the words out. "I'll serve you."

Once the bandits were clear, Berisan released his barrier and sagged to his knees. The arrow sent pain tearing through his shoulder and into his chest, like a badger going after a rat in its burrow. The stench of blood was nauseating. He sucked in several deep breaths, and made himself close a shaking hand on the shaft. Before he could change his mind, he yanked on it.

A high groan, like a stranger's voice, and the arrow was out. A fresh spurt of crimson soaked through his tunic. The pain was worse now, bright and fierce as fire. Berisan felt light-headed, but clamped a hand over his injury, feeling the sticky blood against his skin.

With another gasp, he drew in *vitalis* from the sun's light upon him, and from all the little creatures scattering away from the rockslide. Healing energy flowed through his abused flesh. The pain eased as the puncture sealed itself, but it was still there, stabbing him anew with every heartbeat.

Sweaty and shaking, he looked down the hill. The two bandits had reached the base. Through a screen of rising dust, Berisan saw that one of them had spread his arms and legs wide enough to slow his fall. He tried to get up but then fell back, clutching his left arm. The other one lay unmoving, half-buried in rubble.

Berisan kept up his healing, but he scanned the slope around him. Arrows were scattered nearby. The bow and the other man's sword lay farther away. He spared enough *vitalis* to reach for them. That cavity beneath the waterfall was wet and dark. The weapons would be hard to spot. He tossed them through the screen of falling water and spitefully hoped for the damp to ruin them.

That was all the sabotage he had time for. If he stayed here, they might come back up and have another try at him. Berisan got his feet under him. Loose stones continued rolling free in ones or twos as he staggered across the shifting rocks. Somewhere up there, that big bandit Mogrok would be threatening Yamaya. He had to help her!

Mogrok lounged in the doorway, reveling in his victory. Just because no other men were in sight, he thought he owned her. Yamaya hunched over, stirring the pot of river grain and vegetables. Ducking her head, she spoke in a low, appeasing voice.

"It isn't ready yet."

"Give me some of that, then. And hurry up!"

A harried glance showed Yamaya what he wanted. The barbtail potion, of course. It was the biggest bottle on the shelf. The shiniest glass. She kept her face down as she went to fetch the bottle and a large clay cup. Thick liquid gurgled into it; the fragrance of fermented apricots blossomed in the air.

"Hmmm," Mogrok smacked his lips in disgusting anticipation. Yamaya set the cup on the table and pushed it to the far edge before snatching her hand back, as if she feared he would grab her. He made a show of sipping from the cup. "Not bad for a peasant farmer."

He took a bigger gulp. While his head was tipped back, Yamaya scanned the yard behind him. There was no sign of his two buddies, nor of Sand. It was hard to know if that was good news.

Mogrok smacked his lips and leered at her. "Good stuff."

Yamaya turned her head away, though always alert in case he made a grab at her. She stirred the pot as it boiled. In her memory, she was far away. On a certain day, Bekkera had gathered Yamaya and two other girls whose breasts were starting to develop. It had been a hot day, the sun beating into the canyon even without Bekkera's fire blazing. More important, most of the men were gone on a raid.

Starting that day, Bekkera had taught the girls the facts of life. That in the future they would bleed without having been injured. How to clean and care for their bodies. Later, they would serve the men of the bandit gang as they wanted — food, drink, sex. They would have children to grow up and become bandits like their fathers. Yamaya remembered her disgust at the prospect, which Bekkera claimed was unavoidable. She said the men fought to bring back all the things they needed, and the girls had a duty to repay them.

But, Bekkera also said, there were some men who hurt women more than they needed to. For those men, the women of Cutrock Canyon had a special medicine. Bekkera showed the girls thick, squat barbtail plants that grew in cracks of damp rocks. The flowers curled into wide, hollow pitchers full of sour-smelling fluid. She taught them how to gather that liquid and boil it down into a syrup that was good for pain — and other things.

What Yamaya tried to remember now was how much barbtail syrup it took to knock a man out. Bandits wounded in raids and women in the throes of childbirth were only allowed a small sip at a time. Mogrok was a big, strong man. It was hard to gauge the dose he'd already guzzled down.

Keeping her sullen face on, she flicked a glance his way. Mogrok kept lounging in the door, blocking her escape, still with that hateful smirk. Better to keep him talking while the poison did its work.

"Did Huld send you?" she asked.

"Sure did." Mogrok took another swallow. Yamaya noted that he didn't say what he was sent for. It could be anything.

"To scout for caravans?" she pressed. "Or to shake down the tavern keeper for tribute."

Mogrok shrugged, smirking. "Why not do both?"

"You yelled out Huld's name in front of the town. Not that I care, but Huld might."

"That was Tyar! The idiot," Mogrok grumbled. He drained his cup and slammed it down. "Woman, give me another."

Maybe it was her imagination, but his voice sounded just a bit... squishy. Yamaya didn't pour out as much this time. She only had a limited amount of barbtail, and she wanted to keep most of it for her own needs. Again, she scooted the cup toward him and snatched her hand back. Then she went back to stirring the pot. The river grain was nearly ready. If this worked out, she'd have it all for herself, and maybe Sand, without wasting any on a doomed man.

"Doesn't matter to you," Mogrok sneered once he'd taken another gulp. "Huld will forget all about that when I bring you back to him."

So that was his plan. He thought he could use Yamaya as a decoy to distract from his blundering in Opshar.

"He didn't send you to search for me," she concluded. That meant Huld wouldn't be angry at her for killing Mogrok. Especially in self-defense.

"You think that matters?"

Mogrok's voice definitely sounded slow. He blinked, as if he'd heard it too. Then he raised a hand and gazed at it. Next he favored the cup with a puzzled frown. "What is that stuff?"

"You wanted to be served," Yamaya answered with quiet malice.

"What?" He leaned forward a little, maybe to threaten her, or maybe not quite by his own choice. "Woman! What did you do?"

She quickly gathered her skirt into several thicknesses and used it to lift the pot off the coals. Rising, she patted the folds of fabric to make sure no spark had taken hold. Then she reached through her skirt pockets to draw her knives. The weight and texture summoned her familiar strength and confidence.

"Huld didn't send you to find me," Yamaya repeated, "and you should have left me alone."

"Tell me what you did," Mogrok slurred. He tried to get up, but his knees didn't want to hold him.

As he clutched at the door frame, Yamaya lunged. Steel flashed. Mogrok leaned away, but then his heavy hands clutched at her. She ducked beneath them and drove her shoulder into his chest. Then, while he still scratched at her hair, she was past him, darting down the steps.

"Bitch," he bellowed, stumbling after her.

"Yes I am," Yamaya grimly agreed. "Maybe you should have remembered that."

Heart pounding with exertion, shoulder throbbing with each heartbeat, Berisan made it back up to the farm. He was just in time to see Yamaya bull her way out of the cottage. Steel gleamed as she turned to confront the man who tottered in the doorway. Her two daggers were longer and sharper than what he recalled her showing him in Opshar.

"Bitch!" Mogrok staggered down after her.

"Yes I am. Maybe you should have remembered

that." Yamaya's expression was fierce and alert, alive in a way Berisan had never seen. He drew breath to call out, but then caught it back. This was no time to distract her.

"Come back here, woman!" Big hands clawed the air as the bandit tried to grab her. She deftly twirled aside.

"You'll never touch me again," Yamaya vowed savagely.

There was skill in the economy of her movements. Berisan had guessed right; she was as much a bandit as her foe. Yet surely there was something wrong with Mogrok. His grab was awkward, and he struggled to stand straight while drawing his sword.

"You'll pay for this," he raged. "You'll pay. I'll rip that brat out of your belly!"

Those words squashed whatever faint impulse of compassion Berisan knew. The bandit slashed at Yamaya's belly, trying to carry through on his threat. Steel slithered against steel as she forced his blade aside. Strong as he looked, it shouldn't have been possible.

"Not likely," Yamaya hissed.

With a frustrated roar, Mogrok kicked at her belly. Yamaya again evaded the blow, but in that moment her expression changed. Her thoughts weren't vicious, as she sounded, but cold and intent. Mogrok tottered, grounding the point of his sword to support himself. He babbled threats and curses as a shudder racked his burly frame. The pregnant woman stalked aside, waiting for an opening.

Berisan thought he understood what Yamaya had done. While he watched, she stepped into a kick that struck behind one leg. Mogrok went to his knees, still leaning on his sword, and after a moment slumped the rest of the way.

Groaning, he struggled to rise, but Yamaya was already behind him. The two daggers crossed beneath his chin, then pulled back with a vicious jerk. Blood spattered the ground. Mogrok gasped out a strangled cry. He clawed at

Yamaya's ankles before she jumped clear. Her two blades dripped dark flecks into the dust as she prowled, several feet away.

Berisan watched her face, the set calm as she took in her enemy's last struggles. When Mogrok went still, she gave a little nod of satisfaction. He found it a bit dismaying, how good she was at killing.

Ar-Thea had taught him that every human life had potential, even that of the most cruel mage who had no thought for mercy. Every life lost should be mourned. Still, this particular man was hard to grieve for. Berisan had seen him brutalizing Farri in Opshar, and heard his threats to Yamaya's unborn baby. He'd seen him try to carry out that threat. Yamaya couldn't be blamed for defending herself.

Mogrok had been still for a stretch of heartbeats when Yamaya caught sight of Berisan. She snapped alert, but then straightened when she recognized him.

She tossed her chin and huffed, "It's about time you got here."

"The other two snuck up on me," he started to explain, but Yamaya was frowning at his chest. Glancing down, Berisan saw how his hand was coated in vivid crimson. His shirt was streaked with more.

"They got you. How bad?"

She shook blood off her two blades and approached, frowning with rough concern. Which certainly was better than how she had been looking at Mogrok before she killed him.

"One arrow," he said. Glimmering golden rays of *vitalis* leaked between his fingers. "It's all right. I'm healing it."

A shade of surprise crossed Yamaya's brow. Most people in Skaythe didn't know that magic could heal as well as hurt. Now that he was up by the cottage, his breathing started to even out. The healing would go faster.

Yamaya's dark eyes skinned past him. "Where are they, then?"

"I caused a rockslide. They're at the bottom. I don't know if they'll come up here, or run off." Reluctantly, he turned his eyes to the corpse in the yard. "What about him?"

Yamaya was in the midst of an unusual maneuver with both knives in one hand and the other deep in her skirt pocket. There was a light clink, and a belt fell to the ground. Shaking that out, she strapped it over the outside of her dress. Bending over Mogrok, she wiped her two blades thoroughly on his trousers leg and sheathed them on the belt.

"If they decide to show their faces," she said with a trace of defiance, "they can take him. If not, I'll salvage what I want and bury him in my field. He can fertilize the sweet potatoes. It will be the best thing he ever did with his life."

Berisan nodded, morbidly impressed. It seemed there was history between them. A score had been settled.

Yamaya walked past the corpse, as if dead bodies bleeding into the dirt were nothing unusual or important. "Food's ready. Come in and get cleaned up."

The irony of the situation wasn't lost on Yamaya. For months, she'd been swearing the past was behind her. "*I'm not that person any more.*" What a fool. Being that person had served her well. She was alive, wasn't she?

Anyway, it felt good to wear her knives openly, even if the belt barely squeezed around her bulging middle. She might be a widowed farmer now, but she was hardly helpless. It had been too long since she dressed the way she lived.

Striding inside, she swept up the bottle of barbtail and scowled as she held it up to the light. Mogrok had gulped down almost half of it.

"Greedy pig," she grumbled, before jamming the cork back in and setting the bottle in its place. Turning, she saw

Sand's questioning eyes.

"Something to say?" she demanded.

"You gave him that, didn't you?" His neutral tone made her wonder what he knew.

Hands on hips, she glared at him. Slowly, with exaggerated patience, she explained. "Some guys, when they find a woman by herself, they think that they own her. They start bossing her around. They say 'give me food,' or they say 'give me drink.'" She jabbed a thumb at the bottle, which gleamed innocently on the shelf. "So I gave it to him."

"I'm not questioning," he began, just the way he said it to Aulgrip.

"Good." She cut him off. "Get that shirt off. I want a look at your wound."

"It's healing," he said, while that strange glow leaked between the knuckles.

"Don't be stupid. They shot you," Yamaya snapped. "I've dressed wounds in the field before, you know."

She didn't know what he meant about healing himself. That was a magic she had never heard of. What she could see, that was what she trusted.

Yamaya glared at Sand until he winced and raised his arm to peel the bloodied shirt off. Satisfied, she went to dip a jug of water from the cistern. She filled a small bowl to wash his wound and saved the rest for later.

When she turned back, he was holding the gory shirt as if he didn't know what to do with it. Yamaya took it from his unresisting hand and held it up to the light from outside. After all her battles, she hardly even noticed the sticky dampness saturating the fabric. The arrow had left only a small slash in the fabric.

"Easily mended," she said. "If you wash it before the blood dries, it shouldn't stain too badly."

Yamaya used a wet rag to dab at Sand's shoulder.

The blood came away easily, and she was forced to revise her opinion. As expected, the wound was a straight puncture, slightly reddened about the edges. Only, the bleeding had stopped and there was no swelling. The wound looked several days old.

"This is from today?" she asked, incredulous.

"Yeah."

"Huh. It is healing."

"I said." He shrugged, with that modesty that set her teeth on edge.

"Why?" She propped the wet cloth against her hip. "Why can you do this, and pick people up, and cause rock slides — so you say — but not simply blast those idiots back where they came from?"

Sand winced a bit, then sighed. "That's what Gabrith did, I'm sure. Like I told you, there's more than one kind of mage."

"Bullshit." She glared at him for his nonsense. Everyone knew that all magic was wild and dangerous. The only question was what kind of insanity it would bring. Even Gabrith had had moments when he seemed no more than a hair away from madness.

Sand stepped away, gazing over toward the waterfall in a moment's silence. Slowly, he explained. "A piece of steel can be shaped into a sickle, to cut weeds, or into a knife like one of yours. Right? The smith who holds the hammer decides its shape."

"Okay," Yamaya said, though skeptical.

"So with mages. Our teachers shape us. It's true that most mages draw on dark powers — blood, fear, death. Because their casting is so frightening and so visible, most people think that's the only way it can be. Your Gabrith must have been trained in a temple school, where violence is the only way they know."

She nodded. "He had scars all over. He didn't like

questions, but I saw them." Not that she didn't have a few scars of her own. They were nothing compared to what Gabrith had endured.

"That's the only way they know," he said softly, "so it's the only way they teach. That doesn't mean it really *is* the only way. Me and my brother were lucky that someone else found us before the hunter-guards did. So, we were trained in a different way."

As she washed her hands and wrung out the washcloth, Yamaya frowned thoughtfully. She might not have magic of her own, but she understood when a person had to get off the path laid out for them.

"That's why Gabrith couldn't have done this —" Sand pointed at his half-healed wound — "and I can't blast people back where they came from. We both were shaped to be as we are."

Berisan didn't know if Yamaya understood him, or if she understood but didn't accept it. He just hoped she wouldn't keep arguing about it. Two battles in one day, plus healing his shoulder, had left him feeling spent, shaky and ill. Yamaya seemed to recognize that much.

"You look like hell," she said without accusation. "Sit down before you fall. I'll get something hot to eat."

"That would be nice." Berisan gratefully sank down on the top step. With the dust from the fight settling, he picked out the tempting aromas that wafted around the cottage. He watched his reluctant employer scoop river grain and vegetables from her cook pot. When she handed him a steaming bowl, he barely even blew on the food before stuffing it into his mouth.

Yamaya filled her own bowl and lowered herself slowly, with an awkward grunt. Between bites, she observed, "Gabrith had that look, after some battles."

Berisan nodded, scooping more river grain into his

mouth. "Magic might not seem like hard work, but it really is."

They were interrupted by a muffled groan and the thunk of rocks turning against each other. Both straightened. Yamaya raised another spoonful to her mouth, slowly, while her other hand drifted down to touch her dagger's haft. Already Berisan sensed surges of pain and alarm.

"Sabbin and Tyar," he reported. Yamaya gave an indistinct grunt.

The two bandits came slowly up the steep trail from the fields. Tyar leaned heavily on Sabbin. His breath came in a series of panting groans. Sabbin winced as every step jarred his arm.

"That one has a broken bone," Berisan murmured to Yamaya. "The other one, broken ribs at least."

"You probably want to heal them, too," she snorted. With narrowed eyes, Yamaya watched them come. "They tried to kill you, remember? Don't pity them."

Reluctantly, Berisan acknowledged the truth. He didn't like to think he had injured anyone, even indirectly. What would Ar-Thea have said? Pain seeped into his mind, and guilt followed, but Yamaya had a point, too. The kindness would not be appreciated.

When they reached the level top of the hill, they came to an awkward stop. Tyar could barely lift his head. Sabbin stared at Mogrok's body, dark eyes filled with bewildered shock. Mogrok was one of the toughest men in Huld's band. His strength was like a tree they were used to sheltering under. Now questions beat in Sabbin's mind. What happened with him gone? How were they going to tell Huld?

Yamaya kept eating, waiting for them to speak. Her brilliant black eyes held no mercy. In her mind, Berisan heard her jeer that they weren't sticking together because they cared about each other. It was because they needed a fellow witness, or they would be blamed for Mogrok's death.

The barely conscious Tyar grated out, "You finally got him."

"And?"

Yamaya sounded harsh, but Berisan felt pain inside her, too. Old scars that had never fully healed. He shivered as waves of pain crashed around him. There was nothing for him to do, except let them say what they needed to say.

Sabbin blurted, "We're not going to fight you!"

"I know," Yamaya retorted with thin scorn. That drew a huff of indignation from Tyar, but she just shrugged. "Do you want his stuff?"

Sabbin appeared interested, but shook his head. "I can't, not right now."

"Then get out," Yamaya ordered. "I know you have horses. Head back to Huld. If he asks what happened, you tell him exactly. Got it?"

"Sure, Yamaya." Tyar grunted. In his mind, Berisan sensed, he wasn't even sure he would get to have that conversation.

"Tell them all," Yamaya went on, with more intensity. "I don't want Cutrock people down here bothering me. I'm not part of Huld's band any more. I don't want to see them in Opshar, either."

"But we trade, sometimes." Sabbin summoned a bit of spark.

Berisan couldn't keep quiet at that. "What I saw isn't trade."

Sabbin actually cringed. "Yes sir. As you say."

"Find another village to trade with," Yamaya said. "If anyone else wants to come down here and try me, they know what's going to happen."

"Okay, okay," was Sabbin's irritated reply. With a final glance at Mogrok's body, he started to help Tyar walk away. "Come on."

Berisan watched them pass, waiting for their pain to flow around him and dissipate. Maybe Yamaya was right, and hurting would remind the bandits why they needed to stay away from Weeping Falls. The knowledge didn't do much to ease his conscience.

VI

Desires, Light and Dark

Yamaya watched narrow-eyed as the two bandits shuffled around the cottage, keeping an anxious eye on her. There was a lot she would never forgive them for. Still, it felt good that even these lowlifes were afraid of her. Then she noticed that Sand had stopped eating.

"Hey. Eat. You're still pale, and we don't have food to waste."

"All right." Though distracted, Sand dipped his spoon into the bowl.

Once she saw him chewing, Yamaya decided to straighten a few things out. She took a bite of her own rapidly cooling dinner and said, "Let me tell you about Cutrock Canyon."

His eyes flicked to her with startled attention. "If you don't want to..."

"I'm tired of you watching me like I might come at you for no reason," she complained. "Yes, I'm from there, and yes, they're bandits. But it's not just a rowdy camp. It's a village, built into what used to be a stone quarry. Huld's old man, Hown, moved in after the good stone gave out and the quarrymen left. Huld's the chief now. They can hunt up there, but it isn't good land for farming. That's why they have to raid caravans."

"A village of bandits?" Sand's neutral tone said that he wouldn't condemn her, but Yamaya heard it all the same.

"It's a village where people go when nobody wants

them," she corrected. "They're thrown out, or on the run, and they find their way to Cutrock Canyon. Huld can offer them three things they haven't had for a long time." She held up her fingers, counting off the items. "Good food, warm shelter —" Yamaya glanced over, reminding Sand that this was exactly what he said he wanted, those days ago "— and women who were also desperate for food and shelter."

"The count lets them do that?"

She laughed, a crow's mocking call. "There are two counts, one in Pulgoll and one in Deeve. Cutrock is in the mountains, right between them. They already have a grudge, so if one of them sends his soldiers too close to the border, it might start something worse. Anyway, they both probably want the other one to deal with it. So nobody does much."

"That's where you were born?" Sand eyed her while he ate.

"Well," she answered with mocking cheer, "when you have a bunch of women whoring for some bandits, then sooner or later you get kids. The only good thing about Hown was, he never threw the women out. When the men weren't planning raids, he made sure they got time with their kids. If they wouldn't claim their kids, or if they died in a raid, or if the mother died —" she made a circling gesture to encompass all the things that might happen "— then Hown took care of those kids along with his own. When the time came, Huld took over, and he does the same."

Hesitantly, Sand asked, "What happened to your parents?"

"My mother died after birthing me. My father was one of Huld's best friends, a squad leader, but he got an infected wound." Yamaya shrugged a little. The tale was so familiar, usually she hardly felt anything. Only now that someone cared about her pain, she felt them differently. Irritated, she shook that aside. "So Huld called me his second-daughter, and his wife, Bekkera, acted like my second-mother."

"I'm surprised that a bandit chief would care," he said with honesty.

"Don't be fooled. Huld didn't care." Yamaya didn't like the implication, that she should be grateful. "He uses us. That was one of the ways he got more fighters. The boys all grew up to be bandits, and the girls became the whores he handed out to new men."

Yamaya remembered it clearly, how she had come to realize what happened to her older second-sisters in the feast hall after successful raids. Why they were always pregnant. She'd confronted Bekkera, the nearest thing she had to a mother, and got a slap in the face for her defiance.

"Not you?" Sand's probing was a welcome interruption to those memories.

"Only because I wouldn't let them," she said. "The boys my age were already training with Amery, another of Huld's cronies who got sidelined after he wrecked his back. Amery didn't want me there. He set all the boys against me, but we'd all grown up in a pack, running around the canyon. They already knew I didn't give up easily. So I fought for my place, and then I fought as a raider. If any of them tried to pinch my ass, they got an elbow in the eye. Or more."

Yamaya let her hands brush her dagger handles again. Pride warmed her as she remembered her success. Yet it had never completely relieved the tension of defying what the other women submitted to. She constantly had to watch for bastards like Mogrok, who thought her skill was a bad joke.

Sand asked, "Was Gabrith already there?"

Yamaya shook her head. "He turned up a couple of years ago like most of the men do, asking for a place. Huld was excited when he found out he was a mage. After a couple of fights, when Gabrith had proven himself, suddenly one night it's 'take your pick of my daughters.'" She shook her head, disgusted all over again. "You can guess which one he wanted."

"Well, you are pretty," Sand offered.

"What Gabrith said was, women with knives turned him on." Yamaya smirked a little, but her anger soon rose again. "I worked hard and fought well, and Huld gave me away like some kind of cheap trinket. Instead of front line, I was stuck guarding Gabrith's flank." She let go a frustrated sigh. "You hear that a lot of mages are crazy or violent, but Gabrith was all right. He listened to my advice. We were a good team. When I quickened, he was really happy. I think he even loved me."

Yamaya trailed off. She hadn't meant to say that. Gabrith's affection had been no secret, but she had never felt the same. How could she, when someone else made her most intimate decisions for her?

"He didn't want to raise his son as a bandit," Sand guessed.

Son, he said. Yamaya supposed, if he could tell Tyar had broken ribs, he might be able to tell the sex of an unborn child. Still, that rankled. For all the trouble it meant to be a woman, she hoped for a girl.

"Maybe I didn't want to raise my daughter as a whore." Daughter, she said it defiantly. "The other way Huld keeps his men in line is because he's got control of their families. Once our kid was born, Gabrith knew he would never get loose. We had to get out of Cutrock Canyon while I could still travel and fight. Gabrith scouted around a bit, and found this place abandoned. Then we packed up and went to see Huld. We left with what we were carrying."

"You walked away and took up farming." Sand scraped his bowl for the last bits of river grain.

"And then he died." Yamaya finished. She didn't mean it to sound as bitter as it did.

"I don't know if this helps," Sand said, "but there's a cost to mages who use Gabrith's kind of power. *Lethentros* makes them feel invincible, but it eats them inside. You're right that they eventually they go mad, or other mages kill them. He may even have felt it beginning."

Yamaya frowned a little. There had been a few instances where Gabrith had had trouble sleeping after battles. Afterward, his anger has flashed out more quickly. He'd never turned it on Yamaya, but he'd gotten into fights with Mogrok and a couple of the others.

"You're saying that's why he decided to become a farmer?" She frowned doubtfully.

"Sure," Sand said quietly. "He wanted to be there for you and the kid. Like any decent man would."

Yamaya's throat tightened. She refused to cry. Anger swelled, familiar as the knives that fit her hand. Anger was what kept her alive, even when the brat kicked her, or milk leaked out of her breasts, or she just felt too bloated and heavy to get out of bed — but did it anyway. She hardly knew what to do with any other emotion.

"Stop talking like you knew us," she hissed.

Sand opened his mouth, but then closed it again. It was quiet for a little as they both finished what was left of their food. It would have been nice if she had loved Gabrith, Yamaya thought. Most days, she hardly even missed him. There was too much work for her to mope about it.

Softly, in a soothing tone, Sand said, "You said this farm was Gabrith's dream, not yours. You don't plan to leave?"

"I'm too heavy to go anywhere now," Yamaya countered, "but I wouldn't go back for anything. My kid is going to have better choices than Cutrock Canyon." Setting her empty dish aside, she pushed her hands against her knees to stand up. "I'll go over the body, see what we can salvage. Then, are you well enough to help me dig a grave?"

After they finished burying Mogrok, Yamaya insisted that Berisan go back to the waterfall and scrub his shirt thoroughly. It now hung from a branch nearby, dripping lazily. Lying beneath the lean-to, he watched the pale folds of fabric swirl in a night breeze and tried to quiet his thoughts.

He couldn't seem to find a comfortable position on the rough-made bed. His shoulder might be mostly healed, but the place where the wound had been still ached. Any time he turned over, he had a burst of fear that it would split open again. Then, whenever he began to relax toward sleep, the events of the day came back in jagged flashes. Berisan relived the moment when the arrow struck him. Or yelling warriors charged through his mind. He jerked alert, half-dreaming the rank stench of blood and sour dirt from the grave.

Giving up on sleep, he rolled onto the side that didn't hurt.

Yamaya's connection to the bandits was no surprise. Hadn't he suspected as much? Still, something in her story haunted him.

Who could imagine that bandits would have their own village, full of families — or second-families. Clearly Yamaya had no affection for her second-father, and Berisan couldn't blame her. Still, it was strange to think a hardened killer and bandit chief could be a father figure to the orphans his men left scattered behind them.

It was very different from the way Berisan grew up, in a close household with two devoted parents and an older brother and sister. Yamaya would have laughed to hear him compare their childhoods. Yet beneath the surface, their fathers made almost the same decisions.

Now that he thought of it, Aulgrip did, too. Yes, the headman strutted around with the over-inflated pride of the richest man in a very small town. He lorded it over the rest of them, while he secretly paid tribute to the bandits so his people would be left alone. It was the same reason Aulgrip had been so quick to blackmail Berisan once his magic was revealed.

All that had only happened half a day ago, and so much had gone on afterward that Berisan nearly forgot about it. Now, he had to reconsider whether it was safe for him to stay in Opshar.

Dried weeds crackled as he turned over fretfully. Had he really thought he could offer the people of Opshar a better way? That, if he could only show them all mages didn't have to be insane tyrants, they would be ready to hear Ar-Thea's message of peace? What a foolish dream that was. A child's illusion.

It was like one of Keilos' songs, a romantic fantasy where goodness overcame evil. Berisan had never thought that it could leave him personally vulnerable. Now that he felt an arrow in his own flesh, he had to think again. About everything.

Emotions rose within him, just as they had when Keilos revealed his foretelling. That desperate fear overwhelmed other bonds of family and friendship. It drove Berisan to leave his own brother behind, so he could run and run, all the way to this pitiful farm on a cliff's edge.

Even now, his legs itched deep inside with the need to be moving. He could gather his things, right now, and be gone in the night. It would hardly take any time for Berisan to get ready. Yes, he should run. There was nothing here worth saving.

The night wind shifted, bringing with it a faint froth of mist from the waterfall. It cooled him, so he could simply breathe and try to get his fears under control. Months had gone by. Had he not grown even a little stronger, yet?

Besides, it was wrong to say he had nothing here worth saving.

When Berisan had first encountered Yamaya in Opshar's market, he only thought she was someone who needed help. He had never planned how long he would stay at Weeping Falls. Somehow, he had it in his mind that he could run away if he needed to. That was what the minstrels usually did. They helped people, and then left before the hunter-guards found out.

In the night, with the wind whispering through the trees, he could admit that Yamaya wasn't the only one to be caught by her past. Deluded fool that he was, he had stayed long enough to get tangled up in this thicket of bloodthorns and secrets.

Berisan rubbed his shoulder. That small patch of pain was a nagging reminder of why the minstrels always kept moving. Common sense raged at him to run while he could. Somewhere, his friends were still wandering across Skaythe, waiting for the moment they could gather again. He belonged with them. Yet, how could he leave Yamaya, pregnant and alone?

She would have said she didn't need him, but he knew there was no one else she could trust. That young cockerel, Kinson, had to be reminded about a simple thing like paying for what he took. He would never do something really dangerous on her behalf.

And the people of Opshar? They would still have no one to watch over them. Aulgrip wanted pride of place, but he forced others to do the fighting for him. As a minstrel, Berisan could never be the protector Opshar demanded. He couldn't abandon his principles of nonviolence.

Anyway, hadn't he already gone through the thing he most feared? Berisan had broken his own cardinal rule and allowed himself to get caught. Then he'd been blackmailed, and attacked. Yet, somehow, he was still alive. In the dark of night, he could lie awake and agonize over it all.

As sleep finally settled around him, an insane idea began to take shape.

The next days passed in relentless activity. Yamaya and Sand focused on the tasks necessary to keep the farm going, and didn't speak any more about what had happened. Between them, they picked, pitted and dried a small mountain of cherries. Still others they boiled for juice, and set in crocks to ferment. Once the cherries were down, Sand pruned the trees and wove the fence for the chicken run with a singular will.

Hour after hour, day after day, Yamaya expected him to accuse her of lying. He should have been angry, demanding to know why she waited to tell him she used to be a bandit. Yet he said nothing of the sort. At times he seemed to be wrapped up in his thoughts, but mostly he kept on working.

The man made no sense to Yamaya, but maybe he didn't have to. He had come back to help her when the bandits showed up. He never stopped thinking about the farm. Better yet, he didn't push himself at Yamaya the way Kinson or Mogrok did.

What more could she ask for?

If Sand appeared to have put those events aside, Yamaya certainly hadn't. She was jumpy, reaching for her knives at any unexpected sound or movement. Even after an ambush went bad, she had never been this nervous. Why, she scolded herself, was a minor skirmish so different?

Maybe because killing Mogrok had cut her off from her past life. Yamaya didn't think that mattered, but worry began to gnaw at her as each passing day brought the birthing closer. She had few friends in Opshar, and Monetha, the midwife, was another one of Kinson's aunts. This business with Aulgrip threatening Sand could be a problem.

Everyone Yamaya really knew was back at Cutrock Canyon. Especially Bekkera. Her second-mother might be harsh, but she had overseen a lot of births. If Yamaya had thought about it, she could have sent a message back with Sabbin, to ask if Bekkera would come visit for a few weeks.

But she hadn't. She'd been too focused on survival. Then, in the aftermath, things that should have stayed private just poured out of her. Five times a day, Yamaya berated herself for saying too much. It wasn't as if she needed Sand's approval for her life. Or anyone's!

Regardless, Yamaya had business to finish up in Opshar. Mogrok had interrupted, but Yamaya needed to know if the cradle was ready, or if Monetha was even willing to come as far as Weeping Falls for a birth. If not, maybe Lilia's family would let her come up the hill.

Or if Sand's healing extended as far as childbirth.

Or if... If...

Yes, she had a few things to settle in Opshar.

The next market day, Berisan and Yamaya set off toward town in a glowering dawn. Their waypacks were laden with fresh and dried fruit to trade, plus a bit of food and water for the day. The valley below was hidden by layers of mist from the river. Farther beyond, jagged mountains bared their rocky teeth at the sky.

Step by step on the damp track, the village came closer. When Berisan had first walked in, from the other direction, Opshar had been nothing but a convenient place to hide. He had been a beggar, unseen in plain sight. Now, everyone saw him, and Opshar just might be a place he could call home.

Knowing this, he tried to relax. The sights and sounds were the same as they had ever been. Distant voices echoed over stone walls. Scents of dust and manure from animal pens drifted over the house walls. The breeze carried a hint of the river's clean tang. Echoes of hammer blows made an unsteady rhythm from up ahead. Market stalls were going up for the day. You could almost think that nothing had happened, that last time.

As they came into the plaza, more and more people looked at them sidelong. Mages were always met with concern, and they folk had had a few days to think about what his presence could mean. The other reason was that Yamaya wore her knives openly. After some struggle and cursing, she had rigged a way to belt them across her chest, instead of below her massive belly. She walked differently, too. A confident stride, even commanding, despite her advancing pregnancy.

People might look at them twice, but from Berisan's point of view, the most important fact was the absence of any hunter-guards. As long as no one had set the law on them, he had something to base his hopes on.

Yamaya caught many startled glances as she and Sand made their way to the market square. Did they stare, shocked, that a woman went so armed? Well, let them stare. Yamaya wasn't someone to be trifled with. It was a statement that needed to be made.

Further, she observed with some amusement how many of the women were watching Sand as he passed. No longer was he a mere beggar, but a powerful mage, possibly someone important to the village. Their dark eyes gleamed with a particular speculation. Was Sand with Yamaya, or were they free to seek his attention?

To Yamaya, it was a pointless question. Much as she appreciated Sand's work ethic, they weren't suited as a couple. They never would have been, even if she wasn't swollen with another man's child. Or if Kinson hadn't already tried to stake his claim.

There were benefits to having a mage as your hired hand, though. The space where Yamaya last set up was still vacant, presumably out of respect for Sand having driven the bandits off. She swung her waypack down with a relieved "oof," and straightened to rub her back. The early mist had long since lifted, leaving her sweaty and aching from the long walk.

Immediately, Sand passed her a waterskin. She drank gratefully. They might not be a romantic couple, but she wouldn't say no to just a bit of pampering.

He asked, "Do you want to rest? I can go find

Aulgrip."

There was such a thing as too much doting, though. Yamaya wiped her mouth. She longed to sit down, but if she did, it would be hard to get back up again. Besides, she didn't want anyone to think she needed help.

"No, it's my farm. I'll do it."

"He probably wants to lord it over me, though," Sand suggested wryly.

"Do you enjoy him thinking you're a servant?" Yamaya barked. This was why they couldn't have been a couple. "Make him come to you."

She was about to head for the tavern, but Lilia darted over from the fish stall, where her father and uncle were busy shifting barrels around.

"Yamaya!" The younger girl paused, admiring the two knives on Yamaya's belt. "Wow." Then she shook her curiosity away. "Guess what I heard?"

"Is this important?" Yamaya tried not to be impatient with the chit-chat, but she had her own things to set up.

"Yes." Lilia leaned in urgently. "Listen, you know my big sister, Jenissa? Her house is right behind Kinson's. She said they've been having huge fights. She can hear them over the garden wall."

"What are they fighting about?" Sand looked up from unloading his waypack.

Lilia giggled, and whispered to Yamaya, "You!"

"They are not." Yamaya took an instinctive step back as something like panic flooded her veins. She had just reached a point where she felt like her life was her own. There was no way she would let anyone else make her decisions for her.

"Why?" Sand also sounded concerned.

Lilia grinned, enjoying their confusion. "It sounds to Jenissa like Doloram and Kinson's dad, Kinley, are getting tired of how Aulgrip runs things. Especially since they found out Aulgrip made a deal with the bandits. They want to have a town council instead of just a headman."

"I would, too." Yamaya could understand their wanting to have a say, but she didn't trust that some bunch of men she barely knew were talking about her.

"What do the rest of the villagers think?" Sand wanted to know.

Lilia shrugged, then winced as her father called out. "What are you doing, girl? We need you over here."

"Yes, Papa!" She darted back over, and Yamaya clearly heard him scolding her to "hold this while I tie it down" and "leave them alone."

Yamaya and Sand exchanged glances as they turned their focus to their own setup. After they tossed the odd pebble out of the way, they could flatten out Yamaya's old blanket to serve as a base. She studied the camouflage pattern for a moment, remembering how Mogrok had recognized the weaving as being particular to Cutrock Canyon. If she was going to be trading here regularly, maybe it was time to exchange the blanket for a proper table. A chair would be nice, too. Only, how was she going to get them up and down the ridge from Weeping Falls?

Sand's quiet voice interrupted her thoughts. "Could Aulgrip be trying to get hold of me for something to do with this family dispute?"

"He can't have you," Yamaya retorted. She didn't mean to sound so angry, and quickly modified her tone. "He might think that having you at his beck and call would give him leverage."

"Well, don't worry, I have no interest in changing jobs," Sand assured her. "Then why would their argument involve you?"

"It doesn't, except Kinson's been coming around. Some of his aunts are acting friendly, too." She shrugged, frowning to herself. "Maybe they want to get me on their side. That doesn't make sense, though. I'm barely part of this village. Weeping Falls is too far away."

She gazed angrily across the square, where Aulgrip was running the market under the shelter of the inn's broad porch. "I guess I'd better get over there and ask him."

"Maybe we should both go talk to him." Berisan didn't like the way Yamaya's expression had changed with Lilia's news. Obsidian eyes glittered with a reflection of her ferocity as she finished off Mogrok. That wasn't going to help anything.

"Someone has to finish setting up our goods," she answered, and then gave a curt smile. "Don't worry, I won't hurt him."

Seriously, he said, "When you talk to Aulgrip, don't forget, he was trying to protect his people."

"Right. I'm sure that was the first thing in his mind." Yamaya rolled her eyes and stalked toward the tavern.

Berisan hoped she meant what she said. If not, his hopes of building a different relationship with the people in Opshar could evaporate like water on hot stones.

He finished unloading their packs. A light breeze flipped up one side of Yamaya's blanket, so he held the corners down with empty baskets until he could fill them. Some he mounded with softly gleaming, bright red cherries. Others held the dull and wizened dry fruit. He walked around the display and moved things around until it came close to how Yamaya usually set it up.

By this time, Lilia's father had their stall arranged and was hanging strings of dried fish from upright poles. The dark-eyed girl was busy polishing the wooden trays on the table. He caught another friendly glance from her.

"What do you think?" He indicated his display.

She studied it, then said, "Put the fresh ones closer to

where you're sitting. That way nobody tries to grab them."

"You have a point." He took her suggestion, then folded his leather cloak and settled down with his pipes.

"Lilia," scolded her father. "Come over here and pass me some of the smoked silt-fish."

The girl pouted a little, and Berisan caught the father's wary glance. Not everyone was willing to trust a mage, it seemed.

"Fish," the father yelled to all who might hear. "Fresh or dried fish!"

His suspicion reminded Berisan that it was time to stop lurking like a beggar. Just as Yamaya did with her daggers, he needed to been seen for who he was. Seated on the leather pad, he tilted his hat farther back on his head so that his face was visible. Then he blew through his pipes a little, warming them up to play.

Spurred by what Lilia had said, Yamaya strode off with great energy. Who were these men, Kinson and his uncles, to make her life their business? Aulgrip's power play had to be answered, as well. Sand was her worker, and she wasn't ready to give him up.

Yet, a warrior's instinct wasn't always the best strategy. Yamaya did need to preserve what little good will she had built in Opshar. There was nowhere else she could trade for things she needed. So it was Sand's words that stayed with her as she joined the line of farmers and crafters waiting to sign up for the market.

A low buzz of conversation reverberated beneath the tavern's wide porch. Yamaya listened with half an ear, but heard only idle gossip or talk of the weather. Her feet ached, complaining of the delay. The line moved quickly enough, though, and soon she caught Aulgrip's brief frown around the shoulder of the man ahead of her.

"Good luck with your bargaining," the headman said

as that man moved away. Then he frowned at Yamaya, making only a partial effort to conceal his disapproval. "Mistress Yamaya, surely it isn't necessary to go so armed? People might be frightened."

'People,' she thought sarcastically. Not him personally, just people. However, Yamaya wasn't going to debate with someone who tried to make others do his fighting for him. She casually set her coin on his desk.

"It's Farmer Yamaya," she corrected blandly, "and it surely is necessary. You see, Headman, those bandits followed me home last time."

Aulgrip had taken the coin and put his head down, writing her name in a ledger. Now his startled gaze jumped back up to her.

"They followed you?" She could almost think that his concern was real.

There was a slight lull in the conversation as people stopped to listen. Yamaya neither raised nor lowered her voice.

"Don't worry, I dealt with them. They won't be coming back here again."

Aulgrip frowned, almost by reflex. Mention of the bandits brought up a sore point, and he was clearly aware of people watching them. She also could sense his disbelief, that a mere woman could handle such frightening fellows. His dark eyes rested on the deer-horn handles of her knives before he pulled them away.

"What do you mean, dealt with them?" came a skeptical demand from somewhere in the crowd.

"We talked it over," Yamaya answered in a mockingly sweet imitation of Sand. A few chuckles went through them. Though she was tempted to add some of the gory details, she decided to let them all wonder. "Anyway, I'll be keeping my weapons with me, thanks."

"I see, well, if that's true," Aulgrip trailed off,

unwilling to acknowledge her refusal. Yet his eyes strayed again to the daggers on her sash.

"Headman," Yamaya continued, "I did you a favor by taking care of that. The village is safer now. So I'm asking you, as a return favor, not to steal my hired hand. Sand has a place at Weeping Falls Farm. I can't spare him."

She straightened a little, letting her big belly stick out as a reminder of why that was. Aulgrip's forehead reddened a bit at the crude reminder. He managed a sour chuckle.

"You're made your point, Yamaya."

"Farmer Yamaya," she corrected. "Thanks, Headman. Good luck with your bargaining."

Yamaya headed for the stairs, nodding in response to a few murmured greetings. Sand should be happy to know that she had reached a deal with Aulgrip, and he wasn't bleeding. Not even a little.

Although he probably deserved to. What an ass.

Berisan played a lively tune to attract customers. It was early in the day, and most of the people were circulating to find out what the stalls had before they made their choices. Cheerful greetings cost nothing, however. He traded a few with those who passed nearby.

He enjoyed watching the ever-changing kaleidoscope of people mingling in the market square. On one side was laughter and gossip, on the other side, heated barter. A young girl stopped and began to dance to his music, completely without shame, until her scolding mother pulled her away. Opshar was just like every village where the minstrels had set up their show, and yet it was different. This village was likely to be his very own. He wanted to see all of it.

Berisan listened, too, to see if there was room here for his crazy idea. Yamaya had been shocked that he was able to heal that arrow wound. She had never even considered that magic could heal as well as harm. Hard working people like these in Opshar would hurt themselves, or gather a few sore muscles. He watched for anyone who walked stiffly, or whose mind bristled with complaints about their pain.

When he had been with the minstrels, Tisha used to offer healing services. She had been so skillful, Berisan had never paid much attention to how she did it. But, if he could build his skills, it could be something to benefit the whole village.

He had to be careful, though. Healing had a way of changing people's hearts. Berisan wanted to be accepted in the village, not compel everyone to alter their way of thinking.

If he could do it, though, that would be something fit to honor Ar-Thea's memory.

When Yamaya explained how she got Sand out of Aulgrip's trap, the former beggar nodded with relief.

"It's good to have that settled. Thanks, Farmer." As always, he used the title Yamaya wanted. If only everyone paid that much attention.

A few hours passed, while Sand played his pipes and Yamaya bartered with all who came. She traded the last of her fresh cherries for other foodstuffs, and the carpenter's boy ran up to tell her she could come look at the cradle. Even the midwife, Monetha, came by to inquire after her health. Was that at Aulgrip's request, or did Monetha simply know the birthing time was closer? Regardless of the reason, they made arrangements for Yamaya to call on Monetha later in the day.

Meanwhile, Yamaya was amused by how often Lilia leaned over, chatting to Sand. Her father kept calling her away, but she always drifted back. It wasn't only Lilia, either. As Yamaya had expected, a number of young women made a point of stopping to talk. If Sand took a fancy to one of them? Well, Yamaya wouldn't mind having some company up at the farm.

She was just thinking so when a shadow fell across her blanket. "Yamaya?"

"Farmer Yamaya," she corrected before she looked up and saw Kinson.

As ever, he was handsomely turned out with an embroidered tunic — this one was deep blue — and topknot carefully trimmed and oiled. He had that same confidence, as if he privileged her by being there. Yet, like his uncle, his eyes flitted to her knife handles and then away.

Good. Yamaya had a few questions for him, and the answers might shake loose more easily if he knew he wasn't completely in control.

She answered, "Good day," and to Sand she added, "Watch things for a bit, will you?"

"Sure thing, Farmer," he agreed.

Yamaya gathered her feet, but the weight of her belly made it harder to get to her feet. Sand set his pipes aside and started to help her up, but Kinson scowled and shoved a hand down to her.

"Thanks." Yamaya didn't specify which of them this was for. As she and Kinson moved away, she informed him, "I was going to walk by Monetha's house. Will you walk with me there?"

"Of course." Kinson tried to be smooth, while obviously anxious to get her away from Sand. Indeed, they hardly got a few steps before he reproached her in a low voice. "Why is that man still here? You should have sent him on his way."

That made it sound like Sand had done something wrong. Although Yamaya had her own doubts about Sand's approach, Kinson was being unfair. And fairly uppity, to tell her what to do on her own farm.

"Sand has never threatened me," she retorted. "He

only stepped in to protect Farri, and he didn't even hurt those men." As an afterthought, she added, "That happened later."

Still, Yamaya was pretty sure that wasn't really what bothered Kinson. He didn't know she had no interest in Sand. To him, Sand must seem like quite a rival.

"He's a mage," Kinson answered urgently. "They're dangerous!"

She gave the same reply that she had to his uncle. "Sand is a good worker, and I need him."

"No you don't," Kinson coaxed. "I've told you my brothers and I will be glad to do whatever he does. Sheykin and Kindrik, they're both ready."

Yamaya arched a brow. If she remembered correctly, Sheykin and Kindrik were his younger brothers. He probably assumed they would do the hard work for him. That could explain why the arguments were loud enough to be heard over the garden wall.

"You'd all be willing to sleep under a lean-to and work just for meals?" she teased. Then she put out the same question she had posed to Sand, that first day. "How much farming have any of you done?"

"It can't be that hard." Kinson waved her question away.

So he hadn't done any. That wasn't a surprise. His father, the tailor, wouldn't have trained him in manual labor. Still, something in his tone made her hackles rise. Kinson and two brothers, invading her farm? He sounded just like Mogrok, threatening to take over everything she and Gabrith had made.

"Besides, you must be so tired in your condition," Kinson reasoned. "You deserve to be taken care of. All this —" he waved vaguely — "pretending to be a farmer. Leave that stuff to the men. You don't need those awful knives."

Yamaya stopped walking. She wasn't pretending to be a farmer, and her knives were part of her. She wasn't about to give them up. Kinson walked a step farther, then turned with every appearance of confusion.

"You don't need them," he insisted, so sincerely that Yamaya knew it was fake.

"A woman never knows what's going to happen." She still didn't understand what Kinson was after, and it was about time she got those answers.

"We'll protect you," he insisted. "Yamaya, listen. I thought it was clear —"

"It's not clear," she cut in briskly, "and I don't like guessing games."

"Can't you see that I care for you?" he persuaded. "You're all alone, and in your condition... All I want to do is help."

He reached for her hand, and she pulled it away.

"You don't know me," Yamaya answered flatly. "You have some idea about me, and you expect me to go along without knowing what it is. Besides, I'm really not looking for another man. As you keep mentioning, I'm still dealing with what the last one left behind."

After a quick flash of anger and hurt, Kinson kept up his loving concern. "That's just it. You need someone more reliable than a... a wandering fugitive. When the baby is born, he'll need a father to bring him up. I've got it all figured out. I'll be there, on the farm. My brothers will be there."

The gall of that! Yet, there was an eager undertone that told Yamaya this, at last, was what he really wanted — her farm.

"Oh?" she bit out. "What, exactly, is your plan for bringing up my kid?"

"Why, he can work on the farm. Or her. She can keep house for me."

A stillness came over her. Very quietly, Yamaya

repeated, "For you."

"No, us. I meant us..." He faltered, aware of the blunder and trying to recover. "How can you even think that? You're getting confused."

So he thought to point blame at Yamaya, just the way Mogrok had, but Yamaya wasn't confused. One poor widow, pregnant and alone. Kinson saying he was there to 'take care of her,' along with two of his brothers. If they decided to sieze control of the farm, it would be three against one. Family squabbles aside, these were Aulgrip's kinfolk. He was sure to side with them against an outsider like Yamaya. She would become a prisoner on her own farm. Just another whore, trading her body for an illusion of safety.

"Well, I have a different plan," she informed him. "*My* plan is that *my kid* will inherit my farm."

"Of course," he agreed, far too easily, "but surely there will be more than one child."

Again Kinson tried to take her hand. Yamaya folded her arms and glared at him. Yes, a brilliant plan, to keep her pregnant and — he thought — helpless. He might even assume that if something, somehow, happened to her firstborn, she would be just as happy to have his brats take it all.

This, from a man who knew nothing about farming. Coming from a family that owned so much of Opshar, he might even think he had some right to snatch an outlying farm from the outsiders who brought it back to life.

Her fury rose, but she kept a tight rein. Even now, her lack of cooperation had set him back. Kinson might be a few years older than Yamaya, but he was acting like a child. This wasn't worth her anger.

"Be reasonable," Kinson pouted and huffed indignantly.

"Don't worry yourself about me," she said calmly. "I'll manage."

"But... Yamaya," he sputtered. "Think of your future. My family is important. We can do a lot for you."

"Well, I'm clearly not worthy." Yamaya unleashed a fraction her sarcasm. She briefly rested her hand on a knife hilt. "*This* is who I am, Kinson, and you just told me I'm awful."

She turned away, face burning with anger, and headed in the direction of Monetha's house. For the second time that day, she was aware of people around them stopping to listen. Their expressions were amused, but Yamaya hardly shared their glee. The situation was too embarrassing.

"That isn't what I meant," he scrambled after her. "We can fix this."

Fix her?

"That's enough," was her ruthless reply. "My farm is small and half-made, but it's mine. I have a hired hand, and I'll stand with that."

"No, Yamaya, wait!" Kinson cried with indignant disbelief. He reached to grab her shoulder, but she deftly avoided his hand.

"Did you think I'm some kind of fruit, to be plucked off a tree?" Yamaya yelled, for the benefit of all those people staring. Let them hear this, too. "You have no claim on me."

Kinson stared, as if she had suggested something ridiculous and unreasonable. Yamaya stalked off, and went on to the midwife's house. No man would ever make her decisions for her again.

It turned out that Berisan didn't have to wait long for the opportunity to test his idea. One of the farmers from out in the valley walked by, with his wife scolding at his heels. "At least let me wrap it, Nerric."

"Let me be, Allace. It's nothing."

"Then why won't you let me look at it?"

Berisan extended his thoughts to share a throbbing ache in the farmer's hand. In Nerric's memory a wheel turned suddenly, jamming his hand against the side of a wagon. Then the shock of pain, and the sense of physical violation Berisan knew so well.

"There's nothing you can do," Nerric growled.

"Actually," Berisan spoke up smoothly. His years in the minstrel show had taught him how to catch a man's attention without setting him on edge.

"Leave me be," the farmer began, but faltered when he saw who it was.

"I'll bet that hurts a lot," Berisan murmured sympathetically.

"It's not so bad," Nerric blustered.

"The bone is cracked, and it's getting infected," he corrected mildly. Berisan could feel the swelling, and angry pulses of infection, like a smoldering fire ready to burst into flame. He moved slowly, bracketing the wounded wrist without touching it. A gentle glow sprang up as he drew in *vitalis* and let it flow into the injured flesh. The farmer caught his breath as the pain eased.

"Sure, he'll let you do it," the farmer's wife grumbled, but he sensed her relief.

Berisan nodded, moving the healing deeper to chase out the last malignance. Moments later, the farmer flexed his wrist and then his fingers.

"I don't feel anything," he murmured, baffled but pleased. "I don't know how you did that, but thanks." The unaccustomed word came out stiffly.

"Just don't tell Yamaya. She'll make me charge you." Berisan winked at them.

The couple both laughed, finally able to relax without worry. Berisan could see their moods lifting. There was even a hint of pride, that Opshar had a mage of its own. As Ar-Thea had said, being healed had an effect on people.

Allace offered, "At least let us trade you something."

"You know," Berisan said slowly, "Yamaya's been hoping to get a hen or two. Do you have any to spare?"

She glanced at her husband. "Well, there is the gray one that the others keep pestering."

A short time later, the couple left with an agreement to pick up a chicken on their way back to Weeping Falls. All Berisan had to do was figure out some way to carry it with them. Again, he watched the square, hoping Yamaya would return so he could tell her the news.

Meanwhile, Berisan savored the knowledge that his guess had been right. The people of Opshar might not acknowledge it, but they were hungry for more than mere survival. Even Aulgrip, who thought he was in control of everything, might not be so eager to send for the hunter-guards once the people learned what he could do.

For himself, Berisan had even higher hopes. If he set the example that compassion was stronger than self-interest, it could be the beginning of real change. Ar-Thea's dream had been to save Skaythe from the darkness that shrouded it. Maybe Berisan would be the one to bring it beyond the realm of childish illusion, and into the light of reality.

PRISONERS OF THE
WAILING TOWER

by Deby Fredericks

Dedication

For Alden, with my thanks.

Prisoners of the Wailing Tower

I

The Larder

T here was a tower, swollen black against the dying sun, and there was screaming, a high thin wail without pause for breath. Alemin had sunk into a trance over long hours of enforced travel. Now the screaming clawed him back into his misery. Blinking, he tried to focus his eyes against the relentless glare of sunset. Tried, also, to straighten his legs and shift his arms into a more comfortable position.

No such thing existed, chained as he was in a cage of iron, in the bed of a wagon, rolling on and on down an endless road. The gag in his mouth sucked all moisture out of him, leaving his throat painfully dry. Hunger gnawed at his ribs. Sweat plastered loose hair over his eyes. He tossed his head a little, shaking the dark coils back.

No, there was no comfort for a renegade mage captured by hunter-guards. A juggler by trade, Alemin was especially tormented by having his hands bound. Yet he was also a mage, and he knew his art well enough that he did not need hands free in order to juggle. He could trace it in his mind, the rhythmic dance of fingers and wrists, the balls or fruit or blunted daggers circling before him.

Not long ago, Berisan would have been his partner. Their movements were perfectly coordinated, catching and tossing, joking and jigging before a crowd. It hurt to be stripped of his brother's company. Yet Alemin knew, with bleak certainly, how fortunate the distance was. If they still traveled together, they would both have been jammed into this cage. Alemin wanted his brother to stay safe and free.

Thus he was left with only his magecraft and memory of the art.

Juggling in his mind, he put himself back into the trance, drawing in *vitalis* to wipe away pain and thirst. No matter how often the hunter-guards beat him or jabbed through the bars, his power healed those injuries. Even fear, the yammering hound, fell silent for a time. So Alemin had passed the long days of travel when he had no choice but to wait and endure.

Yet now there was a tower, and a scream. It seemed they were getting somewhere. Alemin was fairly certain he wouldn't like their destination.

The driver cursed and lashed at the oxen. A rough jolt broke up what was left of Alemin's trance. It seemed the wagon crossed over rocky ground. Horse's hooves thudded up beside him. Sergeant Traggan, leader of Boar Squad, sneered with eager malice.

"Taking a good look, pretty boy?"

They had been calling him that for days. Possibly because he had been juggling when it all went wrong. Alemin had been arrested in the clothes he wore for performance, tight leather trousers and an embroidered shirt glinting with beads. The taunt reminded him why he had been spending his days in a trance.

"It's the Larder," added one of the guardsmen who rode in the back of the wagon. That one was responsible for much of the poking and punching. He waited with delicious glee before going on. "Dar-Gothull's Larder."

With the gag in his mouth, Alemin couldn't answer. Still, fear bit into his heart. Dar-Gothull's Larder was the most dreaded prison in all of Skaythe. It was the last stop for renegade mages and madmen. The shrieking went on, as if in agreement. It hadn't stopped this whole time. Alemin was surprised that none of the hunter-guards noticed it.

The driver stopped lashing his oxen long enough to smirk over his shoulder. "You'll have a fine welcome there. The Lizard loves the smart ones."

Someone else snickered, "The Lizard."

The sergeant flashed a cruel grin in the shadow of his helmet. The men of his squad guffawed along with him.

Only a lowly man, often abused, could take such pleasure in a brief moment of power.

Despite the danger, Alemin found their bragging and posturing ridiculous. He was worn down with travel, even a little hysterical. Humor rolled up his spine. It made the fear loosen its jaws. He turned his eyes downward before the guardsmen could see that he was laughing. That impulse, to laugh at the absurdity of the world, was what got him arrested in the first place. But Alemin couldn't keep his mirth from shaking his shoulders. Luckily, the hunter-guards misunderstood.

"Awww, he's crying," one gloated.

"Don't be sad, pretty boy," another said with mock sympathy.

More crude laughter blended in with rumbles and jolts as the oxen drew the wagon over uneven pavement. The rough ride helped Alemin gather his sobriety. The road shouldn't be this bad. They were traveling over the Shining Ones' highway, or had been when he tranced himself at noontime. Common roads might be rutted or rocky, thick with mud, but the ancient highways were different. Created with a silvery gray material no one now living could identify, they remained pristine across untold centuries, and they always gave a smooth, gentle ride.

Alemin shifted around until he could peer between the bars. What he saw was troubling. The road beneath the wagon's wheels was bubbled, marred by inky streaks. It was as if the surface had been melted and then allowed to cool. The two oxen grunted with the effort of pulling their burden over the ravaged paving. He couldn't imagine what might cause this.

A harsher bump made Alemin's forehead slam against the bars. Hunter-guards roared with mirth. He leaned back, blinking against the pain. Bound as he was, he could do nothing to ease himself.

At least, nothing the guardsmen could perceive. Alemin drew a careful breath. The world around him was full of *vitalis*, the energy of all living things. He took it cautiously into himself. Not enough to draw a light — the guardsmen would see that. He only needed enough to banish the headache and blunt his raging thirst. There was no telling what other mages were nearby. He didn't want anyone to sense his working.

As it was, the hunter-guards' leers were slipping. His lack of anguish disappointed them. Again, Alemin's ill-timed humor rose up. He shut his eyes, arching his back to ease stiff shoulders, and threw in a few gasps to make them feel better about themselves.

They all rode closer now than they had in past days. A little defensive, maybe. Alemin could see why.

The ancient highway ran along the edge of a deep canyon, like an axe's bite into the land. That was Yergha Drop. Sunset gave the far cliff a darkened look, just like the road. On the opposite side, Yergha's lush tropical forest had been hacked away to make space for a sprawling town. Smoke from cooking fires hung over it in a shifting, grainy curtain. More fumes rose from mines deep in the canyon. The count's fortress of Yergha glowered over it all.

However, their destination was on this side of the chasm. That tower crouched like a wounded beast on the crest of a hill, right above the void. Everywhere in Skaythe, rumors swirled about the Larder. They said Dar-Gothull devoured his enemies and fed from their very souls. It was how he had maintained his life for more than three centuries.

Alemin didn't want to see that vision of doom approaching. In his mind, his mentor Ar-Thea whispered, *"If you don't look, you will never see things as they are."*

So he looked at the Larder.

At some point, the screaming had stopped. Alemin was relieved, but uncertain. How could he have heard any noise coming from the Larder at that distance? The hunter-guards should have noticed, too. Much as they enjoyed suffering, they should have been teasing him with it.

Maybe he had imaged the cries? He had been half in a trance, after all. Only, a mage's mind was trained against such errors. Even as hungry and thirsty as he was, Alemin wouldn't have invented such a thing. He frowned a little, studying the structure as the wagon rattled ever closer.

The tower itself was tall and round, with a flattened crown. It was slightly sunken, slumped lower on the left side than the right. Narrow black windows were fringed with metallic char. They seemed to have been punched through from the inside. Clearly this was as much a relic of the Shining Ones as the roadway that led to it. Like that road, it had somehow been wounded.

The original tower was surrounded by a few outbuildings, and then high walls with frowning ramparts. A large structure right against the tower probably housed the prison itself. These were modern stonework, rough blocks with crude mortar. They looked like a child's mud pot compared to a porcelain vase. For all they were built around the tower, they could not touch its scarred elegance.

Beyond the Larder itself, Alemin glimpsed a small village huddled at the edge of Yergha Drop. Then the roadway turned toward the prison, and its thick walls blotted out all else. Chains clanked and groaned as a massive portcullis rose to admit them. Passing through, they entered a wide courtyard scented with dust and manure. There was something that might be a vegetable garden, just at the edge of a tower. A servant in a shapeless gray robe moved along the wall, lighting a series of oil lanterns set there. Their yellow glare only partly relieved the deepening dusk.

Another forbidding gate rose before them, accessible by a stairway. The wagon's driver hauled on the reins and cursed his beasts, stopping them at the foot of it. All banter forgotten, the hunter-guards moved with grim purpose. Those who rode dismounted, and the others poured out of a second wagon that followed Alemin's. Bare blades glinted in the lantern light. Bars clanged as the cage door slammed open.

"Out you come, pretty boy," Sergeant Traggan growled, "and no cute tricks."

Alemin nodded eagerly. The moment he knew he would be able to leave the cage, every muscle seemed to cramp at once. When he actually had room to straighten up, pain burned in his legs and up his back. He moaned behind his gag, stumbling, but the hunter-guards grabbed him before he could fall.

Rough hands propelled him to the steps. An armored door gaped wide at the top. Behind them, the portcullis screeched down its rails again. In his confusion, Alemin almost thought he heard the same voice that had cried out before. Then they were through, and the metal door clapped shut like the jaws of some mighty beast.

Something was wrong. Dread settled on Lorrah's shoulders, dragging on her like a water-logged cloak. Her first thought was of ambush. Casually, she turned her head to survey the area.

Wheels rumbled and dust drifted up from the wheels of the prison wagon. Lorrah sat in the front seat, beside the driver. Sethamis held the reins with strong brown hands. In the back of the wagon, the empty cage rattled as they bumped across a rocky patch. The two oxen, Moon and Star, plodded along at the same speed, regardless of obstacles.

The narrow dirt track wound its way through the outskirts of the fabled Hornwood. On both sides, scattered hornpines loomed among thorny brush. Their bark was white as bone. Lorrah immediately saw that the trees were spaced too widely to hide a force of any size. Then why did this foreboding prick at her, like a burr stuck in her boot?

Now she felt stupid. Worse, Sergeant Zathi had noticed her looking around. Hoofbeats thumped nearer as the sergeant brought her sorrel, Ember, up beside the wagon. Black eyes were sharp in her stern face.

"Trouble, Lady?"

Lorrah winced at the title. It was a ruse, no more comfortable than her borrowed mage robe.

"Maybe," she said. "Not near us, though."

The sergeant nodded, accepting her judgment. Lorrah settled nervously back on the bench. She no longer felt that weight of foreboding, and none of the animals seemed worried about anything, either. That was some reassurance.

The robe was crimson, once a bright hue but now faded by the previous owner's use. It was somewhat too large for Lorrah's slim young frame. Black hair, worn loose, rolled down her back in inky waves. She rubbed the shoulder with a restless hand and met the small bumps of a badger's head badge sewn onto the fabric.

Above her seat, a pennant snapped in the breeze. It

was crimson, with the same emblem roughly stitched on. Armored riders moved alongside the wagon. Sergeant Zathi and Giniver were on the right, Jaxynne on the left. The sisters, Keerin and Razeet, rode on a bench to watch behind the wagon.

Odd as it was to wear the mage robe, Lorrah found it stranger to ride among this group of hunter-guards and not fear for her life. She shrugged a little, trying to loosen the tension in her neck.

"You know," Zathi said, "you really need to stop jumping when I talk to you."

Lorrah ducked her head. "I'm not used to any of this."

"It's new to all of us," Zathi countered brusquely. "You must get used to it. Faster."

Lorrah frowned, feeling put-upon. "This was your idea, Sergeant."

"Which you agreed to, so don't whine. If anyone is going to believe that Badger Squad answers to you, we must first believe it ourselves. Or do I need to remind you what will happen if someone doesn't believe it?"

"No," Lorrah mumbled rebelliously.

There would be a battle, which the small band of hunter-guards might not win. In that case, Lorrah would be arrested as a renegade.

She paused, sitting a little straighter. Something in the thought of being arrested caught her attention. The burr in her boot itched again. Whatever it was fled before Zathi's impatience.

"You must act more like a mage, Lady Ar-Lorrah."

"Be rude and demanding," Sethamis said.

In the back of the wagon, Razeet suggested cheerfully, "Call us idiots."

Their words summoned a vivid image of Lorrah's noble father, Ar-Evaus. He was the epitome of a mage, simmering with power even in calm moments. He seized every eye with his handsome face, fine crimson robes, and perfectly oiled hair. When he stalked into a room, everyone stopped what they were doing.

Too often, Lorrah's older sister, Lizelle, would be at his side. Neither of them would skip an opportunity to lord it over someone else. They would only break their arrogant poses long enough to scowl at some lapse on Lorrah's part.

"Really, daughter," Ar-Evaus would sniff, leaving it to her to figure out what she had done wrong.

Lizelle would scoff in her harsh voice, *"Will you ever learn to act like a mage?"*

Now Lorrah hesitated, embarrassed. Did Zathi really want her to act like a mage? She tried to imitate her father. Hands folded just so, chin up, making it easier to look down on people. Never mind that his rank was gone along with his life, and Lizelle's ambition was less than a dream.

"You can't call me that." Lorrah flicked her hand in a gesture of rejection. The cart jolted over an eroded channel, spoiling the effect.

"Wow, that's pretty good," Keerin chuckled. Zathi nodded slightly, but Lorrah insisted.

"I'm serious. You can't call me lady. I haven't earned the title."

Wearing the mage's robe was technically legal for Lorrah. She had power, and some training. The title was a more serious matter. Lorrah hadn't passed the final rite to earn them. In fact, she hadn't passed any of the three rites.

"If you're already a renegade, why does it matter?" Razeet asked. "Nobody will know."

"People who matter will know," Lorrah told them. "Besides which, it's stupid to act like I'm in charge when it's obvious Sergeant Zathi gives the orders. We'll forget, and say lady at the wrong time. Or not say it. Trying to pretend is just a faster way to get ourselves reported."

"You are a mage." Jaxynne drew her red roan, Spark, up the other side of the wagon. "Everyone expects mages to be in charge."

"Mages who haven't passed the rites can still cast magic, just not use the title. We should work with that," Lorrah said. "Tell people straight out that I'm unranked and Zathi hired me to be part of the squad."

"You're right. That will be easier." Zathi nodded, with even a trace of relief on her face. Lorrah realized it probably wasn't comfortable for the sergeant to give up control of her squad, even as a ploy.

Finally, Lorrah let her shoulders relax. She had too many risks in her life already. Why add another if she didn't have to?

"All right, then. I'll be listening, and trying to figure out what's catching at me."

Zathi nodded approvingly. "Very well, but I want to know whatever you find out."

"Yes sergeant."

Alemin had thought they were entering the Larder, but it was more of an inner gate. Platforms to either side held soldiers in red leather jerkins, poised for trouble. On an elevated walkway, archers in similar uniform held crossbows ready. A narrow stair angled down from a door, high on the left. Directly ahead of them, a wide and graceful archway had been bricked up to create another grim portal with its own armored door.

The hunter-guards waited in swaggering poses. Surrounded by their swords, Alemin shivered. Hunger had left him weaker than he realized. He turned his head, seeking any sign of who had been screaming as they approached the Larder. There must be a whipping post or some such. He saw only the archers.

That bothered him almost more than the pain of cramped legs. He had heard so much noise. Surely there should be some sign. He could only detect a very faint odor of char.

Echoes ricocheted in the enclosed space as the door above slammed open. Two people emerged. A woman in crimson mage robes swept boldly down the stairs. She was followed by a younger man in similar attire, carrying a writing board and stylus. He hopped a little to avoid stepping on the hem of her robe.

Sergeant Traggan bowed obsequiously. "Warden Ar-Lizelle, you are beautiful as always."

"Save your flattery for those who want it." The prison warden's voice was at odds with her proud demeanor. High and nasal, it reminded Alemin of an ill-tuned violin.

So this was the person they called "Lizard." He could see why. The woman had a narrow face with a long, pointed nose and prominent, pouchy eyes. Inky hair was coiled so tightly atop her head that it pulled at her brows. She didn't seem very old, now that she was closer, but her cheeks were hollowed and fine wrinkles surrounded a hard mouth. A cruel person might liken them to lizard scales.

"Of course, Warden." Traggan spoke the words, but his fist tightened at his side. Only for a moment, as he offered a folded paper. "We captured this renegade outside Unthur. You'll see the seal of Count Ar-Gammord on the writ."

Ar-Lizelle strolled past, ignoring the document. Her assistant took it with a grand nod. Hunter-guards shifted aside when the warden approached. She circled Alemin, studying him with unfriendly eyes. Their gazes met briefly, and he felt her power as an intense heat. His throat tightened, but years as a performer had taught him to stand straight and relaxed, regardless of circumstances.

When he didn't flinch, the warden turned back to Sergeant Traggan. "Who is this man?"

Her shrill voice brought a bubble of humor up his throat. He turned it into a cough, muffled by the gag. The nearest hunter-guard swatted the back of his head.

"Name's Alemin, Warden. Says he's a juggler. If you can believe what a renegade tells you," Traggan blustered.

Ar-Lizelle turned, frowning slightly. She looked Alemin up and down, taking in his extravagant clothing. He made a little bow, as much as he could while bound, gagged, and held up by thugs. The warden answered with a very small, sharp smile.

"Ar-Chindu will pay the customary bounty." Ar-Lizelle beckoned to the guards on the platforms. "Bring him."

Half of them sheathed their swords and hastened down to her, while the archers above maintained their watch. Hunter-guards now stepped back as the prison guards reached them. They were lightly armored compared to the hunter-guards, but he didn't doubt their swords were just as sharp.

"Go," one of them commanded. Alemin nodded politely.

Ar-Lizelle strode toward the inner door. Prison guards herded Alemin into a kind of parade. Behind them, Traggan called out in a wheedling tone.

"If we may, Warden Ar-Lizelle, it's getting dark out. Hard to get over to Yergha for lodgings before nightfall. If there might be room in the barracks —"

"The last time Boar Squad shared quarters with my guards, the fighting went on all night. I'll not have that again," Ar-Lizelle snapped. "Try the tavern in Haggazes."

Alemin couldn't hear how the sergeant answered that, for the warden swept on toward the inner door, and the prison guards pressed him to keep pace. He was better in control of his legs by now, and didn't resist.

A shield bearing Dar-Gothull's crest adorned the center of the inner door. Ar-Lizelle pressed her long fingers against it. Alemin saw that her nails had been sharpened into something like claws. Then, did she know they called her "Lizard?" Perhaps she accepted the name in order to enhance her own reputation. Alemin had heard stranger things, in his life on the road.

The energy of Ar-Lizelle's casting rasped like sharkskin against his mind. *Lethentros*, the power of pain and death. Alemin bit down on the gag. His instinct was to raise a shield against it, but that might be taken as an attack.

With a kind of tremor, the door swung inward. As they marched Alemin through, he felt a change in the energy. Clear air gave way to tension and bitterness. This, at last, was the true prison.

The space was wide, half-round. Its walls were modern stonework. Archers filed through that small, high door to another walkway where they resumed their vigil. It was like looking up from the bottom of a well. There was no ceiling above, just a high round shaft rising into darkness. A few beams of light, regularly spaced, hinted at windows going up two or three levels.

Directly ahead, oil lanterns blazed on tall tripods. The area they lit had a sandy floor, eerily smooth. A grim metal rack, a whipping post, and an executioner's block were neatly spaced out. There were several benches along the walls, and each one had metal rings where the viewers could be chained in place.

A stage well set, Alemin had to admit. Instruments of torture right in the middle, where sounds would echo upward. No one could avoid hearing the cries of the victims.

Unlike the walls, however, the floor was of the ancient paving. As with the highway outside, the silvery glimmer was churned and marred by tarry streaks. A faint mist seemed to rise, as if something smoldered deep beneath the ground. He blinked, and the haze was gone.

Ar-Lizelle stopped at the edge of the arena. Her assistant scurried through last. With a condescending wave, he pulled the armored door shut. Crashing echoes resounded in the central well. The warden turned to confront Alemin. No word was spoken, but the guards seemed to know what she expected.

Two men held Alemin's arms, while a third harshly jerked at his gag. The sting of pulling hair did nothing to dampen his relief as the gag was yanked out. Moments later, his hands were free of the leather cords. With relief bordering on dizziness, he flexed his arms and worked his tongue in his parched mouth.

Alemin bowed his head, barely able to rasp out, "Thank you kindly."

The warden watched his reaction with a penetrating stare. Now she tensed, as if he had called her something foul.

"I don't know who you were, or where you came from," Ar-Lizelle shrilled, "but you are under my rule here. Whatever you have will be on my sufferance."

At her shoulder, the junior mage nodded righteously. From this, Alemin assumed they wanted him quiet while the warden gloated. That would be typical of Dar-Gothull's regime.

"Warden, will you suffer me a drink of water?" If she gave him that, he would gladly listen to her threats.

"Silence! You don't make demands here," the assistant burst out.

"Keep your place, Ar-Chindu," snapped Ar-Lizelle. The man stepped back, murmuring an apology. The woman's dark eyes bored into Alemin's with surprising focus. "Are you indeed a juggler?"

"Yes." Alemin had the impulse to ask if she thought the prison lacked entertainment.

Again, those onyx eyes roved him up and down. He didn't understand the intensity of her interest. Ar-Chindu frowned, too.

Ar-Lizelle announced, "You will be shaved and bathed, to assure you bring no vermin here. You will answer my questions. Then, perhaps, you will eat and drink."

These words made Alemin's hunger rage in his belly, but what could he say? Ar-Chindu quickly inserted himself.

"Let me see to this, Lady Ar-Lizelle."

"Fine. Be quick with it."

Ar-Chindu beckoned to the guards. He strode ahead importantly, making for a ramp that led upward. Alemin could only follow, flanked by guards. Ar-Lizelle stared after them. Alemin couldn't think why she was so interested in a random prisoner like him.

A mage should never ignore a premonition. So Lorrah's mentor, Ar-Thea, had taught her students. Yet after hours of steady travel, Lorrah sensed nothing more. There wasn't much point in brooding over something that had slipped away from her.

Instead, she joined the women of Badger Squad in the bustle of setting camp for the evening. In a way, it wasn't much different than traveling with the minstrel band. Everyone had their chores. Lorrah's part hadn't been settled yet, but she didn't enjoy dragging equipment out of the storage compartment beneath the wagon. The guardswomen who had horses would see to their animals, but Sethamis had two oxen to care for. So when she started unhitching them, Lorrah offered to lend a hand. Sethamis shrugged and handed her the lead, then led the way to a nearby creek.

"Which one is this?" Lorrah patted her ox's neck as it shoved its muzzle eagerly into the water.

"That's Star. This is Moon." The beast Sethamis led had a slightly darker stripe down its broad brown back. "Have you taken care of animals before?"

"Tisha let me help with her donkey." Lorrah smiled a little, remembering how the wooly gray donkey would nudge her, looking for attention. "Riprap never got tired of being brushed, especially under his pack saddle."

That seemed to satisfy Sethamis. The guardswoman bent over to inspect a half-healed cut on Moon's leg. Lorrah stroked Star's neck as he drank. Anyone watching would have been shocked that a robed mage took part in such menial chores. There was a perverse satisfaction in that.

"Did you travel with them long?" Sethamis spoke idly. Lorrah's stomach tightened at the reminder of things she had been trying to put out of her mind.

"Three years, I think. It was a big transition," Lorrah confessed. "Father served directly under Count Ar-Nithal. Mother's family weren't mages, but they were rich. We had a big mansion, servants, all that. But then, my father led a coup against the count."

Her dark tone made Sethamis glance up. "I'm guessing that didn't go well?"

"We lost everything when he failed." Lorrah kept her tone steady. Nothing would have been better for her if she became a count's daughter. "I barely got my mother away."

"You saved her?" Sethamis asked, impressed.

Lorrah nodded. It hadn't felt very heroic at the time. More like terrifying. "Luckily, someone at her parents' mansion knew how to reach Ar-Thea. She let me apprentice with her."

The change had been jarring. From a life of comfort to Ar-Thea's band of misfits. Constantly on the move. Sleeping in tents or under trees, no matter the weather. Always feeling sweaty and grimy. Lorrah had come to like the Minstrels — though they hadn't been minstrels, then. Even when they ignored her, they were kinder than her own kin had ever been.

Lorrah missed her friends, especially Alemin. He and Berisan were closest to her own age. That was why she tried not to think about them too much. They were scattered. She wouldn't see them for at least a few months more. Dwelling on what she couldn't have would not help her stay alive.

"It was good, as long as it lasted," she said. Sethamis nodded.

They staked the animals with fetlock chains in a

grassy area close to where the tents were going up. Lorrah still had plenty of time to wander around near the camp, gathering firewood and searching for edibles. Following Zathi's orders, she always stayed in sight.

It had only been a handful of days that she traveled with Badger Squad. At least, voluntarily. Lorrah had known someone was trailing her for several days before. She'd been playing her fiddle on the streets of Litholl when she first noticed a pair of women loitering nearby. They whispered to each other as they watched her play.

Carefully, Lorrah worked a spell to make them forget seeing her. Then she moved on to a small town where they let her play in the tavern for tips and a spot to sleep near the fire. A few days later, those same women wandered in, but there had been more of them. Even though they wore peasant clothing, their military bearing came through. Lorrah knew their kind. They were hunter-guards!

Truly frightened, she had left under cover of darkness and retreated to the thickets of the Hornwood. Two years before, the minstrel band had camped at a wood cutter's shack, a place well hidden by bloodthorn and hornpines. She had meant to forage, replenish her supplies, and let those dangerous shadows pass her by.

Yet, again, the group of women appeared. This time she saw their prison wagon. Terror bound her legs as she peered through a chink in the cabin wall. Lorrah hadn't known what to do. Her childhood training demanded that she fight.

In memory, her dead father hissed, *"No true mage would allow these menials to dog her steps."* Ar-Lizelle, not dead but well gone, harped, *"Attack! Make them pay for their gall!"*

But there were so many of them, and Lorrah had never been the fighter. Lizelle had beaten her down at every opportunity. While she dithered, the tallest and fiercest of the hunter-guards stepped forward. Sunlight glinted off the gray steel of her armor.

"Fiddler girl!" she called. "Play us a song."

Bitterness choked her. Even if Lizelle ever gave her a chance, Lorrah was badly out of practice. Ar-Thea would never allow her apprentices to fight each other. *"If it comes to blows, you have already lost,"* as the old women said so often. Lorrah gritted her teeth. Never had the fatality of the old woman's philosophy been so clear.

Another of the guardswomen called out, "It goes like this!" She started to sing, badly. *"The light of your fire draws me ever. A tie that no distance or time can sever."*

Scowling, the sergeant covered her ears, but she nodded along with the tune.

Inside the shack, Lorrah dared to breathe. She knew that song. It was the one Keilos sang at the end of every performance. How could they know it? Her heart thudded as she fumbled for her instrument. The fiddle echoed sweetly inside the barren hut as it sang back to them.

"Sure as the sun rises at dawn, the hope in our hearts will go on."

Through the chink, she saw the stern guardswomen relax. They smiled to each other. At the end, Lorrah's hands shook as she opened the door a crack. This had to be a trap. Did she dare speak to them?

"What do you want?"

Even then, she expected an attack. Surely she was the bounty they were hunting.

"Do you know Keilos?" The officer's brisk voice carried easily.

"Yes..."

Eventually Zathi had explained. How Keilos had been their prisoner. How they came to a grudging accord as they faced the dangers of the Hornwood. How Keilos had died to see them safe.

That had been bitter news. Keilos had told the Minstrels he foresaw being arrested, but not that he would die. His fate was hard to hear. Yet now, Zathi had said, Badger Squad was looking for another mage to work with them. A specific kind of mage. They wanted a minstrel, but more than that, they wanted a woman.

"Why a woman?" Lorrah had asked.

"Men are too much trouble, and mages are the worst," Zathi had scoffed. "He'd try to take over my squad. Or turn us into his private harem. Nobody needs that bullshit."

Hard as it was to believe, Zathi really did want Lorrah among her squad. Lorrah wasn't sure yet if that was good luck or misfortune. Her job was to keep her mage's senses open for any sign of a rogue mage. Exactly what she was supposed to do when she sensed something off, this afternoon. A task she had failed at, Lorrah had to admit.

Still, she felt safer with Badger Squad than in any of the weeks since the minstrel troupe had to dissolve. More than that, she wanted to be part of something where she didn't have to apologize for her presence.

All her life, Lorrah had been the least regarded. Among her kin, she was the weakling daughter, fit only to play her fiddle and amuse family guests. Among Ar-Thea's band, she was the last to be apprenticed, left out of their established friendships. The other Minstrels put up with her, but they never asked what she thought about anything.

If she could prove herself to this small group of women, the very hunter-guards that most mages feared, then maybe she wouldn't have to hide from the world any more.

When they said he would be shaved, Alemin assumed they meant his face. His chin definitely itched after a span of days in the back of the hunter-guards' wagon. Instead, Ar-Chindu gloatingly told him to sit on a bench and bend forward. A guardsman brought the razor and shaved his whole head with quick, hard strokes.

"Ow." Alemin winced when the man cut too close.

"Shut up and sit still." The scraping went on without remorse.

Afterward, while the guard cleaned the razor, Ar-Chindu barked orders. "Get those rags off. Wash." He jabbed a finger at a single bucket of water, and then a low cabinet against the wall. "Get a robe from there."

Alemin rose from the rough bench. The bucket reeked of bitter herb, a plant commonly used to ward off fleas and lice. "Can I please have a drink of water?" he pleaded.

"Not worth my life," grunted the guard, and he took up a position beside the door.

Smirking, Ar-Chindu waved a hand at the bucket. "Drink that, if you can stomach it."

Bitter herb wasn't safe to drink. Everyone knew that. Both men stood and waited, until Alemin realized he wouldn't have privacy to bathe. And of course not. It was a prison.

So he stripped down, humiliated to be leered at the whole time, and was depressed that the guard immediately grabbed his shirt and trousers. Even the boots were snatched away. That was a particular blow. Those boots were nearly new, with many miles left in them. Ar-Chindu made a great display of searching the hems and cuffs of the garments. Alemin knelt by the bucket and washed as quickly as he could. The water was frigid, and the stink of herbs clung to his wet skin. Over by the door, Ar-Chindu casually pulled the shiny beads off the shirt's embroidery.

Dripping, Alemin shivered in the chill of the room, especially with his suddenly-bare head. He hadn't worn his hair as long as some, but he missed its warmth. The guard threw him a threadbare towel. The cabinet held dull gray robes and twine sandals. Harsh fabric itched against his skin.

"Nobody's going to wait on you here," Ar-Chindu taunted. Silvery beads glittered as he stowed them inside the sleeve of his robe.

"Nobody did wait on me," Alemin answered mildly.

"Shut up." The guard shoved a broom at Alemin.

They made him sweep the sad curls of his lost hair off the floor and wipe the wet stones with the towel. Then they marched him down a corridor that curved along the outside wall. There was a shallow basin in the floor, with a small square grate that no doubt drained into a cesspit far below. He tossed his shorn hair in, and washed it down with the herbed water. Gurgles and whispers came up from below.

As they turned back, Alemin caught a glimpse of another gray-robed figure moving slowly away down the corridor. It appeared to be another prisoner. The robe was like Alemin's, and the head was shaven. It surprised him that prisoners were allowed to wander around so freely.

"What are you staring at? Move!" A cuff and a shake

from the guard brought him back to his own predicament.

They walked him back down the corridor. Narrow doors passed on either side, spaced so that none faced directly into the others. The only light came from lanterns fixed to the walls. A pair of guards passed them, going the opposite way.

The ramp came up from below, and also continued upward, but somewhat beyond that was a large door framed with brighter lanterns. Carved letters read WARDEN. A stony faced guard watched them approach. He saluted Ar-Chindu, who knocked importantly. Alemin sensed a hot wave of power. The door swung open and Ar-Chindu shoved him in.

If he meant to throw Alemin off balance, it didn't work. A skilled performer could keep his feet on far more difficult surfaces than these stone blocks. Instead of stumbling, he gave a quick bow.

The office was small, furnished with bare wooden desks and chairs. Ar-Lizelle was at the larger desk, sharpened fingernails meshed beneath her chin. The paperwork Sergeant Traggan had delivered rested between her elbows. A single chair faced her. The guard shoved Alemin into it, while Ar-Chindu swept up his writing board and stylus. He took the extra chair over to the side.

As before, the warden's dark eyes gleamed fiercely. More important to Alemin was the wooden pitcher and cups at her left side. He could smell the water in it. He curled his fingers around the edge of the chair to keep from reaching for it. Ar-Lizelle nodded briefly. The guard took up a position blocking the door.

Ar-Lizelle poured herself a cup of water and leaned back in her chair. She sipped it, taunting him. Alemin cleared his throat quietly. For her, it seemed, this was all a mind game. For him, the torment of thirst was worse than any threat.

"Tell me why you were arrested," she ordered in her sharp, unmelodic voice, "and know that I've read the writ. You'd be well advised to tell the whole truth."

"Talking will be easier if I have something to drink," he countered, and rubbed his throat pleadingly. Sometimes women responded to his pretty face.

Not this one. A sudden pain burst between his eyes. Alemin gasped without meaning to. Ar-Chindu chuckled.

"I don't need your cooperation to get the information," she pointed out, cold as any lizard.

"Ouch, I take your point." However, Alemin wasn't sure she really had that power. Most of the Minstrels could touch minds. It hadn't felt like that. Just in case, he raised a mental screen. If Ar-Lizelle tried to reach into his mind, she would receive impressions of tall grass swaying in a gentle breeze.

She didn't react to the mental screen, but instead repeated, "Why were you arrested?"

"For laughing at the wrong time," Alemin confessed. Ar-Lizelle frowned. He went on, "There was a man in the stocks at Unthur. A boy, really. They said he tried to cheat a tax collector. People were jeering and throwing things, but —"

Both mages were staring at him as if he had grown a second head.

"I saw it. The man who accused him, the tax collector, had the stolen money in his own pouch."

"You interfered with justice," Ar-Chindu burst out. "For some peasant?"

Ar-Lizelle shifted slightly, and her assistant closed his mouth. Alemin made his case to her.

"It wasn't justice," he said urgently. "So when people were throwing fruit and rocks, I just walked over and caught them. And I started to juggle them. The more they threw, the more I juggled." He gave a little shrug. "That was our act, you see. People from the audience threw whatever they wanted. Rocks, rotten fruit..."

There had been more to it, when he worked alongside Berisan. Flipping knives between them, dodging with wild hilarity, while Lorrah on her fiddle and Keilos on his lute would play silly music to match their antics.

"Until eventually something would drop, or they would hit us. Everyone had a big laugh, and they would toss a few coins our way." He shrugged again. "It made us a living."

That act was always popular. It had been working that day in Unthur, too. Alemin smiled, remembering how the crowd's angry jeers had turned into healthy laughter. They even started to follow him away from the stocks. He thought he'd spared the accused boy.

"But then someone jumped into the middle, commanding us to disperse." Alemin's smile faded. How well he remembered it, the glitter of egg white and bits of shell on a crimson robe. Fabric slowly darkening as moisture seeped in, and the face of the man grew dark as well.

"The count?" Ar-Lizelle guessed. She might even have been amused. It was hard to tell from her acid tone.

Alemin nodded, staring at the desktop to conceal his satisfaction. Mages like Count Ar-Gammord needed those little reminders that they weren't immune from the forces of gravity.

"You laughed at him!" Ar-Chindu accused, nearly as indignant as the count himself had been.

"We were already laughing," Alemin reasoned. "We just didn't stop right away. Anyway, it seemed fair. He put the boy in the stocks to have rocks thrown at him. You could say he was bitten by his own dog."

"Very amusing," Ar-Chindu huffed.

Alemin couldn't keep back a grin. "That's what he said."

The die had been cast, of course. The count's guards were already there, and the crowd had grown too large for Alemin to slip away. The rest had followed with predictable, painful speed.

"Disrespect," Ar-Chindu fumed.

However, Ar-Lizelle was smiling, an unpleasant curve of lips. She lifted the pitcher and poured a finger span into the second cup. "For telling the truth."

She pushed the cup across the desk. Alemin reached warily, in case she snatched it away, but she jerked her chin at her assistant.

"Out. I will speak with him in private."

Ar-Chindu's eyes widened with indignation, but then an unpleasant smirk twisted his lip. He and the guard left, while Alemin gulped the precious liquid. There was far too little of it. He felt almost dizzy with relief as blessed moisture penetrated his throat.

Even then, his mind darted with dismay. A cruel mage, being kind? This worried him in an entirely different way.

As the door snapped shut, Ar-Lizelle leaned back in her chair. She studied Alemin, and he sat very still. For all his stagecraft, the fine hairs rose along his arms.

"You must have heard rumors about the Larder," she began. "That our prisoners are the most vicious and depraved in all Skaythe. Traitors and killers. If you aren't insane when you come here, you will be before long."

Vicious and depraved? That described Dar-Gothull's whole regime.

"I've heard a few things." Alemin felt like a cat, carefully stalking a bird on the ground. In truth, he suspected Ar-Lizelle was the cat.

"The Larder is meant to hold the worst of the worst," Ar-Lizelle continued. "We aren't intended for petty vandals. That means, I have discretion to release you."

Interesting that she dangled a carrot instead of a stick. Cautiously, he asked, "What would be the price for that discretion?"

"Information," she replied. "Tell me more about your minstrel troupe."

Through a startled moment, her dark eyes bored into his. Alemin looked aside, dry-throated in a way that had nothing to do with thirst. Too late, he realized his mistake. He'd told them 'our act' instead of 'my act.' The warden had noticed.

"Troupe?" he asked, innocently confused. "I was alone when I crossed Count Ar-Gammord."

Ar-Lizelle's gaze was as flat and unblinking as they lizard they called her. "You have no idea how many lies I hear in this office. They are tiresome and a waste of effort. So please give me credit for my intelligence."

Alemin said nothing. He filled his mind with the swishing of wind and scent of dry grass. What could he say that wouldn't make this worse?

"Yes, I know about your minstrel band." The warden

spoke in a slightly softer screech. "There have been a
number of reports over the past few years. Scattered
incidents. A debt unexpectedly paid in Deeve. A riot averted
in Nibbok. Not everyone pays attention, but when you do, a
pattern appears."

Alemin remembered that riot. It had been a terrifying
situation, but in some ways less dangerous than this one. "If
a riot is averted, isn't that a good thing? Public order is
maintained."

Public order — that was Dar-Gothull's excuse for his
evil reign.

"On a superficial level, it might appear so. However,
in the past few months, the pattern is off. Something has
changed. I want to know why." She stared him down. "What
are you renegades planning?"

"There was never a plan, besides surviving." Swaying
branches, he held in his mind. Rustling leaves.

"So you and your friends look for trouble on a
whim?" Her voice reeked of skepticism.

"That boy was innocent."

"Not according to Count Ar-Gammord."

"I was trying to help, and maybe get a few coins
tossed my way."

"An idealist?" Ar-Lizelle raised her eyes to the
ceiling, disgusted, and flicked the page she had been holding
aside. "This is what they send me," she complained to no one
in particular.

"There is no plan," Alemin repeated. "I'm only trying
to get by, like everyone."

She studied him for a long moment. Alemin held his
mental screen. The Minstrels had hoped to move through the
land unnoticed. It was alarming to think someone had been
paying attention to their small resistances.

"So you claim there is no conspiracy."

"That would be a death sentence," he answered
earnestly.

His heart sank when she smiled at him. "Interesting
you should say that."

Ar-Lizelle opened a desk drawer and drew out a
different set of papers. "Do you deny that you were a student

of the heretic, Ar-Thea?"

He sat silent. After a moment, his head began to pound as if the Warden was banging to get in. "No."

"No, you were not her apprentice?" Black eyes blazed dangerously.

"No, I would never deny Ar-Thea."

Alemin didn't have to pretend at his grief. When he and Berisan first encountered Ar-Thea, she had seemed to be merely a wandering mage, lowest of her kind, with a daughter trailing behind. She claimed to be an herbalist, harvesting plants from the countryside and making poultices or salves to sell wherever she happened to be. The brothers had known she was more from the moment they saw her.

"She died a few years ago," Ar-Lizelle said.

"She was murdered," he corrected.

"Deservedly so. Those who are loyal to the great Dar-Gothull dealt with that renegade, but her apprentices were nowhere to be found. Not long after, the first incident was reported. Curious timing."

Her gaze dared him to argue. He didn't. Instead, he focused on remembering his teacher's round face, the deep-set eyes twinkling with humor. Her tolerance for the antics of her young apprentices, who weren't always patient with each other. The generous rolling laughter that he had first despised, but later taken as his own.

"I miss her," he said with complete truth. "Every day."

The warden gave an impatient sniff.

"A heretic's records are destroyed, so that in the eyes of history they no longer exist. However, according to the fragments I could collect, there were six apprentices. Also six minstrels in the troupe. Again, curious."

Alemin shrugged, worry churning along with his loss. What did Ar-Lizelle want to hear, if she already knew this much? Despite himself, his eyes drifted to her pitcher of water. He jerked them away. No thirst was enough to make him betray his second family, and he couldn't afford another mistake.

She made a show of studying one particular page. "Let me see if any names are familiar to you. Meven.

Tishala. Keilos. Oh — Alemin and Berisan. A brother of yours?" She tried to skewer him with her eyes, but he avoided her gaze. "And Lorrah."

Alemin didn't speak. She glared at his profile. "Nothing to say?"

"You told me not to lie," he murmured, an answer that was no answer. More than ever, her questioning reminded him that the Minstrels shared a bond of loss and hope. He had to protect them, even if it meant his life.

"Clever." She set the sheet down with a papery whisper. "I want to know where they are, and what they're up to." She paused, savoring his discomfort. "There was a large magical event in Seofan Holl, and later in the Hornwood. Rumors from Eshur speak of a castle built all of ice. What are you renegades up to?"

Alemin shook his head. "Seofan Holl and the Hornwood? None of that makes sense." The ice could be Meven. Ice was her hallmark, but it wouldn't be like her to make a display of it. He wouldn't tell Ar-Lizelle that, though. He still didn't know what she was after.

"And Lorrah, where is she?" Ar-Lizelle pressed. Pressure stabbed into the back of his neck.

"We no longer travel together." Alemin heard the pain in his own voice. It felt like a terrible risk to admit even this much. "There was a premonition, just as before Ar-Thea died. We separated. I don't know where any of them went."

Ar-Lizelle gave a little hiss of annoyance, and the pain dropped away. "Truth."

Her features were tight with disgust, but she slowly reached to pour another measure of water. Alemin wanted it desperately, but he was afraid to take it. What else would she ask of him? Her brows twitched.

"You are loyal to your own. I respect that." The warden's voice was brittle. Cautiously, he reached for the cup. As he gulped the tepid water, she went on. "I'll let you think on this. But know, juggler, that I have other ways to acquire the information if you cling to your pride."

He choked a little. Smiling, she called out, "Guard!"

Ar-Chindu swooped in first. His prudish mouth drooped when he saw that Alemin wasn't weeping or bleeding. Ar-Lizelle gestured him back to his seat and restored the second set of papers to her desk drawer.

"Give him bread and water, and take him to the upper level." She smiled wickedly. "Put him in number six."

The guards saluted. "Yes, Lady Ar-Lizelle."

II

The Nightmare

D usk fell over the Badgers' camp outside the Hornwood. Four red tents stood in a neat row, with the Badger Squad pennant hung over the largest one, Zathi's tent. Their wagon was parked behind the tents. Near the center, Keerin had driven a post into the ground. An oil lantern was clamped to the top. The squad's portable stove had been set up beside it, where the light was good. A pot of water was on to boil, so everyone could wash their dishes.

The guardswomen had brought folding stools to share the light and warmth. Lorrah watched lazily as Jaxynne showed Sethamis how to oil and clean a crossbow. Keerin and Giniver were honing their swords. A soft grating sounded as Zathi buffed her breastplate, where a row of dents had recently been pounded out.

It was quieter here than in the minstrels' camp, where everyone would have been tuning their instruments or practicing lines from a puppet play. Also, of course, the Minstrels would never have displayed so much armament.

Lorrah sank into meditation, opening her senses for any trace of magic nearby. Not that this was likely, considering how far they were from any villages. There still was nothing of the premonition she'd had earlier. Lorrah shifted restlessly. Could she have been wrong?

It was almost a relief when her fruitless search was interrupted by Razeet coming back from a perimeter check. Crouching by her sister, she whispered something. Keerin's reply was noncommittal.

"Ask her." Razeet nudged her shoulder.

"You ask, if you want to hear it," Keerin retorted. "You big baby."

How Lorrah envied their easy banter. Her own sister had never treated her as a friend.

"Lorrah?" Razeet asked. Lorrah glanced over. "Will you tell us the story?"

"I'm not really a storyteller." That had been Meven's specialty, with her puppets. Razeet looked so disappointed, she had to ask. "Which one is it?"

"About the Shining Ones."

"What?" Lorrah's thoughts stumbled, from *Keilos told them that bunch of ancient bullshit?* to *Nobody is supposed to know about that!*

All of the guardswomen had turned away from their weapons. Their brown faces were eager, but perhaps a little embarrassed. Even Zathi paused in buffing her armor.

"Keilos told us, but we can't remember it all," Giniver added.

"I don't know if I do, either," Lorrah said. "Ar-Thea only told it once, right before she — well."

Lorrah remembered the night clearly. Ar-Thea had called them all into the kitchen. Mostly she remembered because it was the first time they'd had a kitchen to be called into. That little hut, patched together from a half-burned farmhouse, was their first permanent dwelling. Ar-Thea had kept her apprentices moving, always searching for the freshest herbs. Or for something else. Lorrah had never been sure.

"We don't need a house," Ar-Thea had explained when Lorrah asked, early on. "We are like rascalweed, my child. We blow on the breeze. Many have tried, but no one can stamp out rascalweed."

Ar-Thea had been right, too. As soon as they stopped

moving, the regime had found them.

"Was she arrested?" Giniver's question pierced Lorrah's memory.

"I don't know." Flames lit the sky in Lorrah's mind. "If they tried, it didn't go well."

"When was this?" Zathi frowned slightly. Lorrah saw no reason not to tell them. After all, she was part of Badger Squad now.

"A couple of years ago, outside Dakadoz. Ar-Thea was very gentle. I know," she mocked her own words. "Who ever heard of a gentle mage? But she was." She shook her head. "That's why I can't believe Ar-Thea would have started any trouble. I heard the count was there, though. Ar-Rendon. He'd be the one to set a building on fire and blame the peasants who lived there."

She couldn't hide her bitterness. Around the circle, guardswomen nodded. "Keilos didn't resist," Jaxynne said quietly.

"I guess I didn't, either." Lorrah shrugged, again mocking herself.

"Lucky for you." Razeet shook her fist, teasing. Lorrah smiled back, raising a quick flare of golden energy before she went on.

"Anyway, she sent us off without her the next morning. We would never have left if we thought she was in danger." Tisha and Keilos were especially devoted to the old woman. If they hadn't left, Lorrah couldn't have, either. "Ar-Thea might have known, though. She was foresighted. So that night, before we left, she told us the story."

Lorrah remembered their mentor's fevered urgency. Usually so calm, she suddenly spoke with a zealot's fire in her dark eyes. The story had hit the others hard. They sat up late talking about it, questioning Ar-Thea. Lorrah, on the other hand, had slept just fine. After only a year with the troupe, she'd hardly known Ar-Thea well enough to worry for her.

"Well, what do you remember?" Keerin persisted. "Maybe we can put it together."

"Don't forget what Keilos said," Jaxynne cut in. "Some stories are dangerous to know."

"We already know it," Razeet countered.

Everyone looked to Zathi for permission.

"We should have it straight, if we're going to guide by it," the sergeant decided.

Lorrah gazed at her, disbelieving. Zathi planned to guide by that old load of manure? It was surreal. Yet she couldn't forget how terrifying it had been to have these hunter-guards trailing her. Lorrah had never been the strong one. After what happened to Ar-Thea, she had to stay with the others. Just the same, she needed this new group to like her, and want her among them.

"All right. I'll try." Lorrah folded her ankles under her stool and sat up straighter, as if she was a star of the minstrels' stage. "A long time ago, the people who lived in Skaythe were not like the people now," she recited. "There was no such thing as a division between rich and poor, mages and commons, or even men and women."

She faltered at the impossibility, but Giniver jumped in. "They were magical people."

Lorrah nodded. "Magic flowed to all of the people. It created everything they needed, and everything they made was divided equally. No one was ever left hungry or alone." She faltered, trying to remember more.

"They build great cities," Keerin prompted.

"And their highways," Sethamis added with appreciation. "We still use them."

"Yes." Lorrah pressed on. "Their cities were filled with light, and so we call them the Shining Ones. No sickness or sorrow darkened all those lands. If some were born damaged, unable to summon magic on their own, no one thought any less of them. The Shining Ones cared for them kindly, and shared all things with them."

It was a beautiful dream. Lorrah remembered thinking that. Quite impossible, of course. Yet the hunter-guards were gazing at her with joy in their eyes. Surreal, Lorrah thought again. How could these hardened warriors become trapped in the same vision that had captured the Minstrels?

"But then," Keerin leaned forward with delicious suspense.

"Somehow the Shining Ones were undone. The Devourers came." Lorrah deepened her voice, playing up the drama. "No one knows what they were, those Devourers, but they fed upon all of the magic in the world. The Shining Ones couldn't stop them when their casting made the enemy stronger. They were killed, and all their works crumbled away."

"Every light has its shadow, and after the summer, winter must come." Jaxynne spoke as if she herself was quoting Ar-Thea. Lorrah shivered. Then Zathi spoke with a bitter twist of her lips.

"I remember the next part. How the only ones left were the cripples, those with less magic. They seized power and divided the mages from the commons. Those who wouldn't share their possessions divided the rich from the poor. Those who demanded control of their loved ones divided the men from the women."

Around the circle of lantern light, women rolled their dark eyes and made faces. Giniver said, "Everyone died except the assholes."

"We are left in the dregs of that world," murmured Sethamis.

They sat in silence, yet a fire of determination flickered in their eyes. Lorrah still couldn't believe it. She was surrounded by fools. She'd thought so when the minstrels started their plan of resistance. Wandering Skaythe, doing good deeds and then disappearing?

Ridiculous.

Now Lorrah wondered what Badger Squad, themselves, planned to do with this ancient story. Did they really think they could raise an army against Dar-Gothull's whole regime?

Lorrah had thought she was safe with them. Now she wondered if that was true.

Alemin stumbled along, trying to keep up with his two guards. Number six, Ar-Lizelle said with such relish. Six of what? The worry plucked at his nerves.

The corridor outside the Warden's office again curved to match the outside wall. That was on his left, the ancient paving glinting silver in the lantern light. Only a few wisps of darkness clouded it. Aside from the grinding of their footsteps, the prison was eerily quiet. Perhaps everyone had already been locked in for the night.

They passed what seemed to be a small kitchen. One guard glared at Alemin while the other slammed through cupboards. A thin blanket was shoved at him, followed by a leather bottle and a coarse sack. The bottle sloshed enticingly, and the scent of bread set his stomach clawing at his ribs like a cat stuck in a too-small cage.

Alemin longed to gulp from the water bottle, but the guards shoved him onward. The corridor met a narrow stairway. Clothing rustled loudly in its confines as they climbed.. Breath gusted like angry surf. They soon reached another landing, where a wooden counter faced the steps. Metal bars rose from it to the ceiling. A sharp-eyed guard nodded when he saw them.

The cramped stair continued its upward climb past another guarded landing. Booted steps thundered. The guards' lantern cast shadows that followed them like robbers in the gloomy passage. Alemin's legs burned with fatigue, but there was no pause to rest.

As they climbed higher, the ceiling began to slope in

on them. The dark streaks were thicker here. Alemin remembered how one side of the tower had seemed to sag. They must be coming into that upper level.

The guards ducked a little, then shoved him down a short, straight passage. The guard station was on the right here, with another behind the counter. Past that, the ceiling dipped too low for anything but crawling.

"New friend?" The guard sounded tired. A metal gate rattled as he opened it, emerging from his shelter.

"New," answered the lead guard. "Not friends."

The latest guard followed the other two as they shoved Alemin left, down the corridor. There was more black than silver in the ceiling, and he smelled a faint tang, not unlike burning hair. They pushed him past one door and then another, with narrow grilles imprisoning darkness.

Behind the third door, there came a kind of yip and scrambling. A face appeared at the grill. The prisoner was bald and gaunt, with deep pits about his eyes.

"Let me out!" he demanded.

"Sorry, old man," answered the guard immediately behind Alemin. "Orders."

"Orders? I'll give you orders!" White knuckles wrapped around the bars. "I am the warden. Let me out!"

The prisoner tried to rattle the bars, but the door didn't even budge. Alemin winced, expecting a spell blast, but none came. There was just more shouting, growing in intensity. The guard at the rear kicked at the door.

"Shut up, you lunatic!"

"Don't start, Groff," chided the man in the lead.

"What? He is," came the bitter retort. "You try listening to it for a couple of hours, Stegnor. See what you think then."

"I am the warden," shouted the man in the cell. "How dare you?"

The other guard said, "Groff has a point."

"You know what Lady Ar-Lizelle says about taunting the prisoners." They passed two more doors. "Set one of them off, and you set them all off. Then everyone has to listen to their raving for the rest of the night."

That seemed like a very specific prediction. Alemin wondered how many of the prisoners spent their nights ranting at empty corridors. Was it connected to the noise he'd heard earlier?

They came to the last door before another slump of the ceiling made walking impossible. Two bolts would secure the door from the outside, one low and one high. The lead guardsman, Stegnor, slid them back and jerked the heavy door wide.

"In."

Reluctantly, Alemin stepped to the door. Light from the guards' lantern barely penetrated into the narrow space beyond. He glimpsed a slat bed with a mat of woven reeds, a small side table, and a latrine bucket. He paused there, hugging his blanket and sack.

"What's the Lizard going to say," scoffed Groff. In a high-pitched imitation, he squeaked, "Now you boys be nice to the lunatics."

You couldn't deny how ridiculous Ar-Lizelle's voice was. A laugh burst out of Alemin. He was so tired and scared, what else could he do but laugh? From the other cell came higher, hysterical echoes.

"See?" Stegnor complained, and he shoved Alemin through the door.

Alemin tried to control himself. "Her voice," he gasped, blotting his eyes. "I can't —"

Groff's mouth twitched, as if he held back humor. He stepped up to cuff Alemin, but not very hard. "No talking."

Stegnor barked out a few more rules. "You take care of the stuff in here. Anything gets broken or burned up, your legs will feel the same. There's a lamp in the bag. That's all the oil you get. When it goes dark, you're done until morning. So I suggest you quit laughing and eat fast."

"Thanks," Alemin began.

The door cut him off with an ear-splitting slam. The two bolts slapped into place. The guards immediately vanished from behind the grille, taking most of the light with them. Another bout of yelling signaled when they passed the so-called warden's cell. Soon even that was swallowed by silence.

Alemin's laughter trailed off into a sigh. It was hard to think through a fog of hunger and thirst. With difficulty, he focused enough *vitalis* to create a witchlight. By that radiance, he stepped to the end table and dug in the bag. The lamp was a flat shell with a cover of tarnished metal. A large clay bead held the wick. It wobbled until he fished out a wooden cradle to hold it steady.

Keeping the witchlight up was giving Alemin a headache. He quickly called a spark. Once the wick had caught, he let his own light go and slumped down on the bed.

What was he doing in this dismal place?

He knew every step of the journey, of course. It just hadn't seemed real. Now the weight of it settled upon him, invisible and crushing. Equally so, the silence seemed to muffle his thoughts. This was a place he couldn't joke his way out of.

One thing compelled him beyond all else: his raging stomach. The bed frame creaked ominously as he shifted to sit on the folded blanket. With shaking hands, he wrenched the cap off the water bottle and sucked down a frantic swallow. Relieved a little, he pulled out the food. There was a single strip of salted meat and about a third of a loaf of dry bread. Arid crumbs scraped in his throat. Another swallow of stale water helped it down. After a few frantic bites, he forced himself to stop for another sip of water.

Chewing slowly to make the tasteless loaf last, he

leaned his back against the wall. Food helped him revive a little. The shell lamp's glare revealed the cell in pitiless detail. The inner wall was modern masonry, brown stones crudely worked but better put together than they had appeared during his approach. Even a strong mage wouldn't easily blast through them. The floor was of thick wooden planks, blotched with stains. It was probably best not to know what made those.

Alemin was more interested in the ceiling and outer wall. The smooth surface was so blackened that he only now noticed a very narrow window. No light entered the chamber. It must be fully dark outside.

"They gave me the cell with extra gloom," Alemin quipped aloud. In the stillness of the cell, his voice was boldly out of place. It was foolish, with no one nearby, but he somehow felt embarrassed.

He took another swallow of musty water and examined the furnishings. The slat bed was so ancient and abused that the joints wobbled when he merely crossed his legs. The reed mat smelled of mildew. Beside the bed, the small wooden table had a shelf beneath it that was the right size to hold his sandals and not much more.

A sluggish breeze crawled over his newly-bare head. Reflexively, he raised a hand to flatten his hair, only to find it gone. That was going to take some getting used to.

There was little more to see. The latrine bucket was just a bucket. The sack of food was all too empty by now. Alemin took his time chewing the last bit of salted meat. The scant meal hardly satisfied him. He breathed in, drawing in *vitalis* to ease his lingering hunger. The power responded only slowly. Maybe that was because he was isolated, away from other living things. Or maybe he was just too tired to focus.

Alemin couldn't even create an image of juggling balls in his mind. He yielded with a gasp, and slumped back against the wall. In the corners of his vision, the lines on the walls seemed to twist and writhe. His eyes jumped to the swirling pattern of soot and silver. The darkest patches seemed to radiate from that slash of a window. It looked like a bleeding wound.

"What happened here?" Again his voice felt too loud, out of place in this foreboding chamber. A feeble draft from the window made the lamp's flame jump and bob.

The streaks on the wall were almost hypnotic. His eyes kept going in and out of focus. Alemin shook his head. Exhaustion rose up after days of being frightened and abused. Sold to the prison like a prized horse. Shaved, stripped of his clothing and identity. Then interrogated.

There was something about that, he thought fuzzily. Something he should remember. He tried to think back over what Ar-Lizelle had asked, what he had told her. The number six must mean something. She said she had the power to release him. What did she really want to know?

He couldn't think. Tomorrow would be soon enough to puzzle it out. Alemin leaned forward, feeling stiff as an old man, to untie his sandals and tuck them onto their shelf. He wrapped the threadbare blanket around him and settled on the rickety bed.

The guard had warned that the lamp would go out. Even so, he left it to burn as long as it could. This cell was too dark by half.

Most of the hunter-guards sought their tents as true darkness fell. Only Jaxynne remained on watch. With the lantern turned down to a softer glow, Lorrah sat quietly, hands folded over her knees. She meant to meditate, a practice Ar-Thea had promised would strengthen her magic. Lorrah had been lazy, these past few years. The Minstrels were focused more on survival than spirituality. Now that she was with Badger Squad, it seemed like a good idea to work at it again.

Yet she couldn't concentrate. The tragic tale of the Shining Ones buzzed through her mind like a persistent fly.

Sure, it was a fun story. Who wouldn't like to dream about a perfect world where nobody ever went hungry? You just couldn't think of it as anything real. How did the Shining Ones have children, for one thing?

That wasn't what bothered Lorrah, though. It was how seriously people took the story. The Minstrels questioned the way things were. They thought that Skaythe could be saved from Dar-Gothull's wicked rule. Then, they started taking crazy chances. Wandering the land, secretly doing good deeds. How stupid was that?

Now the Badgers had the same fever. Zathi searched for the remaining minstrels, but what was the plan once she found them?

Ar-Thea had warned her apprentices that this story was dangerous to know. Lorrah had thought that was just drama, a way to get people's attention. Now, she wasn't so sure. Look what had happened to Ar-Thea herself.

Lorrah might have been the youngest of the Minstrels, but she had grown up as a noble mage's daughter. She knew the system from the inside. The Minstrels, the Badgers — what did they really think they could do?

They were all begging to get caught.

The nightmare began with a muted roar, rising and falling like distant surf. Churning clouds, the color and texture of charcoal, billowed past him. They stank of burning. Beneath him, Alemin saw a great disc glimmering in the uncertain light. Was that the sea, so far below? It almost could be the view over the garden wall in his childhood home, overlooking the Bay of Kamuril.

Only, his home had never been wreathed in smoke.

He squinted, trying to make out what lay below. Tooth-like rocks — or was it a ruined wall? — rimmed a circle of black water. There was a slow circulation of water coiling inward to a massive vortex at the center. The roaring Alemin heard was the voice of that raging tide. That liquid did not seem to be water, but something thick and black, steaming like hot oil.

Some force drew him toward it. A sharp wind tugged at his flamboyant sleeves, stitched with glittering beads. It caught and pulled and tore the cloth. Terrified, he wobbled, trying to step back — on what surface, he couldn't have said.

Then, far beyond the swirling hunger of that maw, a flicker of light came. Pale gold rebuked the ash-gray clouds. A spark of *vitalis!* The color was unmistakable. Alemin's feet steadied as hope kindled within him. He saw another, some distance from the first, and now he caught two more. An icy white gleam showed at the opposite pole of the sky.

Emotion clenched at his throat, to see those five stars defying the inky dusk. Five stars — five friends, lost to him. Loneliness and longing surged like the tide so far below. He reached with his mind, calling out to them. *"I am here!"*

Then he choked to a stop. What would he say if they answered? It was too dangerous for the other minstrels to come to the Larder. Would he cry warning, or beg them to save him? Only one of those would be right.

Before he could decide, the nightmare convulsed. Alemin shuddered to wakefulness. The prison cell was frigid, clay lamp guttering with fitful light. He clutched the inadequate blanket and swung his feet toward the floor, but then froze. The walls glinted with movement. Black fluid from his dream trickled down in sullen loops and strings. It pooled on the floor boards, lightless and reeking of scorch.

Impossibly, a few dark streams ran upward, toward the window. There a robed figure held a dripping hand to the narrow gap. A whisper reached him, startling in the silence of the prison.

"None of that, my fine lad." Sinister gloating embodied the rush of the nightmare vortex.

Alemin pressed backward. Rough stones poked through his thin prison robe. Black liquid dribbled down his bare skull, and panic droned in his ears like a hive of angry wasps.

"That's right," whispered the stranger. "You'll stay nice and quiet while I eat you."

That terrifying detail, the hive of wasps, shook the grip of dread on Alemin's mind. This was a jail cell. There were no wasps here. No stranger could come wandering into this bleak prison. The nightmare was not over, only changed.

He sat up, away from the wall and the flowing liquid. Even in dreams, a mage had to be wary. He studied the image before him. Alemin had seen this man — ? — before. The lone figure, shaved bald and robed in gray, that wandered the halls of the Larder.

Cautiously, Alemin asked, "Who are you?"

The entity replied with a raspy, taunting laugh. "Which one do you mean?"

Black mist rose from the floor and billowed from cracks in the walls. Startled, Alemin summoned all his power. Witchlight flared, piercing every corner of his cell.

It was empty, of course. There was no stranger, no sinister fumes. Feeling a little ill, he peered down to be sure there was no sludge on the floor. A shaking hand found nothing on his head. Only his heart kept up a racing tempo to fit one of Tisha's best dances.

Alemin let the witchlight fade. He was truly awake, and would be for some while. Aside from the shell lamp's feeble glow, it was entirely dark. Muffled sobbing echoed down the corridor. He wondered if that was the other prisoner, the one who claimed to be warden. Did he, too, suffer nightmares?

The slat bed creaked as Alemin got up to use the latrine bucket. Floor boards were cool beneath his bare feet. Afterward, he stepped warily toward the window, where that malevolent figure had stood. No lingering traces of energy suggested that a living mage had been there. The thin strip of air showed nothing but velvety blackness. The stars he had seen in his dream were no more real than the rest of it.

Returning to the bed, Alemin lay down. Dawn might be long hours away. Exhausted, he was afraid to sleep. After a few restless minutes, he turned around so that his feet were next to the wall instead of his head. It was foolish, but he didn't want to wake up with anything dripping on his face.

Lorrah tried to shake the gloom away, but the shadows of her friends insisted on creeping into her mind. Keilos with his lute, always knowing exactly when to play a lively song and when the crowd wanted a sentimental one. Tisha dancing as if she was more spirit than human. Meven, so snappish and cold. Only when she got behind the puppet stage could you see her clever spirit.

Best of all, the brothers Alemin and Berisan with their juggling act. Lorrah played her fiddle and tried to keep pace with the flashing knives and pratfalls. Best of all was to work alongside Alemin. With a smile like that, he hardly needed magic to charm an audience.

Lorrah swallowed against a lump in her throat. It had been so long since the Minstrels split up. She was losing track of the months. That was fairly depressing.

She shifted, ready to give up on meditation, when a voice came in the silence. *"Lorrah."*

She jumped a little, thinking Jaxynne had spoken, but immediately realized her mistake. This voice was not from her outer ears. Much like the warning she had sensed earlier, it came from deep within.

Lorrah stilled herself, allowing faint impressions to coalesce. The call was distant, yet a tenuous connection held. The voice was familiar. One of her fellow Minstrels cried out.

"Fear," she sensed. *"Cold."* Then, *"I need you."* In the same moment, *"Don't come here!"*

"Where?" she called back.

Even in her trance, anxiety tightened in Lorrah's gut.

The Minstrels had promised not to contact each other for another month, maybe two. Who was breaking the silence?

No one answered, and the echoes were slipping away. Lorrah searched for an answer. First she thought of the older girls, especially Tisha. But no, she was sure it had been a man's voice.

It couldn't be Keilos. That left the brothers. Instantly, she knew it was Alemin she heard. There was no mistaking his voice, quick and sly, yet sweet beneath it. His square face formed in her mind. The bright eyes and winning smile, a bushy ponytail behind. Slim shoulders, long legs, hands flicking the air almost too fast to see. Alemin never seemed to care if Lorrah was near him, but her heart jumped like a fish on a line.

She caught herself back. This call in the night could be a trick. Dar-Gothull's regime was devious and deadly. Someone could have forced Alemin to cry out. Lorrah had to be prudent. She should guard herself and her new comrades. Yes, she ought to ignore it.

That would never happen.

"Don't come here," Alemin cried, while cold and afraid. What Lorrah heard was, *"I need you."*

"Where are you?" she called into the ether.

Contact shivered away before Alemin could reply. Now she heard nothing but one of the horses shuffling its feet.

Lorrah let go a hard breath and opened her eyes. The camp was silent, red tents dark as blood in the dim lantern light. Above them, tall white trees stood like ghostly guards. Jaxynne stood with her back to the lantern, knees jigging a little in apparent boredom. A bottle glinted briefly as she tipped it back. When Lorrah exhaled, she came alert.

"Find anything?" Jaxynne pitched her voice low.

"Not enough," Lorrah admitted. Lizelle would have said to expect no more. Nothing Lorrah ever did was good enough for her.

Jaxynne paced a few steps, turning her face to the rutted dirt of the road they followed. "Something's better than nothing."

"Someone called out. I think it was Alemin." Lorrah put her hands on her knees and pushed herself up. Her legs were stiff from sitting.

"That's one of the Minstrels?"

"Yes. It sounded like he said 'help me' and 'stay away' at the same time."

"Mm." Jaxynne considered that. "People don't always say what they mean. Or, maybe, don't want to ask for help."

Was that some sort of jab? Lorrah tried to brush it aside. This was Jaxynne, Zathi's second-in-command, not her bullying big sister.

"He needs help," she said. "Alemin does."

"If he's one of your troupe, Zathi will want to know. What else could you tell?"

"He was cold and scared. I couldn't see any details. I just know it was very dark, and far away." Lorrah hated sounding so uncertain. Eyes shut, she reached out with her left hand and slowly turned until some faint sensation brushed her fingertips. "That way."

Together, she and Jaxynne gazed in that direction. Stars glittered in a deep-black sky. Swells of land glimmered faintly under their scanty light. 'That way' was a pathetically inadequate direction. To Lorrah's surprise, Jaxynne took her seriously.

"Between those two ridges? That'll be east or south of east," she mused. "We're in Litholl now. Unthur and Kamuril are due east. South of east could be Yergha."

Something in the sounds tugged at Lorrah's mind. "Did you say Yergha?"

"Yergha," Jaxynne repeated. "That's pretty far."

That just pointed out how pathetically little Lorrah had to offer. She pinched her lower lip between her teeth, holding back apologies. A true mage never apologized. Only weaklings did that.

"So it fits what I sensed." She schooled her voice to make it a statement, not a question.

"It might. I was a scout before Zathi recruited me to Badger Squad. Let me get a better read of the stars. We'll have a look at the charts in the morning."

Lorrah nodded, frustration tightening her shoulders. Morning was a long time away, and Alemin needed her now!

Jaxynne said, "Good work, mage."

"Thank you." Now that Lorrah was standing, exhaustion weighed on her. A yawn dragged at her jaws. Jaxynne chuckled.

"You should get some sleep, and try not to worry. Zathi won't leave your friend hanging."

Lorrah hoped that was true. Hanging was much too dreadful an image! She headed for the tent she shared with Sethamis. As the newest of the squad, she had expected to sleep in the back of the wagon, but Sethamis had room.

As she entered quietly, a new set of worries buzzed in her mind. Lorrah vowed she would use every bit of Badger Squad's resources for Alemin's sake. They were Ar-Thea's apprentices, bound almost as brother and sister. She had to find out what was wrong, and try to save him.

Talk about taking crazy chances.

III

The Prisoners

T he dawn came with pitiful moaning. It was soft at first, but swiftly surged louder. Alemin sat up, dizzy and raspy-eyed. He looked for the source, but there wasn't one. The noise came from everywhere, and nowhere. It almost radiated from the walls themselves.

A shaft of light from the window brought the room into dismal relief. He shivered, clutching his meager blanket to him. Faint mist trickled from the blackened walls, a memory of burning. The ghost of some nightmare prompted him to gaze up at the ceiling. It was black as the roof of an oven, but he saw no hazard there.

The moans grew more intense, rising to a wail much like the screams Alemin had heard the day before. He'd forgotten them in the process of interrogation and installation into this miserable cell. Well, there was no forgetting now. The sounds reverberated into his very bones.

Could all this come from that man down the hall? Gritting his teeth, he tottered to the door. Only darkness lay behind the grille. No guards appeared to be responding.

Alemin shuffled to the latrine bucket. The cries came from all around him, no softer or louder anywhere in the cell. He eased back on the bed and covered his eyes with one arm.

There would be no more rest now. He could only wonder what was happening. Alemin's ears throbbed with the noise, but even more, he wished for an answer. Such cries — they were what a Minstrel was driven to find, so he could heal it. He rolled over, and back again, while sourceless anguish tore at his heart. How could he help, if he didn't know who needed him?

Light brightened in the corridor. Through a rising crescendo, Alemin heard stomping feet and the rumble of voices. He ran to the door, longing to focus on something besides the unbearable lament.

Lamplight pierced the darkness, and a pair of guards scowled through the bars. These were different men from last night, though their red jerkins, slouched caps and indifferent expressions were nearly identical.

Alemin clung to the bars, desperate for answers. "Who is that? What's wrong?"

The guards stepped back, a defensive reflex, then eyed him with disdain. "You want to eat? Then quit babbling."

"Get back from the door," added the other, unhelpfully.

"Don't you hear it?" Alemin stared at them. Then a single word penetrated his confusion. *Eat,* his stomach demanded.

The guards pushed the bolts back and swung the door outward, while Alemin hastily fetched his sandals. He hopped, pulling the twine up behind his heel.

"Hurry up," grunted the second guard.

The first one added sourly, "We're not bringing your food up here. Move it or go hungry."

Other noises echoed down the corridor. More bolts slammed open. Gruff tones ordered the other mage prisoner out of his cell. The two guards bracketed Alemin as he emerged from the cramped cell. He skimmed names from the surfaces of their minds. Endole was in front of him, Tharow behind. That other prisoner shuffled along ahead of them, not entirely steady. He was also penned in by guards.

Everything was a procession in this place, it seemed. Alemin could only summon a ghost of his usual humor.

Descending the narrow stairway, they encountered other small groups. Each mage was escorted by a pair of guards. Alemin counted six prisoners before he got distracted. Ahead of them, one mage walked alone. He'd seen that person before. The gray robe had a gap where the stitching was loose between the back and the right sleeve.

This one prisoner walked unhurried, unguarded. Indeed, they seemed unaware of the people moving around them. They raised a hand to caress the wall. The gesture was intimate, possessive. Alemin faltered as a memory of sticky tar dribbled down his bare head. Was it some apparition who had stood at his window during the night?

He lost sight of them when Tharow jerked on his shoulder. The group turned down a side corridor, descended another stairway. Somewhere along the way, the screaming had stopped as mysteriously as it began. How could he not have noticed?

Alemin no longer knew where he was in the building. However, this stair was the last. It ended in a steel-clad door. Sunlight made him blink as they entered the bracingly cold morning. Across a narrow courtyard, there was a low building tucked between the high modern wall and the ancient prison tower. Farther back, he glimpsed rows of a small vegetable garden. That was something he remembered from the day before.

Heavy doors swung open, and they were pressed into an open hall. Scents of food made Alemin's stomach shriek like the unseen mourners of the prison tower. To his right, at the head of the room, there was a platform with a rail. Ar-Lizelle and Ar-Chindu sat there, in their vivid crimson robes, along with several men who appeared to be officers of the guard. Rows of tables stretched the length of the room. At the nearest one, guards were just finishing their meals. The farthest one held dirty dishes and utensils, signs of a meal already completed. The row down the middle was much shorter, the boards bare. Alemin hoped that meant seating for him and the other prisoners. Every moment he smelled food was a vicious torment.

Guards stayed close as the prisoners filed toward the back of the room. A table there was laden with large bowls and platters. There were no knives or forks, only flimsy wooden spoons. Hunger propelled him until he trod on the heels ahead of him. A scowl over the shoulder warned him back.

Alemin didn't care. He only saw the platters of bread, sliced meat and quartered oranges. A bowl held boiled eggs. He scooped some of everything into his own wooden bowl. Once the prisoners were seated, the guards finally stepped back. Alemin wrapped a scant slice of bread around the meat and tore into it. The guards didn't go far. He was aware of them lined up at the sides of the room, watching relentlessly. From their gimlet stares, you would think that eating breakfast was a deadly crime.

There was no conversation at the table. Everybody ate as fast as possible, glaring at anyone who reached too close to their plate. Cups and pitchers occupied the center of the table. Again, Alemin noted that these were all of thin wood. Nothing pointed or metal that could be turned into a weapon, he supposed.

After he had inhaled his bread and meat, he slowed down and sucked on a piece of orange. It was sour, but he was desperate for the juice. Considering the size of the hall, he was surprised there weren't more prisoners. Including himself, there were eleven of them. All were shave-headed, in drab gray robes. Three women sat in a cluster, slightly apart from the others.

How jarring it was, to sit among these strangers instead of his minstrel band. No friendly eyes met his. Other prisoners eyed him without welcome. To them, he supposed, he was the stranger. Not an ally, but a potential rival. Even Alemin's fellow prisoner of the upper floor showed no recognition. The man hunched over his plate as if he expected to be robbed of his last orange wedge.

Dread coiled inside Alemin. A sensation like the slick scales of a snake glided up his back and around his ribs.

It tightened on his throat until his pulse throbbed and he couldn't get a full breath.

"What the matter with you?" These could have been kindly words, but the prisoner on his left didn't seem to care much about the answer. He was distinguished from the others by a crooked nose and a small cut below one eye that hadn't healed yet.

"It's my first time in a prison," Alemin admitted.

A slight frown crossed the man's forehead, as if this wasn't what he had been asking. Then he shrugged, and picked at something between his teeth.

"Better eat fast. They'll put us to work soon enough, and you'll get no more until nightfall."

Alemin half-expected the guards to tell them to shut up. They were clearly listening.

"Thanks for the advice." He nodded, and cautiously reached for a pitcher of water.

He nearly missed the brush of movement against his shoulder. Alemin jerked back in time to see his neighbor's hand sneaking a boiled egg out of his bowl. In an eye-blink, he had his egg back. Guardsmen tensed, and all down the table, sharp eyes were on them.

"Ask me first," Alemin said calmly.

Spite flared in the man's eyes. "It was worth a try." Then he gave an ugly cackle. "You've got fast hands. You're the one they brought in last night. The juggler."

There was a barely perceptible sigh along the table when violence failed to materialize. Prisoners and guards returned to their own thoughts. Alemin was tempted to start juggling his two boiled eggs, but he was still hungry. The man beside him watched, expectant.

"Yes, I'm Alemin." He moved one egg away, since there was no one else on that side, and tapped the other against his bowl.

"Illen."

"I would say it's a pleasure, but..." Alemin shrugged.

Illen gave another chuckle, this one more natural. It trailed into a bout of coughing. Alemin felt a moment's sympathy. All of the prisoners had pinched faces and dark circles under their eyes. He felt tired enough after one night with his sleep disturbed. How long before he wore that same haggard look?

Illen slurped down some water and asked, "What are you in here for, Juggler?"

"I laughed at the Count of Unthur." Alemin kept his voice light. Others along the table listened with open skepticism. "Really, that's it. I laughed. What about you?"

The man's brows twitched as if he had asked the wrong question. If so, why was it all right for Illen to ask his crime? Little cracks sounded as Alemin peeled his egg, not expecting an answer.

"I aimed a blast at someone. Missed." Illen gave a dramatic sigh. "A foot to the right, and it would all be different."

A mumble of agreement went through the prisoners. Shaven heads nodded with shared grievance. Another man leaned in.

"My own mother sold me out." Alemin sensed a frightening knot of rage pulsing beneath his mild exterior.

"Was that before you killed your brother, or after?" Someone else bantered. Alemin tensed, egg half way to his lips, but the brother-killer accepted the barb.

"He was a weakling. I always took better care of the family. 'Til they sent me here, anyway." The fellow grinned amiably. No light reached his eyes.

Another prisoner growled, "I didn't do anything wrong. Those stupid hunter-guards were supposed to be bribed."

Alemin took a slow bite of his egg and listened with more than just his ears. This was much like Unthur. The tax collector's thoughts had been so smug, certain of success as he stole and made another bear the cost of his crime. If any of the prisoners felt guilt, they buried it deep. Their chief emotion was simmering resentment at being caught.

Well, this was the Larder, after all. These men and women were in prison for a reason.

One of the women spoke up from the far end of the table. Her lovely face was twisted by burn scars. "They stuck you up at the top, right? Up there with old Wharon."

The man in question jerked upright. "It's Ar-Wharon! I'm the warden." He aimed a volcanic glare at Ar-Lizelle, seated at the head table.

"Then I'm Ar-Duessa," the woman retorted. "That's Ar-Haafeth. Until we're not."

"And we all know why." Illen's sinister growl was barely audible.

Wharon scowled. Alemin could feel his rage spiraling hotter and tighter. Others were getting agitated, too. Violence felt imminent, like a bubble about to burst. Alemin wondered just how quickly the guardsmen could intervene.

Duessa's scars did nothing to mute the glitter of her bright black eyes. "Well?" She prodded Alemin.

"Yes, we're both up there." Alemin was happy enough for a change of subject. "That reminds me, what's all the screaming about? I heard it last night, when we were coming in. Woke me up pretty fast this morning."

To his surprise, the hostile and curious eyes suddenly slid away. Some pretended to eat, when their bowls were bare of even the smallest fleck of food. Alemin couldn't believe it. These were all mages. They must have heard it.

He turned to Illen. "You know what I mean."

"Nobody knows." The man shrugged, pushing his question aside.

Duessa laughed. "That's a question for the ages."

"We don't talk about that." Unspoken words drummed in Alemin's mind. *"It's always been that way."* Across the dining hall, he caught a glance between the two guards who had brought him down. *"These mages are crazy,"* they silently jeered.

"You can hear it," Alemin insisted.

Why would they not talk about something that disturbed everyone in the place. He glanced past Illen to Wharon. He claimed to have been warden. Wouldn't he know the Larder's history?

"So what?" said Haafeth, the man who had killed his own brother. "We can't do anything about it."

Alemin looked down the table lined with shaven heads and fevered eyes. Reluctantly, he opened his senses to them. The jagged edges of Illen's malice slashed at his mind. Duessa's sullen, throbbing bitterness matched her scars. The lightning of Wharon's rage, barely held back. The signs were different, but the same sickness gripped them all.

Yet they shifted away, glowering as if his mild touch of *vitalis* was an intrusion. The lightless pit behind Haafeth's eyes promised a hideous retaliation for the trespass. Immediately he retreated, dismayed.

As an entertainer, Alemin depended on making connections with people. Listening to the prisoners' kidding, harsh as it was, he actually wanted to like them. Yet these were killers and thieves. Haafeth and Wharon hovered on the brink of insanity. Who would make a connection with them?

Lorrah's body was heavy with sleep, but her mind buzzed with ideas to convince Zathi they should try to rescue Alemin. However, when she emerged from her tent, Jaxynne already had the charts out. She and Zathi studied them, while the rest of the squad broke their fast with dried cakes made of grain mixed with meat and fruit.

Lorrah was poised to blurt out her strongest arguments, but Zathi only asked, "Yergha, you think?"

She had Lorrah repeat everything, although she had no new details to add to what she'd told Jaxynne at the time of her sensing.

"Did he call out to you, personally, or to anyone who might have heard?" Zathi probed.

"Alemin always ignored me." It stung Lorrah to admit that. "I don't think this was intentional. We're not supposed to reach out yet." She had explained this to them, days ago. "I did sense it, though."

Keerin breathed a short laugh. "The last time a mage sensed something, it was that giant badger."

"I thought it was the drakanox," Razeet said.

"One of the two."

By the end of the following day, Keilos had been dead. Around their circle, the guardswomen sagged a little. Giniver's eyes were on the map, but she wasn't seeing it. Loss and regret lurked behind Zathi's flinty gaze. Lorrah couldn't think about that, not in connection to Alemin. She had to believe he could still be saved.

"It sounds like your friend's been taken," Sethamis said.

"Yes." That was obvious. It was also Lorrah's greatest fear.

"If he's anything like Keilos, he'll be charming them already," Jaxynne said wryly.

"I don't think so." That didn't fit with what Lorrah had sensed. Still, she smiled a little. Alemin was such a showman. It was something to hope for. To Zathi, she said, "I know it isn't much."

Zathi stopped her with a frown. "No more apologies. This is more than we knew before."

Jaxynne took out a leather cord, knotted at careful

intervals, and stretched it across the chart. Lorrah ate quickly, listening as they talked softly, fingers brushing the chart's face. Sethamis joined the discussion, reminding them how far the animals could go without water and a rest.

Lorrah listened anxiously. What if they said no, that it was too far?

Giniver caught Lorrah's eye. "We wanted a mage along with us. It would be pretty stupid if we didn't listen to you."

Lorrah wished she could believe that. All her life, everybody second-guessed her.

Zathi was saying, "We can't make straight for Yergha. There's no direct route."

"There's a guard station south of Litholl." Jaxynne touched a spot on the chart. "We can check in there, see if anyone's bragging about a big catch."

Gratitude tightened Lorrah's throat. "Thank you. Alemin is... my favorite brother."

"Oh, your favorite." Razeet smirked and bumped Lorrah's shoulder.

"I didn't say I'm his favorite." Lorrah tried not to blush. "The Minstrels aren't really brothers and sisters. We're Ar-Thea's apprentices, but she always wanted us to act like family. Tisha and some of the others really believed in that." She shrugged uncomfortably. "I was the last one there, so I couldn't really argue."

"It still sounds better than a temple school," Sethamis answered.

"Maybe." Lorrah had never been to one. Young mages of common stock were trained in the brutal competition of the temple schools. As daughters of nobility in Prowth, she and Lizelle had studied first with tutors and later under their father's critical eye. Then a new thought struck her. "If we find him, what are we going to do?"

"That," said Zathi, "is an excellent question. Because

you know the biggest thing in Yergha, don't you?"

Puzzled, Lorrah thought about it. Then her heart froze. "Oh. Oh, no."

The others around her were equally grim. Keerin said it first. "The Larder is in Yergha, isn't it."

Lorrah hadn't even thought about that. If she had, she wouldn't have slept as well as she did. But, as she'd said to Jaxynne last night, it fit with what she had sensed.

Giniver whistled tunelessly. "How are we going to get him out of there?"

"Well," Jaxynne said slowly, rolling up her charts, "we'll have time on the road to think about it."

"First things first." Metal greaves thunked as Zathi slapped her knees. "Gear up, and get running."

Playful groans echoed through the camp as the guardswomen stood up from their stools. "We have to train now?" Razeet complained.

"You whine like a bunch of little boys," Zathi barked. "Move it!"

The guardswomen were already in their armor, with weapons at their sides. Lorrah had only seen them without their arms when they were in disguise, following her across Litholl. The warriors stretched out their legs and backs, while the archers set up targets. Zathi led them off down the road at a jog, so that Lorrah and Sethamis were left to watch the camp.

Lorrah jumped up, too. Adrenaline prickled in her veins, just thinking of Alemin in that awful place. She couldn't sit and do nothing!

"Hey, Setha." The driver looked up from setting out the crossbows and targets. "How far from the horses do I need to be if I practice casting?"

"At least go across the road. Do you want to use one of our targets?"

Lorrah studied the crude human shapes stuffed with field grass. She shook her head. "I might be setting it on fire, so... no. I'll find something else."

"Good idea," Sethamis chuckled. "Don't make too much noise, though. Ember is the only one that's trained, and Spark will take any excuse to fight his lead."

A quick look around showed Lorrah that the road itself was the best place to cast, since it was mostly bare of the grass and brush around the camp. There was even a convenient rock sticking out of the ground, about twenty feet away from the wagon. She set up her folding stool where she could see the camp, and sat down to work.

The very tips of the tallest hornpines flared with light as the sun began to rise. Patches of pale mist drifted above the creek. Chilly air flowed into Lorrah's lungs as she began the first phase of meditation. She released it slowly, the way Ar-Thea had taught her. What to work on first, that was the question. Lorrah reviewed all the spells that might be useful.

There was fire, of course. Fire was everyone's favorite. Ar-Evaus had a flame-lash that was his specialty. It had been a particular terror to the servants. However, her father hadn't been a patient teacher. At the first sign of a fumble, he would order her to sit down and watch her sister do it properly. Oh, how Lizelle had loved that!

Because she was constantly interrupted, Lorrah had never been very good with fire. It had always seemed unfair to practice on the servants, who had no way to defend themselves.

There was one skill where Lorrah could out-do her sister, though. Their first tutor, , had favored spells to reach into people's minds and disrupt their senses. Lizelle could give people bad headaches, but Lorrah could make them dizzy enough to fall, or stop them from noticing things that were right in front of them. All of that was subtle, invisible. Ar-Evaus had scorned such casting because magic was meant to be seen. He believed that true power should cause panic and chaos.

Despite his scornful opinion, Lorrah had used those exact spells to escape when everything went bad in Prowth, and again to elude the hunter-guards before she knew that they might become allies.

Badger Squad returned from their run, breathing lightly. They quickly split into teams. Keerin sparred with Giniver while Zathi watched critically. Jaxynne, Razeet and Sethamis shot crossbows at their targets.

The hunter-guards made a choice, Lorrah thought. Sword or crossbow? Just so, Lorrah needed to make a choice. Mind or flame?

"Focus, Lorrah," she scolded herself. Time was slipping away.

The problem with mind casting was that she would have to hone her skills on someone. The hunter-guards were her friends, and Zathi probably wouldn't appreciate her tampering with their senses. The horses would probably run away if she tried it on them. Perhaps the oxen? They didn't seem to mind much of anything.

Lorrah shook her head. Once she found shelter with Ar-Thea, her success had come to an end. The old woman had taught that it was a grave wrong to influence the minds of others. Lorrah's skill at listening had improved greatly, though. The Minstrels could communicate without words, when they needed to.

Irritable fingers drummed on her knees. Why must there always be someone holding her back?

She tried to shrug that off and summon fire. Fire was easy. You just needed *lethentros*, the energy of death and pain. She studied the rock that stuck out of the track for a moment, then rested her hands on her knees and closed her eyes. Lorrah pictured what she wanted in her mind: orange and blue flames curling around the gray stone. Opening her eyes, she willed it.

"Fire!"

A witchlight appeared, bright gold rays blending with

the sunrise. Lorrah released a disgusted snort and dismissed the light. Again she focused on what she wanted.

"Fire!"

Again the witchlight popped in. Over and over, she called for fire and summoned a light. Fists clenched, Lorrah tried different names for it.

"Flame!"

"Heat!"

It made no difference. Stymied, she shook her hands to loosen them. Lorrah growled to herself. What was she doing wrong?

Not far away, Zathi had switched in and was sparring with Keerin. The women circled, probing and blocking. Lorrah watch with keen envy. None of them had to manage these stubborn energies. All they had to do was move their bodies.

Complaining silently, Lorrah turned back to her target, which remained peacefully untouched by fire. Ar-Thea would have told her to relax and let the power flow to her. She didn't have time for that, and anyway, Ar-Evaus said you had to bind the magic to your will.

Frustrated and angry, Lorrah glared at the rock. Her chest felt tight with the intensity of it. *"Burn!"* she demanded.

The glow was different, red-orange instead of yellow-white. Then something slipped. Instead of flames, black fumes billowed out. Lorrah groaned and let it dissipate. She rubbed at a knot in her neck. She could picture what she wanted. Why didn't the *lethentros* come?

Zathi called a hold, demanding of Keerin, "Why does your greave squeak like that?"

"It has since the badger tossed me," Keerin said. "I'll work on it more."

"See that you do," Zathi said, and then called, "That's

enough. Time to break camp and move out." She glanced over at Lorrah. "You, too."

Lorrah nodded, humiliated that she couldn't even finish a beginner's spell. Everyone must have seen her failing. If her sister had been there, she would have been hysterical with laughter. Lorrah turned toward that damned rock. Without even trying, she stretched out her *vitalis* and wrenched the jagged stone out of the ground.

That was so easy, it was infuriating. Why couldn't she call fire like that? Lorrah huffed petulantly and flung the rock out across the plain. Then she snatched up the folding stool and stalked toward camp. Sarcastically, she wondered if throwing rocks at people counted as an attack. Ar-Evaus would have been humiliated.

It didn't matter if Lorrah was out of practice. That was no excuse. She had to get better, a lot better. For Alemin's sake.

Mercifully, the clang of a bell brought Alemin out of his thoughts. Around him, the other prisoners brushed crumbs off their robes and stacked empty dishes at the center of the table. Alemin still had his last boiled egg. Remembering Illen's warning, he stuffed it into his sleeve.

By then, everyone was watching the head table. As the bell's last echo faded, Ar-Lizelle stood. Ar-Chindu and her other companions did the same. Guards closed in behind the prisoners. When the other captives stood to face the head table, Alemin quickly did the same.

"Prisoners to your work," came her strident command.

Controlled turmoil broke out as the prisoners edged past each other. Nobody wanted to get too close to anyone else. Guards followed them, wary and alert.

Seeing Alemin's confused expression, Illen said, "We work if we want to eat."

"It's rehabilitation," Duessa corrected with sarcastic precision.

"Scrubbing floors and weeding the warden's garden," someone grumbled on the other side of Haafeth. "Very educational."

Wharon hissed, "The garden is mine!"

"Sure, sure." The scarred Duessa brushed past him.

Under his breath, Illen muttered, "Not any more."

There was a story there, Alemin guessed. Maybe if they were assigned together he would find out what it was. The prisoners quickly sorted themselves into groups of two and three. Alemin assumed someone would give him a task as well.

He jumped when a heavy hand gripped his shoulder. Tharow snickered at his reaction.

"The warden wants you."

"Have fun," Illen waved as the guard shoved Alemin toward the dais. Ar-Lizelle and her hangers-on looked down their noses from above.

"Did you sleep well, Juggler?" the warden mocked. Ar-Chindu's lip quirked with sly humor as he paged through a short stack of documents

"Terribly." Alemin called up images of waving grasses to block her from probing more deeply.

"Good." Her lizard-like stare bored into him. "Then is there anything you want to share with me this morning?"

Alemin caught barbed glances from the prisoners nearby. He suppressed his irritation at how she made sure they knew he was in a special circumstance. It didn't take great people skills to know it would be bad for him if the other prisoners thought he was cooperating with the Lizard.

He answered with a charming bow. "I don't know any more than I did last night."

Let them all hear it, and know he wasn't her spy.

"If you ever want to get out of the Larder, you'd better think of something," Ar-Lizelle warned. "Tell a guard if you change your mind."

She strolled away, trying to act as if there was no urgency. Something in that made Alemin think that actually she was in a hurry. He bowed again to her retreating back.

His guard, Tharow, muttered, "Kiss-ass," and yanked on his arm "Come on. You want to eat here, you work."

"So I hear," Alemin replied pleasantly. "Where do you want me?"

"Kitchen." Tharow was obviously put out that he didn't complain. With unnecessary force, he steered Alemin to a set of unmarked doors that probably led to the kitchen. Three other prisoners and their guards were already waiting there. Duessa was the only one he recognized. She also appeared to be in charge.

"Juggler, get over here. That's Kyanon. Noluss." She punctuated their names with sharp jabs of her thumb. "I'm Duessa, if you didn't get it before."

"Hello, I'm Alemin." He was getting a little tired of being labeled solely as "juggler."

One of the guards barked, "Get to work."

The job was self-explanatory. Duessa showed Alemin where a couple of large reed baskets were stored beneath a table. Noluss and Kyanon dumped serving bowls and platters into one of them, along with the bigger utensils. Alemin followed Duessa around the tables. He tried not to stare at her scars as they swept dishes and spoons into the other basket.

Guards prowled watchfully, sometimes uncomfortably close. In his mind, Endole coached himself, *"Mages want range. Can't give it to them."*

Now that he'd eaten, Alemin was feeling better. The nightmares were just that — figments of his imagination. He amused himself by flipping a couple of the spoons before letting them rattle into the basket. His companion awarded a tight smile, but the guards tensed, scowling. They always seemed to do that. Alemin was starting to wonder who was more nervous, the prisoners or their guards.

Tables cleared, he carried the basket into the kitchen, which was lined with cabinets and had a work table down the middle. A huge fireplace of chiseled stone occupied the outside wall. An iron cauldron hung there. That was the only metal object in the kitchen. Kyanon leaned into it, both hands flat to the iron. Perhaps he called on some remembered fury, for Alemin felt the heat he was pouring into the cauldron. Farther down was a wide, deep sink with a water pump over it. Noluss worked the pump. Alemin got splashed with icy water when he went to dump the dishes in.

While they waited for the cauldron to heat, Alemin grabbed a couple of spoons in each hand and flipped them to find the balance. Noluss frowned as much as the guards were doing.

"Don't you have anything better to do?"

"Not until the water's hot." Alemin idly juggled the four spoons. Now that he'd found the rhythm, it would have been hard to put them down. There was a tightness down his arms, a pinch in his wrists. He needed this movement.

Duessa shook her head, amused and annoyed at the same time. "Why do you keep doing that?"

"It's —" He caught himself. Nobody needed to know that he built up his magic by juggling. "It's fun. Don't you do that here?"

"What most of these guys call fun?" Duessa's scars twisted her mouth awry.

Noluss grunted agreement. The guards hadn't stopped frowning for a moment. Alemin admitted there was a certain pleasure in tweaking them. Besides, the activity renewed his spirit. He'd woken up so drained with all the shrieking. He should have done this the night before, instead of lying awake and sweating in fear.

While the sink filled, Noluss leaned a little closer, veiled hostility in his eyes. "What did she mean, juggler?"

It took a moment for Alemin to understand the question. "Ar-Lizelle?" His hands moved steadily, while his mind fumbled for an answer. From the gleam in Noluss' eyes, silence wasn't a good option. "Uh... There are some people. On the outside. She wants to know about them."

The guards loitered a little closer, no doubt hoping to pick up the information Ar-Lizelle desired.

"You're staying in here for them?" Duessa appeared completely baffled.

"That's stupid," Noluss sneered, but his aggression dissipated. "If you can get out of this place, you should."

"And don't look back," Duessa added.

Alemin shook his head and focused on his spoons. The rise and fall, ever changing. People like this, who bragged about who they had killed, would never understand loyalty among friends.

"They must have something on him," Noluss said to Duessa.

She teased, "What do you owe them, Juggler?"

Alemin still didn't know what to say. He owed the Minstrels everything — life and love and purpose. How could he explain that a band of minstrels wandered Skaythe with a secret mission. The longer he thought about it, the more foolish it sounded.

"They're my friends," he finally said.

"Friends." Noluss slowly shook his head.

Duessa gazed at Alemin with a mixture of admiration and disgust. "You seem a lot smarter than that."

"Hey," Kyanon's cranky voice broke into his thoughts. "Quit goofing off and help me."

Alemin caught the spoons — one, two, three, four — and flipped them into the sink. Then he went to join Kyanon. Between them, they got the heavy pot of water across to the sink. Great billows of steam stung his face as they tipped it in.

As the newest prisoner, Alemin was nominated to do the scrubbing. The soap was crude, reeking of bitter herbs, and the water was unpleasantly warm. He worked as fast as he could. Noluss rinsed the dishes, while Duessa and Kyanon dried them with swatches of ragged cloth. Soon all the dishes were stacked in one cabinet, and the spoons filled a clean basket.

If Alemin thought that was all the work, the guards quickly corrected him. Their next task was to wash down the tables and stack up the chairs, then scrub every foot-scuff off the flagstones in the dining hall. If all the prisoners did such work, he could see why the Larder was so unnaturally clean.

Since the minstrels were used to walking long distances, Alemin had thought he was strong and healthy. It seemed there was a great difference between that and the hard work of scrubbing floors. Soon his arms and shoulders burned with the relentless effort, while his back and knees ached from kneeling. The guards never offered a rest, even for a sip of water from the kitchen pump.

Alemin lost track of time. The only relief came when he turned the scrubbing into a circular motion and imagined it as juggling. He drew some *vitalis* from that. Not so much that the other prisoners might think he was up to something, but enough to ease the throbbing of his knees. Duessa sent him wary glances from time to time. If she knew what he was doing, she kept it to herself.

Sometime before noon, the hunter-guards' supply base rolled up over a hillside. It appeared to be little more than a handful of wooden buildings penned up behind a stone wall. Red and silver banners waved sulkily above a blocky gatehouse. A small horse shed stood against the outer wall. A few animals grazed in pastures alongside it.

Despite the peaceful scene, Lorrah's stomach was tight with worry. It was one thing to travel with Badger Squad, knowing they all held a secret goal. Trying the ruse on strangers was something else. What if they figured it out?

"I'm doing this for Alemin," she reminded herself, and settled her shoulders in a relaxed posture. Lorrah had gone into dozens of settlements across Skaythe, both with the Minstrels and alone. This was no different.

Sentries ambled along the top of the wall. Two of them converged on the gate as Sethamis guided the wagon toward it. Zathi, Jaxynne and Giniver brought their horses up into flanking positions. Lorrah hoped all of this was normal.

"We're here for information?" She pitched her voice low, in case the sentries were listening.

Zathi answered, "Hunter-guards don't just wander around. We must account for our movements. There are two things we have to do here. We report significant incidents, if there are any, and we ask about new reports that need to be investigated."

"We can't be diverted," Lorrah protested.

"Not to worry," Zathi's mouth hardened. "We are not in good favor, and the best assignments will be kept from us. That's why we rove, picking up tips from the locals."

A sentry hailed them before Lorrah could ask why Badger Squad wasn't in good favor. "Halt and state your business!"

"Badger Squad, for a routine report and resupply." Zathi spoke firmly, making herself heard without having to yell.

That must have been what they expected to hear. Already the gate was rising with a series of sharp clanks. A thick metal door swung open behind it. Sethamis cried "Hup boys, hup!" and the oxen heaved the wagon forward. A light breeze swept wisps of dust from the packed earth of a wide courtyard. Lorrah looked around boldly.

On the side where the pasture was, she saw a large stone trough and water pump. Sethamis steered toward it. Three plain wooden buildings stood opposite the trough. Each had an overhanging roof, creating all the shade there was in the barren courtyard. At the far end, a row of straw targets hinted at military training. As the gate clattered down behind them, Zathi gave her orders.

"We'll water the animals and take on supplies. Jaxynne, see to that."

"Yes, Sergeant."

Lorrah glimpsed movement in the shade of the overhang. Two or three men sat at a table. From the faint rattle of knuckle bones, they were playing a game of some sort. One of the men jumped up and yelled something into the door behind him. Zathi marked that with a brief narrowing of her eyes.

Sethamis was busy steering the wagon, so Lorrah turned to Razeet. "Is that a barracks? Why don't we stay there, instead of camping out every night?"

Razeet chuckled with grim humor. "You'll see."

"Badgers, help Jaxynne or Setha. Keerin, keep watch. Stay close and mind your own business. We don't want these men to remember much about us."

"Yes, Sergeant," they chorused. As the wagon slowed, Razeet jumped down from the bed. Giniver swung off her horse.

"What about me?" Lorrah asked.

"We check in at the office. This way."

Door hinges squealed as they entered the nearest building. There was a small waiting area, with a pair of benches facing the counter. Everything was polished dark by age and use. The officer behind the counter was armored almost exactly as Zathi was. He was considerably thicker in the waist, with a haze of silver over his short black hair.

"Yes?" He scarcely glanced up, then did a double-take. "Who are you?"

"Badger Squad, checking in to resupply," Zathi said.

"Badger, eh? Haven't heard of you." Skepticism flavored his tone.

"You won't have." Zathi spoke blandly.

The officer heaved himself out of his chair. A large book lay open on the counter. He pulled ink and stylus out from under the counter. Zathi took these, and wrote briskly in the book. Lorrah watched the officer watching Zathi. His gaze touched her, and then darted back to Zathi. Eager questions flitted across his face.

"You're all girls, then?"

Lorrah didn't like his question. He acted as if there was something salacious about women being hunter-guards. She was about to retort, but Zathi gave a dry snort.

"We're not girls." Her tone held a hint of warning. "Anything going on around here? New writs or bounties?"

"Let me think." The man stroked his chin, as if he had power by delaying his answer. Lorrah remembered how Zathi had said she wouldn't be told about the best assignments.

"Pardon me, Sergeant," Lorrah said. "We already have a lead."

Let him take that for his petty power. Zathi frowned slightly at Lorrah, but then nodded. "As you say."

"Where did you get it?" The officer scoffed, disbelieving. In the surface of his mind, Lorrah felt his scorn, that she was too young to wear the crimson robe. No more than he thought a woman should hold the rank Zathi had.

"By my craft." Lorrah made her voice drip with arrogance, as a true mage would do.

In the same moment, Zathi closed the log book firmly on his hand.

"Hey!" The officer jumped, and they scowled at each other for a moment. "Good luck with it," he grumbled, while clearly wishing the opposite.

Lorrah flicked her fingers in dismissal, and followed Zathi out the door. Once it had slammed behind them, she murmured apologetically, "Too memorable?"

Ahead of them, Jaxynne had the cargo bins open. Giniver and Razeet carried empty boxes and crates into one of the other buildings, and returned with full ones. Keerin stood guard beside the wagon, while Sethamis pumped water for the horses. Half a dozen guardsmen were at the rail outside their barracks, hooting and leering.

Lorrah watched, disgusted. Nobody should have to put up with such behavior. She followed Zathi down the steps. "I guess this is why we don't stay in the barracks."

"Correct." Zathi moved purposefully into the courtyard, taking a position between the two sides. She said nothing, and made no visible threat, but the rowdies quieted down. Lorrah thought about helping Sethamis with the oxen, but decided a mage's intimidation was better used on Zathi's behalf. By the time she got there, the men were slinking into their barracks. Sergeant's stripes and crimson robes had influence, no matter who wore them.

They stood for a moment, in that space where they could observe both the wagon and the barracks. Then Zathi spoke with grim quiet.

"We walk a line, Lorrah. Most hunter-guards would say that women don't belong here. They'll mock our skill and assign us lowly tasks. We can't allow that, and you were right to speak up."

That made sense. It was Dar-Gothull's law that everyone fought for what they wanted. Still, Lorrah thought there was more.

"But—?"

"If we are too pushy, too soon, some of the sergeants will hold a grudge. The hunter-guards are spread out, searching for rogue mages, so it can be hard to maintain communication. Still, a vendetta could spread among the squads. Badger Squad is small. If it comes to a battle, and we lose —"

Zathi bit off with a bitter curl of lip. Lorrah could guess the rest.

"They'll say you reached too far. That you deserve to fail." It was a familiar refrain.

"And this would prove that women are only fit to manage documents and wait on the men, yes." Zathi glanced toward the office door. Her voice was dry and hard.

"I'll be careful," Lorrah promised.

"I know." Zathi's gaze was not unkind. "You'll learn, as we all do. The most successful battle is the one never fought."

"Huh." Lorrah chuckled. "That sounds like something Ar-Thea would say."

Zathi didn't know how to take that, but she seemed to be pleased.

Eventually, the guards ran out of things to be scrubbed. The four prisoners lined up against a wall, while Guard Captain Morthem inspected the dining hall. Alemin fidgeted. Much as he tried to be patient, his mind seethed at the prospect of any more chores. However, the inspection ended with the officer's neutral nod.

"This will do."

The prisoners were ordered back outside. Alemin dreaded being taken back to the stale air and blackened ceiling of his cell. But in fact, they were marched through the narrow gap between the outer wall and inner tower. This widened into a small formal garden, a startling contrast to bare walls and trampled ground. Scents of greenery and turned earth washed over the weary prisoners. There were strictly lined blocks of vegetables, freshly weeded and watered. Flowering vines grew up the sides of a tiny arbor. A small table with a single chair completed the tantalizing vision.

This garden clearly wouldn't yield enough food for the prison's inhabitants. It must be a retreat for Ar-Lizelle alone. Still, it was an effective display of comforts the prisoners weren't allowed.

Guards pressed them on until a stone wall confronted them. Sentries let Alemin's group in through a metal gate. Beyond that was another narrow courtyard with packed earth below their feet. Stone benches lined both sides. Alemin winced as the gate's metallic clang reverberated in the confined space.

"What now?" he asked Duessa.

"It's our rest period," she answered in a mocking sing-song.

A wobbly table held pitchers of water and wooden cups. Exhausted and a little light-headed, Alemin gladly poured a cup and gulped it, then poured more and backed away. Some of the pitchers were already empty.

The only sliver of shade was against the outer wall. The benches there were already taken. Prisoners spread out in groups of one or two, with only fitful conversation between them. A few appeared to be dozing off, then jerking back to alertness. The women formed their own group, sitting apart from the men. Two of them rested while the third, Bettain, watched for trouble. In a prison full of mages, nobody could rest easy.

As it was, Alemin's eyes were blurring and his head throbbed. He spotted a vacant bench right against the Larder wall, where the sunlight was most brutal. When he settled on it, he found it strangely short, so that he couldn't lie down. Sharp edges of chiseled stone bit into his ass.

Alemin shifted, trying to find the least painful seat. Now he understood Duessa's sarcasm. This was no rest period, merely a different kind of torment. The sun baked this barren courtyard. No breeze could get past the walls. In the rainy season, there would be no shelter from the weather. All this time, he had been afraid Ar-Lizelle would have him beaten or tortured, but it seemed she was more devious than that. The train of discomforts would wear down most prisoners, until they did what she wanted.

With little hope of rest, he set his cup of water on the bench, where his shadow might keep it from getting too warm. Then he pulled his knees up so that his legs could cross. This forced his back against the surface of the Larder's main tower. Fierce heat immediately penetrated his thin robe. Sweat soon trickled between his shoulders. For a moment, he wished Meven was there. Meven, the ice witch, would have been able to chill his drink even in this sweltering courtyard.

It was no good thinking about his friends. He didn't think these mages could pry into his thoughts, but why take the chance? Alemin let his hands rest on his knees and drew in a deep gust of heated air. As when he rode in the hunter-guards' cage, his best hope was in meditation. He could forget the painfully bright sunlight, and the headache it gave him, at least for a while.

Wooden spoons spun in his mind, just as his worries did. Ar-Lizelle seemed to be very well informed about the Minstrels. She knew how many there were — and now he saw why she had put him in "number six." Six was the number of Ar-Thea's missing apprentices. Very sneaky of her.

The things she accused them of were pretty far-fetched. Still, he sensed this was a personal issue for the warden. She was especially interested in Lorrah. He couldn't think why. Lorrah was the youngest of them, a bit of a brat in some ways. She always butted in with comments that showed she didn't understand what they were talking about. Lorrah had never been involved in planning anything the Minstrels did. Then why should Ar-Lizelle focus on her?

Fabric rustled, intruding into his mind. Alemin

shifted, damp fabric sticking to his back. He sipped his cup
of water and eased one eye open. Illen was just sitting on the
next bench over. A reek of the stables suggested what his
morning's work must have been. Immediately, Alemin felt
concern. Even if he was a thief, Illen didn't look well. He
was pale beneath his brown skin tone. Sweat drew glinting
tracks down his shaved scalp.

"Have you had any water?" Alemin's own voice
sounded harsh as the desert.

Illen glared in reply, then slumped down facing
away.

Alemin didn't care if he was shunned. To tell the
truth, it was almost a relief. He shifted again, and something
hard pressed into his side. He fought through the headache to
remember the egg he'd put inside his sleeve. The morning
meal had been good enough, but it felt like years ago. Now
his empty stomach awakened.

He slipped his fingers into the sweat-dampened
sleeve. The shell shifted beneath his fingers. Scrubbing must
have cracked it. He'd better eat it before it went bad.

Reluctantly, he looked at Illen's stubborn back. His
fellow prisoner sagged on the bench, leaning away from the
Larder wall as much as he avoided Alemin.

"Eat it, it's yours!" The imperative raged in Alemin's
mind, but he knew Illen wouldn't be able to draw on *vitalis*
to ease his hunger and thirst. He squinted up at the sentries
on the wall and wondered what happened if a prisoner
collapsed. Would they do anything at all?

Alemin's fingers tightened around the smooth
eggshell. His stomach screamed at the faint aroma of it. He
swallowed, drawing in a breath.

Before he could speak, Illen rasped, "What the hell
are you doing over here?"

At first, Alemin thought he meant the egg, but as in
the morning, Illen wasn't asking about surface things.

"I'm just meditating." When a trembling hand, Alemin kept the egg inside his sleeve. Illen raised a skeptical brow. "It makes the time go by."

Even soft voices bounced off the walls. Other prisoners were watching them, some suspicious and others merely bored.

"Don't give me that bullshit," Illen croaked. "We can all feel it. What are you doing?"

"Meditating."

Illen tried to spit, but there was little moisture left in him. Alemin only received a dry puff of breath. The other man choked as Alemin drew his hand out of his sleeve. The egg gleamed shockingly white in the harsh sunlight.

"You snuck food?" Illen whispered, furiously jealous.

"Nobody said not to." Alemin hoped none of the guards were about to swoop down and take it. He kept his prize close to his body, concealing it from them and the other prisoners. His fingers didn't want to move, but he levered them open. "Take it."

"You're insane." Illen stared at the egg as if it might poison him.

"I can wait," Alemin said. "That's what the meditation is for."

Illen's hand moved before he finished speaking. Alemin didn't resist as he clawed the egg away. Bits of shell sprayed around them. Illen stuffed the treat into his mouth before it was fully peeled.

"You know what? I think that's the same one you tried to steal this morning." Alemin's dry lips stung as he tried to smile. "Congratulations."

Illen glared, unable to reply because his mouth was full. Alemin sipped his water, trying to make it last. Most of the prisoners in the courtyard seemed unaware that someone had food. Duessa, however, pierced Alemin with her accusing stare.

Now he didn't know where to look. Stirring on the bench, he found that his ass had gone numb. With a sigh, he unfolded his legs and tried again to find a comfortable seat. By this time, Illen had swallowed the egg and was spitting bits of shell onto the ground.

"I don't owe you for that," he growled, but already he looked a little better. Pieces of shell stuck out against the shadow of the bench. He scuffed them with his sandal, as if they represented a shameful secret.

Something rattled over the ground and bounced off Alemin's foot. It was a large pebble, flat on one side. He leaned over to pick it up. From the color and texture, it was a piece broken off the wall. Alemin tossed it lightly, getting a feel for the weight.

Illen huffed out an angry breath. "You're the weirdest one yet."

"That's true." Alemin smiled a little. Ar-Thea had infected him with her rebel ideas long ago. Besides, in a way, Illen had already paid him back. If they found another pebble like this, he could juggle with his hands, not only in his mind.

Illen himself replied with an exasperated wheeze.

Lorrah brooded as the wagon rolled across the plains of Litholl. Now that she had seen what the Badgers put up with, she was even more determined to build her power. It wasn't enough to be the youngest and let the other minstrels do the hard work. Nor could she accept that her big sister was right, and she was a failure. She had to do more. Lives were at stake — Alemin's, the guardswomen's, and her own. She couldn't give up. If summoning fire didn't work, then she had to try something else.

What other casting did she know? Ar-Thea had been a kind mentor, but her teaching had been all too limited. She didn't approve of mages going into battle — hence her being labeled as a heretic — and only taught defensive spells.

The barrier had been Ar-Thea's favorite. For lack of anything better, Lorrah practiced that. She drew a breath and felt *vitalis* flowing. Then she pictured the barrier. Lorrah raised a hand and clenched a fist. *Vitalis* flared. The barrier formed as a small rectangle, smooth and flat, glowing gently. Sethamis looked around, startled. Lorrah shrugged a little, and released her fist.

At least something she did worked. She raised the barrier again, then let it drop, several times in a row. Sometimes she placed it behind the driver's back, as if to protect her. Maybe later someone could throw rocks at the barrier to test its strength.

The spell wasn't exactly difficult, so it didn't tire her. Still, as the sun rose ever higher, she grew bored with the repetitive work. The highway dipped slightly to ford a stream, and Zathi ordered a halt to eat and let the animals rest. Before they got back in the wagon, Lorrah cast about for something else to work on.

The cage in the back of the wagon was closed with a metal padlock. She unhooked that and sat with it in her lap. As the vehicle jolted back into motion, Lorrah explored the smooth, cold iron with her mind. She used the same *vitalis* she had used to lift the rock, earlier in the day. Reaching through the keyhole, she probed at the shapes within it. Razeet leaned over from the back of the wagon to watch.

Lorrah tried not to let that distract her. After several minutes, she pushed the tumblers into the right order and pulled on the hasp. It opened with a snap.

"That's handy," Razeet commented.

"It's not much good in a fight," Lorrah grumbled.

"Not every battle is fought with weapons," Sethamis said.

"Sometimes you have to be sneaky," Razeet agreed.

Lorrah thought about her mind powers again, and couldn't disagree. She kept practicing, locking and unlocking the padlock. How much easier this was. *Vitalis* flowed like water, smooth and yielding. Why was calling fire such a problem? *Lethentros* wasn't that much different.

The answer came to her suddenly, and her stomach sank. In fact, *vitalis* was very different from *lethentros*. Most mages drew on *lethentros* easily, because they were constantly angry or braced for an attack. Ar-Thea had kept her apprentices away from such lethal competition. Sheltered them, even.

Because Ar-Thea taught only with *vitalis*, Lorrah hadn't used *lethentros* in years.

She sat in the lumbering wagon, staring at the road before her. This couldn't be, but it was. She had always thought Ar-Thea saved her. Instead, she was crippled!

IV

Boar Squad

S omewhere high above them, a bell rang. Its flat, unmelodic clanking drew groans of relief all around the courtyard. With shuffling and much complaint, the prisoners gathered in a line against the wall. Alemin stuffed the pebble into his sleeve. It was a miserly substitution for the boiled egg.

He went to find Duessa. "More rehabilitation?"

"Nope." She flicked him a smile. "Housekeeping."

The gate slid aside. Guards came in, yelling at the mages to put their backs to the wall even though most of them were already there. Soon Alemin found himself bracketed by guards. He and Wharon were pulled out of the line and marched off together. Alemin couldn't help noticing how sleek and healthy the guards were, almost plump compared to the sun-parched prisoners. The man behind Alemin even had a shine of grease on his chin. So they were allowed a meal, while the prisoners went hungry? He tried not to let that bother him. Anger would only play into Ar-Lizelle's hands.

They were taken to a back room in the tower. Wharon fetched a grimy rag from a shelf and a wooden bucket from a stack, so Alemin did the same. They filled the buckets from a water pump. Alemin longed to gulp from the pump, but Wharon didn't, so he restrained himself.

With heavy buckets, they labored up several fights of stairs. Once, Alemin allowed his bucket to slosh water on the steps. That got him a clout to the head. "Watch what you're doing, scum!"

His legs burned and he was gasping for breath by the time they reached the upper level. This time, their task was to scrub their cells down. The guards stood in the hall, gossiping about whether another guard had a girlfriend down in the mines. Alemin was desperate enough to scoop up a gulp of water before he started scrubbing. When the floor was clean, they had him take his latrine bucket to a floor drain, empty it, and scrub it out. Now he was relieved that he had stolen his drink beforehand.

With empty buckets, he and Wharon were run down the stairs to the pump room. With the empty buckets put away, they ran straight back up. By the time they completed this second trip, Alemin was too winded to resist being shoved into his cell. The door banged shut and bolts slammed home. The guards left without so much as a word.

Panting, he eased down on the unsteady bed. He had no idea what was supposed to happen next, and there was nobody he could ask. Although it was better than sitting in the sun, the cell was half-dark and stuffy. It reminded him a lot of when he was a kid, in the seaside town of Kamuril.

Until they met Ar-Thea, he and Berisan had lived a hidden existence. Their magic could erupt without warning. It was a danger to everyone. No one else in their family had been mage born. Nobody knew how to help them. The brothers' secret had dominated everything in the family's life.

Mother dreaded that she would be blamed for birthing two monsters. Father, perhaps kinder, refused to lose both of his sons into the dark pit of a temple school. Their older sister, Salima, had resented all the attention on her "useless brothers" and made every day a misery. She broke things and blamed it on their powers. If Mother wasn't watching, she made them do her chores. In jealousy and spite, she called them names and accused them of ruining her life. If they argued back, she threatened to tell the temple priests and let them be arrested.

The threat had been all too credible. Before their

magic, they had seen other boys and girls dragged away from weeping families. There was a reward for turning in secret mages — and an equal punishment for hiding them. Nobody could be trusted to keep a secret like that.

Over time, the brothers' world had contracted to the walls of their family's house and the walled garden behind it. Whenever strangers appeared, they had to hide in the root cellar, where it was chilly and dark. They'd keep the door open a crack, letting in little more light than the slotted window of this cell admitted now.

Waiting among the onion bins, the two brothers had begun juggling as a way to pass the time. As years passed, the boys grew taller. There was barely enough room in the root cellar for both of them. It was getting harder to hide.

That was when Ar-Thea had come. The old woman arrived at their back gate with a basket of herbs for sale. She wore a mage's crimson, but it was sun-faded and ragged at the hem. A sullen teenaged girl trailed at her heels. Meven, although they didn't know her yet.

The appearance of a wandering mage had been terrifying. Berisan had grabbed Alemin's arm and dragged him off to hide. It was Father who went to confront this stranger. Mysteriously, he decided to let her in. Soon he sent Salima to fetch them from the root cellar.

Somehow, Ar-Thea got the truth from them. Father wept to let them go — but not in the way those other families had. In her traveling camp, they weren't judged and silenced, but encouraged to find their strength. Until then, the brothers had viewed the world through the eyes of frightened children. Ar-Thea had taught them to breathe again.

Now, Alemin was back in prison. A different and harsher one.

He mulled over the day so far. The other inmates had been so disgusted that he would endure all this to protect his friends. Illen had pronounced him insane for the simple kindness of sharing a boiled egg. Alemin had thought it was a good way to build bridges. Maybe there was no such thing here. In the Larder, Alemin was just one more prisoner, ground down by lack of sleep, short rations, hard work, and brutal sun exposure. The tension of being constantly watched was one more weight upon his soul.

Yet there were hints that the rumors about this place were not entirely true. If the prisoners seemed fearsome, perhaps instead they were fearful. Anyone might attack, and who would come to help them? A man might boast of killing his own brother, if it meant his neighbors wouldn't try to start something.

If the inmates seemed savage, perhaps instead they were exhausted. He had seen them longing to sleep, but afraid to lower their guards. The women clustered together, bracing for who knew what abuses. In this setting, his meditation — or what they sensed of it — might appear as one more threat. What other way did they know?

If Ar-Thea had been there, she would have scolded Alemin for thinking he knew anything at all about these men and women. The rumors could have been exaggerated, an excuse for the harsh treatment. He supposed that they also worked to cow the prisoners before they even reached the Larder. It seemed like the kind of strategy Ar-Lizelle would employ.

Before she died, Ar-Thea had told her apprentices a fantastic story. It was tragic and grand and impossible. Then she had sent them out into the world with a mission to change the dismal state of Skaythe. Alemin's fellow prisoners were clearly not ready to hear such a tale. Yet he was still bound by Ar-Thea's calling. If anyone in Skaythe needed to be saved, it was these mages of the Larder, so desperate and lost.

Alemin groaned at the very idea. What madness was this, to think they even wanted to be saved?

Yet, like it or not, he was stuck here. Unless he gave in to Ar-Lizelle's cruel persuasions, of course. Even then, there was no assurance that the warden would keep her word and release him. People who went into the Larder didn't come back out. So where was the exit for Alemin?

The day dragged, and Lorrah didn't want to think about spell casting any more. Even meditation was too much of an embarrassment. What could she do about her sudden handicap? While the sun sank below the horizon, and guardswomen tended their gear, she turned to the only other thing that might keep her hands busy — her violin.

The guardswomen watched with interest as she took the instrument out of its soft leather case. Lorrah quickly inspected the fiddle and wiped its body with a soft rag. Fortunately, the bow didn't need resin. Lorrah didn't have much left. The fiddle's mellow voice vibrated through the strings as she tuned them. Then she went into a sequence of scales that always started practice sessions.

"Play something real," Keerin complained.

Lorrah raised her head enough to speak past the chin rest. "Do I tell you how to sharpen your sword?"

As punishment, she dropped into the one tune she had played more often than any other. It was a dreary melody with tedious rhythm that Mother always wanted her to play when noble ladies came to visit. Left to herself, Lorrah could begin to improvise from that, but her mother hadn't appreciated her taking the liberty.

"You're just trying to get attention," she would scold.

After a few verses of Mother's favorite dirge, the guardswomen were looking confused and unhappy. "Come on, let's hear some real fiddling!" Razeet booed.

Lorrah chuckled to herself. Mother would have been disgusted to hear it called that. She had bought her younger daughter a good quality violin, not some peasant's fiddle. Knowing how Lorrah struggled to reach Ar-Evaus' standards as a mage, Mother sought to instill some gentle virtue that might at least offer Lorrah the security of a favorable marriage. With an alliance for the family, of course.

Still, Lorrah took pity on the guardswomen, and perhaps on herself. She slipped into a walking song, the kind the servants would sing among themselves. Those weren't good enough for her mother's fine guests, but they served Lorrah well when she played for work-worn peasants in taverns. Or in this case, some tough hunter-guards, who tapped their feet to the beat. From there she passed through a series of quick dances, pausing to say she had learned them in Deeve, or Nimthar, or Sloram.

"You've been all over," Giniver marveled.

Lorrah paused. "Haven't you?" Hunter-guards went everywhere in Skaythe.

Giniver pretended to pout. "Not to any *fun* places."

Jaxynne grinned over the crossbow she was inspecting. "Yeah, Sergeant. You never take us anywhere nice."

"Shut up," Zathi said, but fondly. "You bunch of babies."

Smiling, Lorrah moved into to one of the slower, sultry dances that Tisha favored. She never failed to captivate the men in the audience. Last of all, she played Keilos' signature ballad — the same Keerin had sung for her not so long ago. Now there were smiles and approval around the glowing lantern.

"Well played," Zathi murmured, while Lorrah tucked her fiddle into its case.

Lorrah nodded gratefully. Music might not have been her own choice, but at least she could relax with it. Ar-Evaus and Lizelle had regarded it so little that they hadn't bothered to interrupt and tell her she was doing it wrong.

It was good to know she could succeed at something. She just wished it was a skill that might actually help her friends.

Alemin tried to sleep through the long, hot hours. Sinister whispers flitted through his mind, keeping him from truly relaxing. The single stroke of light from the window crept down the wall and across the floor. That was the only way to tell time was passing.

Eventually, the window dimmed. Alemin sat up, rubbing behind his ears. There was a tightness there, and a warning pinch at the back of his neck. He schooled himself to relax and listen to what his senses were telling him.

Minutes passed as he sweated in the oven-like cell. He had begun to believe it was nothing when a faint, sobbing moan echoed around him. Then another. The cries quickly escalated, even more than in the morning. Vibrations washed around him, through him. Someone unseen wailed with... what? Not merely pain. It went deeper. A loss from the very soul.

In fact, it might not be just one person. There were many voices, layers of them. A slight dissonance separated them in his mind. A ragged chorus howled with grief too raw for words.

Alemin remembered that figure in his nightmare. "Who are you?" he had asked. The specter had retorted, "Which one?"

"If you don't look, you will never see things as they are." Just so, if he shut his mind to this chaos, he would never understand what it was trying to tell him. Alemin grimaced and sat up straighter, then pressed both palms against the soot-streaked wall.

He gasped as emotion rolled through him. Agony, terror, the shock of betrayal. Stabbing pain surged up his arms. Tears overflowed, but these extremes were not *his* emotions. Where did they come from? Who was it that wailed so horribly?

Alemin tried to hold on, but it was too much. The chaos was overwhelming, and it felt like the blood in his veins was scalding him. He snatched his hands back and sagged forward, to sniffle and wipe his eyes with threadbare sleeves.

He didn't understand what was happening. The tormented cries went on, everywhere around him. Alemin felt as if he was literally sitting inside a scream. He blinked at the window, a slot with black runnels around it, and the scorched ceiling.

Strangely, he had sensed the deluge coming this time. A new question slowly emerged.

What if he really *was* sitting inside the scream? It couldn't come from a person, or people. No one was there. It had to come from the Larder itself.

Was the Larder... alive?

He shook his head and pressed a sleeve to stinging eyes. That was absurd. A building was not alive.

And yet.

How many generations of mages had been kept prisoner here? Alemin hadn't seen anyone tortured so far, but he'd been there less than a day. It must have happened many, many times. Those tormented mages would have lashed out and been subdued, and cried out with all their anguish. What impression would that make on a tower that was already steeped in ancient sorcery?

Voices echoed in the corridor. Alemin shook off the shreds of speculation as he realized that these voices were real. Dusk had fallen outside the window. He hoped the guards were coming to take him down for a meal.

Regardless, the puzzle remained. Trapped as he was, Alemin was sure to have plenty of time to work it out.

Alemin was to learn that life in the Larder held two constants: the nightmares, and a relentless routine. The schedule was an unbreakable chain that bound them all. The prisoners rose at dawn, to sourceless shrieks and a morning meal watched by vulture guards. Grueling labor would

follow: chopping wood, scrubbing the kitchen, mucking out
the stables.

Afternoon offered only a few sips of water to keep
them alive in the roasting pan of the courtyard. Then up to
their cells for hours of unending boredom. Alemin managed
to scavenge a thick wooden button with a crack in it, and a
bit of bone left over from a ham. These let him juggle to
restore some of his strength. Yet, without an audience, he
could only do that for so long before it lost its appeal.

At length, the dusk would bring renewed screaming.
Alemin listened, trying desperately to understand who cried
out and what they needed. There was never an answer, only
shrieks that left his mind raw. Then the prisoners would be
marched down for another scant meal, and more chores to
see the dining hall spotless before they were caged for the
night.

This routine locked each day to the last, and on to the
one to come. It would have been difficult enough, but
Alemin was to learn that nowhere in the Larder was free
from nightmares.

However weary his body might be, there could be no
rest. Deadly sharks swam in the waters of the nights. Often,
Alemin dreamed of that malevolent vortex he'd seen the first
night. Distant, flickering lights dangled a rescue that could
never come. And there were plenty of other nightmares. The
cell's narrow window turned into a lurid eye. The ceiling
became a maw of jagged teeth. Alemin dreamed that the
floor was flooded with vile sludge, where the harder he
struggled the more quickly he sank. He dreamed that he was
left in his cell forever, and no guards came when he called.
Some dreams had him running, pursued by that elusive
specter of the tower. It was shouting threats and demanding
answers. When he woke, sobbing for breath, he couldn't
remember the questions.

Other prisoners suffered just as much, he could tell.
Their hollow cheeks and sunken eyes told the tale. Alemin
found an odd kinship in that. Mornings, as they all sat bleary,

Illen or Haafeth would seek him out. The conversation was seldom cheerful. However, now that Alemin had done it, one or another of the prisoners often attempted to smuggle food out of breakfast. If the guards caught on, they would take back the prize with heavy fists. Yet if someone succeeded, it was a triumph for them all — even when the winner refused to share their snack.

At some point in the day, Ar-Lizelle would saunter through, silently offering the escape that could only come with betrayal. Alemin endured the sudden headaches and screened his thoughts, while pretending not to know what she wanted. Each time, he wondered how long her patience would last.

Day after day, Badger Squad traveled. The dark curtain of the Hornwood dipped lower behind them as the squad crossed the broad Litholl Valley. Lorrah was surprised at the fearful deference the squad received in the many little towns they passed through. It was far different for a troupe of wandering minstrels!

Mornings were for running, sparring, trying and failing to summon fire. Evenings were for music and tending their gear. Soon rocky peaks loomed to the south and east. Jaxynne directed them to a track so narrow that a merchant caravan had to back up some distance to let them by.

Lorrah sympathized, but Sethamis told her, "Don't feel bad. This is the road going up. See that one?" She pointed across a sharply carved valley, where a line of switchbacks angled lower. "That side is for going down."

"Were they trying to get down faster?" Lorrah asked doubtfully.

Razeet shrugged. "There's probably a tax collector at the bottom on that side."

A lone fort guarded the wind-torn pass. After that, they were on Unthur Plateau, a place bare of trees but rich with sheep and goats. Every few days, they came to another guard post. Even with the guardswomen hunting and foraging, there were supplies they needed. Each time, Zathi and Lorrah checked in. They were never offered any bounties.

However, at every post, there was some sort of cat-calling and harassment. Men challenged Keerin to arm wrestle. They tried to switch a sickly ox for one of Sethamis' lovingly cared for beasts. The only time a soldier offered to help them load supplies, it was so he could pinch Giniver's ass — and get a bloody nose in return.

It became routine. Lorrah no longer worried about whether she was enough like a "real mage." After they'd made a few such stops, she realized there was always one thing in common. While the wagon rumbled along, she turned it over in her mind, making sure it wasn't a silly waste of time. That evening, while they shared a stew made from a pair of pigeons Jaxynne shot, she gathered her courage.

"I have an idea," Lorrah announced.

Around the circle, spoons clinked against metal bowls. Zathi picked a fragment of bone out of hers. "What about?"

"Getting Alemin out of the Larder," she said. "All we need is a writ."

The sergeant nodded. "Go on."

"Every time we stop, you ask them about open writs and bounties," Lorrah explained. "You'd have to have documents to put someone in the Larder, right? So if we have a writ, you can take him out."

"Maybe," Zathi answered. Then she admitted, "I've never fetched a prisoner, only turned them over."

"We don't have a writ," Giniver quickly pointed out.

Keerin snorted. "How hard is it to make a fake one?"

"Not hard, for me." Lorrah gave a modest shrug. "My father served the Count of Prowth. He made me handle a lot of documents that he didn't want to bother with. I can make us a very official-looking writ. It will be in the formal script and everything."

"I see two problems," Jaxynne said. "Writs are on parchment, not the reed paper most people use. Plus, you need a count's personal stamp."

"I know all the official stamps for Prowth, and some of the ones for Ebruc and Prizom." Lorrah had never thought the humble chores her father dumped on her would have any value. "If I have the right sized stick, I can carve the one we want. Prizom's, I think. They're farther away, less known around Yergha. There's also a special ink they use. Mages see a glow, and others don't."

"I suppose you know how to make that ink," Zathi said.

"I sure do." Lorrah was feeling confident. This idea could work. "Besides, Ar-Thea used to tell us that people will see what they expect to see."

Sethamis asked, "Can we get parchment with our other supplies?"

"Not likely," Jaxynne answered promptly. "Parchment is expensive. We'd need a reason for wanting it."

Lorrah let go a little, frustrated sigh and blew on a bite of her stew. Surely they could think of some reason. Razeet chuckled.

"Don't feel bad. It's better than what I was thinking."

Her sister raised a brow. "Do I want to know what you were thinking?"

Razeet sent Lorrah an apologetic glance. "Act like we arrested Lorrah."

"What?" Lorrah choked on her food.

"Only pretending," Razeet hastily assured her. "Just to get inside the Larder, but I couldn't think what we would do next, so..." She shrugged.

Still coughing, Lorrah brushed at drops of stew that

had spilled on her robe. Zathi eyed her sympathetically.

"There's no point leaving one mage behind so we can get another out, but there might be something we can use in both ideas. Let's keep working on it."

During a withering afternoon in the courtyard, Duessa and the other two women gathered in their usual group. Alemin, passing by to see if any water was left, realized they were playing a guessing game, such as children used to learn their letters. All of them groaned when he casually gave the answer.

Duessa mock-scowled, "If you're going to play, then sit down, Juggler."

Alemin joined them. By now he knew the other women's names. Elldri had broken teeth that made her speak with an embarrassing lisp. Bettain was prickly and stubborn. The game went well enough, despite Alemin's back hurting from scrubbing the stairs. He even managed a puzzle that stumped his rivals.

Duessa grumbled, "You've got me there. Too bad I don't have any coin for you to win."

"Well," Alemin leaned in a little. Coin wasn't the only thing of value here. "You could tell me something."

She was instantly wary. "What do you want to know? Tell me and I'll decide."

"There's something I've been wondering." Alemin glanced around and spotted his topic crouched alone, muttering to himself. In a low voice, he asked, "Wharon keeps saying he's the warden. That's not true, is it?"

The other women stiffened. Duessa's hand flew up to touch her cheek, where scars puckered from nose to chin. Her black eyes glittered with fury.

"You really know how to hurt someone." She gathered herself to stand, but he put out a hand.

"How should I know that, if no one will talk about it?"

"Then listen." Her legs quivered as she crouched, her face just a few inches from his. Her voice was deadly soft. "Yes, he was the warden. Then he went crazy and started burning everyone."

"Oh." Alemin had heard mages who used *lethentros* could go mad, but this was the first specific story he had heard. It put her scars into a very different light. "I should have asked someone else."

"Yeah, you say that now," she bit out. "There used to be about 30 of us. See how many are left?"

"He killed a couple of the guards, too," Bettain added. "They wouldn't follow orders."

Illen knelt to join the conversation. "I heard that order. He wanted them to herd us in for him to kill, one by one."

That explained why the Larder had so few prisoners for a building of its size. It also fit with some of the stories people told about this place. *"If you aren't mad when you get here, you soon will be."*

Alemin shook his head, glancing back at Wharon's pitiful figure. "Did he really do that?"

Bettain nodded. "It happens here. I've seen two or three go bad."

"Why?"

"Who knows? He kept saying the tower was hungry," Duessa quoted bitterly.

Illen corrected her. "He said we're being devoured, and this made it quicker."

That was like something from one of Alemin's nightmares. "How did you stop him from doing it?"

"We fought like hell," Bettain retorted.

Duessa cut in. "It was Ar-Lizelle who did it. She was his second, but she shut him down."

"How?" That could be useful information.

"You'd have to ask her." Illen prodded Alemin's shoulder. "She likes you. Maybe she'd even tell the truth."

"Er, no," Alemin choked. They guffawed.

Duessa seemed to be over the worst of her anger. "People make fun of her voice, and call her names, but she saved us."

"The Lizard makes us work, but nothing like when Wharon was warden," lisped Elldri.

"She should have killed him, though," Illen said. "You aren't safe after that."

"Hey!" A harsh voice snapped down from above. Startled, the prisoners looked up to meet a guard's suspicious squint. "Do you have food down there?"

"We're just talking," Bettain answered. The others began to scatter, though they were guilty of nothing. Alemin caught up with Illen.

"So he was the warden, but he went mad. How do you come back from that?"

"You don't," Illen grunted. "Haven't you noticed, he only talks about one thing. 'I'm the warden.' And that screaming in our heads? It's his voice."

"Really?" Alemin thought back to the all-too-familiar cries. Was Wharon's voice part of the cacophony?

"They hold him up at the top to dampen his magic. The building is like that, see? The higher up you go, the more it sucks your will."

"Oh..." That could explain why Alemin woke in a haze each morning, but felt relatively clear-headed the rest of the day. When he was in his cell, he had a hard time summoning *vitalis* even if he juggled.

"I don't know why she put you up there, though." Illen eyed him sideways.

"The Lizard wants to know something. If I tell her, people will die."

"So you'd rather be here?" Illen snorted. "I forgot how weird you are."

The bell clanged, echoes painfully loud in the small courtyard. Alemin's mind was busy as everyone shuffled toward the gate to line up. He hadn't thought Ar-Lizelle would fight for the prisoners whose lives she dominated. He almost felt bad about calling her Lizard.

The afternoon sun blazed down as Badger Squad rode into yet another outpost. Lorrah was more concerned with finding a place in the shade than whatever coarse jokes the locals might try. This time, a surprise awaited them.

Another squad already filled up much of the courtyard. There were two wagons, one holding the usual cage and the other for guardsmen to ride in. Armored men went back and forth, toting bales and crates from the storage shed.

Zathi cursed softly. Lorrah turned, surprised. The sergeant was always stern, but never angry. Now she wore a hard scowl.

Sethamis slowed the wagon, calling, "Ho boys, ho now!"

The guardsmen with the crates seemed glad enough to set them down and let her ease the wagon by. When they saw who drove that wagon, and who rode beside it, the familiar nasty grins began to spread.

"Hey, look who it is," a man exclaimed. Another called, "Come for another party, girls?"

Jaxynne and the other riders came in close, a guarded formation. Lorrah leaned back to ask Keerin, "Who are they?"

"Boar Squad," she replied in a bitter growl.

"They stole a catch from us a while back." Razeet's knuckles whitened around the stock of her crossbow.

Lorrah could see their pennant now. It was red with silver bars, the same all hunter guards displayed. A black boar's head leered on top of that. Lorrah's eyes roved the courtyard, taking in the number of men Boar Squad claimed. Zathi's caution, those weeks ago, about battles she couldn't win, took on a new meaning.

"Get us turned around," the sergeant ordered, flat and cold. "We'll be quick inside, and come back out to you."

"Yes, Sergeant," Sethamis was already tugging on the reins.

As the wagon trundled slowly around, Lorrah watched for a chance to jump down. On her left, Jaxynne turned her horse, the red roan Spark, toward what looked to be her counterpart on Boar Squad.

"Are you here for a while, or heading out?" Her bland voice barely penetrated the background noise in the courtyard.

"Whatever Sergeant says." The man shrugged, but with a sly little smirk. Like the desk sergeant back in Litholl, he savored the power of a non-answer.

"Are you going to leave any supplies?" Jaxynne pressed.

"I've got a lot of hungry men to feed." He rubbed his chin, pretending to think. "Unless, what would you give for them?"

Jaxynne rolled her eyes at the vulgar suggestion in his tone. "That's what I thought."

She was reining Spark around when Lorrah spotted a gap and jumped down from the wagon. Straightening her robe, she looked for the office. That's where Zathi would be headed. It was slightly unnerving, though, that the crowd remained so thick. Most people gave way before a mage's crimson robe. Boar Squad seemed to feel no such concern.

"Hey, you're just a young thing," said a fellow with a gap between his teeth.

"Are you lost?" Someone else bantered. "I'll help you find your way."

Lorrah's heart thumped in her chest. After traveling with the Minstrels, she should be used to these crude advances. Although, normally, their attention would be reserved for the beautiful dancer, Tisha.

"No need," she answered pleasantly. "The office is always in the same place, right?"

Their buddies laughed and thumped each other as Lorrah walked on. As she hoped, Zathi was at the foot of the steps, frowning over the crowd. Relief flashed in her dark eyes when she saw Lorrah.

"We shouldn't be alone here."

"I got that impression." Lorrah matched her stride up the steps. She meant to ask more, but the door banged open and a hunter-guard came from the office. Zathi halted, rigid. His breastplate was of better quality than the men's, and sergeant's bars were stamped into the shoulder. He paused, startled, and then a broad grin broke over his brown face.

"Zathi! Long time no see." The jovial greeting rang through the courtyard, answered by chuckles from his guardsmen.

"Not long enough, Traggan." Her tone was tight, unfriendly.

"Ah, so harsh!" Rather than being upset, Sergeant Traggan seemed entertained by her retort. He made no move to clear the steps. "We made good on that bounty for you. I should pay you back. Join me and my boys for a drink."

There was no mistaking his gloating tone. Zathi spoke curtly. "We're here to water our oxen and sign the log book."

Lorrah felt heat rising in Zathi's core. She knew, all too well, the helplessness of being out-numbered. Lorrah, too, felt the urge to strike back at the braggart and show him not to tangle with the Badgers.

In her memory, Ar-Thea whispered, *"Child, you must never strike in anger or fear."*

"Let us pass." Zathi spoke in a warning tone.

Still, Lorrah had some skills a guardswoman might not. Minstrels didn't have much luck on the road if they couldn't gather information from people they met. Even the rude ones. So she kept her professional smile and stepped up beside her sergeant.

"Someone you know, Sergeant?"

Traggan modified his swagger at the sight of a mage's crimson. He bowed, although not very long or low. "May Dar-Gothull show you favor."

"May he never know your name." Lorrah replied with a country saying. That brought a grim smile to Traggan's lips. Lorrah flicked her fingers at Zathi. "Go on. Sign your book."

Zathi strode on up, unimpeded. To keep Traggan busy, Lorrah said, "This is a large squad. Are they all your men?"

"Yes, Boar Squad's all mine," he straightened his shoulders and swaggered a little.

"Impressive," Lorrah murmured.

The praise revived Traggan's bravado. He folded his arms and surveyed the courtyard, where some of the men were idling, trying to strike up conversations with Badger Squad's women.

"Get to it, you louts!" he bellowed. Once the work was going at a quicker pace, he squinted down at Lorrah with his own sly query.

"You hired Zathi, did you?" His voice held a faint

undertone. Maybe it was suspicion, since mages and hunter-guards were traditional enemies. It might also have been envy.

"They hired me," Lorrah corrected. Feigning bitterness, she added, "It was suggested that I travel outside the temple school to broaden my experience."

"Ah, that's rough." Traggan nodded. A mage who failed in the temple school would never rise to any rank of note. That much was widely known.

Of course, Lorrah's tale was a lie, except for the part about who hired who. Minstrels often spun such tales to shield themselves from hunter-guards exactly like this one. Lorrah even had a false name ready, in case he asked. Meanwhile, she could practically hear Traggan trying to calculate what Zathi was paying her, and whether he could make a better offer.

She resumed her flattery. "With so many guardsmen, you must make some big arrests."

"Oh, yes indeed." He swayed on his heels, smirking toward Badger Squad. Lorrah stopped him before he could regale her with her friends' humiliation.

"What have you done recently? Caught anyone important?"

"Don't know about important," he shrugged with false modesty. "The most interesting one was a pretty boy trying to pass himself off as a juggler."

"A juggler?" Lorrah choked. Alemin! It couldn't be anyone else. This bunch of two-legged pigs had taken him in? Before she revealed too much personal involvement, she forced a scornful laugh. "A juggler. I'll never sink that low."

"Real weakling," Traggan sneered. "Never even fought back."

Of course he wouldn't. Ar-Thea taught her students to resist without turning to violence.

"We took him down to the Larder all the same.

Turned him over to the Lizard herself." He chuckled lasciviously. "Maybe she'll make a man out of him."

"Lizard?" Lorrah covered her disgust with pretended curiosity.

"Warden Ar-Lizelle," Traggan corrected himself with mockingly exact pronunciation.

"What?" Now Lorrah was stunned indeed. Her older sister was the Larder's warden? This was terrible! It was easy to keep up her performance with an outraged shriek. "When did *she* get a promotion!"

Traggan eyed her, startled, then shook his head with rough sympathy. "The rotten ones get all the breaks."

"That snake," Lorrah hissed, playing up the rivalry. Inside, she grappled with what this meant.

"Lizard," Traggan corrected. No doubt he thought himself clever.

"What's wrong?" Zathi was at Lorrah's shoulder. Her murderous gaze was fixed on Traggan. The other sergeant held up his hands and took a joking step backward.

"Don't look at me."

"Let's go, Sergeant." Lorrah had lost all taste for this charade. Something must have shown on her face, because the men of Boar Squad got out of her way when she reached the bottom of the stairs.

Zathi was not to be put off. "Tell me what he did."

"I found out some things. Tell you later," Lorrah growled back.

As they got closer to Badger Squad's wagon, the crowd was packed even tighter. Lorrah wondered what the men of Boar Squad were up to. Then she heard Razeet's cheerful voice through the babble of the courtyard.

"We did so fight off a giant badger." She was in the bed of their wagon, crossbow propped over her shoulder. "It's how we got our name."

"A giant badger," one of the guardsmen scoffed. "There's no such thing."

"It was a giant," answered Giniver, sitting on her horse, Cinder. "I ran up its tail and across its back."

"No way," they jeered. And, "You're shitting us."

"Oh, for..." Zathi started pushing her way through. "Out of my way, guardsman."

Razeet was enjoying the attention. "See my sister's armor? Those are tooth marks, friend."

Keerin turned around. Much as she had tried to buff out the row of gouges across her breastplate, they were still plainly visible. Wryly, she said, "Monster tried to bite me in half. That was a fun time. So... much... fun..."

Around them, some of the men chuckled. For once, it wasn't in an ugly way. Someone Lorrah couldn't see called out, "If it was that big, how did you kill it?"

"I didn't say we killed it. We just fought it off." Getting more into the telling, Razeet gestured broadly."Our mage stuck a ball of light on its nose, so it couldn't see."

That had been Keilos, but the men were looking skeptically at Lorrah, the only mage in evidence. A shaft of sorrow pierced her heart. Keilos had always been kind to her. Now he was dead, and Alemin might be next.

"Stop wasting time," she called, but Razeet was still in the midst of her dramatic story. She should have been a minstrel, Lorrah thought sourly.

"Then, it tried to eat Sergeant Zathi —" Razeet made a sharp upward motion, "— but she stabbed it through the roof of its mouth. It spit her out and ran away."

Men grumbled. "No way." "I still don't believe it." "Well, what made those marks, then?" "Probably fell on some rocks."

Zathi managed to get through the crowd. "Badgers, form up," she called as she swung up on Ember's back. "If there's no room at the watering trough, we'll be on our way."

At these words, Lorrah hurried to her seat in the front of the wagon. The sooner they got out of here, the better. She had to figure out what to do about Lizelle.

V

The Revenant

A lemin unbuttoned his gray robe and shrugged it off to bare his chest and arms. That was little help as he sweated in the stifling heat of his cell. The odd pieces he had to juggle with sat loosely in his palm. Using them was too much effort. The afternoon crawled by. Vague images swam in the dark behind his eyes. Nightmares, waiting to fall upon him.

The tale Duessa and Illen had told, of Wharon wielding fire and death, was just one more evil dream to drive from his mind. With great effort, Alemin dragged his thoughts to other things, such as his hopeless quest to understand what was happening in the Larder. Day after day, he pressed his palms to the wall in meditation. Breathing slowly, he opened his mind and tried to listen to the tower.

Today, he had little hope. After waking from nightmares several times each night, he was simply exhausted. Prodded by routine, he pressed his forehead to the wall. Vague murmurs came to his ears. A stray puff of wind had managed to find his window, or some echo came from down the hall.

Perhaps that very lack of focus allowed him to cross a threshold. He found himself in the corridor outside his cell, walking that tight curl toward the stair. There was a sort of light, more than the single lantern at the guard station would account for. Alemin passed Wharon's cell. Soft whimpers drifted through the bars. No doubt he babbled, "I am the warden," yet again. Ar-Thea would have urged compassion for such a broken soul, but Alemin remembered Duessa's vivid scars and the agony she must have endured.

He moved on, aware that he wasn't walking so much as gliding. Wondering about that might break this trance, so he pushed the question away. A slight swirl of energy caught his attention. Without effort, Alemin drifted downward, through the scarred boards of the floor.

He was in the center level of the three that housed prisoners. The mages were in their cells, guards ensconced in their stations. Haafeth and Noluss spoke idly through the bars in their doors. Many other cells were empty. Somehow Alemin could see it all.

He sensed that ripple again, a wave of energy markedly cooler than it should be. Ahead of him, Alemin glimpsed that mysterious prisoner who haunted the Larder. Curiosity gave way to caution. Steps led downward on his right. He took the opportunity to move away from that other phantom.

Next was the lower level, where the less dangerous prisoners were held. Illen and a man called Calsith surreptitiously lobbed sparks across the corridor, laughing when the other one yelped. Elldri sat with her back against the wall, flapping the front of her robe to cool her sweaty face. Two cells farther, Duessa sat on her bed, knees crossed, in a familiar meditative posture. Alemin glided to a stop. He hadn't realized she knew how, but it did make sense that she would hide it from the other prisoners.

This dreamlike experience was much more detailed than Alemin was used to. He almost thought he could talk to her.

Before he decided whether to try it, a cold current flowed around him. That specter again. It seemed to be tracking where he moved. An image came to Alemin, half remembered. A robed figure at the window saying, *"Be quiet while I eat you."*

Nightmares within nightmares. Alemin sped down

the corridor, seeking a way out. The revenant persisted, amused by his effort to escape. It might be safer if he returned to his cell, but that was two levels up. The revenant would intercept him all too easily.

Alemin dropped through the floor, into the level of barracks and offices, anywhere he might be able to hide. A familiar door came up on his left. WARDEN. She wasn't the worst of his troubles at the moment. He slipped through the door.

Ar-Lizelle and Ar-Chindu were at their desks, with documents spread across both surfaces and their chairs slightly turned to face each other. Ar-Chindu was speaking, but Alemin heard it only as a distorted rumble. The warden answered with a shrill quip, equally unintelligible.

He began to think that this was more than some sort of dream. The soft light around him was very like the silvery gray of the ancient tower, where it hadn't been polluted. His mind was roaming the tower. In some way, the Larder itself made this possible.

Astonishing — but Alemin disciplined his emotions. Such a trance could be fragile, easily broken by his own reactions. He moved further through the office, wondering how long this could last. As he passed behind Ar-Lizelle, she abruptly sat up straight.

"Quiet!" Her voice remained muffled, but the single word was clear enough.

Ar-Chindu jerked back, offended by her abruptness. The Warden rested her hands on her desk. Her shoulders sank in a deep sigh. Then she rose slowly — only, her body remained seated. A second Ar-Lizelle stood above the first, this one seemingly molded of blood red glass. Her spirit form was clouded and scratched, with many dark flecks suspended inside it.

"Who's there?" Ar-Lizelle's demand was easy to hear now, but it was different. The sharp edge was softer on the ear. She prowled toward the door.

Alemin glanced down at himself. He also glowed, but with a pale gold radiance. *Vitalis*, he thought. Ar-Lizelle's form was red because her power was based on *lethentros*.

Meantime, Ar-Chindu leaned forward a little. No longer servile, he stared greedily at the warden's still body. Perhaps he hoped to steal this technique somehow. Alemin noted odd ripples in the scene around him, as if a pebble had been dropped into a pool of still water. Only, maybe, he was the pebble.

Seeing no one at the door, Ar-Lizelle stalked back toward her desk. For half a moment, he wondered if she wouldn't see him. Then the onyx eyes narrowed.

"A spy." She hissed like a lizard in truth.

Alemin was too surprised to make up a lie. "I thought this was a dream."

She snarled at him, but Alemin saw movement behind her. An awful presence swelled into the space around them. That wandering prisoner entered just as Alemin had, without opening the door. Instantly Ar-Lizelle spun in that direction, and she choked on whatever she was going to say.

The revenant advanced casually. It wore the same tattered gray robe he had seen before, and its head was shaved bald, just like all the prisoners. Something was wrong with the face, though. It was strangely bland and generic, less an individual than an effigy carved from soft wax. When it smiled, its teeth were those of a shark, jagged rows receding into darkness.

"Who is your friend, Ar-Lizelle?" The voice, too, had a waxy smoothness. "Did you take an understudy and not introduce us?"

"A blundering fool is what he is," Ar-Lizelle answered curtly. Alemin hardly noticed the insult. Even in this spirit form, his knees wobbled with relief that the entity wasn't speaking to him.

"Do you think to deceive me? Here is one who walks the ether."

"By mistake." Ar-Lizelle made a slashing gesture to reject the accusation.

The specter strolled a little aside. Ar-Chindu jumped when it moved past him, but his eyes didn't focus on any of them in their spirit forms.

"Perhaps it is time that you came to me." The revenant spoke almost gently.

"No." Her voice was brittle, a little breathless. The words of someone bracing for a fight. Her hands fell to her sides, with long strips of bright energy coiling out. Whips of flame.

No matter how Alemin disliked Ar-Lizelle, he couldn't let her face the revenant alone. He gathered *vitalis* as best he could.

"Wait! Tell me who you are."

"Quiet, fool!" Ar-Lizelle glared at him, incredulous that he interrupted. "I'll handle this."

The revenant ignored her. It grinned with its shark's mouth. "You poor child. Do you not know? I am the Devourer."

Surely this was no mere phantom. Waves of chill came off of it. Alemin shivered as its lightless gaze bored into his will. He drew a gasping breath. His knees wanted to fold and bow, begging for mercy.

"Let him be," Ar-Lizelle demanded. "I'm not done with this one yet." She might have remained silent, for all the regard the creature showed.

"Shall I show you the meaning of my name?" grinned the revenant.

Vitalis seemed a weak and pathetic flicker against the ageless dark. Yet somehow Alemin summoned the words. "No thank you."

He braced himself for the assault, but to his shock, the revenant spun and leaped at Ar-Lizelle. All semblance of humanity shredded away. Two arms became many, octopus tentacles lined with shark teeth, flung wide to engulf her. The warden jumped away, slashing with her flaming whips.

"Look out!" Alemin leaped to her side. One hand clenched into a fist, raising a barrier between her and the monstrosity. His other hand grabbed her arm. Ar-Lizelle's power also surged in self-defense, and the two sorceries clashed like fire against water. There was a brilliant flash; a roar sounded from the very core of the tower. He and Ar-Lizelle yelled as they were flung apart.

How could it be, that Lorrah came so far only to be thwarted? Worse, it was by the one person she never wanted to see again, her bitch of a sister.

As the fortress walls receded, she sat stiff on the wagon's hard bench. Her fingers crooked together in her lap so tightly that the bones pinched against each other. The riders of Badger Squad stayed close, worried eyes pricking at her.

Lorrah had thought she was ready to hear about Alemin's capture. She knew he had been taken, after all. That dismissal — "real weakling" — still smarted. What did a bunch of bullies know about true strength? Then to hear that Lizelle was in charge of the Larder? Lorrah's mind whirled with despairing fury.

Of course Lizelle was in the way. She always was.

"What did you find out?" Zathi demanded. "Don't pretend it's nothing."

The interruption came as a relief. Lorrah drew a harsh breath. "I can't go to the Larder."

"You can't?" Giniver burst out.

Keerin said, "What?"

"Let her talk," Jaxynne scolded.

"You can't go to the Larder, because —?" Zathi

prompted.

A tight band closed around Lorrah's throat. "My sister is there."

"Your sister." Zathi's face held a wealth of skepticism.

"As a prisoner?" Sethamis hazarded.

"As the warden. That's what he said. Sergeant Traggan. My sister is the warden at the Larder." Lorrah could hardly get the bitter words out. "They call her the Lizard. It sounds just like her." Unless — A sudden hope caught at her heart. "Would he lie about something like that?"

"How would he know she's your sister?" Razeet asked.

Zathi thought about it, then shook her head. "He'd have nothing to gain."

Disappointment sank snake-fangs into Lorrah's heart.

"Why can't you trust her?" Keerin looked at her own sister, Razeet, as if that meant anything.

"Not everyone is lucky enough to get a good family," Lorrah retorted. All the poisoned years flowed through her mind, the daily mockery and interference. "Even if we did, it's different with mages. Everything is about clawing your way up. What one has, the others are denied. Lizelle would do anything to keep me down." She bit out a quote from her sister. "Only a weakling would make allowances for family."

"That's not actually so different," Giniver said quietly.

With mock cheer, Razeet said, "So I guess you can't ask her to let him go as a favor."

"After our father died..." Lorrah's shoulders bowed, but then she jerked upright. "Which was his own fault! But Lizelle tried to blame me. Nothing she ever said was true. I swore I would never listen to her screeching again."

Dust rolled up under the cart wheels to make her eyes burn and tear up. She blotted them angrily with the sleeve of her robe. This was no time for whimpering. Ar-Evaus had brought on his own downfall.

"We were going there to help your friend. Have you decided to leave him behind?" Zathi kept a neutral tone, but the accusation was plain. The words pierced Lorrah like a spear.

"I don't know!" Lorrah glared at her. "If Lizelle finds out Alemin is my friend, she might kill him out of spite. Or do something else. Torture him, I don't know."

Sethamis winced. "That bad?"

Lorrah's chin jerked in a nod. Alemin! She cried it in her mind. She couldn't turn her back on him. That was exactly what her sister accused her of. There was no way out of this. Confronting Ar-Lizelle would make everything worse.

Keerin offered a slightly crooked smile. "I guess we'll have to arrest you after all."

"I can still make the writ," Lorrah flared. "I just can't go into the Larder when you deliver it."

"It sounds like that would be an unnecessary complication," Zathi agreed. "How long until we get there, Jaxynne?"

"Without looking at the charts, I'd guess another week."

Lorrah's heart sank. "That soon?"

"Give or take."

She bit her lip. Earlier today, the question would have been reversed. *"That long?"* It had become something of a daydream for her, to imagine the first moment with Alemin. No other mages around to distract him. Lorrah pictured his eyes lighting up at the unexpected sight. He would call her name with joyous surprise. Perhaps he would faint into her arms, letting her soothe his injuries.

All that was dust, unless they did things exactly right.

"We're close, then." Zathi seemed to be thinking out loud. "Not to be harsh, but we aren't here only for you, Lorrah."

Again, the words stung. Lorrah sat sullen and forced herself to listen.

"We set out to honor Keilos' memory," Zathi said. "To do that, we needed to find another mage like him. One of the minstrels. Someone who deserves the strength of our blades. One who can lead us forward."

They had found Lorrah. Humiliated, she knew that she was no leader. Then she realized two things. If she was no leader, maybe it was because her father and sister kept telling her so, relentlessly. Also, that Zathi wasn't actually speaking to her. On horseback, and in the back of the wagon, the women of Badger Squad watched their sergeant intently.

"There were only six Minstrels to begin with, and Keilos is dead." Zathi's jaw tightened, and Lorrah sensed the dull throb of her regret. She hadn't realized the sergeant has such feelings for Keilos. "We found one, and now there's a chance to find another. Maybe you've wondered what will happen afterward. I can't tell you that I know.

"What I do know is that nothing will change unless we're willing to take some risks. Skaythe will stay a cesspit where everyone claws their way out of the muck. What lies before us now is to choose what risk to take, and when."

Stern black eyes swept over the group. They all sat up a little, alert for her instructions. Lorrah had heard her father make speeches like this on several occasions. Usually it involved furious ranting and death threats. Zathi's version was calm, practical, but somehow more inspiring that any verbal fireworks. Lorrah found herself drawn in. She wanted to believe it, too.

"We've gathered the materials we need," Zathi went on. "Lorrah can forge the writ. While she does that, the rest of us will decide how to deliver it and get our 'prisoner' out of the Larder. You have until tonight's camp to think of ideas." She darted a wry glance at Razeet. "Nothing is too stupid."

"Yes, Sergeant." Lorrah joined in the chorus.

It was like that night when they begged to hear Ar-Thea's ridiculous legend. Lorrah still couldn't believe they took it so seriously. Yet, they had known the details better than she did.

More, Lorrah knew that Alemin believed it. Her knotted fingers sent phantom pain in streaks up her arms. There was no way she could give up on him, when a bunch of strangers were committed. In her eyes, the guardswomen were beautiful. Fearless in their banged-up gear. Lorrah's heart swelled with pride to sit among them.

Reluctantly, she spoke up. "I'm almost done carving the count's stamp, but we still don't have the parchment."

"Actually, we do." Zathi allowed herself a small smile. "I got three sheets at the last outpost. The desk sergeant was so busy with that pig Traggan emptying out his stores, he didn't even ask why I wanted them."

Lorrah's jaw dropped, but then she grinned. "You thief, Sergeant."

"It was a perfectly normal requisition," Zathi retorted.

Laughter rippled through the small squad. Giniver said, "That must be the first helpful thing Traggan ever did."

"Let's hope they're that lazy at the Larder, too," Jaxynne said drily.

Alemin struggled back to his senses with something tangled around him. Half-wrapped in nightmare, he thought he was back in Boar Squad's wagon, bound and gagged and caged. Only when he heard fabric ripping did he realize he had torn his gray robe, and the flimsy bed was shaking beneath him as if it was about to give way.

Panting, he sat up. For certain, that had been no dream. It had been far too elaborate. Breathing slowly, trying to calm himself, he drew his robe back up around his shoulders. The guards had told him if he broke anything he would pay for it. A hasty search revealed only a small tear. Nothing they would notice immediately.

It was more important to understand what he had just experienced. His spirit had been wandering around the tower, as it seemed. That wasn't anything Ar-Thea had ever suggested a mage could do, but this was the Larder. Alemin had a feeling that not all the rules were the same here.

So, the Larder allowed him to... reach through it. If that was what he'd done. Ar-Lizelle seemed also to have some ability, although it had been more difficult for her. In the same way, during their first interview, it had appeared she could cause mental pain, but not perceive his thoughts. This could be a weakness of hers, something it would be helpful to know about in the future.

Alemin was struck by an unpleasant coincidence. In her tale of the Shining Ones, Ar-Thea had said the Devourers were responsible for destroying everything good and beautiful in Skaythe. Because of them, mages ruled by violence, with no check on their cruelty. Those without magic were easy prey for them.

Now it seemed that this malevolent entity roamed the Larder. Alemin had been aware of it from the first hour he arrived, but it hadn't noticed him until today, when it hunted him through the tower. "Devourer," it called itself, exactly like in Ar-Thea's story.

It wasn't that Alemin didn't believe her. The old renegade was right about so many things. He just hadn't thought the tale could be true in a literal sense. Knowing this, he had to question everything. If the tale of the Shining ones was a true history, and not some wishful romance, then what did that mean?

Alemin straightened, startled, as heavy footsteps echoed down the corridor. Guards were coming. A surge of panic gripped his throat. He might not be certain what he'd done, or how, but Ar-Lizelle had seen him. There was going to be a reckoning.

He straightened his robe and pulled his sandals on. The backs of his knees clenched tightly, as they sometimes did before performances. He hopped a few times, loosening his body. This might possibly be the most important performance of his life.

Boots thumped louder, nearer. It was a big contingent, six guards led by Sergeant Rhodec.

"Out."

Alemin didn't resist as they took him down the hall. Guards bracketed him, closer than usual, and Groff, behind him, made sure Alemin saw that his blade was bare and ready. They passed Wharon's cell. The former warden was at the grille. He pierced Alemin with a fierce and accusing gaze.

"You saw it."

The guards pushed Alemin by before he could decide how to respond.

"You saw!" Wharon yelled after them.

All the way down through the Larder, the imprisoned mages watched him marched by. And of course they did. Every one of them must have felt that burst from deep within the tower. You'd have to be drained of all magic to avoid sensing it. Some, like Duessa, stared through the bars without a word. Others called out, "What was that?" and "What did you do?" Haafeth mocked him, "Oooh, Juggler, you've been a very bad boy!" Alemin shrugged, afraid to say anything, while the guards yelled at them to mind their own business.

Inevitably, they took him to Ar-Lizelle's office. Ar-Chindu opened the door before they got there. Everything had been cleared from the desks. Ar-Lizelle was seated, outwardly calm, but to a mage's sight she pulsed with fury. As on the night of Alemin's arrival, a single chair faced the main desk. He settled into it without being told.

Razor-sharp eyes stabbed past him, to the row of guards. "Rhodec, Groff." Those two took up stations beside the door. The other four trooped out.

There was a long pause. Not knowing what to say, Alemin kept silent. When Ar-Chindu laid out a sheet of paper, the rustling fell like thunder into the tense silence.

"I should whip you bloody." Ar-Lizelle's lips barely moved as she spoke.

Remembering the flaming whips she had tried to use, Alemin merely nodded.

"Tell me what you did."

"It was an accident," he answered slowly.

"Accident."

The muscles in his neck tightened painfully. He forced himself to relax, as he did when the crowd in front of the stage was getting ugly.

"It was hot in my cell. I felt like I couldn't breathe. To distract myself, I imagined that I was walking through the Larder." All the time, he screened his mind with the rustle of branches in the wind.

"Yes, I hear you have a great fondness for meditation." Ar-Lizelle tapped a claw-like fingernail on her desk.

Alemin felt a prickle of indignation. Who had told her that? Maybe it was Illen. He couldn't think about that now. Better to focus on the problem in front of him.

"I found that I was seeing more detail. People moving around in their cells, the guards walking patrol." One of Ar-Lizelle's brows flicked upward, but she said nothing. "I also sensed that someone... or thing, was following me. It felt dangerous. I kept moving downward, but it was getting closer.

"When I got to your office, it wasn't to spy. I needed

a place to hide. You sensed me." Alemin allowed a hint of question.

"Of course I did," she snapped. "This is my domain."

Ar-Chindu sat at his desk, writing it all down. Now he glanced up with a baffled sneer. He didn't know what they were talking about, and he resented it.

"The revenant followed me into your office, and — you know the rest." Alemin was afraid to ask, but he needed to know. "I didn't understand some of what it said. Do you? What is it?"

"I've known it was there." The warden's lined face twisted with disgust, maybe at Alemin. "What it is? No. In fact, this is only the second time I've seen it. Today is the most I've heard it speak. You do have a special way," she sneered.

"Ahem." Ar-Chindu set his pen down. Ar-Lizelle speared him with her glare. Apologetically defiant, he said, "Forgive me, Warden. What are you talking about?"

In silence, Ar-Lizelle studied her assistant. Alemin seized the moment to look behind him, at the two guards flanking the door. Groff, the younger one, tried to keep a blank face, but his confusion was evident in a slight pinch of the brow. However, from Rhodec's wary gaze, he knew exactly what they meant. Alemin quickly turned back to the warden.

Ar-Lizelle must have decided to trust her assistant. "There is an... entity here in the Larder. A revenant, you might say." She mocked Alemin with a glance.

"This 'revenant' was responsible for what happened?" The junior mage appeared doubtful, but interested.

"In part." She flicked a grim eye at Alemin, who spread his hands in apology.

"It's real." Rhodec unexpectedly spoke up. "If you've been in the tower long enough, you know."

"That will do," Ar-Lizelle said, but she nodded to

acknowledge his support. "It doesn't seem to care about us. Most of the time, it simply roams the halls. I thought it harmless, before —"

She broke off, and Alemin wondered, *"Before what?"*

"Perhaps it was focused on Ar-Wharon, since he was warden," she went on. "Now that I'm in charge, I hear it more often. It whispers, walking in my dreams."

Alemin hunched his shoulders in sympathy. Ar-Lizelle frowned.

"You see it, too?" Then she rolled her eyes, disgusted. "Of course you do."

"I don't suppose there's any way to verify this?" Ar-Chindu complained. His tone was resentful, even jealous. "He could be lying. This one likes the attention."

"Not from that thing," Alemin retorted.

Ar-Lizelle wasn't happy to be questioned. "You're the one in charge of records. Do some research," she snapped. Ar-Chindu bowed obsequiously, but his eyes glinted with anger. The warden turned back to Alemin. "As for you, if you rouse that creature again, I'll have you whipped bloody. Understand?"

Alemin winced, but she brought up something he'd been wondering more and more.

"Er," he ventured. "Not that I want that, but why haven't you?"

Ar-Chindu's jaw dropped with almost childish fury, and behind him Alemin heard a scraping of booted feet preparing to pounce. Ar-Lizelle spoke with deadly quiet.

"Oh, I truly wish I could treat you all as you deserve. Sneaking food everywhere, the shoddy work you do. It would make so many things easier. However —" Her eyes blazed as if she would burn two holes through Alemin. "That creature is already far too dangerous, and I suspect that every moment of pain or fear makes it stronger. Until I know how to stop it, or dispel it, I can only try to weaken it by shortening its feed."

Alemin nodded slowly. "That makes sense."

"I don't need your approval!" The warden came to her feet, the flats of her hands slamming the desk top. "Mark me well. If I ever sense you in my office again, I'll have you thrown into the canyon. Maybe the revenant will follow you down there!"

She nodded sharply, and the two guards hauled Alemin up from his seat. He wasn't completely sorry about that. Ar-Lizelle did make an effort at fairness, but she was more frightened by the revenant's attack than she wanted anyone to know.

Wet stone gleamed as Lorrah mixed the ink. The makeshift grindstone on her lap held shards of charcoal, bloodthorn leaf, skyberry juice, and a bit of oleya oil in a shallow depression. She focused, setting the spell that would render this ink impermeable and make it shine in the eyes of those who could see. All the while, she wished she was smashing the mortar stone into Ar-Lizelle's smug face.

Lorrah glanced around the camp site, where the guardswomen did their evening chores with little jokes and smiles. She envied that they were so relaxed.

For herself, knowledge was a sullen inner ache, like a bad tooth throbbing. She couldn't bear that Alemin was in the clutches of her hateful sister. What was Ar-Lizelle doing to him, even at this moment? The Larder had such a grim reputation. Beatings, torture — the possibilities were as endless as they were terrible. Lorrah couldn't shake the fear away.

At last, she carefully tilted the stone to dribble the finished ink into one of Jaxynne's empty bottles. This part was done. Lorrah rose and took her two stones down to the creek bed where she'd found them. The remains of the ink couldn't be washed away now that she had enchanted it, so she turned the stones over and buried them deep in the stream bed, out of sight.

Cold water did little to relieve Lorrah's worry. Shaking off the last moisture, she returned to settle on a stool. She ought to meditate, but her foreboding was so strong that she knew she could never relax that much. Over all these days, the road had carried them closer to Yergha. Surely she would be able to reach Alemin by now. He'd want to know that help was coming.

That was just an excuse. Lorrah could admit it. She wouldn't be at peace until she knew he was all right.

She let a breath go and sank into meditation. Images blossomed in her mind. Alemin and Berisan strolling down the long trail between villages. Their graceful fingers flicking pebbles back and forth in those clever circles. Sometimes Alemin would smile at her in the sly way he usually directed at the peasant girls who crowded up to the stage.

Lorrah remembered the extra training Peremain had given her, before Ar-Evaus dismissed her from his service. She held to the memory of Alemin's smile, and she reached.

Far across the land, something gleamed like a distant campfire. She willed herself closer, but turbulence broke against her. A barrier, trying to keep her away. The harder she pressed, the more it cut at her. She quieted herself and inched closer until the resistance no longer held against her mind.

Lingering daylight outlined a tall, round tower, its roof partly collapsed. The faint glow she traced brought her to a narrow window. She eased up to it.

The cell beyond was tiny and cramped. Its walls were blackened as if by fire. A man lay on a narrow cot. Lorrah's heart crashed in her chest. Alemin was barely recognizable. His fine, glossy curls had been hacked away, and his face was so thin and tired! A shapeless gray robe hung on his skinny frame.

Lorrah hovered, as if she sat on a chair beside the cot.

She whispered, "What have they done to you?"

His eyelids had been sagging, but now dark eyes snapped open. "Lorrah?" An incredulous smile tugged at his lips. Then dismay wiped it away. "No. No, you can't be here."

"Well, I am." She would have hugged him if she could. It hurt so much to see him worn down. "And I call that gratitude, telling me to leave when I barely found you."

"Don't." The strained whisper tore at her. An unsteady hand reached out, and Lorrah reached back. Even though she was only present in spirit, their hands met. A thrill went through her. Then he swallowed, and she felt his terrible thirst as if it was her own.

"You have to go." His normally glib voice was a raven's croak. "She's looking for you."

"You mean Lizelle? Yes, I know about her," Lorrah cut in bitterly.

"Every day she wanders by. She asks without saying a word. At first I thought she wanted all of us, but there's only one she keeps mentioning." Alemin's hollow eyes gleamed with urgency. "Why is she after you?"

"We're sisters. We hate each other." Lorrah felt slightly ill, but she didn't want to burden Alemin with more than he already had to deal with.

"I can see it now. Your chin and your ears are so alike." The corners of his mouth twitched, trying to form a smile. Lorrah brushed at her right ear, suddenly bashful. "Me and Berisan, our sister hated us, too."

"It doesn't matter." Lorrah rallied herself. "Tell me where you are in the prison. How can we find you?"

"Find me?" He sagged a little. "You can't."

"Were getting you out of there." Lorrah projected all the confidence she could muster.

"How?" he breathed, full of wonder and doubt.

"We're still planning," she admitted. "It's why I need to know —"

Something inside him crumbled. Alemin clung to her hand, desperation flooding into her. "It's horrible here. You can't imagine. We're hungry all the time, thirsty as camels. They work us... And they stare at us... But it's the nightmares. Always nightmares. No wonder people go insane here."

He was babbling, exhausted. It broke Lorrah's heart to see the ruin of this man, whose sense of humor had carried them all through so much.

"We'll save you," she vowed.

"Berisan and the others? Has it been six months already?"

Lorrah felt a twinge of pain. Berisan was his brother, but it hurt that he cared more for the rest of the minstrels, when she was actually doing something to help him.

"No," she began, but broke off as an unseen shock rippled around them. Alemin's image shuddered in her mind's eye. Was it that barrier again, seeking to drive her from the Larder? The vibration expanded into a sobbing moan and quickly rose to a keening whine.

"What is that?" Lorrah cried.

"It's the Larder. It does this." She could barely hear Alemin through the din. "Nobody will talk about it."

A pull was growing, like the current racing to a waterfall. It was trying to tear them apart. The wailing rose to a howl of unimaginable agony. Lorrah couldn't tell if it was one person crying out, or a chorus of them, or some kind of monstrous gale. From Alemin, she received a brief image of a foaming whirlpool surrounded by broken rocks. It sucked at them both, greedy to drag them in.

Every instinct was to drop contact and save herself. Somehow Lorrah found the strength to tighten her grip. "Hang on!"

"This won't hurt me." She barely heard him. "Lorrah, let go."

"No," she screamed into the maelstrom. Lorrah tried to hold his mind, not with childish infatuation but as if she held a drowning man above the waves. "I won't let it take you."

"Something is happening here. I have to —"

Alemin was torn away, and Lorrah flung back to herself with a wail. "No!"

She jolted backward on the stool and her head slammed into the dirt. For a moment she could only stare into a swirl of lantern light and pain. Then the faces of Badger Squad crowded around her. Lorrah was dizzy, confused about where she was. She let the guardswomen sit her up and bat the dust off her robe. It took a while longer to separate their questions from the cacophony that still rang in her ears, even as she knew it wasn't truly there.

"What happened?" Jaxynne's voice broke through, angrily concerned.

"Spell gone wrong?" Giniver guessed.

"Hope that sister of hers didn't get hold of her," Razeet said.

"It wasn't Ar-Lizelle." That was the only thing Lorrah could be sure of.

Zathi watched, stoic as ever. When she caught Lorrah's eye, she asked, "Your friend. Not dead, I hope."

"There's something. In the Larder, where they have him. It was screaming, like —" Lorrah shivered and dug her fingers into the hair at her temples. "Maybe a defense? I'll have to pick through it, try and figure this out."

The women exchanged glances. They must all be thinking the same that she was, that prisoners were tortured in a place like the Larder. Old anger flared in Lorrah's chest. If Ar-Lizelle was responsible, she was going to pay for everything Alemin had suffered!

Even as she made that promise, Lorrah knew how hollow it was. She couldn't risk confronting her sister personally. There was good reason for that. Snatching Alemin from her prison would have to do as revenge.

For now, the grim truth was, Lorrah could do nothing to help him. Alemin was on his own.

Alemin stumbled up from his cot, emotionally torn. He was ashamed to break down like that, yet it was an incredible relief to touch Lorrah's mind and feel her genuine concern. It was alarming to think she might have exposed herself on his account.

The howling that marked each day's end had shattered his concentration. The noise was never easy to listen to, but tonight it was worse than usual. The cries were visceral, and much, much closer. Alemin didn't only hear psychic screams, but actual sounds. He clutched the bars in his door and jammed his face against them, trying to see down the darkened corridor.

It was Wharon's voice screaming, he was sure of it. Though they weren't friends, he couldn't bear to hear the noises the former warden was making. Alemin sucked in a breath, marshaling his minstrel's voice that could be heard across a noisy square.

"Guards!" He yelled. "Help him! Something is wrong!"

His words were lost in Wharon's dreadful cries. Alemin didn't hear any response. Not such much as a booted footstep. Ar-Lizelle had warned him not to send his spirit into the tower again, but surely she hadn't been thinking of something like this when she said it.

He couldn't wait for help. With a groan, Alemin stuck his arms through the grille. Then he blew out a breath and slumped against the rigid boards. His spirit was down the corridor in a moment. At the door to Wharon's cell he froze and couldn't make himself go any farther.

The ceiling was a maelstrom of dagger-like rocks and seething waves, exactly what he had seen in so many nightmares. Tentacles lined with shark's teeth stretched down to clutch Wharon like so many nooses. The man hung suspended, his arms splayed and head thrown back. His eyes were wide and white, mouth stretched in a hideous gurgling shriek.

Whatever this was, Wharon fought it. He tried to focus his magic. Red flames swirled around him, but they were drawn up toward the ceiling. A mist rose from his eyes and mouth, grayish wisps streaked with crimson. Wharon screamed. Lightning lashed the air. He convulsed. Vapor streamed upward, sucked into the throat of the vortex.

In his spirit form, Alemin felt the cyclonic pull. He focused on the door frame, as if it could shield him. His own voice panted and whined along with Wharon. This had to be the Devourer that haunted the Larder. Nothing else had such tentacles. It had no human shape at all. Perhaps this was its true form.

Everything in him wanted to flee back to his cell. Or to keep still as a spider in a crack. Anything to keep that horror from noticing him. A last shred of courage held him in the door. Any bit of information might help him, or Ar-Lizelle, or one of the other mages, to defeat this horror one day.

Wharon's flames had snuffed out. He still struggled, feeble twitching without strength behind it. Even the ruddy mist was nearly gone. Dark skin went sallow, the face wizened and slack as the peel of an over-ripe fruit. All life and power had been sucked out of him, trailing away with the last wisps of vapor that vanished into the ceiling.

The Larder's screaming faded along with it, echoing into a lingering moan of grotesque satisfaction. The vortex slowed and coalesced to the center, where a human face appeared. Alemin was sickened, but not surprised, to recognize that evil specter that called itself Devourer. The tentacles loosened carelessly. With a final exhalation, the maw on the ceiling closed entirely. The husk of Wharon's body slid to the floor with a dry, rasping sigh.

Alemin's spirit fled at last, back to his own body. He remained slumped against the door, while the cell twisted and shifted around him. He swallowed, and swallowed again, sweating with more than the heat of the closed space.

"How. Why," he rasped, unable to form a whole thought. "What. That. That —"

His knees wobbled. Alemin struggled to free his arms and sank to the floor. It was like one of those nights in the carnival, when he and Berisan and Keilos tried to see who could drink the most. There was nothing in his stomach, but still he clamped his teeth to keep from retching.

Alemin bent his head and lay down, taking meager comfort in the stability of the floor boards. He lay there trying to make sense of what he'd witnessed. It was the revenant, yes, making the same attack it had attempted against Ar-Lizelle. Was that only a few hours ago?

His thoughts skittered away from that, seeking refuge in mundanity. Alemin had been yelling for the guards, but none had come. Was that out of self-preservation, or as a punishment for his affront to Ar-Lizelle? Regardless, they would arrive soon to take him down for supper. Their ironclad schedule bound them. They wouldn't care if Alemin had no appetite.

First, they would find Wharon dead. What would they do? If they blamed Alemin, how could he possibly explain? He wondered, too, if the warden would be surprised. Well, and why would it matter? She'd once defeated Wharon in order to secure her position as warden. The man's fate was nothing to her.

A long time had passed. Alemin was beginning to think that the guards weren't coming. He often had that fear, that he would be left to starve in this wretched cell. At last, he heard the thump of boot heels, and unfriendly fists banging on a door down the hall. Words echoed down to him, oddly refracted. Then came a cry of disgust, followed by extended cursing.

Groaning, Alemin got his hands under him and pushed himself up. Still dizzy and weak, he clung to the grille for support. A lantern approached. Rhodec and Groff again, scowling as they undid the bolts, but not with the usual defensive anger.

"Back it up, Juggler." Groff's command was almost gentle. When Alemin walked out, stiff as an old man, he didn't curse him for a sluggard. "Come on," was all he said.

Passing Wharon's cell, Alemin glimpsed Stegnor and another guard wrapping something in the blanket from the bed. He didn't need to ask what it was.

Down the stairs and across the courtyard, he walked in a daze. Twice he clutched the wall when his knees suddenly wobbled. There was no talk in the corridors, or in the line to get food. Everyone seemed to know that something dreadful had happened. Alemin felt their eyes on him, quick jabs of curiosity and suspicion. He couldn't bring himself to care what they thought. It was all too much, this hideous prison full of savages.

The smell of food troubled Alemin's stomach, so that he took only a bit of dried bread and a bowl of boiled peas. Haafeth, behind him in line, took the chunk of over-cooked meat Alemin had skipped over. "No sense wasting it," he declared with mercenary cheer. Nobody bothered to argue about it.

At the table, he found himself hemmed in by Illen and Duessa, with Elldri and Bettain opposite. It was a protective seating arrangement, something Alemin could appreciate. Though he had to wonder if they were being considerate or just grabbing the best gossip for themselves. Neither possibility would have surprised him.

Alemin's mind felt dull as the wooden spoon in his hand. The peas steamed fitfully, but their smell made his stomach worse. He pushed the bowl away. The others ate, and eyed him warily. Finally, Duessa leaned in.

"You look like shit."

"Thanks," Alemin answered automatically. He tore off a bit of his bread and compressed the white fluff between his fingers.

Impatiently, Illen asked, "It was Wharon, wasn't it."

"Why Wharon?" Bettain snapped.

"Everybody else is here," Illen replied scornfully.

Alemin nodded silently. He couldn't bear to look and see that Illen was right. In the morning, there had been eleven prisoners. Now there were just ten. Cautiously, he tasted the wedge of flattened bread to see if his stomach could manage it.

"One less worry, then." Illen sneered, pretending he didn't care, but then darted a glance at Duessa.

Her dark eyes glittered. "Couldn't have happened to a nicer guy."

Illen nodded with sour agreement. The bread didn't turn Alemin's stomach, so he ate the rest of it. Elldri silently reached over to take his bowl of boiled peas. She set a pair of orange wedges in its place.

"You're really out of it." Duessa frowned at Alemin's lack of protest. She jabbed her own spoon at him. "If you aren't eating, then start talking."

"Yeah, Juggler," Haafeth interrupted from Illen's other side. "We know you didn't do it, so what happened?"

Everything in Alemin's body went painfully tight. His legs, back, neck, jaw. He couldn't pull in a breath. All down the table, eyes were on him.

"Come on," Bettain chided. And Illen said, "Spit it out."

Alemin took another bit from his bread and methodically pressed it into a pasty white cube. His mind felt mired in a bog, so many thoughts shouting to be heard. How could he explain, who should he trust? What would they do with the knowledge? Ar-Lizelle was up on the dais, watching him along with everyone else. Maybe she wanted him to keep it a secret. Alemin didn't need a whipping on top of everything else.

Yet, all their lives were at stake. Even Haafeth, who chewed his meat in eager anticipation of a gruesome story.

Much as Alemin reached out and tried to befriend the prisoners, that was just a strategy for staying safe. He didn't trust them at all. Could that change?

"Tell us." Elldri lisped. Everyone looked in surprise, since she hardly ever talked. Somberly, she urged, "You have to tell, or it will eat you alive."

Alemin grimaced at the horribly appropriate image. The prisoners deserved to be warned about the revenant that haunted the Larder, but the story was so bizarre, why would they believe him?

Then again, they lived in the Larder. They probably had some idea, but didn't want to put a name to it. Alemin swallowed heavily and began.

"There is a revenant that haunts the Larder. You might have seen it. Or dreamed about it. It looks like one of us, a prisoner. Shave-headed, gray robe?"

He searched their expressions for recognition or rejection. The prisoners eyed each another. Nobody wanted to admit anything.

"There are lots of nightmares." Illen didn't answer the question.

"This afternoon, the revenant attacked me and Ar-Lizelle." Alemin decided not to mention exactly how that had happened. "Well, it went for Ar-Lizelle and I got in the way."

"It went for the Lizard and you stopped it?" Bettain asked, incredulous.

"Hey," Duessa scowled. "She saved my life."

"One time," her friend shot back.

"That's when she dragged you down?" Duessa asked.

"After. We fought it off, more or less by accident," Alemin hurried on, before anyone could figure out he had been in his cell at the time, and wondered how this alleged battle was possible.

Illen said, "Yeah, I felt something."

"Like an explosion," Haafeth said, and belched. "I love explosions."

The other prisoners groaned and laughed, but heads were nodding along the table. The joke relaxed them enough to admit they had felt the burst, too.

"That's why she marched me down in front of everyone. To figure it out," Alemin went on. "She said if it happened again, she would throw me into the canyon and see if the revenant followed me down. I thought that was all of it."

"But then?" Noluss prodded from the other side of Illen.

Alemin absolutely couldn't mention his conversation with Lorrah. If the prisoners knew there was hope for him, but none for them, there might not be enough guards to stop them from killing him.

"The revenant came back, right at dusk. It went after Wharon instead of me." Just saying those words made his throat close up in a hard knot. Alemin swallowed, and swallowed again. "Have you —" He coughed. "Uhm, have you had the nightmare where the ceiling in your cell is like a whirlpool full of shark's teeth and lightning?"

Furtive stillness settled over the table. That was an answer, of sorts.

"That was there," Alemin continued. "It filled his whole ceiling. Tentacles came out of it, holding him trapped.

They were lined with shark's teeth. Wharon was fighting, summoning fire, but it turned into mist and was sucked into the whirlpool. No matter how much he fought, it consumed his power and then, I think, his soul. It dropped him, and he was dead before he fell."

The prisoners were tense, rapt. Alemin cleared his throat and rubbed his nose. Sudden, sarcastic applause made all of them jump.

"Well, Juggler. A thrilling tale," Ar-Lizelle declared from up on the dais. "Shall I throw money?"

Alemin was tired, but not so much he couldn't hear the warning. Hear — and defy it.

"Yes please," he answered wearily. Someone muffled a laugh.

Ar-Lizelle ignored that and proclaimed to the hall in her shrill tone. "You have all heard that a prisoner has died. We will finish this meal with a special ration of beer." A surprised murmur went through both prisoners and guards. "No one is to enter the top of the tower until I know it is safe. That means you — " she slanted an eye at Alemin "— will be moved one level down."

Was that a bribe, to stop him telling the story? Surely she knew that would only make it easier for him to talk to the other prisoners.

At her side, Captain Morthem said, "We'll see to it, Lady."

Ar-Lizelle moved to sit down, but Illen burst out, "Did it really have tentacles with shark teeth on them?"

Her expression stiffened, but Alemin knew how much she valued telling the truth. "It did. And that is all the discussion I wish to hear."

So the warden said, but from the prisoners' expressions, Alemin was fairly sure the discussion had only begun.

VI

Lost Echoes

L orrah's head pounded, and her neck twinged from gritting her teeth. The guardswomen sparred and archers shot at targets, seemingly without effort. It was only Lorrah who couldn't control her working.

Now that she had seen Alemin's face, and knew the toll his captivity was taking, she was desperate to build her skills. Yet still, after days of practice, no flame blossomed about the rock that served as her latest target. Only light, or a haze of noisome smoke. She let go a gust of frustration and rubbed her neck.

Ar-Evaus had made it seem so easy to wield his favorite spell, the fire-lash. He would brag to Lizelle how that cord of pure malice would wrap around whatever it touched, and then ignite. "They will burn and not escape the flame!"

Lizelle had applied herself ruthlessly, while just the idea made Lorrah wince. Maybe that was the whole problem. Even as angry as she sometimes became, she had never wanted to burn anyone.

The lash itself, Lorrah formed perfectly — but only with *vitalis*. She could lift a heavy stone from twenty feet off, or pluck a cluster of skyberries from a high branch. Could she summon fire? Ha.

Jaxynne stood nearby, one eye on Lorrah and another watching Sethamis practice with the crossbow. Razeet pulled back with string, raised it, and shot in a smooth series of motions. A hiss and a thud, and the bolt stood in the practice dummy. All while Sethamis fumbled to nock the bolt. Lorrah knew exactly how she felt.

Absently, Jaxynne asked, "Why do you even need that?"

"It's how we're meant to fight," Lorrah answered tightly. Mages threw fire blasts. Everyone knew that.

Lizelle wouldn't have hesitated to point out her weakness. She was always so confident and strong. Her own sister, and her eternal foe. Something coiled in Lorrah's stomach when she thought about it.

Giniver wandered up, blotting sweat from the back of her neck. She and Keerin had just finished sparring with Zathi. "You know, if I had to fight Zathi for real, I wouldn't be using the skills she taught me. She can anticipate what I'd do."

"That's true," Jaxynne agreed. She glanced at Lorrah. "Maybe you don't want to practice what your sister already knows. What you need are moves she won't expect."

Reluctantly, Lorrah nodded. Inside, she fumed that they didn't know what they were talking about. To show them, she reached past Sethamis, who was aiming her shot, and grabbed the practice dummy. Light weight, it was easily hoisted into the air.

Sethamis jumped and cursed. Her bolt went far aside. The dummy's head was only propped on, and it tumbled down as the straw body flew. Razeet's white teeth flashed as she bellowed laughter. "Lorrah, you're such a brute!"

Embarrassed, Lorrah tried to set the dummy back down where it had been. It teetered, then slowly fell over. She had no choice but to join in the merriment. Zathi shook her head and sheathed her sword.

"That's enough. Ready for the road."

Laughter did make Lorrah feel a little better, but Jaxynne still eyed her thoughtfully. "You know, Keilos did more with his barriers than any attack."

"This is all Ar-Thea had time to teach me," Lorrah grumbled.

Zathi moved past, pulling her helmet off and running a hand through her short black hair. "You want to be your own person, Lorrah. I understand that. Just make sure you don't waste the little time we have, being someone you're not."

Lorrah shrugged, deflated. She stood, brushing dust from her robe. Keerin strolled by. "Besides, we're the warriors. Fighting is what we're here for."

"Yeah, don't take our job," Razeet teased.

That seemed less likely with every passing day.

Wharon's death forced a re-ordering of the Larder's inexorable routine. Alemin was placed in a different cell, as promised. This one was on the inside of the tower, with only blackness beyond the slot window. Several empty cells separated him from the other mages, though stray currents of power still reached him sometimes.

On the other hand, his nightmares were less intense. Even the shrieking at dawn seemed easier to bear.

After the morning meal, Alemin found himself on a different work crew. No doubt Ar-Lizelle wanted to sever the ties he was building with the prisoners on the kitchen work crew. He was teamed with Ferrant, a prisoner he barely knew. Nor was he likely to. The man kept darting anxious glances at Alemin, and crept around as if he expected an attack.

They were sent to tend Ar-Lizelle's garden. When Alemin asked what to do, Ferrant jumped away. "Don't talk to me!"

Alemin laughed wearily. It hurt to be blamed for Wharon's death, but the work itself was some consolation. Familiar scents of earth and vegetation brought back the days he and Berisan had spent tending their family's garden.

Hidden as they were, it had been the only job they were allowed. Cool dirt ground under Alemin's fingernails as he plucked the weeds. Then he and Ferrant carried bucket after bucket of water from the pump nearby. The burden got heavier with every trip.

Once, when the guards turned away, Alemin dared to drink a swallow from the bucket before he poured it over the plants. Ferrant watched with an anxious frown. Alemin winked. You'd think he had cursed the man from how quickly Ferrant scurried back to the water pump.

While Alemin's hands were busy, his mind juggled ideas. If the Devourer was quiescent after making a meal of Wharon, maybe Alemin would have a chance to learn more about it.

That would be easier if he had help. Since most of the prisoners didn't believe what he had seen, he didn't think they would cooperate. Besides which, there was still Ar-Lizelle's threat to throw Alemin in the canyon if he disturbed the revenant again. No, this would have to be his own project.

Once they were escorted down to the courtyard, Ferrant scurried away as fast as he could. Alemin followed his usual habit of gulping water and refilling the cup. Illen caught up with him before he even sat down with Duessa and the other women.

"What are we going to do?" Illen demanded in a low voice.

"I don't know what we can do," Alemin dodged.

Other prisoners seemed to be loitering closer than usual. Noluss and Kyanon to one side, Haafeth on the other. Maybe they believed more than they wanted to admit. Alemin kept quiet. He didn't like the number of guards tramping around on the walkway directly above them.

"The problem won't go away," Bettain cut in, "and I don't plan to wait for some specter to take me out."

"It'll pick us off one by one," Kyanon predicted

dourly.

Haafeth radiated skepticism. "What are we supposed to do about some invisible creature?"

Alemin didn't have an answer to that, but Duessa did.

"Learn to see it," she retorted. "We're mages. We live by mind and will." Duessa turned to Alemin. "How did you do it?"

She'd hit on something with that. The prisoners could build on this without risking Ar-Lizelle's wrath. Slowly, Alemin reached into his sleeve and brought out the bits of scrap he'd gathered for juggling. The chip from the wall, the button, the bit of ham bone. Let the guards think he was passing the time with this diversion.

"It's about the tower," he told them once the pieces were moving. "You've all been here longer than me. Some of you already know that the Larder has its own voice. Sometimes you can get it to answer you. That's how I saw the Devourer. I was meditating and I listened to the tower."

"What bullshit," Haafeth turned away. Alemin was just as glad to let him go.

"We're all mages." He nodded to Duessa. "Each one of us can connect with the Larder. If I'm right, then through the Larder, we can connect with each other." He kept the stones moving, but glanced around the watchers. Duessa's scarred face lit.

"We can talk to each other, and the guards won't hear?"

"Ar-Lizelle might," Alemin cautioned. "I don't know how often she listens. Not Ar-Chindu, though."

"He'd think it was beneath him," Bettain said.

"You just want to make us all meditate," Illen complained.

Alemin grinned, and did a few fancy tricks for the sake of the lurking guards. The three women clapped dutifully. He blessed them for helping keep the appearance going.

"Not all of us at once. They'll figure out we're up to something. Just three or four. Whenever you can, touch the tower." He leaned back a little, pressing his back to the hot surface. "Try to connect with it. Building the link takes time."

"When we're alone in our cells," Noluss suggested.

Alemin purposely dropped the wooden button. As it skittered away, he caught the other pieces. He went to collect his button, and left them with that. What they did with the idea was up to them.

"Got your barrier set?" Giniver jumped a little, armor rattling lightly as she prepared for the match.

In the dusk light, Lorrah examined her glimmering golden shield critically. Raising the barrier was second nature, now that she had practiced it so much.

"Come ahead."

Giniver stepped up, flexing her mailed fingers. She set her feet and jabbed at the barrier. Lorrah felt the bump. The barrier flickered, but stayed firm. Behind Giniver, Zathi was sparring with Keerin, but Lorrah could tell Zathi had an eye on them.

"Harder," Lorrah encouraged her partner.

"You asked for it." Next came an explosion in the form of a mailed fist. Several hard blows rocked the barrier. "That's good, not squishy at all," the guardswoman approved.

"Who are you calling squishy?" Lorrah laughed back at her.

More days had passed as their wagon rolled over one of the ancient highways. A dim shape now rose on the horizon, and there was a shadow across the land. Yergha

Drop, and the Larder. Badger Squad was getting close. There wasn't much time left. Sweat trickled between Lorrah's breasts, and her neck felt tight from holding the casting. She reminded herself to draw deep, even breaths.

"What else?" she asked her training partner.

Giniver drew her sword. Instinctive fear gripped Lorrah, to see that sharpened steel pointed at her. She tightened her shield and nodded. "All right."

Sword jabs were different, a sharper blow, but the blade skidded aside. Then a bash with the shield, which bounced back. Giniver adjusted her footing to account for that, and glided aside, probing to find the edge of the barrier. Lorrah turned with her, confidence rising. She could do this.

Then, movement from the other side. Zathi! A rock, thrown hard. Startled, Lorrah extended her barrier to block the missile, while Giniver made a serious lunge at the barrier. Lorrah pushed it back. Whooping, Keerin and Razeet also started to throw rocks. Lorrah trembled a little.

"All of you?" she complained.

"Keep it firm!" Zathi barked. "Do you think the prison guards will go easy on you?"

She too drew her sword and charged. Golden lights flared. Lorrah held against the four of them, but her heart was pounding harder. She had to bring her barrier closer, lapping around all sides. Lorrah didn't dare look at Zathi, to see her ruthless expression. How far would they push her?

Through the buffeting, she heard a sharp click. A droll voice put in, "That's not all of us."

Jaxynne cocked her crossbow and raised it to leisurely take aim.

"Agh!" Real fear surged in Lorrah's veins. She couldn't tell if Jaxynne was aiming directly at her, or a bit to the side. Surely she wouldn't risk shooting Lorrah! Before the guardswoman could fire, Lorrah reached past her barrier and yanked the crossbow out of her hands.

"Whoa!" Jaxynne cried. She scrambled after her weapon. "Good one."

But Lorrah's barrier wavered, and suddenly there was a pair of armored women crashing against her. Giniver had her arm behind her, steel at her throat. All of them breathed lightly.

"Damn it," Lorrah said.

Giniver let go, then flexed her wrist ruefully. Zathi nodded and stepped back.

"Good effort, mage. Keep working at it."

"Yes Sergeant." For someone who had lost the bout, she felt pretty good. *Who's helpless now, Ar-Lizelle?"*

When afternoon chores were over and Alemin was alone, he followed his goal. The new cell didn't have a wall of the ancient tower, but he couldn't let that stop him. He knew it was there, just a few yards away. Alemin sat on the cot, which fortunately was not as rickety, and settled himself to meditate.

A slight tug of flowing energy drew him to his goal. The ancient walls were honeycombed with small connecting chambers. Wisps of energy trickled between them, a circulation of sorts. To his surprise, he recognized *vitalis*, though soured in some way.

There also was a resonance from below the earth. Some hidden chamber balanced the upper structure. From this dark well, plumes of a different power rose up, musty and stagnant. Alemin's immediate thought was of the Devourer. He didn't let his mind linger with that.

It was hours until the outburst that would come at dusk. That should help him reach deeper into whatever awareness the Larder possessed. Alemin drifted, trying to quell his impatience. After a time he couldn't measure, a faint echo reached him.

Shrieks again, but he held himself steady. This chaos

was part of the Larder as much as the specter evidently was. He couldn't run from it if he hoped to understand. Tentatively, he moved himself toward the faint cries and pressed out a gentle query. The same question he had asked that very first night.

"Who are you? Why do you weep?"

Something quieted in the tower. A mental presence rippled back to him. No, he realized — a multiplicity. Shreds of memory and shadows of personality mingled and overlaid each other. Many minds were answering him. Dozens of voices whispered, different words but all with the same meaning.

The tower had been a tranquil place, made for community and sharing. Alemin saw it in a hazy fashion. People in circles, holding hands. So many circles overlapped each other, he couldn't bring individuals into focus, yet he perceived their essence. These shadows had once been members of a community that followed each other into service over decades, each group in turn. No matter the passing of seasons or centuries, they were as one.

Could it be? Wrapped in this vision, Alemin trembled. Incredibly, he was hearing from the Shining Ones themselves. Even after so long, this echo of them still existed. Awestruck, he felt his vision waver. If he clung too tightly, he would lose it.

"Breathe," he reminded himself, and he took up their rhythm, letting their thoughts blend with his own.

Without words, they showed him their purpose. Breathing in, breathing out. Taking in and holding. Letting go and sharing. Beneath it all was a humming, like the echo if you stepped too hard on the ancient roadways. A succession of circles formed and faded. Rings crossed without breaking one another. It was a timeless rhythm, like a heartbeat or a song spanning generations.

Through it all, *vitalis* was the flowing blood. Incredibly, it all passed through the roads, which weren't roads at all, but channels made to guide and contain *vitalis*. Alemin couldn't tell where it came from, but he saw how the ancient mages received the bountiful energy and distributed it to any who needed it. For these were the Shining Ones, and whatever one had was free to all.

He listened, hardly daring to believe. Ar-Thea's tale was true, in its essence. It was wonderful, unbelievable. Much as he longed to bask in their presence, it didn't answer his most urgent question.

Though dreading the answer, he whispered across the centuries, *"But what happened?"*

The ancient spirits clung to their memories of paradise. They didn't want to remember the rest. Alemin understood. He felt the same. Still, he forced himself to repeat it.

"What happened to you?"

A shudder rolled through the spirits, and resonated through the ancient tower. It had begun with a terrible mystery. The flow of *vitalis* had stopped, without warning or explanation. People gathered to the tower over a period of days, worried by the loss of the magic that sustained them. Alemin could see vague shapes of them, linking their hands and minds. They weren't afraid, not then. They only wanted to help.

From the north, a blackness cloaked the sky. What their eyes saw might have been no more than a few people approaching, yet a wave of incomprehensible evil blanketed the land. The Shining Ones sang a welcome, blessing the strangers, for hospitality was always their way. Perhaps they hoped to calm the storm and bring it to peace.

With the dusk, the Devourers descended on them. Scattered screaming began as uncounted inky coils snatched the hapless people, tore them from their circles into a fatal embrace. Rapacious tentacles bit deep, tearing through flesh to gouge out their very souls. The largest one disdained such little fare and fastened itself to the tower. Its unholy maw gorged on the remaining *vitalis* in that reservoir.

The Shining Ones were massacred, stripped of their magic and their lives. Some struggled, despairing. Others fled, but there was no escape. Their mystical essence lit the darkness and betrayed them to their ruin. By daybreak, nothing was left but their bones, and the screaming.

The tower sagged, drained of its marrow, but it was not empty. That greatest Devourer lingered, lurking like a spider inside a hollow log. While the lesser devourers scattered, seeking fresh prey, it waited there, a hunter forever hungering.

Over many ages the screaming went on, an endless wail of heartbreak and terror. For those of the Shining Ones who had been bound to serve this tower were trapped along with it. Their spirits hung in anguish through the centuries, while the Devourer perverted and defiled all they once had loved.

New folk came to live in the tower. They built it a new skin of stones and mortar, but still the tormented spirits wailed with grief that no one now could hear.

Sharp banging summoned Alemin from his trance. He was glad enough to get free from the experience. Croaking a protest, he pried his eyelids open. His throat felt raw, as if he had been screaming along with the ghosts of the Larder.

"Juggler!" shouted a rough voice. "Damn you, don't make me come in there."

Dazedly, Alemin blinked into focus. Stegnor, leader of the afternoon watch, was behind the bars in the door. Farther back, in the corridor, other voices called out as well. Alemin felt a dull surprise that anyone was concerned about his welfare. He sat up, every muscle seizing. No matter what had happened, he had to be careful what he said.

"I'm..." He coughed. "It was only a nightmare."

"Keep it to yourself, then," Stegnor yelled. "No more screaming."

Alemin nodded, but a bitter chuckle rang through his mind. *"If only that was possible."*

From down the corridor, a voice that might have been Haafeth's rang out. "Is he dead yet?"

Someone else called, "Shut up!"

"That's right!" Stegnor gave Alemin a last, disgusted look before he stormed back down the corridor. "He's fine, so all of you shut up!"

Alone again, Alemin flopped back in his cot. His mind was still whirling, past and future blurred together. One moment he longed to reach back into that long-lost community and tell them that, after so long, someone knew their suffering. Absurdly, that it would be all right. He would save them.

The next moment he understood the vanity of that. The Shining Ones could not be saved, when they were centuries dead. He couldn't lose himself in their ancient struggle. No, it was the living he must think of. They who might still be saved.

As he calmed, Alemin tried to sort through what he had learned.

The Larder had been the center of community. True to its name, the Devourer and his parasites had destroyed them, body and soul. What remained were merely shadows. Echoes of their suffering.

Souls, Alemin thought again. Souls. There was something about that.

With a chill, he put it together. Only one person was known to devour the souls of his enemies. That was Dar-Gothull, the tyrant who held all of Skaythe in his bloody grip.

His mind faltered, shying from what this might mean. One of the great questions in Ar-Thea's story was what had happened to the devourers after they consumed all the magic in Skaythe. Ar-Thea said they might have turned on each other when the Shining Ones had been wiped out. Or they simply starved and died. That had always seemed a bit too easy.

Now Alemin had encountered a revenant who called itself the Devourer. Based on what he had experienced, it was possible that Dar-Gothull *was* that greatest of the Devourers.

His heart pounded as he sifted through other bits of lore that didn't, at first, appear connected to Ar-Thea's. Dar-Gothull was supposed to be more than 300 years old. He was said to extend his life by absorbing the souls of any who challenged his reign. That was the most terrifying part of his legend. The entire regime encouraged mages to war against each other, to fight for rule — ultimately, to raise the banner of challenge that would make them Dar-Gothull's prey.

Alemin didn't know anyone who believed Dar-Gothull's soul-eating claim was true. Not until the previous night, when he had seen it for himself.

He shuddered, and logic interposed itself. Dar-Gothull lived in the capital, Dakadoz. That was on the opposite side of Skaythe. The tyrant would have to travel across the land to take his feast at the Larder, and frequently. People would speak of such movements, much as they did a bandit incursion or similar hazard. He had never heard of anyone encountering a royal entourage making the trek.

Except, as Alemin had discovered, there were those ancient highways, which once had transmitted *vitalis* across the land. What else could an ancient sorcerer transmit? It had been some time since Alemin saw a map of all Skaythe, but he recalled that Dakadoz lay at a nexus of several highways. Could Dar-Gothull use those to reach across the land and devour a mage's soul?

Ordinary people who crossed the law, those without magic, were simply executed. Only mages were transported here, to the wailing tower. Ar-Lizelle had said something like this, on the night Alemin arrived. The other prisoners had warned that your power was weakened when you were held high in the tower. Dar-Gothull must be draining them, day by day. That was the vortex Alemin saw in his darkest dreams.

All the while, in daytime, hard work and scant meals kept them exhausted and desperate. Ar-Lizelle must have placed up Alemin there to sap his will and force him to cooperate.

He wished that he knew more about the other prisoners in the Larder. Had any of them tried to take on the tyrant? Illen and Haafeth claimed murder, but it was hard to believe that the wary, lisping Elldri would do such a thing.

Perhaps it didn't matter. If Alemin was right, Dar-Gothull maintained his connection with the Larder in order to feed. For his purpose, innocence or guilt were irrelevant. After all, everyone knew the Larder housed the worst, most vicious and despicable mages in Skaythe. Nobody would care what happened to them.

When Wharon was prison warden, he must have stumbled upon the information. No wonder he'd gone mad. Like Ar-Lizelle, he would have wanted to fight back. His attempt to kill all the prisoners in the Larder might have been a misguided effort to weaken the Devourer.

Whatever the case, Wharon had been partly correct. Alemin now understood that as long as the Larder existed, Dar-Gothull would, too. If Skaythe was ever to be freed from his tyranny, the Larder had to fall.

"Come on, I'm not doing this work for you," Ferrant complained.

"I'm just stretching," Alemin replied. After hours bent over, pitching hay in the stable, he straightened and twisted his torso to ease his lower back. Ferrant made a huffing noise. The man was as bad as the guards, harping on every moment's rest. No doubt that was Ar-Lizelle's intention.

Grudgingly, Alemin bent over his pitchfork again. It

had been several days since he communed with the tower. The nightmares hadn't been away for long, and he didn't want to try it again if the Devourer might be roaming the Larder. Nor had any of his fellow prisoners hinted at success in attuning themselves to the building. For all he knew, they weren't even trying.

Alemin tried not to show his doubts. He cracked jokes at meals, juggled to relieve the courtyard's stifling heat. When he was alone in his cell, he brooded over the problem before him. How could anyone destroy the Larder?

Despite the damage it long ago sustained, the core of the tower was of the Shining Ones' construction. It had stood for millennia. The Larder had been built around it because ordinary hammers and saws could not touch it.

True, the Larder stood on a hilltop overlooking a great canyon. An earthquake or landslide might pull the ground out from under it and sever its connection with the network of highways. However, that would require a joint effort of many mages — a collaboration not easily achieved — and uncounted lives would be at risk, including the miners who toiled in the depths.

A better option would be to abandon the Larder. Ar-Lizelle was already worried about the Devourer. There was a remote possibility she could be persuaded to remove the prisoners to another site and leave the tower vacant.

It wasn't something she could bring about on her own, though. There would be permissions, and the process of building a new prison. Since Dar-Gothull benefitted from the current arrangement, that was obviously not going to happen. Ar-Lizelle would probably be devoured if she even suggested such a thing.

Still, Alemin had one asset the despot would never imagine. He had friends, both inside and outside the Larder. Unlikely as it might appear, the prisoners were a tight group. Even if they couldn't access the building at will, Alemin suspected they were more connected than they realized. They might mock him for meditating, but escape was one idea they were sure to like. And he knew very well that Lorrah was still coming to aid him, despite being told not to.

Considering all that, the best way to weaken Dar-Gothull was by escaping. It couldn't be just Alemin — everyone had to escape. Illen, Duessa, Noluss, Bettain. Even the unfriendly ones, like Ferrant, and the unstable ones, like Haafeth. Releasing them was a big risk. Who knew what crimes they might commit, once free? Alemin would have to carry those on his conscience. But the reward was greater.

The six Minstrels said they were working against Dar-Gothull. What good did they really do in their pathetic scramble, always hiding from the hunter-guards? On the other hand, if they took the old monster down, that would be a service to Skaythe far beyond Ar-Thea's pacifist dreams.

As Alemin raked the dung out of the horses' stalls, he murmured to himself, "I have not been thinking big enough."

"What?" Ferrant demanded suspiciously.

Alemin merely shrugged, but he knew what had to happen. The first step to getting rid of Dar-Gothull was breaking the mages out of the Larder.

Just one more day of travel. Badger Squad had crossed the Yergha Drop on a toll bridge, and now passed through cultivated land. Narrow dirt trails led from the highway toward small hamlets tucked between orchards of spice wood and oranges. As the dusk deepened, flickering lights outlined the walled city of Yergha itself, and the rising tower of the Larder. Whatever came of their desperate mission, it would be done soon.

Cautiously, Lorrah extended her thoughts across the darkening land. She had to be careful. Ar-Lizelle might be alert for the intrusion. Lorrah shifted her shoulders restlessly. It was hard to think of Lizelle having an adult's name. Difficult as their relationship had been, Lizelle was her sister. Ar-Lizelle was a stranger, and her enemy. That was Dar-Gothull's way.

Best not to dwell on that. What she needed was to make sure Alemin was all right. He'd broken off so suddenly. This would be their last chance to plan ahead.

So she whispered, like a lover in the night. "Alemin."

"Lorrah!" His immediate answer reassured her. "I was hoping — I need your help."

"I knew that." Lorrah quipped, but she sensed an extra urgency. "What else is wrong?"

"I have so much to tell you, and there isn't time. Are you almost here?"

"We are close." Out of caution, Lorrah didn't give a specific location or names. "Someone will be there tomorrow. They'll get you out."

"Not only me," Alemin cut in. "There are ten of us."

"...Ten?" Lorrah must not have heard right.

"Yes, ten. You have to get us all out."

"No," Lorrah choked. He didn't know what he was asking. "Alemin, that's not possible."

"Nobody can be left behind. It's important."

She could feel how much he believed it, but that didn't make it realistic. "You don't understand. They're coming to transport one prisoner. Only you."

"It's not enough. Lorrah, listen —"

She gasped as he flowed into her mind, pressing in so much information at once that she could hardly track it. That nightmarish figure, a man's murder, and then the knowledge of what the Larder truly was.

"I don't like most of these people. I don't trust them," Alemin rushed on, "but if even one prisoner is left behind, then Dar-Gothull will still be in a position of power."

"I can see what you're saying," Lorrah answered, flustered. There wasn't enough parchment, even if she stretched the ink to make nine more writs. To say nothing of the time it would take to carve several more stamps. "Even if I could, it wouldn't make sense to take out all the prisoners at once. Nobody will ever believe it."

"Isn't there any way?" Alemin begged.

Lorrah's mind whirled. She wanted to see Alemin so much. She also wanted to reach through their bond and slap him. Badger Squad had a good plan. What he wanted to do piled risk on top of chance, and balanced it all upon a teetering stack of danger.

Yet, in the back of her mind, Zathi rallied her squad: *"We must choose what risk to take."*

When Lorrah didn't answer, hope glimmered in Alemin's thoughts. Very reluctantly, she said, "I'll ask."

She dropped the contact as if it had burned her. When she opened her eyes, the guardswomen were around her, watching in the lantern light. This was becoming a familiar sight.

"He's ready?" Zathi spoke with her usual brisk snap.

Lorrah forced a laugh. "Maybe too ready. He wants us to get them all out."

"All?" Zathi's brows rose, and a little buzz went around the circle.

"I know, that's what I said!" Lorrah realized her hands had been clawing into her knees as she worked. She stretched them against each other to relieve the tightness.

"Aren't they all madmen?" Giniver asked.

"According to Alemin, they mostly aren't. He's had time to study the Larder. I mean, the building itself."

Quickly, Lorrah laid out Dar-Gothull's connection to the Larder. Zathi listened silently, her dark eyes impassive. There was a brief silence when she was finished.

"He has a point," Keerin said. "Taking out Dar-Gothull's food supply would be a pretty bold move."

"Only if we're ready to follow up," Jaxynne countered. "We aren't."

"There's no way we could match the force in the Larder," Zathi said.

"Them escaping would create a lot of confusion, though," Sethamis said. "They'd have to chase all the prisoners down. Does that count as follow-up?"

"A bunch of maniacs should keep them busy," Razeet agreed.

Zathi cautioned, "Whatever happened, there's no way we'd keep our name out of it. Any hope of rescuing Lorrah's other friends would be gone."

That drew somber reactions. Like the Minstrels, Badger Squad tried to operate out of the regime's sight.

"We don't know they need rescuing," Keerin answered, but with some doubt.

Zathi turned to Lorrah. "What did you tell him?"

"That it's impossible, but you said, that time, nothing will change if we never take a risk."

"I did say that." Zathi's face was unreadable. Another stir went around the circle, this one alert and even excited. "Options?"

"Not a frontal assault," Jaxynne answered at once.

"Unless we can split them up somehow," Giniver countered.

The women leaned in, urgently offering suggestions. "We can talk our way in the gate, and then —" "None of us know the layout —" "This Alemin can make a fuss and distract them —"

Lorrah felt sick as the answer came to her. "Don't forget who the warden is. My sister will come after me, no matter what. That would split them up."

"I thought you can't face her," Sethamis said.

Lorrah tried to act nonchalant. "I don't want to, but it still might be useful."

"So, you lure Ar-Lizelle out of the Larder," Jaxynne said thoughtfully. "Then what?"

"The rest of you follow our plan. Present the writ and get Alemin out," Lorrah said. "He's the one with direct information. We need him free, no matter what."

"If the warden leaves, an underling will be in charge," Zathi mused. "I think I can handle that. What about the rest of them?"

"Alemin is the one who wants this," Lorrah said, a bit testily. "Let him plan with them to create the distraction."

"From what I've heard of the Larder, it's going to get bloody," Razeet warned. "The prisoners might even attack us. They'll think we're more hunter-guards."

"Do we try to take them all in the wagon?" Sethamis asked doubtfully.

"The rest of them will probably scatter," Keerin said. "It's what I'd do, if I broke out of prison. Just get as far away as possible."

She spoke so firmly that Lorrah wondered if she actually had been in that situation.

"What if Lorrah is captured?" Zathi asked, impartial.

Everyone went quiet. Lorrah managed a casual shrug, although her stomach was tying itself in knots. "Then I guess I'll find out what my dear sister wants."

Nobody liked that idea. "How will you get back out?" Jaxynne asked.

"That's not a concern," Lorrah tried to sound as calm as Zathi did. "I don't think she plans to capture me. Anyway, Alemin is the one with the information."

There was another silence, but now Lorrah saw respect in the eyes of her fellow Badgers. She wasn't a weakling to be protected, or a friend of Keilos who had died, but a warrior like the rest of them.

"So. I guess I'll tell him the good news."

Lorrah closed her eyes and settled back into meditation. She just wished she was sure this *was* good news.

Excitement thrummed in Alemin's veins at the thought of what was to come. If there was even a chance of escape, he had to let his fellow inmates know. That meant it was time to test their efforts.

With great caution, he extended his thoughts. The evening meal and attendant chores were done, the prisoners locked in for the night. Without an exterior window, it was impossible to know the hour, but he hoped the Devourer wasn't roaming about. Above all, he must not catch that fiend's attention.

He didn't try to penetrate the tower, so much as listen to whatever might be about. At first there seemed to be nothing. All was still, empty of thought. Then came a mere tickle of sound, a voice heard in the distance. He felt his way toward it. Alemin began to see, in hazy patches. Illen lay on his side, drowsing. Haafeth played with the flame of his lamp, causing it to flare brightly and then sink nearly to extinction. Alemin sensed Kyanon and Noluss, too, but none made any effort at meditation. That shouldn't have been as disappointing as it was.

Still, the distant tone was familiar. Alemin stretched past the empty cells to Bettain, who knelt on her bed, hands pressed against the wall. It was her voice he heard, an impatient snap. Then he sensed the others. Duessa was present, and Elldri! In a way, he wasn't surprised. The three women were closer than the men, who were ruthlessly trained to stand or fall alone.

Unfortunately, their communication wasn't what Alemin expected. There were no ghostly images, as he had projected to Ar-Lizelle. Brief impressions of emotion brushed past him, and an occasional fleeting image. The women were like fish moving below the surface of a pool, sensed but not truly seen.

It seemed they sensed him as well, for those elusive thoughts scattered away.

Friend, Alemin projected soothingly.

Recognition. A careful return. Alemin didn't try to impose his own ideas, but to communicate on their level. Bettain, especially, would not like to be told she was doing it wrong. So he placed the images and emotions he needed them to receive.

Help coming.

What help? demanded a shadow that might have been Duessa. The others queried, *When? Who?*

Lorrah hadn't told him much, out of concern they would be discovered. *Unknown,* he sent back, but with certainty. *Something will happen. Everyone should be ready.*

Confusion. That might be Elldri. *Disbelief.* That sounded like Bettain. Before they could fully articulate, they all felt a pressure rising, as it did before a nightmare began. Someone else approached — or some thing!

Alemin dove away, and felt the others scatter as well. He came back to himself gasping, as if he had been swimming in deep water and barely made the surface before his breath gave out. Shivering, he huddled on his bed and waited to see if the Devourer would appear to confront him.

Whatever Lorrah had planned, it couldn't happen soon enough.

VII

The Raid

L orrah left the Badgers' camp early. Sethamis moved about in the lantern light, tending the animals, while Zathi stood watch. Lorrah didn't know if the sergeant had planned it that way, but she was glad of it. They ate quickly while reviewing the charts one final time. The city of Yergha was not far off, and the Badgers planned to stop there first. Now that they knew more escapees would be coming, additional supplies must be had.

However, Lorrah would not be with them. Zathi saw her off with a brief caution: "Be careful."

"Yes, Sergeant."

No more easy rides for Lorrah. She had packed the mage robe away and was back in the peasant dress she had worn before Badger Squad caught up with her. The tight bodice fitted oddly now, and her heavy waypack rattled when she shifted its weight. Only her boots felt the same as she remembered.

What mattered was that she was anonymous, just one more vagabond wandering the land. Lorrah quickly fell into the steady pace that had carried her all across Skaythe. She was vulnerable, the way she had been when the minstrels separated. Strange, how she had forgotten the stress of this feeling.

While the Badgers acquired what they needed, Lorrah walked ahead. She would reach the village of Haggazes, alongside the Larder, and be in position before the

Badgers arrived. She would draw Ar-Lizelle out and keep her distracted, leading her farther away from the Larder. If that failed, Lorrah wouldn't have Badger Squad to back her up. She could only try to escape, and make her way to their arranged meeting place at a waterfall pool.

As the sun broke the horizon, Lorrah felt roughness beneath her boots. The highway's silver face was raddled and darkened as if by fire. Daunting as that was, she couldn't turn back. She stayed on the track as it paralleled the chasm of Yergha Drop. The deep canyon had a voice of its own, a diffuse roar of wind echoing in the deep. Occasionally, a distorted clang would issue from the mines far below. Stone walls frowned on the far side of the gap. The city of Yergha might as well have been a mirage for all the shelter it appeared to have.

Meanwhile, the Larder hulked on the near horizon. It was as damaged as the ancient roadway, wrapped in bandages of parapets and walls. Lorrah didn't hear any screaming such as Alemin had referred to. She wasn't sure what that meant, if anything.

Sweating and breathing deeply, she trudged under the swiftly rising sun. There was no water on this plain, and she allowed herself a hasty pull from her waterskin. The village lay past the Larder, on the opposite side of the roadway. It had no walls, but the stone houses were packed together so tightly that there might as well have been one.

The town was like many Lorrah had wandered through, with the minstrels or on her own. There was a square paved with ill-tended stones, lined by workshops and stalls selling basic foodstuffs. Guards in leather jerkins stalked around. She couldn't tell if they were town guards or part of the prison's garrison. People came and went around the square. She kept her head down, and they seemed to dismiss her as no more than a beggar.

Lorrah spotted a tavern with a wide porch. She spread a cloth near the steps and got out her violin. The landlord hadn't come to chase her off by the time she tuned it, so she started playing bits of folk songs and lilting tunes to speed the work. A few patrons thumped their tankards, but no one tossed a coin. Such was a minstrel's lot.

Once they were used to her music, she peered between the houses and fixed her gaze on the Larder. Lorrah slipped into her mother's favorite tune, the one she always had to play for guests. Lorrah had played it so often, she didn't need to think about it. Ar-Lizelle would know it, too. With all her will, Lorrah projected the sound toward the prison. According to Alemin, the walls had a special resonance. They ought to amplify the sound and draw her sister's attention.

It sounded like pleasant music, but it was a dare. "You want me? Come and find me!"

Every nightmare that had ever plagued the Larder returned to harry Alemin that night. Black rivulets dribbled down the walls and across the floor. A hideous eye appeared in place of the window slot. He dreamed of racing through the Larder, desperate to escape the Devourer, only to have the circular hallways deliver him straight to its lethal embrace.

New fears tore his sleep as well. Everything that might go wrong played out in his nightmares. It seemed the Devourer knew he had hope, and was determined to stamp it out.

He woke with the chorus of anguish at dawn. Walking down, Alemin felt fevered and anxious. Warden Ar-Lizelle seemed especially intent today. How could she suspect? Duessa, too, had questions in her eyes that she was too smart to speak aloud. Alemin didn't want to talk to any of them. The guards were always near, always listening. He couldn't risk a slip of the tongue so close to the time.

Again, he was teamed with Ferrant, whose desperate unfriendliness undermined Alemin's mood. They cleaned the stables, as usual, right near the main gate. Alemin was tense and alert, ready to jump, but hours passed without anything unusual happening. Endless, heavy loads of droppings and sour hay reeked under the baking sun. The stench hung around him like a poisoned cloud.

Gradually, he began to hear soft music. Alemin straightened, wiping sweat from his bare skull. The heat must be making him dizzy.

"Do you hear that?" he mumbled.

"Get away from me," Ferrant snapped.

The guards growled, "No slacking off."

Alemin's hands moved by rote. Bend and stick the wooden rake under the pile, straighten and pitch it into the dung cart. In his mind, he strained to pick up the elusive sound. A single violin played a calm melody with a steady, measured pace. No one in the Larder even had a violin, as far as he knew. Lorrah did, though.

Impatience nibbled at his ribs. How did this help anyone escape? Maybe Lorrah had changed her mind.

No. No, he couldn't think that.

One of the prison guards dashed in. "The warden wants her horse, Captain Morthem's, and four more."

"Out of the way." Alemin's and Ferrant's guards pushed them into the middle of the courtyard, while the guards on stable duty hastily saddled the horses.

"I didn't know she had a horse," Alemin murmured to his fellow prisoner.

"She doesn't live in the Larder, you know," Ferrant growled back. "She lives in the town. Most of them do."

"Quiet!" snapped the nearest guard.

The best horse in the stable was a bright chestnut. Alemin should have known who it belonged to. Ar-Lizelle must come in early, even before dawn, since she was always present at breakfast. By the evening meal, it was only Ar-Chindu strutting around. She must be off to whatever home she kept in Haggazes.

This raised the obvious question: Where was Ar-Lizelle going now, in the middle of the day?

The prison warden swept into the courtyard, followed by Captain Morthem and four guards. Manacles rattled against the swords on their hips.

"Remember, she can't hide from me," Ar-Lizelle declared with eager spite. She got up on her horse, while the guards went to their own.

Ar-Chindu came last, sputtering, "Lady Ar-Lizelle! We haven't finished the report."

"It can hold until after my long-awaited family reunion." Ar-Lizelle's gaze fell on Alemin, and her smile widened to a cruel smirk. "All your silence for nothing."

Alemin didn't have to pretend his shock. He had been right — it was Lorrah playing the violin. She hated her sister so much, and now everything she feared was riding down on her.

Was this part of her plan?

As a traveling musician, Lorrah had developed a fine sense of how much time she had between a bystander pointing a finger and when the guards actually arrived. She started moving a little sooner than that. Scooping up the few bits thrown at her, she stowed her violin and stuffed her cloth into the waypack. No one paid any attention to a beggar shuffling off with a dejected slouch.

Out of sight from the guards, she cut between the buildings. A few streets up and through another narrow alley, until she found a spot where she could see that tavern through the backyard fences. Rumbling hooves reached her before she spotted horses circling around where she had just been. A red-robed figure stood in the stirrups of a bright chestnut horse. She appeared to be talking to the inn's landlord.

Ar-Lizelle! Lorrah's heart skipped an anxious tune. Her plan had worked, at least so far.

She eased aside, propped her pack against her feet, and tucked her violin beneath her chin. Lorrah fixed her eyes on an intersection some way down the street, marking her escape path, then sent soft, taunting notes through the narrow crevice between buildings. She put no power behind them. The music alone was enough of a lure.

Across the street, a woman looked out an upper window. No doubt the music puzzled her. Lorrah couldn't have anyone giving her away too soon. Even as her fingers and bow moved, her power gently swirled around the watcher to blur her sight, make her dizzy. The woman shook her head, confused, than reacted as most people would: she banged the shutters closed. Nobody wanted to get involved with trouble that wasn't their own.

Along with that noise, horse hooves began again. Lorrah peered between the fences in time to see the last horse passing by at a trot.

Time to move.

The heavy portcullis clanked downward after Ar-Lizelle rode through with her escort. One of Alemin's guards cuffed him.

"Back to work, you," barked the guard who oversaw the stables.

Alemin followed Ferrant toward the stable. His mind was a whirlpool of concern. If only he could touch the tower, even for a moment. He would warn Duessa and the others that events were in motion. After Ar-Lizelle singled Alemin out, Ar-Chindu watched him with angry suspicion. He would be sure to notice any casting Alemin did.

Just as he took up his rake, Ar-Chindu barked, "Stop." Alemin and Ferrant both tensed, but the bluster was directed to their guards. "Get them to the courtyard."

"They're not done." One of Ferrant's guards pointed at the hayloft, where fresh straw waited to be distributed among the stalls.

"Don't argue with me." Ar-Chindu's chest swelled with indignation. "I don't trust this. It's too sudden. We'll take no chances while Lady Ar-Lizelle is out of the Larder. Now move it. Move them all!"

"To their cells?" Alemin's guard, Endole, had him by the arm.

"The courtyard. If this turns out to be nothing, they'll be back to work soon enough."

Word was passed and bells were rung, and Alemin found himself being crowded into the courtyard along with all the other prisoners. He tried not to let his dismay show. How could they escape, if they were penned up here?

Stay calm, he reminded himself. This could still work. Ar-Chindu didn't know anything. If the prisoners were together, he wouldn't need magic to tell them what was happening. Alemin clung to that thought as the prisoners were pulled from their scattered work stations and shoved into the courtyard.

It was earlier in the day than usual, so the walls cast some shade to relieve the burning sun. However, there was no water on the table. That caused a great deal of grumbling.

"What's all this for?" someone complained. Another grumbled, "I didn't do anything."

"Not yet, you mean." Haafeth's rough laughter echoed between the hard walls.

Similar comments filtered down from the walkway above. The change of routine set the guards on edge. The firmest answer came from Rhodec. "Who cares? All we have to do is follow orders."

While the prisoners shouldered each other for a patch of shade, Alemin sensed a familiar energy converging on him. Duessa and the other women, and Illen from the other side.

"Did you..." Duessa faltered, unable to put words on his message of the night before.

Alemin nodded. Bettain opened her mouth to speak, but Illen interrupted. "What?"

Alemin didn't want to explain to every one of them individually. He fell back on his usual plan and reached into his sleeves.

"Hup, ho!" He started the button and the rock chip circling one-handed. "I can juggle anything. Come on, try me." Duessa scowled at the lack of an answer. "Throw something," he urged.

Reluctantly, Noluss snuck a small orange out of his sleeve. "I'd better get this back."

"That's the spirit." Alemin worked the orange into his rotation. Some of the prisoners gazed at him with confusion or disgust. At least he had all their attention. In a low voice, not one to reach the guards, he said, "My friends are coming. We're all getting out."

The prisoners showed surprise, and then avid interest. Someone muttered, "No way." Ferrant, of course.

"Don't crowd around," Alemin cautioned. "They'll get suspicious."

"What's the plan?" Illen said.

"We'll know our chance when we see it."

"Funny thing," Duessa said. "I had that same thought last night." Elldri and Bettain nodded.

"Because you pay attention," Alemin answered. He balanced on one foot and made the orange pass under his other leg.

Haafeth grinned on the other side. "You'd better not be messing with us."

Alemin shrugged a little, dropped back to both feet,

and then repeated the trick while standing on the other foot.

"The Lizard just left, though," Kyanon said warily. "She was in a hurry."

"Listen, I know it's not much to go on," Alemin told them. "We didn't share details because Ar-Lizelle might have been paying attention, too. Everyone needs to work together if you want to get out of here."

"Work together," Noluss snorted. "Do you think we're stupid?"

Guards prowled closer on the walkway above them. With false cheer, he cried, "Come on, give me something tougher!"

A large stone and three sandals flew at him. Laughing, Alemin ducked aside. "Not so fast. Give me one at a time." As he caught each new object, he went on more quietly, "Whoever gets left behind will be fodder for the revenant. So to weaken him, we all have to go."

"Sounds like fun." Bettain spoke with disturbing focus.

Alemin quickly added, "You can't kill each other, or the guards."

Haafeth bellowed with laughter. "You must be kidding!" He threw an even larger rock, something Alemin couldn't believe he managed to hide in his sleeve. As Alemin fumbled to keep his pieces in motion, Illen leaned in.

"No, he's right. What makes a guard madder than anything? Hurting another guard."

"Just try," Alemin added, "and be ready."

One object at a time, he tossed back the sandals and stones. A small scramble greeted Noluss' orange, but he quickly reclaimed it. The prisoners separated, darting suspicious glances at Alemin.

In a bitter hiss, Illen said, "This had better not be one of your jokes."

Lorrah kept moving. She ducked between buildings and made tracks in the gardens as a false trail. Since she didn't know the area, she sometimes had to scramble back from a dead end. Somehow she always found a new vantage to play a few bars on the violin. When she could see the ancient highway, she tried to watch it. How long until the Badgers arrived? Had they already come, and she missed them?

Despite her worries, the game was almost fun. Lorrah and Ar-Lizelle hadn't played much when they were girls. Their studies had been too important. This was like making up for lost time, if only the stakes weren't so high. Lorrah tried to pace herself so she wouldn't get tired. She rested briefly when she could, listening for even the faintest echo of horses' hooves. They seemed to come more and more quickly.

Ar-Lizelle was as persistent as she had expected. A sensing sweep rolled down the street toward Lorrah. She ducked between two fences and froze. Borrowing one of Tisha's tricks, she made her mind still. *"I am just a sunbeam,"* she whispered to herself until it had passed.

This was getting a bit too close. She moved on, staying beside walls and fences, anywhere she could conceal herself.

Pausing to breathe, she glimpsed the highway between buildings. There was the wagon flanked by riders. Even over this distance she recognized a familiar sorrel horse, Ember, and Zathi riding!

Lorrah found a space between two buildings to let her music echo in another direction. She had to keep Ar-Lizelle's attention, no matter how dangerous it got.

The prisoners wandered away when Alemin finished juggling. Each one was restless with anticipation of their freedom. He wondered again what he was about to unleash on the world, but there was no way to change it now.

Alemin went to his accustomed bench and leaned his back against the wall. Immediately, a faint buzz of voices rose around him. He knew, in some way he couldn't identify, that what he sensed was at the main gate. Ar-Lizelle hadn't returned yet, but someone else was arriving. A small squad of hunter-guards.

Was this the rescue Lorrah had promised? He stirred on his bench, feeling itchy and anxious. Until it started, he was going to jump to that conclusion about every little thing.

Hunter-guards and prison guards conferred. The prison guards were surprised. Boots thudded rapidly up the steps and along the corridor to the warden's office. Ar-Chindu hurried back down, radiating satisfaction that he had the chance to make the decisions for a change.

The junior mage reached the gate. Parchment crackled as he snatched it from one of the guards. "Who requested this?" he demanded imperiously.

"It says on the writ." The sergeant's voice was strong, and yet somehow feminine.

"Why now?"

"I didn't ask." She paused before adding, "Mages don't like it when we ask too many questions. Or take too long."

A nearby guard asked, "Shouldn't we wait for Lady Ar-Lizelle?"

That seemed to strike at Ar-Chindu's pride. "The writ is valid. Go get him." Alemin sensed Ar-Chindu's satisfaction. *"I'll do what the Lizard can't — get that trouble-maker out of here."*

Alemin slid his eyes open, to find the three women loitering nearby. "Trouble-maker? I am not a trouble-maker."

Bettain snorted. "Keep telling yourself that."

Distant bars clanged. Part of his mind still heard the woman sergeant ordering the cage made ready. Alemin didn't like the idea of getting into another cage, even if it meant escape. Again, booted feet thudded closer. He straightened away from the silvery stuff of the ancient tower.

To Illen, he murmured, "Wait til they take me out. Count to 100 and then make your move."

"Why should we wait?" Kyanon demanded in a low, angry voice.

"Their eyes will be on him," Duessa retorted.

Alemin nodded. "Pass it on."

Outside the gate, guards were talking. Alemin stretched his arms and rolled his head to ease the tension. His stomach rumbled. Alemin was so hungry all the time now, he was almost used to it. Now that the moment was upon him, he thought to wonder what strength he had, if it came to a fight.

A ripple of tension went through the courtyard as the gate clanged. "Juggler, get up here!"

That was Rhodec, head of the guards if Morthem was out of the Larder. Just beyond the gate, a guard named Pelasil smirked unpleasantly. "You have a date with justice."

"Didn't I already?" Alemin tried to act confused. The guards grabbed him and bound his hands. "Ow."

"Quiet," Rhodec barked as he pushed Alemin forward.

As the gate slammed, Alemin sensed many mental voices counting to 100.

Lorrah walked down a nameless street, hunched over in her guise as a beggar. Her breath came hard, and the rhythm of trotting hooves sounded too close for comfort. How long did the Badgers need to rescue the mages? How much risk should she take?

She stopped, startled, as a gust of wind buffeted her. The edge of the chasm was just a few yards ahead. Its windy voice shouted threats. Stone railings offered little protection from a very long fall. A gate to one side hinted at a path down, toward the mines.

Lorrah hadn't realized the town went so close to the edge. She turned, skipping into a run, but then skidded to a halt. Six riders trotted toward her. Behind their advance, people ran into houses and ducked behind walls. Shouted warnings echoed between buildings, but it was too late to do Lorrah any good.

The woman on the bright chestnut horse dominated everything. She sat stick-straight, robed in red, hair coiled high to add the impression of height. Certain of victory, she let her horse amble forward.

Ar-Lizelle.

If Lorrah hadn't recognized her sister's confident aura, she wouldn't have known her. Her fact was thin, and seamed with fine lines. What could have happened? Ar-Lizelle was older, but not by that much. Lorrah let her waypack slide down her shoulder, and straightened her own back. She spaced her feet for balance. This was just like old times, preparing for battle while certain of defeat.

So her sister must think.

Ar-Lizelle reined in, leaning her forearms on the saddle horn. "Well, well, well. My dear little sister. How I've missed you!"

Behind her, the guards shared startled glances. They must not have known who Ar-Lizelle led them after. The officer spoke to his men. Four of the guards dismounted. One man took the reins, while the remaining three spread out, blocking the street.

"You must come up and see my prison," Ar-Lizelle's high, sour voice hadn't changed a bit. "Your friend Alemin is waiting to see you."

"You'd better not have hurt him," Lorrah flared.

"I haven't done anything." Ar-Lizelle gave a shrill chuckle. "However, I'm afraid he's quite the expert at hurting himself."

Lorrah's throat felt tight. Her heart thudded in her chest. One of the guards was getting close to the miners' gate, blocking her escape down that path. In her mind, Zathi whispered advice. *"Relax. Breathe. Wait for the moment."*

"Yes, I'm sure your thugs had nothing to do with it," Lorrah answered tartly. Her voice was high, like her sister's, but melodious in comparison. She took a little satisfaction in that.

"My prison is quiet and orderly, as long as you don't pry into things you shouldn't," Ar-Lizelle retorted. "Come along, dear sister. See for yourself."

It wasn't an invitation, but an order. Much as Lorrah tried to control her feelings, old rage boiled up within her. Their lives had never been fair in the past. Ar-Evaus was always looking past Lorrah, favoring only his first daughter. Lizelle, so smug, had accepted the attention as her natural right.

"No thanks," Lorrah answered. "I believe you."

"Don't be an idiot." Ar-Lizelle let go some of her fake courtesy. The officer moved up, as if to protect her, while the other guards began to close in. Lorrah glanced behind herself, making sure she wasn't too close to the cliff edge.

"What cause do you have to arrest me? I've broken no law." *Yet,* Lorrah silently amended.

"Aside from consorting with renegades and heretics? I can beat the evidence out of you, little sister." Ar-Lizelle's eyes blazed with eagerness to prove it.

The guards quickened their pace. Lorrah raised her hands, fingers spread. They hesitated. She pulled her hands down into fists. A barrier sprang up between her and the guards.

"Show me a writ," Lorrah demanded, "or I'm not going anywhere, *dear sister.*"

The guards drew their swords, but looked to Ar-Lizelle for direction. Her mocking laughter echoed off the nearest walls. "Do you think that will hold me back?"

Lorrah made a little shrug. All this time she'd been running, avoiding her past, but she wasn't a child any more. Anger and fear could not control her. Staring into her sister's haughty face, she discovered that she had a few things to say after all.

"I never did anything to you," Lorrah said. "Why are you after me? Tell me what this is really about."

Ar-Lizelle's glare deepened to darker fury as she expected weakness and discovered strength.

"Don't play stupid with me. You're a traitor, not only to Dar-Gothull but to our family." The words rushed out, dark with spite. "Father was fighting for his life. I stood at his side, but where were you? You turned your back on your own, and I'll see you pay for that."

One of the guardsmen probed the barrier cautiously with his sword. Lorrah casually shoved him back.

"Loyalty? Father was trying to overthrow Count Ar-Nithal, and you were at his side because you thought it would be a prime opportunity. After you'd both spent every day telling me how useless I am, did you really think I'd run into the middle of that?"

"You betrayed us," Ar-Lizelle hissed.

Three guards were at the barrier now, striking harder with their swords. Lorrah slapped her hands sharply outward. The barrier sent the guards staggering.

"I went back for Mother!" Lorrah shouted. "The two of you didn't leave anyone to protect her. Maybe you didn't think she was important because she wasn't a mage."

"You witch!" Fire lashed from Ar-Lizelle's hands — their father's favorite spell. Guards ducked aside as the flaming lash struck Lorrah's barrier three times, four. She felt the impact, but her barrier held. Meanwhile, sparks flared and crackled. Ar-Lizelle's horse snorted anxiously, but it stood still under her. The others began to squeal and caper.

"A hand here!" cried the guard who was trying to hold them.

When Ar-Lizelle paused, Lorrah shouted into the gap. "I did my fighting when I got Mother back to Grandfather's estate, through all the count's guards and patrols. Father knew what he was doing when he plotted against the count. So did you when you supported him. But he lost, and he died, and the brilliant career you had planned went down with him. Didn't it!" Lorrah swept out a hand to the guards around her. "You thought you'd be a countess one day, and now you just work in a prison. Don't blame me for that!"

Ar-Lizelle's knuckles were white on the reins. Her chestnut and the officer's bay seemed to have some training. They stood in the face of her fire, though wild-eyed and sweating.

"So you ran away like a coward, and joined some wanderer." Ar-Lizelle tried to take control of the conversation.

"I couldn't stay there. They'd never believe I wasn't part of your scheme," Lorrah said. "It was just lucky one of Grandmother's maids knew about Ar-Thea."

"Oh, yes. Ar-Thea," Ar-Lizelle smiled spitefully. "I've been doing some research on your petty little band. I'm going to find them, every single one, and you're going to watch them suffer."

What could Lorrah say to such a threat? All that came to her mind was, "What a bitch!"

"What's going on?" Alemin tried to speak in a normal voice. It wasn't easy when anticipation tightened his chest like a drum.

Neither guard answered. They just muscled him past the garden, with its false promise of serenity, and then the dining hall. As they rounded the Larder's great curved side, Alemin saw the hunter-guards.

Doubts assailed him. So few of them! Three with swords drawn, two crossbowmen. In the bed of the wagon, a grim cage yawned wide. It took a moment before Alemin realized that all of them were women. He had never seen so many women in armor. He didn't know what alarmed him more, being rescued by women or that there weren't enough to get the job done.

Again he had to wonder — was this really Lorrah's plan?

Ar-Chindu stood beside the female sergeant, arms folded and a smug smirk on his lips. It slipped when a loud crash echoed behind them. The alarm bell began to clank, and a pulsing vibration rolled across the courtyard. Attuned to the tower as he was, Alemin heard faint shrieks of agony or alarm.

Immediately the two guards grabbed Alemin's arms and rushed him forward. Ar-Chindu ran to meet them.

"What was that?"

"I don't know, my lord. As soon as we cage this one, we'll investigate."

"Hurry and catch up." Ar-Chindu paused long enough to yell at the men in the gatehouse. "Shut the gate as soon as they get out."

A vague reply drifted down to them. "The Warden's not back yet."

Ar-Chindu was already running past. Louder bangs and screams reached them. Although the area was relatively quiet, Alemin had the distinct impression of Duessa yelling, "Head for the gate!"

The hunter-guards strode to meet the prison guards. The female sergeant fixed an intense gaze on Alemin. "This is him?"

"Yes, take him."

One of the archers leveled her crossbow at Alemin, while two of the female warriors moved forward. The other archer asked, "Situation?"

"I don't know, so hurry up." Rhodec moved restlessly, clearly anxious to follow Ar-Chindu.

"I think we can handle one man," the sergeant told them blandly. "You go ahead."

Female warriors came in to take over for the prison guards. They paused over that, but not more than a moment. Another loud bang echoed between the prison walls. Rhodec nodded briefly.

"We appreciate it." He and Pelasil charged after Ar-Chindu.

"Don't speak too soon," one of the guardswomen muttered.

"Quiet," the sergeant warned. More loudly, she commanded, "Into the cage, scum!"

"What's going on?" Alemin protested in a similar tone. The guards on the wall were starting to move toward the noises, their attention divided between the prisoner transfer and what else was happening. More quietly, he asked, "You're Lorrah's friends?"

"Don't say her name here," hissed one of the other female warriors.

Another one muttered, "I thought there were going to be more of you."

"They separated us," Alemin told her.

Swords bared, they pushed Alemin up into the back of the wagon. He bent his head to get into the cage. Flashes of light and more shrieks rang out behind the tower. A sensation of searing heat seemed to brush across his back. Ar-Chindu's distant yell could be heard. "Stand down! This will not be tolerated."

"Tolerate this!" Haafeth laughed back at him.

"That will be them now," Alemin said.

From the wall, prison guards fired down at something in the courtyard. A wave of bald, gray-robed figures raced around the tower. Lightning lanced upward, forcing the archers to scatter. Only a few guards still tried to hold them back. Bettain released a burst that sent one of them flying into the wall. Alemin couldn't see Ar-Chindu.

Haafeth stretched his arms wide, building a huge ball of fire. Alemin yelled to him, "Quit playing around. This is our way out."

Illen and Duessa took up the call. "Get on the wagon. Everybody move!"

The guardswomen were on their horses, spreading out, as the prisoners rushed at the wagon. On the wall, the guards had seen their intention. One of them tried to get back to the gatehouse, but Haafeth's fireball sent him staggering away.

"Yes. Yes! Ha ha haaaaa!"

"I take it all back." Ferrant paused long enough in scrambling aboard the wagon to clout Alemin's shoulder.

"Just get on." Alemin scanned the courtyard, trying to see if any prisoners had been left behind.

Ar-Chindu staggered out from behind the tower. He leaned on the wall, and his crimson robe was scorched. A red glow rose around him, until a crossbow snapped. The bolt took him in the chest and he fell, shrieking. Alemin winced, but there was nothing he could do about it.

On the back of the wagon, Duessa said, "I'll give them something else to think about." She aimed her own fire bolts at the stable.

"Hup! Hup, boys!" The driver cracked her whip. The oxen lowed in complaint at the heavy load, but wheels rumbled as the wagon surged into motion. The mounted hunter-guards closed in behind it.

They rolled under the shadow of the gate. Alemin's heart pounded as they emerged into sunlight again. He raised a barrier in case anyone shot at them from above. Even then, he joined the other prisoners in yelling and pumping fists with glee.

Lorrah had really done it. They were free!

"Oh no, you called me a bitch!" Ar-Lizelle's mocking laughter rang from the walls.

Lorrah firmed her barrier, preparing to hold off the three guardsmen. She glanced behind herself, then backed up. Let them think she was afraid.

Abruptly, Ar-Lizelle broke off. "What?" She stood up in the stirrups and squinted toward the Larder.

Lorrah wouldn't have a better opening. She curved her hands inward, turning the barrier into a sort of scoop. The guards were caught by surprise. They yelled as Lorrah slammed them together and flung them away. She took a solid step forward and followed up with a mental burst that would stun anyone whose mind was undefended.

The guards near her fell to the ground, while the officer sagged in the saddle. Four horses scattered, squealing, as the man holding their reins went to his knees. Ar-Lizelle and the officer's horses stayed still, barely.

Looking up at her, Lorrah said, "Who's a weakling now?"

Ar-Lizelle shook her head a little, but kept her seat. "This means nothing," she began.

Lorrah wasn't listening. In memory, she heard Keerin's advice: *"Use a move she doesn't know."*

Lorrah sucked in a breath and focused all her will at the horses. *"Flame."* She shut her eyes, but still saw crimson through her eyelids. Witchlight flared on their headstalls, as powerful as she could make it. Ar-Lizelle cried out in pain.

When Lorrah opened her eyes, the scene was chaos. With the officer barely conscious, he couldn't control his horse. The bay squealed and backed wildly away. It crashed into Ar-Lizelle's chestnut. Temporarily blinded and struck from behind, the chestnut kicked and fought the reins.

Ar-Lizelle cursed viciously A bolt grazed by Lorrah, but without much power behind it. It seemed her sister was also blind. The chestnut bucked, and Ar-Lizelle toppled with a screech. To her own surprise, Lorrah flung a barrier beneath the falling woman. Ar-Lizelle landed badly, but on her side rather than her head.

"Get up! What's happening?" On the bay horse, the officer blinked, trying to see.

Lorrah darted forward, avoiding the panicked horse. Her sister's eyelids flickered. She wouldn't die. Lorrah didn't want to think if that was a good thing or not. Around her, the guards were groaning, trying to stand. Lorrah reached out to all of them, a deeper strike that sent them the rest of the way into darkness.

Hoofbeats clattered as the other horses darted around, but the chestnut had stopped not far away. It shook its head, confused, and danced back as Lorrah approached with her waypack. She reached for the reins, projecting thoughts of kindness and calm.

"Come here, pretty thing. Let's get out of here."

The chestnut's training seemed to help. It let her lead it aside from the immediate confusion. She murmured to it, and allowed a flow of *vitalis* to clear its eyesight. As soon as it was safe, Lorrah mounted. As a daughter of nobility, she knew how to ride. She just hadn't done it in a few years.

"Good boy. So smart." She urged the chestnut forward, letting it choose its own pace for the moment. A couple of the loose horses seemed willing to follow. Those would mean a lot to Badger Squad, so Lorrah clucked to them over her shoulder.

Now that things were quiet, heads popped up from windows and walls. A small crowd lurked at the mouth of the nearest street. They pressed back at Lorrah's approach. One or two voices even cheered, until their neighbors cuffed them. Lorrah knew her way through the town much better by now. She headed for the Larder, with two of the loose horses trailing her.

As she emerged from between buildings, Lorrah saw a thin column of smoke snaking upward from behind the prison walls. On the road ahead, a wagon loaded with people was bouncing and jolting away from it. Badger Squad! Mages, too — she sensed the wild energy of their escape. Alemin was there, raising a shield to protect their rear.

Joyful and relieved, Lorrah permitted herself a triumphant grin. It had all happened so fast, she hadn't even had time to think about being afraid. She'd fought Ar-Lizelle and won! It felt great to take something back from her bitch of a sister. She pushed the chestnut to a gallop and angled to meet the wagon.

VIII

Possibilities

The oxen made their best speed, which wasn't much. Once they were away from the Larder, Alemin let his barrier down and slumped wearily against the side of the cage. Ironically, he had more room than the other nine prisoners, who were jammed together in the back of the wagon. They jostled each other, uncomfortable to have anyone so close to them. It didn't help when the wagon lurched over the craggy road.

"Can't we just shove the cage out of here?" Illen complained.

"I'll help," Bettain added.

"Hey," Alemin joked. "I'm in here!"

"That thing cost us money," said a guardswoman in the front seat.

"Anyway, we might still need it." This was an archer, who stood facing backward to watch the rear. A crossbow was angled over her shoulder. Other guardswomen on horseback flanked the slow-moving wagon.

Another rough jolt knocked Ferrant into Duessa. She angrily shoved him away. Kyanon meanwhile, noticed the obvious.

"Hey, you're all girls."

"We're not girls," answered the guardswoman who sat beside the driver.

Kyanon grinned lewdly. "Juggler! You didn't say

there would be girls here."

A few of the men whooped gleefully. None of the hunter-guards liked that. The tall, thin one with sergeant's bars on her shoulder drew rein beside the wagon.

"That's enough of that." Her no-nonsense tone quieted the noisy wagon. "We don't know you, and you don't know us, and the wagon is overloaded. Most of you are going to have to get off. Whoever keeps up that noise will be first to go."

She might have said more, but the archer facing backward called out, "Riders."

Alemin scrambled around to peer through the bars. There was dust from three horses, but he could only see one rider. The sight was enough to dismay him. A red horse was in the lead, and there was only one red horse in the Larder's stable.

"The Lizard," someone muttered ominously.

"I'll take care of it." Haafeth stood up, clinging to the sideboard with one hand while flames wreathed the other. Alemin saw that the rider wasn't wearing a mage's crimson. He reached out with his mind and sensed someone familiar.

"No!" he called. "Stop, that's Lorrah."

Now it was the guardswomen who whooped and slapped each other's shoulders. "I knew she'd be all right," one of them crowed.

Disappointed, Haafeth released his casting and lowered himself to the bed of the wagon. "You're no fun."

Illen leaned toward the cage. "Who's Lorrah?"

"A friend." Alemin left it at that. The Minstrels and Shining Ones were too much to explain in this noisy, crowded wagon.

The sergeant called out, "All right, listen. There's a bag with spare clothes under the front bench. You'll want to get out of those prison rags. Try to find something that fits you. But don't you set my wagon on fire." She narrowed her eyes at Haafeth, who smiled with the deceptive serenity he could put on when he wished to.

There was a period of irritable babble as the prisoners passed around shirts and trousers, and occasionally argued over them. Peasant hoods, which would conceal their shaved heads, were especially fought over. The male prisoners bumped and jostled each other as they got out of their coarse robes and into the cast-offs. Bettain complained that there was no women's clothing in the lot. Still, no spells flew. That was something.

Alemin watched as two of the guardswomen rode back past Lorrah and started trying to catch the loose horses. Lorrah soon rode up alongside the wagon. She was dressed in the sturdy peasant clothes he remembered from the minstrels' time on the road. Her curly black hair was pulled into a thick ponytail, but with many loose strands making a halo behind her ears. Dark eyes searched the crowded wagon until she found Alemin.

"Why are you in the cage?" Lorrah cried out. Then, "You're so thin! I was hoping my vision was wrong."

"It's comfy in here," Alemin assured her. "Much gratitide to you and your friends."

Her face lit with pleasure, until Illen interrupted with a pathetic plea, "They starved us, miss."

Lorrah turned to glare backward. "I should have hit her a lot harder."

Alemin was startled. Lorrah had never shown a lot of fighting spirit before.

"Lorrah." The sergeant was there.

"You have to tell me everything," Lorrah demanded to Alemin, but she reined around and rode off beside the sergeant. "Did you see I brought you a present?"

Alemin watched her, amazed. Gone was the childish, petulant expression he knew so well. Lorrah greeted the other hunter-guards with confidence. Even in peasant attire, she spoke up as an equal. How had she grown so much, in just a few months?

A bridge of stout planks crossed a small stream, just below a waterfall. Sethamis pulled off when Zathi agreed to let the animals rest. Lorrah watched the confusion as the escaped prisoners jumped down and spread out. They seemed anxious to get away from each other. Some of them went to wash in the waterfall pool. Others wanted to know if there was anything to eat.

Jaxynne had parcels of food for those who were going their own way. Indeed, some of them already were striking out on the road, or heading across country. Only Alemin and the women prisoners still wore their gray robes. Jaxynne hadn't expected there would be women included when she scrounged through the rag-pickers in Yergha. As for Lorrah, she quickly tossed her crimson robe on over the peasant clothes that had been her disguise.

Of the three women, the scarred one seemed to be in charge. She said to Alemin, "When you say go, how far do you mean?"

"Good question, Duessa." He glanced around, and Lorrah's heart lifted to think that he was looking for her. Then Zathi interposed.

"If you aren't joining us, we can't tell you."

The second woman with her scowled, but Duessa said, "That makes sense." The third one nodded somberly.

Another man sidled up to Alemin. "Juggler. I'll be off. My home town isn't far from here, relatively speaking."

"Aiming more to the right this time?" Alemin teased.

The man grinned, but it quickly faded. "Going to see if the place is still standing, and who's in it. Then I'll decide what I'm aiming at."

So these were the people Alemin had shared his

ordeal with. Lorrah felt a little sad as she listened to their banter. He was right; they didn't seem evil as much as famished and exhausted. Still, it was another whole group of people that didn't include her.

To escape that thought, Lorrah took Ar-Lizelle's horse to the waterfall pool. Actually, it was her horse now. Mages took what they wanted, and it was up to the owners to defend it. That was Dar-Gothull's law.

Sethamis was already making a fuss over the two new horses, a dun and a bay, that had followed Lorrah out of Haggazes. Lorrah borrowed a brush and worked on getting some of the sweat off the chestnut while it dipped its nose in the water.

"You're a good one, aren't you," Lorrah crooned. "You worked so hard today."

It raised its head, the liquid eye focused on her. Clearly the beast knew she was a stranger. However, a kindly one.

"What should I call you?" Lorrah asked, brushing its neck. "We have an Ember, a Spark and a Cinder. Are you a Flame?" That would be an ironic name. "Maybe a Bonfire. Or a Torch."

Unfortunately, they couldn't rest for long. Someone would come after them, either prison guards or city guards out of Yergha. The guardswomen took to their horses — even Keerin and Razeet, who didn't have their own horses and obviously hoped they would get to keep these new ones.

Of the prisoners, only the three women lingered. They now approached Zathi as a group. Duessa asked, "Am I seeing right? You are all women."

Keerin, who was standing nearby, feigned surprise. "Really? Where?"

"Yes, that's right." Zathi's dark eyes roved over the three escapees. "I see that you're also women."

"Women who are sick of men," interrupted the other

woman.

"Now just a minute," Alemin complained.

They all laughed. That was Alemin all over, making people laugh. Lorrah had really missed how he put people at ease.

A kind of understanding passed between Zathi and the escapees. Lorrah could see how the three of them stuck together. It was exactly like how the guardswomen protected each other at the outposts.

When the wagon rolled away, the three women were on it. They joined Alemin in the cage, although they weren't bound or gagged. It was just a ruse. The four of them still had their prison robes on, and anyone who saw them would wonder why a bunch of prisoners weren't in the cage.

Lorrah rode her new horse with pride, but her heart was glum. She should have been bursting with triumph. After all, she had done what she set out to do. Alemin was safe. They had taken a bold risk, just like Zathi said to. Nothing was going to be the same.

It was hard to know what they might have started. Except, Lorrah had come all this way, only to find Alemin surrounded by other women. Even with her scars, Duessa was lovely. Maybe Lorrah had never had a chance at all.

The age-old highway smoothed out as they got farther away from the Larder. The gentle ride was very lulling. Elldri and Bettain did the only logical thing, which was to sleep in the cage. Duessa sat awake, guarding them as she always did. Alemin was tempted by sleep, but the excitement of the escape still fluttered in his belly.

Lorrah rode her chestnut proudly alongside the wagon. She didn't say much, but she obviously didn't want to leave any more space between her and Alemin than she had to. Thinking back to their years as minstrels, it had always been that way. He just hadn't seen it.

Duessa spoke softly. "Juggler."

"Alemin is fine." He wasn't locked up with that bunch of killers any more.

"Alemin," she said slowly. "When they first brought you in, did the Lizard ask all kinds of questions about someone called Ar-Thea?"

"Lizard." Lorrah snickered, until she heard the end of the question. Then she sat a bit stiffer in the saddle.

"How did you know?" Alemin pretended innocence.

"She asked all of us. Every new prisoner."

"She wanted to know about Ar-Thea?" Lorrah was concerned.

Only as a way to find Lorrah, that Alemin was certain of. He caught himself before he blurted out that Ar-Lizelle and Lorrah were sisters. That was Lorrah's tale to tell.

If Duessa noted Alemin's reaction, it didn't matter to her. "The thing is," she went on, "my old teacher, Ar-Lannon, had a sister named Ar-Thea."

"A sister?" Lorrah shared a startled glance with Alemin before blurting, "Ar-Thea was our teacher."

"Really." Duessa studied the two of them, eyes narrowed in thought.

"She never mentioned having any family," Alemin replied cautiously. "Did Ar-Lannon have several other apprentices?"

"Three of us."

"Did he want you to call them brothers and sisters, even though you weren't related?" Lorrah demanded.

Duessa's stunned silence was answer enough.

"I wonder if our teachers were both trained the same way," Alemin watched her as he spoke. "Wandering around, collecting stray magelings. Listening to people when nobody else cared."

"I knew there was something familiar about you," Duessa half-accused. "Meditating, connecting through the tower."

Lorrah broke in, staring hard at Duessa. "Did your teacher tell you some ridiculous story about —"

"It's not ridiculous," Alemin protested.

Duessa was already nodding. "The Shining Ones." Her dark eyes fixed on Alemin. "That was really the Devourer?"

"It claimed to be." Alemin slumped back against the bars. "If this is all true, it means..." He trailed off, trying to understand.

"It means there are more than five of us left." Excitement rose in Lorrah's voice.

"Maybe a lot more," said the driver. Alemin hadn't realized she was paying attention. "Way to find a solution, Lorrah!"

Lorrah grinned, but she said, "If it's all true."

"If," Duessa agreed.

This discovery had huge implications. Alliances, support — assuming they could find Duessa's fellow students. They shouldn't jump to conclusions. Yet Duessa didn't seem to be luring them into anything. She would have been much more glib and eager. Still, these hunter-guards and prisoners were strangers to each other. It would take time for the two groups to trust each other.

They all fell into their own thoughts, grappling with the possibilities. Shortly after, the driver chose a side road, an ordinary dirt track that curved down a hill. The bottom lands of Yergha spread before them, rich with fields and pastures. Groves of spice wood and citrus blanketed the hillsides. There were more people here. Perhaps it would be easier to lose themselves. If nothing else, they could trade for more clothes so Alemin and the others could get out of this cage.

Then where? Their sergeant, Zathi, had yet to say.

Reluctantly, Alemin looked backward, where a dark blot receded from the horizon. It was hard to believe anything good could come out of that place.

When he focused, he could practically hear Ar-Lizelle screeching at someone for failing to stop the prisoners. Alemin wondered if the stable had burned down and how many of the guards had been hurt, or even killed. There was no other outcome. He knew that. The reasons that they had to leave were the same, even if Ar-Chindu or some of the others died.

Dramatic clouds veiled the sun. Alemin wondered if, when dusk fell, he would still hear the chorus of wailing. Now that he had connected to the trapped souls of the Larder, would he ever truly be free?

The wind gusted with a hint of the Devourer's malevolent chuckle. *"Run while you can, ant."*

Alemin turned away with a jerk. He couldn't keep staring at the Larder, reaching back with his senses. No good would come from holding that bond, even if it also contained a precious link to the Shining Ones. Ar-Lizelle was smart enough to use it against him one day.

Hopes and doubts chased each other around in Alemin's head. Was it truly over? Could he ever escape from the nightmares of the Larder?

No. Alemin was safe, against all the odds. He had to believe there was a future worth escaping to.

Instead of the Larder, he looked for Lorrah, who had gotten him out of that horrible place. She darted a wistful glance in his direction. As their eyes met, the warmth of admiration and gratitude flowed through him. Far better to repay the debt he owed Lorrah and her friends, than to cling to the pain he had suffered in the Larder.

He smiled, just for her.

People and Places of Skaythe

Places

Skaythe — A tropical island continent.

Fang Marsh — mangrove swamps inhabited by the water-folk

Gavalar Mountains — the highest peaks in Skaythe, where ice and snow persist all through the year

The Hornwood — an area of dry, dense forest in the center of Skaythe, inhabited by the Drakanox and other fell creatures

Temple Schools — training sites where young mages are indoctrinated into Dar-Gothull's laws; Attendance is compulsory

Governance

Dar-Gothull — tyrant and wizard-king, who rules through domination and cruelty

Dakadoz — Dar-Gothull's capital city

The Minstrels — renegade mages who work to undermine Dar-Gothull's tyrannical regime

Ar-Thea, a very wise and kind mage, who trained the Minstrels before she was assassinated

Alemin, juggler and older brother of Berisan

Berisan, juggler and younger brother of Alemin

Keilos, lutenist (deceased)

Lorrah, violinist

Meven, puppeteer

Tisha, dancer and healer

Badger Squad — an independent squad of hunter-guards;
        women only
Zathi, sergeant and warrior
Jaxynne, second in command, archer and tracker
Giniver, warrior
Keerin, warrior, older sister of Razeet
Razeet, archer, youngersister of Keerin
Sethamis, ox driver and archer
Thersa, warrior (deceased)

Hawk Squad — formerly Count Ar-Dayne of Sloram's
        personal guard, now independent hunter-guards
Piyaro, sergeant
Cothyr, second in command
Guardsmen: Cylass, company scribe (former), Ennow
(deceased), Hyurei, second in command (former), Ragis,
Rowlan, Saylor (deceased), Tallon (deceased)

Boar Squad — an independent squad of hunter-guards
Traggan, sergeant

The Larder — a dreaded prison for the most violent wizards
Ar-Lizelle, warden
Ar-Chindu, second in command (deceased)
Ar-Kyanon, second in command (formerly a prisoner)
Guards: Captain Morthem, Endole, Groff, Rhodec
Prisoners: Alemin, Bettain, Calsith, Duessa, Elldri, Ferrant,
Haafeth, Illen, Noluss, Wharen

The Counties — autonomous, but under Dar-Gothull's
control

Busaren	**Deeve**
Ar-Cadrun, count	Ar-Gevant, count
Dakadoz — capital city	**Dunsaph**
Dar-Gothull, wizard-king	Ar-Hespaas, count

ABOUT THE AUTHOR

Deby Fredericks has been a writer all her life, but thought of it as just a fun hobby until the late 1990s. Her first sale, a children's poem, was in 2000. Since then she has published seven novels through two small presses. She self-publishes her short story collections and novellas.

She also writes for children under the byline Lucy D. Ford. Ford's short stories and poetry have appeared in magazines such as *Boys' Life, Babybug, Ladybug*, and *Cricket*. Her middle-grade novel, *Masters of Air & Fire*, came out from Sky Warrior Book Publishing in 2015 and was re-issued in 2023.

FIND OUT MORE

Follow her blog: wyrmflight.wordpress.com

Official web site: www.debyfredericks.com

Facebook author page:
www.facebook.com/AuthorDebyFredericks.

www.ingramcontent.com/pod-product-compliance
Lightning Source LLC
Chambersburg PA
CBHW070918260626
47162CB00007B/2713